FARRAR
STRAUS
GIROUX

BY LEONARD MICHAELS

Time Out of Mind: The Diaries of Leonard Michaels, 1961–1995
A Girl with a Monkey
To Feel These Things
Sylvia
Shuffle
The Men's Club
I Would Have Saved Them If I Could
Going Places

EDITED BY LEONARD MICHAELS

West of the West: Imagining California (with David Reid and Raquel Scherr)
The State of the Language (with Christopher Ricks)

the collected stories

the collected stories

LEONARD MICHAELS

FARRAR, STRAUS AND GIROUX · NEW YORK

FARRAR, STRAUS AND GIROUX
19 Union Square West, New York 10003

Copyright © 2007 by Katharine Ogden Michaels
All rights reserved
Distributed in Canada by Douglas & McIntyre Ltd.
Printed in the United States of America
First edition, 2007

Library of Congress Cataloging-in-Publication Data
Michaels, Leonard, 1933–
  [Short stories]
  The collected stories / Leonard Michaels.
    p.   cm.
  ISBN-13: 978-0-374-12654-4 (hardcover: alk. paper)
  ISBN-10: 0-374-12654-2
I. Title.

PS3563.I273A17   2007
813'.54—dc22

                                        2006102556

Designed by Gretchen Achilles

www.fsgbooks.com

1   3   5   7   9   10   8   6   4   2

The editor wishes to dedicate this volume to

Ethan, Jesse, and Louisa

and

to Anna, always

contents

FROM SHUFFLE (1990)

STORIES FROM TO FEEL THESE THINGS (1993)
AND A GIRL WITH A MONKEY (2000)

THE NACHMAN STORIES

editor's note

Throughout his career, Leonard Michaels (or Lenny, as he was known to his friends and family) was constantly experimenting with different ways to tell a story. Perhaps for this reason, he was a habitual reviser of his own writing, often creating more than one version of the same situation or story, and also producing collections that juggled different narrative forms and genres: *Shuffle* (1990) and *To Feel These Things* (1993) include essays and memoirs as well as fiction. The present volume comprises only Lenny's fiction, though in the elastic sense that underlies his particular form of storytelling. The versions of individual stories included here are those that (as far as I can tell) Lenny finally preferred.

Lenny's first two collections, *Going Places* (1969) and *I Would Have Saved Them If I Could* (1975), appear in their complete and original form. "Journal" incorporates revisions and additions made by Lenny after *Shuffle* was originally published. Three of the four stories from *To Feel These Things* and *A Girl with a Monkey* (2000) are reprinted as they appear in these collections. However, the version of "Viva la Tropicana" included here is the original form of the story as it was published in *Zyzzyva* and *The Best American Short Stories, 1991*.

One day in November 1997, Lenny sat down and, in just seven hours, wrote a story about a mathematician named Nachman. Uncharacteristically, he made very few changes to "Nachman," which appeared the next spring in *The Threepenny Review*. Subsequent stories about the same character were published in *Partisan Review* and *The New Yorker*; Lenny was completing a volume of Nachman stories when he died in 2003. They are collected here for the first time. In a few cases, I have followed Lenny's manuscript versions of these stories where they differ from the published versions.

—Katharine Ogden Michaels

going places
(1969)

manikin

AT THE UNIVERSITY SHE MET A TURK who studied physics and spoke foreigner's English which in every turn expressed the unnatural desire to seize idiom and make it speak just for himself. He worked nights as a waiter, summers on construction gangs, and shot pool and played bridge with fraternity boys in order to make small change, and did whatever else he could to protect and supplement his university scholarship, living a mile from campus in a room without sink or closet or decent heating and stealing most of the food he ate, and when the University Hotel was robbed it was the Turk who had done it, an act of such speed the night porter couldn't say when it happened or who rushed in from the street to bludgeon him so murderously he took it in a personal way. On weekends the Turk tutored mediocrities in mathematics and French . . .

He picked her up at her dormitory, took her to a movie, and later, in his borrowed Chevrolet, drove her into the countryside and with heavy, crocodilean sentences communicated his agony amid the alien corn. She attended with quick, encouraging little nods and stared as if each word crept past her eyes and she felt power gathering in their difficult motion as he leaned toward her and with lips still laboring words made indelible sense, raping her, forcing her to variations of what she never heard of though she was a great reader of avant-garde novels and philosophical commentaries on the modern predicament . . .

In the cracking, desiccated leather of the Chevrolet she was susceptible to a distinction between life and sensibility, and dropped, like Leda by the swan, squirming, arching, so as not to be touched again, inadvertently, as he poked behind the cushions for the ignition key. She discovered it pulling up her pants and, because it required intelligent speech inconsistent with her moaning, couldn't bring it to his attention; nor would she squat, winding about in her privates, though she hated to see him waste time bunched up twisting wires under the dashboard.

Despite her wild compulsion to talk and despite the frightened, ravenous curiosity of her dormitory clique, whom she awakened by sobbing over their beds, Melanie wasn't able to say clearly what finished happening half an hour ago. She remembered the Turk suddenly abandoned English and raved at her in furious Turkish, and she told them about that and about the obscene tattoo flashing on his chest when she ripped his shirt open, and that he stopped the car on a country road and there was a tall hedge, maples, sycamores, and a railroad track nearby, and a train was passing, passing, and passing, and beyond it, her moans, and later an animal trotting quickly on the gravel, and then, with no discontinuity, the motor starting its cough and retch and a cigarette waving at her mouth already lighted as if the worst were over and someone had started thinking of her in another way.

The lights of the university town appeared and she smoked the cigarette as the car went down among them through empty streets, through the residential area of the ethical, economic community and twisted into the main street passing store after store. She saw an armless, naked manikin and felt like that, or like a thalidomide baby, all torso and short-circuited, and then they were into the streets around campus, narrow and shaky with trees, and neither of them said a word as he shifted gears, speeding and slowing and working the car through a passage irregular and yet steady, and enclosed within a greater passage as tangible as the internal arcs of their skulls. At the dormitory he stopped the car. She got out running.

Quigley, Berkowitz, and Sax could tell that Melanie Green had been assaulted with insane and exotic cruelty: there were fingerprints on her cheeks the color of tea stains and her stockings hung about her ankles like Hamlet's when he exposed himself to Ophelia and called her a whore. So they sucked cigarettes and urged her to phone the Dean of Women, the police, and the immigration authorities, as if disseminating the story among representatives of order would qualify it toward annihilation or render it accessible to a punitive response consistent with national foreign policy. Though none of them saw positive value in Melanie's experience it was true, nevertheless, in no future conversation would she complain about being nineteen and not yet discovered by the right man, as it happened, to rape with. Given her face and legs, *that* had always seemed sick, irritating crap, and in the pits of their minds, where there were neither words nor ideas but only raging morality, they took the Turk as poetic justice, fatal male, and measure for measure. Especially since he lived now in those pits vis-à-vis Melanie's father, a bearded rabbi with tear bags. "What if your father knew?" asked Quigley, making a gesture of anxious speculation, slender hands turned out flat, palms up, like a Balinese dancer. Melanie felt annoyed, but at least Quigley was there, sticking out her hands, and could be relied on always to be symbolic of whatever she imagined the situation required.

She didn't tell the rabbi, the Dean of Women, police, or immigration authorities, and didn't tell Harry Stone, her fiancé, with whom she had never had all-the-way sexual intercourse because he feared it might destroy the rhythm of his graduate work in Classics. But once, during Christmas vacation, she flew East to visit him, and while standing on a stairway in Cambridge, after dinner and cognac, he let her masturbate him and then lay in bed beside her, brooding, saying little except "I feel like Seymour," and she answering, "I'm sorry." Quigley, Berkowitz, and Sax called him "Harry the fairy," but never in the presence of Melanie, who read them his letters, brilliantly exquisite and full of ruthless wit directed at everything, and the girls screamed and could hardly wait till he got his degree and laid her. "It'll be made of porcelain," said Sax, and Melanie couldn't refute the proposition (though the girls always told her everything they did with their boyfriends and she owed them the masturbation story) because they were too hot for physiology and wouldn't listen to the whole story, wouldn't hear its tone or any of its music. They were critical, sophisticated girls and didn't dig mood, didn't savor things. They were too fast, too eager to get the point.

She didn't tell the rabbi or any other authority about the rape, and wouldn't dream of telling Harry Stone because he tended to become irrationally jealous and like homosexual Othello would assume she had gone out with armies of men aside from the Turk, which wasn't true. The Turk had been a casual decision, the only one of its kind, determined by boredom with classes and dateless weekends, and partly by a long-distance phone call to Harry Stone in the middle of the night when she needed his voice and he expressed irritation at having been disturbed while translating a difficult passage of Thucydides for a footnote in his dissertation.

Furthermore the Turk was interesting-looking, black eyes, a perfect white bite of teeth between a biggish nose and a cleft chin, and because he was pathetic in his tortuous English going out with him seemed merely an act of charity indifferently performed and it was confirmed as such when he arrived in the old Chevrolet and suggested a cowboy movie. He held the door open for her, which she could never expect Harry to do, and he tried to talk to her. To her, she felt—though it was clear that his effort to talk depended very much on her effort to listen.

She went to parties on the two weekends following the rape and sat in darkened rooms while a hashish pipe went around and said things too deep for syntax and giggled hysterically, and in the intimate delirium of faces and darkness asked how one might get in touch with an abortionist if, perchance, one needed one. She didn't talk about the rape but remembered the Turk had held her chin and she felt guilty but resistless and saw that his eyes didn't focus and that, more than anything, lingered in her nerves, like birds screaming and inconsummate. She asked her clique about the signs of pregnancy, then asked herself if she wasn't peeing more than usual. It seemed to spear down very hot and hard and longer than before, but she ascribed it to sphincters loosened upon the violent dissolution of the veil between vaginal post and lintel. When she asked the girls about an abortionist they laughed maniacally at the idea that any of them might know such a person, but, one at a time, appeared in her room to whisper names and telephone numbers and tell her about the different techniques and the anesthetic she might expect if the man were considerate or brave enough to give her one. "They're afraid of the cops," said Sax, a tough number from Chicago who had been knocked up twice in her freshman year. "They want you out of the office as soon as possible."

Harry surprised her by coming to town during his intersession break and she was so glad to see him she trembled. She introduced him to her house mother and her clique and he ate dinner with her in the dormitory the first night. The next day he went to classes with her and that evening they ate in the best restaurant in town, which wasn't nearly as good as some Harry knew in the East but it was pretty good, and then they walked in the Midwestern twilight, watching swallows, listening to night hawks whistle, and she felt an accumulation of sympathy in the minutes and the hours, which became an urge, a possibility, and then a strong need to tell him, but she chatted mainly about her clique and said, "Quigley has funny nipples and Berkowitz would have a wonderful figure except for her thighs, which have no character. I love Sax's figure. It's like a skinny boy's." Harry made an indifferent face and shrugged in his tweeds, but quick frowns twitched after the facts and she went on, encouraged thus, going on, to go on and on. In his hotel room they had necking and writhing, then lay together breathless, tight, indeterminate, until he began talking about his dissertation. "A revolution in scholarship. The vitiation of many traditional assumptions. They say I write uncommonly well." She told him about the rape. He sat up with words about the impossibility of confidence, the betrayal of expectations, the end of things. He was amazed, he said, the world didn't break and the sky fall down. As far as he was concerned the ceremony of innocence was drowned. While he packed she rubbed her knees and stared at him. He noticed her staring and said, "I don't like you."

Wanda Chung was always in flight around corners, down hallways, up stairs, into bathrooms, and never spoke to people unless obliged to do so and then with fleeting, terrified smiles and her eyes somewhere else. She appeared at no teas or dances, received no calls and no boys at the reception desk, and Melanie and her clique gradually came to think of her as the most interesting girl in the dormitory. One afternoon after classes they decided to go to her room and introduce themselves. She wasn't in so they entered the room and while waiting for her casually examined her closet which was packed with dresses and coats carrying the labels of good stores in San Francisco. Under her bed there were boxes of new blouses and sweaters, and they discovered her desk drawers were crammed with candy and empty candy wrappers. They left her room, never returned, and never again made any effort to introduce themselves to her, but Wanda, who for months had harbored a secret yearning to meet Melanie, decided, the day after Harry Stone left town, to go to Melanie's room and present herself: "I am Wanda Chung. I live downstairs. I found this fountain pen. Could it be yours?" She bought a fountain pen and went to Melanie's room and an instant after she knocked at the door she forgot her little speech and her desire to meet Melanie. The door gave way at the vague touch of her knuckles and started opening as if Wanda herself had taken the knob and turned it with the intention of getting into the room and stealing something, which is how she saw it, standing there as the door unbelievably, remorselessly, opened, sucking all motion and feeling out of her limbs and making her more and more thief in the possible eyes of anyone coming along. And then, into her dumb rigidity, swayed naked feet like bell clappers. She saw Melanie Green hanging by the neck, her pelvis twitching. Wanda dashed to the stairs, down to her room, and locked herself inside. She ate candy until she puked in her lap and fell asleep . . .

When the Turk read about the suicide he said in a slow, sick voice, "She loved me." He got drunk and stumbled through the streets looking for a fight, but bumping strangers and firing clams of spit at their feet wasn't sufficiently provocative, given his debauched and fiercely miserable appearance, to get himself punched or cursed or even shoved a little. He ended the night in a scrubby field tearing at an oak tree with his finger-nails, rolling in its roots, hammering grass, cursing the sources of things until, in a shy, gentle way, Melanie drifted up out of the dew. He refused to acknowledge her presence but then couldn't tolerate being looked at in silence and yelled at her in furious Turkish. She came closer. He seized her in his arms and they rolled together in the grass until he found himself screaming through his teeth because, however much of himself he lavished on her, she was dead.

city boy

"PHILLIP," SHE SAID, "THIS IS CRAZY."

I didn't agree or disagree. She wanted some answer. I bit her neck. She kissed my ear. It was nearly three in the morning. We had just returned. The apartment was dark and quiet. We were on the living-room floor and she repeated, "Phillip, this is crazy." Her crinoline broke under us like cinders. Furniture loomed all around—settee, chairs, a table with a lamp. Pictures were cloudy blotches drifting above. But no lights, no things to look at, no eyes in her head. She was underneath me and warm. The rug was warm, soft as mud, deep. Her crinoline cracked like sticks. Our naked bellies clapped together. Air fired out like farts. I took it as applause. The chandelier clicked. The clock ticked as if to split its glass. "Phillip," she said, "this is crazy." A little voice against the grain and power. Not enough to stop me. Yet once I had been a man of feeling. We went to concerts, walked in the park, trembled in the maid's room. Now in the foyer, a flash of hair and claws. We stumbled to the living-room floor. She said, "Phillip, this is crazy." Then silence, except in my head, where a conference table was set up, ashtrays scattered about. Priests, ministers, and rabbis were rushing to take seats. I wanted their opinion, but came. They vanished. A voice lingered, faintly crying, "You could mess up the rug, Phillip, break something . . ." Her fingers pinched my back like ants. I expected a remark to kill good death. She said nothing. The breath in her nostrils whipped mucus. It cracked in my ears like flags. I dreamed we were in her mother's Cadillac, trailing flags. I heard her voice before I heard the words. "Phillip, this is crazy. My parents are in the next room." Her cheek jerked against mine, her breasts were knuckles in my nipples. I burned. Good death was killed. I burned with hate. A rabbi shook his finger: "You shouldn't hate." I lifted on my elbows, sneering in pain. She wrenched her hips, tightened muscles in belly and neck. She said, "Move." It was imperative to move. Her parents were thirty feet away. Down the hall between Utrillos and Vlamincks, through the door, flick the light and I'd see them. Maybe like us, Mr. Cohen adrift on the missus. Hair sifted down my cheek. "Let's go to the maid's room," she whispered. I was reassured. She tried to move. I kissed her mouth. Her crinoline smashed like sugar. Pig that I was, I couldn't move. The clock ticked hysterically. Ticks piled up like insects. Muscles lapsed in her thighs. Her fingers scratched on my neck as if looking for buttons. She slept. I sprawled like a bludgeoned pig, eyes open, loose lips. I flopped into sleep, in her, in the rug, in our scattered clothes.

Dawn hadn't shown between the slats in the blinds. Her breathing sissed in my ear. I wanted to sleep more, but needed a cigarette. I thought of the cold avenue, the lonely subway ride. Where could I buy a newspaper, a cup of coffee? This was crazy, dangerous, a waste of time. The maid might arrive, her parents might wake. I had to get started. My hand pushed along the rug to find my shirt, touched a brass lion's paw, then a lamp cord.

A naked heel bumped wood.

She woke, her nails in my neck. "Phillip, did you hear?" I whispered, "Quiet." My eyes rolled like Milton's. Furniture loomed, whirled. "Dear God," I prayed, "save my ass." The steps ceased. Neither of us breathed. The clock ticked. She trembled. I pressed my cheek against her mouth to keep her from talking. We heard pajamas rustle, phlegmy breathing, fingernails scratching hair. A voice, "Veronica, don't you think it's time you sent Phillip home?"

A murmur of assent started in her throat, swept to my cheek, fell back drowned like a child in a well. Mr. Cohen had spoken. He stood ten inches from our legs. Maybe less. It was impossible to tell. His fingernails grated through hair. His voice hung in the dark with the quintessential question. Mr. Cohen, scratching his crotch, stood now as never in the light. Considerable. No tool of his wife, whose energy in business kept him eating, sleeping, overlooking the park. Pinochle change in his pocket four nights a week. But were they his words? Or was he the oracle of Mrs. Cohen, lying sleepless, irritated, waiting for him to get me out? I didn't breathe. I didn't move. If he had come on his own he would leave without an answer. His eyes weren't adjusted to the dark. He couldn't see. We

lay at his feet like worms. He scratched, made smacking noises with his
mouth.

The question of authority is always with us. Who is responsible for
the triggers pulled, buttons pressed, the gas, the fire? Doubt banged my
brain. My heart lay in the fist of intellect, which squeezed out feeling like
piss out of kidneys. Mrs. Cohen's voice demolished doubt, feeling, intellect. It ripped from the bedroom.

"For God's sake, Morris, don't be banal. Tell the schmuck to go home
and keep his own parents awake all night, if he has any."

Veronica's tears slipped down my cheeks. Mr. Cohen sighed, shuffled,
made a strong voice. "Veronica, tell Phillip . . ." His foot came down on
my ass. He drove me into his daughter. I drove her into his rug.

"I don't believe it," he said.

He walked like an antelope, lifting hoof from knee, but stepped down
hard. Sensitive to the danger of movement, yet finally impulsive, flinging
his pot at the earth in order to cross it. His foot brought me his weight
and character, a hundred fifty-five pounds of stomping shlemiel, in a
mode of apprehension so primal we must share it with bugs. Let armies
stomp me to insensate pulp—I'll yell "Cohen" when he arrives.

Veronica squealed, had a contraction, fluttered, gagged a shriek,
squeezed, and up like a frog out of the hand of a child I stood spread-
legged, bolt naked, great with eyes. Mr. Cohen's face was eyes in my eyes.
A secret sharer. We faced each other like men accidentally met in hell. He
retreated flapping, moaning, "I will not believe it one bit."

Veronica said, "Daddy?"

"Who else, you no good bum?"

The rug raced. I smacked against blinds, glass broke, and I whirled.
Veronica said, "Phillip," and I went off in streaks, a sparrow in the room,
here, there, early American, baroque, and rococo. Veronica wailed, "Phillip."
Mr. Cohen screamed, "I'll kill him." I stopped at the door, seized the knob.
Mrs. Cohen yelled from the bedroom, "Morris, did something break?
Answer me."

"I'll kill that bastid."

"Morris, if something broke you'll rot for a month."

"Mother, stop it," said Veronica. "Phillip, come back."

The door slammed. I was outside, naked as a wolf.

I needed poise. Without poise the street was impossible. Blood shot
to my brain, thought blossomed. I'd walk on my hands. Beards were

fashionable. I kicked up my feet, kicked the elevator button, faced the door, and waited. I bent one elbow like a knee. The posture of a clothes model, easy, poised. Blood coiled down to my brain, weeds burgeoned. I had made a bad impression. There was no other way to see it. But all right. We needed a new beginning. Everyone does. Yet how few of us know when it arrives. Mr. Cohen had never spoken to me before; this was a breakthrough. There had been a false element in our relationship. It was wiped out. I wouldn't kid myself with the idea that he had nothing to say. I'd had enough of his silent treatment. It was worth being naked to see how mercilessly I could think. I had his number. Mrs. Cohen's, too. I was learning every second. I was a city boy. No innocent shitkicker from Jersey. I was the A train, the Fifth Avenue bus. I could be a cop. My name was Phillip, my style New York City. I poked the elevator button with my toe. It rang in the lobby, waking Ludwig. He'd come for me, rotten with sleep. Not the first time. He always took me down, walked me through the lobby, and let me out on the avenue. Wires began tugging him up the shaft. I moved back, conscious of my genitals hanging upside down. Absurd consideration; we were both men one way or another. There were social distinctions enforced by his uniform, but they would vanish at the sight of me. "The unaccommodated thing itself." "Off ye lendings!" The greatest play is about a naked man. A picture of Lear came to me, naked, racing through the wheat. I could be cool. I thought of Ludwig's uniform, hat, whipcord collar. It signified his authority. Perhaps he would be annoyed, in his authority, by the sight of me naked. Few people woke him at such hours. Worse, I never tipped him. Could I have been so indifferent month after month? In a crisis you discover everything. Then it's too late. Know yourself, indeed. You need a crisis every day. I refused to think about it. I sent my mind after objects. It returned with the chairs, settee, table, and chandelier. Where were my clothes? I sent it along the rug. It found buttons, eagles stamped in brass. I recognized them as the buttons on Ludwig's coat. Eagles, beaks like knives, shrieking for tips. Fuck'm, I thought. Who's Ludwig? A big coat, a whistle, white gloves, and a General MacArthur hat. I could understand him completely. He couldn't begin to understand me. A naked man is mysterious. But aside from that, what did he know? I dated Veronica Cohen and went home late. Did he know I was out of work? That I lived in a slum downtown? Of course not.

Possibly under his hat was a filthy mind. He imagined Veronica and I might be having sexual intercourse. He resented it. Not that he hoped for the privilege himself, in his coat and soldier hat, but he had a proprietary interest in the building and its residents. I came from another world. *The other world against which Ludwig defended the residents.* Wasn't I like a burglar sneaking out late, making him my accomplice? I undermined his authority, his dedication. He despised me. It was obvious. But no one thinks such thoughts. It made me laugh to think them. My genitals jumped. The elevator door slid open. He didn't say a word. I padded inside like a seal. The door slid shut. Instantly, I was ashamed of myself, thinking as I had about him. I had no right. A better man than I. His profile was an etching by Dürer. Good peasant stock. How had he fallen to such work? Existence precedes essence. At the controls, silent, enduring, he gave me strength for the street. Perhaps the sun would be up, birds in the air. The door slid open. Ludwig walked ahead of me through the lobby. He needed new heels. The door of the lobby was half a ton of glass, encased in iron vines and leaves. Not too much for Ludwig. He turned, looked down into my eyes. I watched his lips move.

"I vun say sumding. Yur bisniss vot you do. Bud vy you mek her miserable? Nod led her slip. She has beks unter her eyes."

Ludwig had feelings. They spoke to mine. Beneath the uniform, a man. Essence precedes existence. Even rotten with sleep, thick, dry bags under his eyes, he saw, he sympathized. The discretion demanded by his job forbade anything tangible, a sweater, a hat. "Ludwig," I whispered, "you're all right." It didn't matter if he heard me. He knew I said something. He knew it was something nice. He grinned, tugged the door open with both hands. I slapped out onto the avenue. I saw no one, dropped to my feet, and glanced back through the door. Perhaps for the last time. I lingered, indulged a little melancholy. Ludwig walked to a couch in the rear of the lobby. He took off his coat, rolled it into a pillow, and lay down. I had never stayed to see him do that before, but always rushed off to the subway. As if I were indifferent to the life of the building. Indeed, like a burglar, I seized the valuables and fled to the subway. I stayed another moment, watching good Ludwig, so I could hate myself. He assumed the modest, saintly posture of sleep. One leg here, the other there. His good head on his coat. A big arm across his stomach, the hand between his hips. He made a fist and punched up and down.

I went down the avenue, staying close to the buildings. Later I would work up a philosophy. Now I wanted to sleep, forget. I hadn't the energy for moral complexities: Ludwig cross-eyed, thumping his pelvis in such a nice lobby. Mirrors, glazed pots, rubber plants ten feet high. As if he were generating all of it. As if it were part of his job. I hurried. The buildings were on my left, the park on my right. There were doormen in all the buildings; God knows what was in the park. No cars were moving. No people in sight. Streetlights glowed in a receding sweep down to Fifty-ninth Street and beyond. A wind pressed my face like Mr. Cohen's breath. Such hatred. Imponderable under any circumstances, a father cursing his daughter. Why? A fright in the dark? Freud said things about fathers and daughters. It was too obvious, too hideous. I shuddered and went more quickly. I began to run. In a few minutes I was at the spit-mottled steps of the subway. I had hoped for vomit. Spit is no challenge for bare feet. Still, I wouldn't complain. It was sufficiently disgusting to make me live in spirit. I went down the steps flatfooted, stamping, elevated by each declension. I was a city boy, no mincing creep from the sticks.

A Negro man sat in the change booth. He wore glasses, a white shirt, black knit tie, and a silver tie clip. I saw a mole on his right cheek. His hair had spots of gray, as if strewn with ashes. He was reading a newspaper. He didn't hear me approach, didn't see my eyes take him in, figure him out. Shirt, glasses, tie—I knew how to address him. I coughed. He looked up.

"Sir, I don't have any money. Please let me through the turnstile. I come this way every week and will certainly pay you the next time."

He merely looked at me. Then his eyes flashed like fangs. Instinctively, I guessed what he felt. He didn't owe favors to a white man. He didn't have to bring his allegiance to the Transit Authority into question for my sake.

"Hey, man, you naked?"

"Yes."

"Step back a little."

I stepped back.

"You're naked."

I nodded.

"Get your naked ass the hell out of here."

"Sir," I said, "I know these are difficult times, but can't we be reasonable? I know that . . ."

"Scat, mother, go home."

I crouched as if to dash through the turnstile. He crouched, too. It proved he would come after me. I shrugged, turned back toward the steps. The city was infinite. There were many other subways. But why had he become so angry? Did he think I was a bigot? Maybe I was running around naked to get him upset. His anger was incomprehensible otherwise. It made me feel like a bigot. First a burglar, then a bigot. I needed a cigarette. I could hardly breathe. Air was too good for me. At the top of the steps, staring down, stood Veronica. She had my clothes.

"Poor, poor," she said.

I said nothing. I snatched my underpants and put them on. She had my cigarettes ready. I tried to light one, but the match failed. I threw down the cigarette and the matchbook. She retrieved them as I dressed. She lit the cigarette for me and held my elbow to help me keep my balance. I finished dressing, took the cigarette. We walked back toward her building. The words "thank you" sat in my brain like driven spikes. She nibbled her lip.

"How are things at home?" My voice was casual and morose, as if no answer could matter.

"All right," she said, her voice the same as mine. She took her tone from me. I liked that sometimes, sometimes not. Now I didn't like it. I discovered I was angry. Until she said that, I had no idea I was angry. I flicked the cigarette into the gutter and suddenly I knew why. I didn't love her. The cigarette sizzled in the gutter. Like truth. I didn't love her. Black hair, green eyes, I didn't love her. Slender legs. I didn't. Last night I had looked at her and said to myself, "I hate communism." Now I wanted to step on her head. Nothing less than that would do. If it was a perverted thought, then it was a perverted thought. I wasn't afraid to admit it to myself.

"All right? Really? Is that true?"

Blah, blah, blah. Who asked those questions? A zombie; not Phillip of the foyer and rug. He died in flight. I was sorry, sincerely sorry, but with clothes on my back I knew certain feelings would not survive humiliation. It was so clear it was thrilling. Perhaps she felt it, too. In any case she would have to accept it. The nature of the times. We are historical creatures. Veronica and I were finished. Before we reached her door I would say deadly words. They'd come in a natural way, kill her a little. Veronica, let me step on your head or we're through. Maybe we're through, anyway. It would deepen her looks, give philosophy to what was only charming in her face. The dawn was here. A new day. Cruel, but change is cruel. I could bear it. Love is infinite and one. Women are not. Neither are men. The human condition. Nearly unbearable.

"No, it's not true," she said.

"What's not?"

"Things aren't all right at home."

I nodded intelligently, sighed. "Of course not. Tell me the truth, please. I don't want to hear anything else."

"Daddy had a heart attack."

"Oh God," I yelled. "Oh God, no."

I seized her hand, dropped it. She let it fall. I seized it again. No use. I let it fall. She let it drift between us. We stared at one another. She said, "What were you going to say? I can tell you were going to say something."

I stared, said nothing.

"Don't feel guilty, Phillip. Let's just go back to the apartment and have some coffee."

"What can I say?"

"Don't say anything. He's in the hospital and my mother is there. Let's just go upstairs and not say anything."

"Not say anything. Like moral imbeciles go slurp coffee and not say anything? What are we, nihilists or something? Assassins? Monsters?"

"Phillip, there's no one in the apartment. I'll make us coffee and eggs . . ."

"How about a roast beef? Got a roast beef in the freezer?"

"Phillip, he's *my* father."

We were at the door. I rattled. I was in a trance. This was life. Death!

"Indeed, your father. I'll accept that. I can do no less."

"Phillip, shut up. Ludwig."

The door opened. I nodded to Ludwig. What did he know about life and death? Give him a uniform and a quiet lobby—that's life and death. In the elevator he took the controls. "Always got a hand on the controls, eh, Ludwig?"

Veronica smiled in a feeble, grateful way. She liked to see me get along with the help. Ludwig said, "Dots right."

"Ludwig has been our doorman for years, Phillip. Ever since I was a little girl."

"Wow," I said.

"Dots right."

The door slid open. Veronica said, "Thank you, Ludwig." I said, "Thank you, Ludwig."

"Vulcum."

"Vulcum? You mean 'welcome'? Hey, Ludwig, how long you been in this country?"

Veronica was driving her key into the door.

"How come you never learned to talk American, baby?"

"Phillip, come here."

"I'm saying something to Ludwig."

"Come here right now."

"I have to go, Ludwig."

"Vulcum."

She went directly to the bathroom. I waited in the hallway between Vlamincks and Utrillos. The Utrillos were pale and flat. The Vlamincks were thick, twisted, and red. Raw meat on one wall, dry stone on the other. Mrs. Cohen had an eye for contrasts. I heard Veronica sob. She ran water in the sink, sobbed, sat down, peed. She saw me looking and kicked the door shut.

"At a time like this . . ."

"I don't like you looking."

"Then why did you leave the door open? You obviously don't know your own mind."

"Go away, Phillip. Wait in the living room."

"Just tell me why you left the door open."

"Phillip, you're going to drive me nuts. Go away. I can't do a damn thing if I know you're standing there."

The living room made me feel better. The settee, the chandelier full of teeth, and the rug were company. Mr. Cohen was everywhere, a simple, diffuse presence. He jingled change in his pocket, looked out the window, and was happy he could see the park. He took a little antelope step and tears came into my eyes. I sat among his mourners. A rabbi droned platitudes: Mr. Cohen was generous, kind, beloved by his wife and daughter. "How much did he weigh?" I shouted. The phone rang.

Veronica came running down the hall. I went and stood at her side when she picked up the phone. I stood dumb, stiff as a hatrack. She was whimpering, "Yes, yes . . ." I nodded my head yes, yes, thinking it was better than no, no. She put the phone down.

"It was my mother. Daddy's all right. Mother is staying with him in his room at the hospital and they'll come home together tomorrow."

Her eyes looked at mine. At them as if they were as flat and opaque as hers. I said in a slow, stupid voice, "You're allowed to do that? Stay overnight in a hospital with a patient? Sleep in his room?" She continued looking at my eyes. I shrugged, looked down. She took my shirt front in a fist like a bite. She whispered. I said, "What?" She whispered again, "Fuck me." The clock ticked like crickets. The Vlamincks spilled blood. We sank into the rug as if it were quicksand.

crossbones

AT THE END OF THE SUMMER, OR THE YEAR, or when he could do more with his talent than play guitar in a Village strip joint . . . and after considering his talent for commitment and reluctance she found reluctance in her own heart and marriage talk became desultory, specifics dim, ghostly, lost in bed with Myron doing wrong things, "working on" her, discovering epileptic dysrhythmia in her hips, and he asked about it and she said it hurt her someplace but not, she insisted, in her head, and they fought the next morning and the next as if ravenous for intimacy and disgraced themselves yelling, becoming intimate with neighbors, and the superintendent brought them complaints which would have meant nothing if they hadn't exhausted all desire for loud, broad strokes, but now, conscious of complaints, they thrust along the vital horizontal with silent, stiletto words, and later in the narrowed range of their imaginations could find no adequate mode of retraction, so wounds festered, burgeoning lurid weeds, poisoning thought, dialogue, and the simple air of their two-room apartment (which had seemed with its view of the Jersey cliffs so much larger than now) now seemed too thick to breathe, or to see through to one another, but they didn't say a word about breaking up, even experimentally, for whatever their doubts about one another, their doubts about other others and the city—themselves adrift in it among messy one-night stands—were too frightening and at least they had, in one another, what they had: Sarah had Myron Bronsky, gloomy brown eyes, a guitar in his hands as mystical and tearing as, say, Lorca, though Myron's particular hands derived from dancing, clapping Hasidim; and he had Sarah Nilsin, Minnesota blonde, long bones, arctic schizophrenia in the gray infinities of her eyes, and a turn for lyric poems derived from piratical saga masters. Rare, but opposites cleave in the divisive angularities of Manhattan and, as the dialectics of embattled individuation became more intense, these two cleaved more tightly: if Sarah, out for groceries, hadn't returned in twenty minutes, Myron punched a wall, pulverizing the music in his knuckles, but punched, punched until she flung through the door shrieking stop; and he, twenty minutes late from work, found Sarah in kerchief, coat, and gloves, the knotted cloth beneath her chin a little stone proclaiming wild indifference to what the nighttime street could hold, since it held most for him if she were raped and murdered in it. After work he ran home. Buying a quart of milk and a pack of cigarettes, she suffered stomach cramps.

Then a letter came from St. Cloud, Minnesota. Sarah's father was going to visit them next week.

She sewed curtains, squinting down into the night, plucking thread with pricked, exquisite fingertips. He painted walls lately punched. She bought plants for the windowsills, framed and hung three Japanese prints, and painted the hall toilet opaque, flat yellow. On his knees until sunrise four days in a row, he sanded, then varnished floorboards until the oak bubbled up its blackest grain, turbulent and petrified, and Monday dawned on Sarah ironing dresses—more than enough to last her father's visit—and Myron already twice shaved, shining all his shoes, urging her to hurry.

In its mute perfection their apartment now had the air of a well-beaten slave, simultaneously alive and dead, and reflected, like an emanation of their nerves, a severe, hectic harmony; but it wouldn't have mattered if the new curtains, pictures, and boiling floors yelled reeking spiritual shambles, because Sarah's father wasn't that kind of minister. His sermons alluded more to Heidegger and Sartre than to Christ; he lifted weights, smoked two packs of cigarettes a day, drove a green Jaguar, and since the death of Sarah's mother a year ago in a state insane asylum, had seen species of love in all human relations. And probably at this very moment, taking the banked curves of the Pennsylvania Turnpike, knuckles pale on the walnut wheel, came man and machine leaning as one toward Jersey, and beyond that toward love.

Their sense of all this drove them, wrenched them out of themselves, onto their apartment until nothing more could make it coincident with what he would discover in it anyway, and they had now only their own absolute physical being still to work on, at nine o'clock, when Myron dashed out to the cleaners for shirts, trousers, and jackets, then dressed in fresh clothing while Sarah slammed and smeared the iron down the board as if increasingly sealed in the momentum of brute work, and then, standing behind her, lighting a cigarette, Myron was whispering as if to himself that she must hurry and she was turning from the board and in the same motion hurled the iron, lunging after it with nails and teeth before it exploded against the wall and Myron, instantly, hideously understood that the iron, had it struck him, had to burn his flesh and break his bones, flew to meet her with a scream and fists banging her mouth as they locked, winding, fusing to one convulsive beast reeling off walls, tables, and chairs, with ashtrays, books, lamps shooting away with pieces of themselves, and he punched out three of her teeth and strangled her until she dissolved in his hands and she scratched his left eye blind—but there was hope in corneal transplantation that he would see through it again—and they were strapped in bandages, twisted and stiff with pain a week after Sarah's father didn't arrive, and they helped one another walk slowly up the steps of the municipal building to buy a marriage license.

sticks and stones

IT WAS A BLIND DATE. SHE MET ME AT THE DOOR and smiled nicely. I could tell she was disappointed. Fortunately, I had brought a bottle of bourbon. An expensive brand, though not a penny too much for a positive *Weltanschauung*. I felt disappointed, too. We finished the bourbon and were sitting on the couch. She stuttered the tale of her life and named her favorite authors. I'd never met a girl who stuttered. Our hands became interlocked and hot, our knees touched. Both of us were crying. I cried for her. She, moved by my tears, cried for me. Beyond the room, our sobs, and her breaking, retrogressive voice, I heard church bells. I squeezed her hands, shook my head, and staggered from the couch to a window. Glass broke, I fainted, and minutes later awoke on a porch just below the window. She was kneeling beside my head, smoking a cigarette. I heard her voice repeating consonants, going on with the story of her life—a bad man, accident, disease. Broken glass lay about me like stars. Church bells rang the hour, then the half hour. I lay still, thinking nothing, full of mood. Cloth moved smoothly across her thighs as she breathed and rocked to the measures of her story. Despicable as it may seem, that made me sexual. I lifted on an elbow. The sight of my face with the moon shining in it surprised her. She stopped telling her story and said, "No, I d–don't want t–to . . ." Our eyelids were thick with water. We shook like unhealthy, feverish things.

There was a reason for not having called her again. Shame, disgust, what have you? When I saw her in the street I would run. I saw her there often, and I ran hundreds of miles. My legs became strong, my chest and lungs immense. Soon I could run like a nimble dog. I could wheel abruptly, scramble left or right, and go for half the day. I could leap fences and automobiles, run from roof to roof, spring deadly air shafts, and snap in middle flight to gain the yard that saved my life. Once, I caught a sparrow smack in my teeth and bit off his head. Spitting feathers and blood, I felt like an eagle. But I was not, and good things, however vigorous, come to an end. At least for me. I was neither Nietzsche, Don Juan, nor Chateaubriand. My name was Phillip. As I resolved to stand and started practicing postures, a friend who knew the girl came and said she wasn't reproachful. I ought to call her on the phone. It didn't sound true, but he insisted. She wanted to see me again, at least as an acquaintance. She would be spared the implications of my flight. I could rest in body and mind. Next time I saw her in the street I ran faster than before, my hair flying, my eyes big. I ran half the day and all that night.

My friend came again. Running alongside, he shouted that he had had her, too. We stopped.

"Do you mind?" he asked. It had bothered him so much he couldn't sleep.

"Mind?" I kissed him on the cheek and slapped his back. Was I happy? The answer is yes. I laughed till my sight was bleary. My ribs, spreading with pleasure, made a noise like wheezy old wood. My friend began laughing, too, and it was a conflation of waters, lapping and overlapping.

A crooked nose and small blue eyes—Henry. A nose, eyes, a curious mouth, a face, my own felt face behind my eyes, an aspect of my mind, a habit of my thought—my friend Henry. The sight of him was mysterious news, like myself surprised in a mirror, at once strange and familiar. He was tall and went loose and swinging in his stride. Degas dreamed the motion of that dance, a whirl of long bones through streets and rooms. I was shorter, narrower, and conservative in motion. A sharp complement striding at his side. As Henry was open, I was closed, slipping into my parts for endless consultation, like a poker player checking possibilities at the belt. He and I. Me and him. Such opposite adaptations contradict the logic of life, abolish Darwin, testify to miracle and God. I never voiced this idea, but I would think: Henry, you ought to be dead and utterly vanished, decomposed but for the splinter of tibula or jawbone locked in bog, or part of a boulder, baked, buried, and one with rock. I meant nothing malicious; just the wonder of it.

Now, in company, Henry would grin, expose his dearly familiar chipped front tooth, and whisper, "Tell them how you fell out the window."

"Out the window," people would shout. "You fell out the window? What window?"

I told the story, but declined the honor of being hero. "No, no, not I—this fellow I know—happened to him. Young man out of a job, about my age, depressed about life and himself. You must know the type—can't find meaningful work, spends a lot of time in the movies, wasting . . .

"It was suggested he call a certain girl named Marjorie, herself out of work, not seeing anyone in particular. He asked why out of work. They told him she had had an accident and lived on the insurance payments. Pretty girl? 'Not what you would call pretty. Interesting-looking, bright.' So he called and she said glad to see him, come by, bring something to drink. She had a stutter. It annoyed him, but not so much as her enthusiasm. Anyhow, he was committed. He went with a bottle, and though she was interesting-looking, he was disappointed and began straight in to drink and drink. Perhaps disappointed, too, she drank as fast and as much. The liquor qualified their sense of one another and themselves. Soon they sat on the couch and were full of expectations, drinking, drinking, chatting. He told her about his life, the jobs he had lost, how discontented he felt, and about his one good friend. She followed in a gentle, pleasing way, ooing and clucking. He said there were no frontiers left, nothing for a man to do but explore his own mind and go to the movies. She agreed and said she spent a lot of time just looking in a mirror. Then she came closer and told him about her life. He came closer, too, and fondled her fingertips. She had been raised in an orphanage. He pressed her palms. She had gone to work in a factory. He held her wrists. In an accident at the factory, her leg was bashed and permanently damaged. His hands slid up and down her arms. She limped slightly but the company paid. She didn't mind the limp. He shook his head no. The scars on her face made her look a bit tough; that bothered her. He moaned. She pulled up her dress, showed him the damage, and he began to cry as he snapped it down again. She cried, too, and pulled it back up. He stumbled from the couch, crying, punching his fists together as he went to the window. Trying to open it he fell through and was nearly killed."

People loved the story and Henry cackled for more.

"You're such a jerk," he said. My heart lunged fiercely with pleasure.

———————

How I carried on. Henry urged me. I carried on and on. Everyone laughed when I fell out the window. No one asked what happened next. Anyhow, the tale of abused and abandoned femininity is pathetic and tediously familiar. Only low, contemptible men who take more pleasure in telling it than doing it would tell it. I stopped for a while after I had a dream in which Henry wanted to kill me.

"Me?" I asked.

"That's right, scum. You!"

Only a dream, but so is life. I took it seriously. Did it warn me of a disaster on the way? Did it indicate a fearful present fact? I studied Henry. Indeed, his face had changed. Never a handsome face, but now, like his face in the dream, it was strangely uncertain, darker, nasty about the edges of the eyes and mouth. Dirty little pimples dotted his neck, and the front chipped tooth gave a new quality to his smile, something asymmetrical, imbecilic, and obscene. He looked dissolute and suicidal.

He rarely came to visit me anymore, but we met in the street. Our talk would be more an exchange of looks than words. He looked at me as if I were bleeding. I looked at him quizzically. I looked at him with irony; he returned it with innocence. He burst out laughing. I smiled and looked ready to share the joke. He looked blank, as if I were about to tell him what it was. I grinned, he sneered, he smiled, I frowned, I frowned, he was pained. He looked pained, I looked at my shoes. He looked at my shoes, I looked at his. We looked at one another and he mentioned a mutual friend.

"An idiot," I said.

"A pig."

"Intolerable neurotic."

"Nauseating . . . psychotic."

Then silence. Then he might start, "You know, his face, those weirdly colored eyes . . ."

"Yes," I would say. They were the color of mine. I yawned and scratched at my cheek, though I wasn't sleepy and felt no itch. Our eyes slipped to the corners of the squalid world. Life seemed merely miserable.

Afterward, alone in my apartment, I had accidents. A glass slipped out of my hand one night, smashed on the floor, and cut my shin. When I lifted my pants leg to see the cut, my other leg kicked it. I collapsed on the floor. My legs fought with kicks and scrapes till both lay bleeding, jerky, broken, and jointless.

Lose a job, you will find another; break an arm, it soon will heal; ditched by a woman, well,

> *I don't care if my baby leaves me flat,*
> *I got forty 'leven others if it come to that.*

But a friend! My own felt face. An aspect of my mind. He and I. Me and him. There were no others. I smoked cigarettes and stayed up late staring at a wall. Trying to think, I ran the streets at night. My lungs were thrilled by darkness. Occasionally, I saw Henry and he, too, was running. With so much on our minds, we never stopped to chat, but merely waved and ran on. Now and then we ran side by side for a couple of hundred miles, both of us silent except for the gasping and hissing of our mouths and the cluttered thumping of our feet. He ran as fast as I. Neither of us thought to race, but we might break silence after some wonderful show of the other's speed and call, "Hey, all right." Or, after one of us had executed a brilliant swerve and leap, the other might exclaim, "Bitching good."

Alone, going at high moderate speed one night, I caught a glimpse of Henry walking with a girl. She seemed to limp. I slowed and followed them, keeping well back and low to the ground. They went to a movie theater. I slipped in after they did and took a seat behind theirs. When the girl spoke, I leaned close. She stuttered. It was Marjorie. They kissed. She coiled slow ringlets in the back of his head. I left my seat and paced in the glassy lobby. My heart knocked to get free of my chest and glide up amid the chandeliers. They seemed much in love, childish and animal. He chittered little monkey things to her. There was a coy note in her stutter. They passed without noticing me and stopped under the marquee. Henry lighted a cigarette. She watched as if it were a spectacle for kings. As the fire took life in his eyes, and smoke sifted backward to membranes of his throat, she asked, "What did you think of the m-m-movie, Hen Hen?" His glance became fine, blue as the filament of smoke sliding upward and swaying to breezes no more visible, and vastly less subtle, than the myriad, shifting discriminations that gave sense and value to his answer. "A movie is a complex thing. Images. Actors. I can't quite say." He stared at her without a word. She clucked helplessly. All was light between them. It rose out of warmth. They kissed.

Now I understood and felt much relieved. Henry cared a great deal about movies and he had found someone to whom he could talk about them. Though he hadn't asked me to, I told my story again one evening in company. My voice was soft, but enthusiastic:

"This fellow, ordinary chap with the usual worries about life, had a date to go to the movies with a girl who was quite sweet and pretty and a wonderful conversationalist. She wore a faded gingham blouse, a flowery print skirt, and sandals. She limped a bit and had a vague stutter. Her nails were bitten to the neural sheath in finger and toe. She had a faint but regular tic in her left cheek. Throughout the movie she scratched her knees.

"It was a foreign movie about wealthy Italians, mainly a statuesque blonde and a dark, speedy little man who circled about her like a house-fly. At last, weary of his constant buzz, she reclined on a bed in his mother's apartment and he did something to her. Afterward she laughed a great deal, and near the end of the movie, she discovered an interlocking wire fence. Taking hold with both hands, she clung there while the camera moved away and looked about the city. The movie ended with a study of a street lamp. It had a powerful effect on this fellow and his date. They fell in love before it was half over, and left the theater drunk on the images of the blonde and the speedy little man. He felt the special pertinence of the movie and was speechless. She honored his silence and was speechless, too. Both of them being consciously modern types, they did the thing as soon as they got to her apartment. An act of recognition. A testimony, he thought, to their respect for one another and an agreement to believe their love was more than physical. Any belief needs ritual; so this one. Ergo, the beastly act. Unless it's done, you know, 'a great Prince in prison lies.' Now they could know one another. No longer drunk, they sat di-sheveled and gloomy on her living-room floor. Neither looked at the other's face, and she, for the sake of motion, scratched her knees. At last, she rose and went to take a shower. When the door shut behind her, he imagined he heard a sob. He crushed his cigarette, went to the window, and flung himself out to the mercy of the night. He has these awful headaches now and constant back pains."

People thought it was a grand story. Henry looked at me till his eyes went click and his mouth resolved into a sneer.

"Ever get a headache in this spot?" he asked, tapping the back of his head.

"Sometimes," I answered, leaning toward him and smiling.

"Then look out. It's a bad sign. It means you've got a slipped disc and probably need an operation. They might have to cut your head off."

Everyone laughed, though no one more than I. Then I got a headache and trembled for an hour. Henry wanted me to have a slipped disc.

Such a man was a threat to the world, and public denunciation was in order. I considered beginning work on a small tract about evil, personified by Henry. But I really had nothing to say. He had done me no injury. My dream, however, was obviously the truth: he wanted to kill me. Perhaps, inadvertently, I had said or done something to insult him. A gentleman, says Lord Chesterfield, never unintentionally insults anyone. But I didn't fancy myself a gentleman. Perhaps there was some aspect of my character he thought ghastly. After all, you may know a person for centuries before discovering a hideous peculiarity in him. I considered changing my character, but I didn't know how or what to change. It was perplexing. Henry's character was vile, so I would change mine. I hadn't ever thought his character was vile before. Now, all I had to do was think: Henry. Vile, oh vile, vile. It would require a revolution in me. Better that than lose a friend. No; better to be yourself and proud. Tell Henry to go to hell. But a real friend goes to hell himself. One afternoon, on my way to hell, I turned a corner and was face to face with Marjorie. She stopped and smiled. Behind her I could see flames. Fluttering down the wind came the sound of prayer.

There was no reason to run. I stood absolutely rigid. She blushed, looked down, and said hello. My right hand whispered the same, then twitched and spun around. It slipped from the end of my arm like a leaf from a bough. She asked how I had been. My feet clattered off in opposite directions. I smiled and asked her how she had been. Before she might answer anything social and ordinary, a groan flew up my throat. My teeth couldn't resist its force and it was suddenly in the air. Both of us marveled, though I more than she. She was too polite to make anything of it and suggested we stroll. The groan hovered behind us, growing smaller and more contorted. While she talked of the last few months, I nodded at things I approved of. I approved of everything and nodded without cease until my head fell off. She looked away as I groped for it on the ground and put it back on, shouting hello, hello.

How could I have been so blind, so careless, cruel, and stupid? This was a lovely girl. I, beast and fool, adjusting my head, felt now what I should have felt then. And I felt that Henry was marvelous. "Seen any movies lately?" I asked.

She stuttered something about a movie and Henry's impressions of it. The stutter was worse than I remembered, and now that I looked her face seemed thin, the flesh gray. In her effort not to stutter, strain showed in her neck. As if it were my habitual right, I took her hand. She continued to stutter something Henry had said about the movie, and didn't snap her hand back. Tears formed in my nose. "Thank you," I whispered. "F-for what?" she asked. We were near an empty lot. I turned abruptly against her, my lips quivering. She said, "Really, Phillip, I d-don't w-want . . ." With a rapid hand I discovered that she wore no underpants. We fell together. I caught sight of her later as she sprinted into the darkness. Groans issued from my mouth. They flew after her like a flock of bats.

It was a week before Henry came to see me, but I was certain I had heard the bell a hundred times. Each time, I put out my cigarette and dragged to the door, ready for a punch in the face, a knife, or a bullet. In the middle of the night, I found myself sitting up in bed, my eyes large and compendious with dark as I shouted, "No, Henry, no." Though I shouted, I had resolved to say nothing or little when he finally came. Not a word would shape my mouth if I could help it. A word would be an excuse. Even self-denunciation was beyond decent possibility. If he flung acid in my face, I would fall and say, "Thanks." If he were out in the hall with a gun and fired point blank into my stomach, I might, as I toppled, blood sloshing through my lips, beg forgiveness. Though I merited no such opportunity, I hoped there would be time for it. If I could, while begging, keep my eyes fixed on him, it would be nice.

After three days passed and he still hadn't come, I thought of hanging myself. I tied a rope to the lightbulb, made a noose, and set a chair under it. But I couldn't, when I experimented, manage to open the door and then dash to the chair and hang myself without looking clumsy, as if I were really asking to be stopped. On the other hand, I didn't want to practice, become graceful, and look effete. I considered poison: open the door, hello, down it goes, goodbye. Or fire: set myself on fire and shrivel, spitting curses on my head.

Despite all this I slept well most of the week, and on several nights I dreamed of Marjorie. We did it every time. "Is this the nature of sin?" I asked. "This is nature," she said. "Don't talk." I discovered a truth in these dreams: each of my feelings was much like another, pity like lust, hate like love, sorrow like joy. I wondered if there were people who could keep them neat. I supposed not. They were feelings and not to be managed. If I felt bad I felt good. That was that.

The idea made me smile. When I noticed myself smiling, I chuckled a bit, and soon I was cackling. Tears streamed out of my eyes. I had to lie on the floor to keep from sinking there. I lay for a long time digging my nails into my cheeks and thought about the nature of ideas. Pascal, Plato, Freud. I felt kin to men like that. Having ideas, seized as it were. I had had an idea.

When I heard the doorbell I knew immediately that I had heard it. The ring was different from the phony ringing during the week. It was substantial, moral, piercing. It set me running to answer, dashing between tables and chairs, leaping a sofa, lunging down the hall to come flying to the ringing door, where I swerved and came back to where I had been. A voice more primitive than any noise the body makes, said:

"Let the son of a bitch ring."

My lips slid up my teeth, my ears flattened to the skull. I found myself crouching. Muscles bunched in my shoulders. I felt a shuddering stiffness in my thighs. Tight as bow strings, tendons curled the bones of my hands to claws. The bell continued to ring, and a hot, ragged tongue slapped across my muzzle. I smelled the sweet horror of my breath. It bristled my neck and sent me gliding low to the ringing door, a noiseless animal, blacker and more secret than night.

Henry out there stood dying in his shoes, ringing in gruesome demise. My paws lifted and lopped down softly. Blood poured me, slow as steaming tar, inevitably toward the door. My paw lay on the knob. It turned. I tugged. Nothing happened. He rang. I shouted, "Can't open it. Give a shove." I tugged, Henry shoved. I twisted the knob and he flung himself against the other side. A panel dislodged. I had a glimpse of his face, feverish and shining. A blaze of white teeth cut the lower half. The door stayed shut. We yelled to one another.

"All right. Give it everything."

"Here we go."

The door opened.

Henry stood in the hall, looking straight into my eyes. The crooked nose, the blue eyes. The physical man. Nothing I felt, absolutely nothing, could accommodate the fact of him. I wondered if it was actually Henry, and I looked rapidly about his face, casting this and that aside like a man fumbling through his wallet for his driver's license while the trooper grimly waits. Nothing turned up to name him Henry. Even the familiar tooth left me unimpressed. Henry's features made no more sense than a word repeated fifty times. The physical man, Henry, Henry, Henry, Henry. Nothing. I wanted to cry and beg him to be Henry again, but only snickered and stepped back. He came inside. I took a package of cigarettes from my pocket and offered it to him. He stared, then shook his head. The movement was trivial, but it was no. No! It startled me into sense. I put the cigarettes back into my pocket and sighed. The breath ran out slowly, steadily, like sand through an hourglass. This was it. He followed with a sigh of his own, then said, "I guess this is it."

"I guess," I murmured, "it is."

"Yes," he said, "it is," and took a long, deep breath, as if drawing up the air I had let out.

I began to strangle. Neither of us spoke. I coughed. He cleared his throat in a sympathetic reflex. I coughed. He cleared his throat once more. I coughed a third time, and he waited for me to stop, but I continued to cough. I was barely able to see, though my eyes bulged. He asked if I wanted a glass of water. I nodded and doubled forward wiping my bulging eyes. When he returned with the water I seized it and drank. He asked if I wanted another glass. I said, "No thanks," coughed again, a rasping, rotten-chested hack. He rushed for another glass. I saw it trembling in his hand. His sleeve was wet to the elbow. "Thanks," I said, and seized it.

"Go on, go on, drink."

I drank.

"Finish it," he urged.

I finished it slowly.

"You ought to sit down."

I went to a chair and sat down. My head rolled in a dull, feeble way, and a moment passed in silence. Then he said:

"There has been enough of this."

I stood up instantly.

He looked at me hard. I tried to look back equally hard, as if his look were an order that I do the same. His height and sharp little eyes gave him the advantage. "Yes," I said, shaking my head yes.

"Months of it. Enough!"

"I'm responsible," I muttered, and that put force into my look. "All my fault," I said, force accumulating.

"Don't be ridiculous. I don't blame you for anything. You want to kill me and I don't blame you for that. I'm no friend. I betrayed you."

"Kill you?"

"I came here expecting death. I am determined to settle for nothing less."

"Don't be absurd."

"Absurd? Is it so absurd to want justice? Is it so absurd to ask the friend one has betrayed to do for one the only possible thing that will purge one?"

He moved an inch closer and seemed to be restraining himself, with terrific difficulty, from moving closer.

"Shut up, Henry," I said. "I have no intention of killing you and I never wanted to do such a thing."

"Ha! I see now."

"You don't see a thing, Henry."

"I see," he shouted, and slapped his head. "I see why you refuse to do it, why you pretend you don't even want to do it."

He slapped his head again very hard.

"I see, Phillip, you're a moral genius. By not killing me you administer cruel, perfect justice."

"Henry, get a hold of yourself. Be fair to both of us, will you."

"Don't hand me that liberal crap, Phillip. Don't talk to me about fair. You be fair. Do the right thing, the merciful thing. Kill me, Phillip."

I started backing toward the door, my hands stuffed deep between my lowest ribs. Henry shuffled after me, his little eyes wild with fury and appreciation. "No use. I will follow you until you show mercy. I will bring you guns and knives and ropes, vats of poison, acids, gasoline and matches. I will leap in front of your car. I will . . ."

Whirling suddenly, I was out the door. Henry gasped and followed, tearing for a grip on the back of my head. We went down the night, Henry ripping out fists of my flying hair and jamming them into his mouth so he might choke. The night became day, and day night. These a week, the week a month. My hair was soon gone from the back of my head. When it grew in he ripped it out again. The wind lacerated our faces and tore the clothes off our bodies. Occasionally, I heard him scream, "I have a gun. Shoot me." Or, "A rope, Phillip. Strangle me." I had a step on him always and I ran on powerful legs. Over the running years, they grew more powerful. They stretched and swelled to the size of trees while my body shrank and my head descended. At last my arms disappeared and I was a head on legs. Running.

the deal

TWENTY WERE JAMMED TOGETHER ON THE STOOP; tiers of heads made one central head, and the wings rested along the banisters: a raggedy monster of boys studying her approach. Her white face and legs. She passed without looking, poked her sunglasses against the bridge of her nose, and tucked her bag between her arm and ribs. She carried it at her hip like a rifle stock. On her spine forty eyes hung like poison berries. Bone dissolved beneath her lank beige silk, and the damp circle of her belt cut her in half. Independent legs struck toward the points of her shoes. Her breasts lifted and rode the air like porpoises. She would cross to the grocery as usual, buy cigarettes, then cross back despite their eyes. As if the neighborhood hadn't changed one bit. She slipped the bag forward to crack it against her belly and pluck out keys and change. In the gesture she was home from work. Her keys jangled in the sun as if they opened everything and the air received her. The monster, watching, saw the glove fall away.

Pigeons looped down to whirl between buildings, and a ten-wheel truck came slowly up the street. As it passed she emerged from the grocery, then stood at the curb opposite the faces. She glanced along the street where she had crossed it. No glove. Tar reticulated between the cobbles. A braid of murky water ran against the curb, twisting bits of flotsam toward the drain. She took off her sunglasses, dropped them with her keys into the bag, then stepped off the curb toward the faces. Addressing them with a high, friendly voice, she said, "Did you guys see a glove? I dropped it a moment ago."

The small ones squinted up at her from the bottom step. On the middle steps sat boys fourteen or fifteen years old. The oldest ones made the wings. Dandies and introverts, they sprawled, as if with a common corruption in their bones. In the center, his eyes level with hers, a boy waited for her attention in the matter of gloves. To his right sat a very thin boy with a pocked face. A narrow-brimmed hat tipped toward his nose and shaded the continuous activity of his eyes. She spoke to the green eyes of the boy in the center and held up the glove she had: "Like this."

Teeth appeared below the hat, then everywhere as the boys laughed. Did she hold up a fish? Green eyes said, "Hello, Miss Calile."

She looked around at the faces, then laughed with them at her surprise. "You know my name?"

"I see it on the mailbox," said the hat. "He can't read. I see it."

"My name is Duke Francisco," said the illiterate.

"My name is Abbe Carlyle," she said to him.

The hat smirked. "His name Francisco Lopez."

Green eyes turned to the hat. "Shut you mouth, baby. I tell her my name, not you."

"His name Francisco Lopez," the hat repeated.

She saw pocks and teeth, the thin oily face, and the hat, as he spoke again, nicely to her: "My name Francisco Pacheco, the Prince. I seen you name on the mailbox."

"Did either of you . . ."

"You name is shit," said green eyes to the hat.

"My name is Tito." A small one on the bottom step looked up for the effect of his name. She looked down at him. "I am Tito," he said.

"Did you see my glove, Tito?"

"This is Tomato," he answered, unable to bear her attention. He nudged the boy to his left. Tomato nudged back, stared at the ground.

"I am happy to know you, Tito," she said, "and you, Tomato. Both of you." She looked back up to green eyes and the hat. The hat acknowledged her courtesy. He tilted back to show her his eyes, narrow and black except for bits of white reflected in the corners. His face was thin, high-boned, and fragile. She pitied the riddled skin.

"This guy," he said, pointing his thumb to the right, "is Monkey," and then to the left beyond green eyes, "and this guy is Beans." She nodded to the hat, then Monkey, then Beans, measuring the respect she offered, doling it out in split seconds. Only one of them had the glove.

"Well, did any of you guys see my glove?"

Every tier grew still, like birds in a tree waiting for a sign that would move them all at once.

Tito's small dark head snapped forward. She heard the slap an instant late. The body lurched after the head and pitched off the stoop at her feet. She saw green eyes sitting back slowly. Tito gaped up at her from the concrete. A sacrifice to the lady. She stepped back as if rejecting it and frowned at green eyes. He gazed indifferently at Tito, who was up, facing him with coffee-bean fists. Tito screamed, "I tell her you got it, dickhead."

The green eyes swelled in themselves like a light blooming in the ocean. Tito's fists opened, he turned, folded quickly, and sat back into the mass. He began to rub his knees.

"May I have my glove, Francisco?" Her voice was still pleasant and high. She now held her purse in the crook of her arm and pressed it against her side.

Some fop had a thought and giggled in the wings. She glanced up at him immediately. He produced a toothpick. With great delicacy he stuck it into his ear. She looked away. Green eyes again waited for her. A cup of darkness formed in the hollow that crowned his chestbone. His soiled gray polo shirt hooked below it. "You think I have you glove?" She didn't answer. He stared between his knees, between heads and shoulders to the top of Tito's head. "Hey, Tito, you tell her I got the glove?"

"I didn't tell nothing," muttered Tito, rubbing his knees harder as if they were still bitter from his fall.

"He's full of shit, Miss Calile. I break his head later. What kind of glove you want?"

"This kind," she said wearily, "a white glove like this."

"Too hot." He grinned.

"Yes, too hot, but I need it."

"What for? Too hot." He gave her full green concern.

"It's much too hot, but the glove is mine, mister."

She rested her weight on one leg and wiped her brow with the glove she had. They watched her do it, the smallest of them watched her, and she moved the glove slowly to her brow again and drew it down her cheek and neck. She could think of nothing to say, nothing to do without expressing impatience. Green eyes changed the subject. "You live there." He pointed toward her building.

"That's right."

A wooden front door with a window in it showed part of the shadowy lobby, mailboxes, and a second door. Beyond her building and down the next street were warehouses. Beyond them, the river. A meat truck started toward them from a packing house near the river. It came slowly, bug-eyed with power. The driver saw the lady standing in front of the boys. He yelled as the truck went past. Gears yowled, twisting the sound of his voice. She let her strength out abruptly: "Give me the glove, Francisco."

The boy shook his head at the truck, at her lack of civilization. "What you give me?"

That tickled the hat. "*Vaya*, baby. What she give you, eh?" He spoke fast, his tone decorous and filthy.

"All right, baby," she said fast as the hat, "what do you want?" The question had New York and much man in it. The hat swiveled to the new sound. A man of honor, let him understand the terms. He squinted at her beneath the hat brim.

"Come on, Francisco, make your deal." She presented brave, beautiful teeth, smiling hard as a skull.

"Tell her, Duke. Make the deal." The hat lingered on "deal," grateful to the lady for this word.

The sun shone in his face and the acknowledged duke sat, dull green eyes blank with possibilities. Her question, not "deal," held him. It had come too hard, too fast. He laughed in contempt of something and glanced around at the wings. They offered nothing. "I want a dollar," he said.

That seemed obvious to the hat: he sneered, "He wants a dollar." She had to be stupid not to see it.

"No deal. Twenty-five cents." Her gloves were worth twenty dollars. She had paid ten for them at a sale. At the moment they were worth green eyes's life.

"I want ten dollars," said green eyes, flashing the words like extravagant meaningless things; gloves of his own. He lifted his arms, clasped his hands behind his head, and leaned against the knees behind him. His belly filled with air, the polo shirt rolled out on its curve. He made a fat man doing business. "Ten dollars." Ten fingers popped up behind his head, like grimy spikes. Keeper of the glove, cocky duke of the stoop. The number made him happy: it bothered her. He drummed the spikes against his head: "I wan' you ten dol-lar." Beans caught the beat in his hips and rocked it on the stoop.

"Francisco," she said, hesitated, then said, "dig me, please. You will get twenty-five cents. Now let's have the glove." Her bag snapped open, her fingers hooked, stiffened on the clasp. Monkey leered at her and bongoed his knees with fists. "The number is ten dol-lar." She waited, said nothing. The spikes continued drumming, Monkey rocked his hips, Beans pummeled his knees. The hat sang sadly: "Twany fyiv not d'nummer, not d'nummer, not d'nummer." He made claves of his fingers and palms, tocked, clicked his tongue against the beat. "Twan-ny fyiv—na t'nomma." She watched green eyes. He was quiet now in the center of the stoop, sitting motionless, waiting, as though seconds back in time his mind still touched the question: what did he want? He seemed to wonder, now that he had the formula, what *did* he want? The faces around him, dopey in the music, wondered nothing, grinned at her, nodded, clicked, whined the chorus: "Twany fyiv not t'nomma, twany fyiv not t'nomma."

Her silk blouse stained and stuck flat to her breasts and shoulders. Water chilled her sides.

"Ten dol-lar iss t'nomma."

She spread her feet slightly, taking better possession of the sidewalk and resting on them evenly, the bag held open for green eyes. She could see he didn't want that, but she insisted in her silence he did. Tito spread his little feet and lined the points of his shoes against hers. Tomato noticed the imitation and cackled at the concrete. The music went on, the beat feeding on itself, pulverizing words, smearing them into liquid submission: "Iss t'nomma twany fyiv? Dat iss not t'nomma."

"Twenty-five cents," she said again.

Tito whined, "Gimme twenty-five cents."

"Shut you mouth," said the hat, and turned a grim face to his friend. In the darkness of his eyes there were deals. The music ceased. "Hey, baby, you got no manners? Tell what you want." He spoke in a dreamy voice, as if to a girl.

"I want a kiss," said green eyes.

She glanced down with this at Tito and studied the small shining head. "Tell him to give me my glove, Tito," she said cutely, nervously. The wings shuffled and looked down bored. Nothing was happening. Twisting backward Tito shouted up to green eyes, "Give her the glove." He twisted front again and crouched over his knees. He shoved Tomato for approval and smiled. Tomato shoved him back, snarled at the concrete, and spit between his feet at a face which had taken shape in the grains.

"I want a kiss," said the boy again.

She sighed, giving another second to helplessness. The sun was low above the river and the street three quarters steeped in shade. Sunlight cut across the building tops where pigeons swept by loosely and fluttered in to pack the stone foliage of the eaves. Her bag snapped shut. Her voice was business: "Come on, Francisco. I'll give you the kiss."

He looked shot among the faces.

"Come on," she said, "it's a deal."

The hat laughed out loud with childish insanity. The others shrieked and jiggled, except for the wings. But they ceased to sprawl, and seemed to be getting bigger, to fill with imminent motion. "Gimme a kiss, gimme a kiss," said the little ones on the lowest step. Green eyes sat with a quiet, open mouth.

"Let's go," she said. "I haven't all day."

"Where I go?"

"That doorway." She pointed to her building and took a step toward it. "You know where I live, don't you?"

"I don't want no kiss."

"What's the matter now?"

"You scared?" asked the hat. "Hey, Duke, you scared?"

The wings leaned toward the center, where green eyes hugged himself and made a face.

"Look, Mr. Francisco, you made a deal."

"Yeah," said the wings.

"Now come along."

"I'm not scared," he shouted, and stood up among them. He sat down. "I don't want no kiss."

"You're scared?" she said.

"You scared chicken," said the hat.

"Yeah," said the wings. "Hey, punk. Fairy. Hey, Duke Chicken."

"Duke scared," mumbled Tito. Green eyes stood up again. The shoulders below him separated. Tito leaped clear of the stoop and trotted into the street. Green eyes passed through the place he had vacated and stood at her side, his head not so high as her shoulder. She nodded at him, tucked her bag up, and began walking toward her building. A few others stood up on the stoop and the hat started down. She turned. "Just him."

Green eyes shuffled after her. The hat stopped on the sidewalk. Someone pushed him forward. He resisted, but called after them, "He's my cousin." She walked on, the boy came slowly after her. They were yelling from the stoop, the hat yelling his special point, "He's my brother." He stepped after them and the others swarmed behind him down the stoop and onto the sidewalk. Tito jumped out of the street and ran alongside the hat. He yelled, "He's got the glove." They all moved down the block, the wings trailing sluggishly, the young ones jostling, punching each other, laughing, shrieking things in Spanish after green eyes and the lady. She heard him, a step behind her. "I give you the glove and take off."

She put her hand out to the side a little. The smaller hand touched hers and took it. "You made a deal."

She tugged him through the doorway into the tight, square lobby. The hand snapped free and he swung by, twisting to face her as if to meet a blow. He put his back against the second door, crouched a little. His hands pressed the sides of his legs. The front door shut slowly and the shadows deepened in the lobby. He crouched lower, his eyes level with her breasts, as she took a step toward him. The hat appeared, a black rock in the door window. Green eyes saw it, straightened up, one hand moving quickly toward his pants pocket. The second and third head, thick dark bulbs, lifted beside the hat in the window. Bodies piled against the door behind her. Green eyes held up the glove. "Here you lousy glove."

She smiled and put out her hand. The hat screamed, "Hey, you made a deal, baby. Hey, you got no manners."

"Don't be scared," she whispered, stepping closer.

The glove lifted toward her and hung in the air between them, gray, languid as smoke. She took it and bent toward his face. "I won't kiss you. Run." The window went black behind her, the lobby solid in darkness, silent but for his breathing, the door breathing against the pressure of the bodies, and the scraping of fingers spread about them like rats in the walls. She felt his shoulder, touched the side of his neck, bent the last inch, and kissed him. White light cut the walls. They tumbled behind it, screams and bright teeth. Spinning to face them she was struck, pitched against green eyes and the second door. He twisted hard, shoved away from her as the faces piled forward popping eyes and lights, their fingers accumulating in the air, coming at her. She raised the bag, brought it down swishing into the faces, and wrenched and twisted to get free of the fingers, screaming against their shrieks, "Stop it, stop it, stop it." The bag sprayed papers and coins, and the sunglasses flew over their heads and cracked against the brass mailboxes. She dropped amid shrieks, "Gimme a kiss, gimme a kiss," squirming down the door onto her knees to get fingers out from under her and she thrust up with the bag into bellies and thighs until a fist banged her mouth. She cursed, flailed at nothing.

There was light in the lobby and leather scraping on concrete as they crashed out the door into the street. She shut her eyes instantly as the fist came again, big as her face. Then she heard running in the street. The lobby was silent. The door shut slowly, the shadows deepened. She could feel the darkness getting thicker. She opened her eyes. Standing in front of her was the hat.

He bowed slightly. "I get those guys for you. They got no manners." The hat shook amid the shadows, slowly, sadly.

She pressed the smooth leather of her bag against her cheek where the mouths had kissed it. Then she tested the clasp, snapping it open and shut. The hat shifted his posture and waited. "You hit me," she whispered, and did not look up at him. The hat bent and picked up her keys and the papers. He handed the keys to her, then the papers, and bent again for the coins. She dropped the papers into her bag and stuffed them together in the bottom. "Help me up!" She took his hands and got to her feet without looking at him. As she put the key against the lock of the second door she began to shiver. The key rattled against the slot. "Help me!" The hat leaned over the lock, his long thin fingers squeezing the key. It caught, angled with a click. She pushed him aside. "You give me something? Hey, you give me something?" The door shut on his voice.

intimations

MAMMA WAS COMING. SARAH WAS STIFF AND PALE. Myron walked circles saying chicken chow mein. If Mamma asks say chicken chow mein. There was a knock. Sarah said chicken chow mein, opened the door. Mamma. Stockings rolled in rubber bands just below the knees. She had something for them in a shopping bag: lox, rye bread, salami, chocolate cake . . . Then it was 5:00 a.m. Light hung about their heads like iron. Naked, staring at Myron, Sarah was poignant with the need to pee. Myron talked about pain, Sarah, and the need we must feel, Sarah, to accept pain. Yet he had suffered doubts. He had been less than cool. Indeed, shiksa blonde or purple eggplant, she was his wife and had made a delicious dinner. Mistake or not, Sarah. Yet he'd been doubtful when he said, if Mamma asks—which she did—say chicken chow mein—which they did. He'd been doubtful when Mamma was eating it, pork casserole, but he babbled distractions and filled the wineglass from which she drank nothing, Sarah, because she was eating misgivings away—hers and theirs, Sarah. And yet in the loving momentum of Mamma's teeth didn't everything seem fine, Sarah, hugging goodbye, gimme-a-call, Sarah. Then the door was locked, Sarah, and Mamma was in the subway tunneling out of mind and he took Sarah, Sarah, and stripped her like a twig and came trip hammers and sprawled all bones until the phone rang weirdly oh God, Sarah. And a hideous bird voice said Mamma had had a trichinol seizure and he screamed filthyfucking-middlewesternswinepeddlers, Sarah, waking, to stare at Sarah's gray eyes staring at him out of sleep and nightmare. I'm talking about pain, Sarah. How the old must suffer, Sarah, because we grow, we change, and we honor them, Sarah, by acknowledging and making clear to ourselves that we accept life's inexorable sophistication and cruel, natural, inevitable growing away from primitive intimations of kindness, Sarah, and the phone rang. From the bathroom she yelled acknowledge it, Myron. And it rang, Myron.

making changes

THE HALL WAS CLOGGED WITH BODIES; none of them hers, but who could be sure? The light was bad, there was too much noise, too much movement. Too many people had been invited. More kept arriving. I liked it, but it was hard to get from one room to another. Conversation was impossible. People had to lean close and shriek. It killed the effect of wit, looking into nostrils, shrieking, "What? What?" But it was a New York scene. I liked it. Except she was missing; virtually torn out of my hands. Cecily. I would have asked people if they had seen her, but I was ashamed to admit I had lost her. I was afraid she was someone's date or inextricably into something. I was afraid she was copulating. She had been dressed, but it was a New York scene. Minutes had passed. I shoved through the hall—hot, dark, squealing with bodies—and looked for her. I shoved into the kitchen and saw just one couple, a lady in a brown tweed suit talking to a short dapper man in spats. She was stout, fiftyish, had fierce eyes. Flat, black as nailheads. Her voice flew around like pots and pans. The man glanced at me, then down as if embarrassed. The lady ignored me. I ignored her and busied around the wet, sloppy counter looking for an unused glass and a bottle of something, as if I wanted a drink. The lady was saying, slam, clang:

"Sexual enlightenment, the keystone of modernity, I dare say, can hardly be considered an atavistic intellectual debauch, Cosmo."

"But the perversions . . ."

"To be sure, the perversions of which we are so richly conscious are the natural inclination, indeed the style, of civilized beings."

I found a paper cup. It was gnawed about the rim, but no cigarettes were shredding on the bottom. I sloshed in bourbon and started to leave, afraid she was pervulating.

"Wait there, you."

I stopped.

"What sort of pervert are you?"

I shrugged, mumbled, hoping she'd forgo.

"What sort of pervert are you?"

I shrugged, mumbled.

"Speak up, fellow."

"I mug yaks."

"You hear, Cosmo? A yak mugger."

"Are you married, young man?" asked Cosmo, dreamily.

"No."

"Good question," she cried, "for we observe, as necessarily we must, that marriage encourages perversity—assuming the parties agree on specified indulgences, Cosmo, which is paradoxical."

"Indeed, Tulip, the natural perversions themselves, one might well assume," he said, whispering.

"Let me continue."

"Please, please do."

Something shadowy and mean in her voice wanted to spring, to rip off his head. I wanted to leave.

"Let me continue."

"Please, please do."

"Paradoxical, I repeat, for the prime value of sex, to an advanced view, lies precisely in its antagonism to society. What, then, dare one ask, must we make of marriage?"

"An antisocial perversion," he said.

"Yes, clearly," I added, "clearly."

The words burst out of themselves with a wonderful feeling. I love logic. Its inevitability, its power of consummation.

"Cosmo," she said, ignoring me, "you're a horse's ass."

She looked at me. I nodded my head. "Clearly."

"I say, fellow, is much going on in the living room?" Her black eyes, like periods, stopped mine.

"I just came the other way, actually. From the back of the apartment."

I pointed.

"How fascinating. Do publish a travel book. In the meantime, look behind you."

I turned and looked through the dining room over scattered struggling to the living room. It was piled and dense with sluggish, sliding spaghetti.

"It's mainly in there now." I pointed.

"Good. The orgy, Cosmo, our oldest mode of sexual community has moved closer. Let's go watch now that we needn't poke about the rooms like vulgar tourists. Oh, Cosmo, what better solvent have we for the diversity of human beings? And, needless to add, it's such a chic way of breaking the ice."

They left the kitchen, her smashing voice flinging in all directions, and hesitated at the edge of the toiling pile with spray in their eyes. Figures cast up like tidal garbage lay quivering at their feet.

"Cosmo, the view is breathtaking. Tell me your impressions."

"Breathtaking, a view of the infinite mind. Indeed, the mind, that ocean where each kind . . ."

"Yes, yes . . . where every sort its own sort shortly finds."

I pushed by them down the edge of the mind, squatting, peering at whatever caught light—blades, nails, paps, hips, tips—looking for her blond hair, her gray eyes, her legs.

I pushed beyond the mind, back into the clogged hall, and looked into a bedroom. Three mirrors showed me looking. I went on, looked into a study, and saw a wall of whips, barbells on the floor, framed diplomas, photos of movie stars and contemporary philosophers. I found a bathroom. I knocked, stepped in. A naked man sitting pertly in the tub said, "I'll bet you're Zeus. I'm Danaë." I shook my head, backed out muttering, "I'm Phillip." Again in the hall, rump to rump, hip to hip, between moaning, writhing walls; pardon me, so so sorry, until a knee plugged under my crotch and I pitched to a side and down, elbow deep in churning, hands smack on a hot face. Eyes gleamed through my fingers, teeth nibbled my palm, fingers clapped my thigh, squeezed to nerve, and my fist swung back like a hoof. Struck neck. "You want to hit?" There was a punch, a slap, a gibbering girl tumbling over me and nails raked my spine. I scrambled for space, slammed nose flat into shivering thighs, pinwheeled, flapped cha-cha-cha like a sheet in the wind, and fell out against bare wall, wheezing, whistling into virtual black. Tulip's voice slashed it like tracers:

"I will say one thing, Cosmo, you meet people in an orgy. Not like conventional sex, sneaking in corners, undermining human society, selfish, acquisitive, dirty. I mean every time one gets laid, as it were, it's conservative politics, don't you think? On the other hand, orgies are liberal, humane. The ambience of impulse, the deluge of sensation, why orgies are corporate form, the highest expression of our catholicity, our modern escape from constrictive, compulsive, unilinear simplifications of medieval sex. Don't you think?"

"They give me a certain cultural feeling."

People were sliding across my legs.

"Precisely."

A pulsing hole went by.

"Precisely a feeling of mind, as it were."

People were sliding across my legs like lizards. I was inching one buttock at a time toward the foyer. A squeal of recognition needled my ear. My hands flew up, slapped a breast, belly, weedy groove.

"You!"

She collapsed into my arms and we went sliding down the molding like snakes, sliding out of massy sucking foliage. But she quit, suddenly dead as a ton. I dragged. She babbled encouragement, "Gimme, gimme sincere." I reached the door with her, opened it, and light swept her body. Bruised, vaporous, shining with oils, more limp than any deposition I'd ever seen, more tragic than Cordelia in the arms of Lear. But she wasn't Cecily.

She was all right. Whoever she was, squalid enervation made easy lines like vines; lips, like avocado pulp, hung lovey in her face. Nose, belly, legs, all in good repair. I helped her stand, then turned her about to consider another prospect. I smiled. She smiled. Both of us a smidgeon self-conscious, confronting one another this way, a couple in the eyes of the world, standing apart, she and I, and it wasn't easy to think, to ignore the great pull of the worm bucket and pretend to individuation. She gave way shyly under my glance, and leaned toward the wall. There was no wall. Her hands flailed like shot ducks, her eyes grabbed for mine, flashing fright and dismay, and I flung after her into the sticky dismal, thrashing, groping like Beowulf in the mere for a grip on Grendel. I seized a wrist. I dragged, dragged us up to light. She whimpered so at the injustice, the imbecilic ironies. For her sake I contained my own distress. It wasn't exactly she. Like her, like her in many ways. Not a speck worse. But another girl. I released her, simpered an apology.

"You must love me very much," she said. "My name is Nora."

Such tender imperative. Another time, another place, who knows what might have been. If circumstances were slightly different, the light better, noise a little less, if, if, if I hadn't shoved her back in, furious with myself, we might have had a moment, a life . . .

"To think, Cosmo, how we build on merest chance—marriage, society, great societies—as if there weren't ever so much to choose from, so much that any choice at all must seem fanatical in its limitation. Isn't it that which makes the satyr frightfully amusing, his perpetual hard-on?"

"Ho, ho. A singular notion. But awfully true, Tulip. Awfully true, indeed."

I stumbled past them at the titillating margin. She was mushing his little rear in her fist.

"Cosmo, Cosmo, I think I see a perversion. You'll have to tell me what it's called. If only there were a bit more light. My, how it smells. Cosmo, what would you call that smell? The vocabulary of olfaction is so limited in English."

"Communism?"

"I adore your political intelligence, Cosmo. Why is it on every other subject you're such a horse's ass?"

I shoved into a bathroom to wash and look for fungicide, slammed the door, flicked the light. *Voilà!* A girl. She was bent over the sink having spasms. I pressed beside her, ran the water, snapped a towel off the rack.

"May I?"

She presented her chin, flecked, runny as it was, and didn't make an occasion of it. Her eyes were full of tears. Elegant gray eyes like hers; blond hair to the shoulders, in love with gravity. In less than a minute there was a bond, soft and strong as silk, holding us. I wiped her chin, we laughed at nothing, chatted, smoked a cigarette, and felt embarrassed by our luck in each other. I peed, and one of us said, "Let's get out of this party," and the other said, "Yes, right now." Holding hands tightly we left the bathroom and worked down the hall and through the living room. More people were arriving, thickening the stew; dull raging continued all around. At the door stood a big man.

"I'm glad you came tonight, Harold."

"I'm glad you're glad," I said. "Name is Stanley."

He wore a shirt and tie, nothing else. He had bloodshot eyes, a beard, a cigar in his mouth. Fumes drifted from his nostrils as if from boiling sinuses.

"I'm sorry you're leaving."

"I'm sorry you're sorry."

"I feel as if you want to say something nasty to me, Harold."

"Not at all, I assure you."

His legs were black and wild with hair. Burning meat looped on his thigh.

"You must have had a fight with one of your girlfriends. And I have to pay for it, eh, Harold? Well, what's a fuck'n friend for if you can't mutilate him every ten minutes, eh?"

He laughed, winked at her.

I edged by him, nodding agreeably, grinning, slapping his shoulder lightly. Not too intimate. I knew the signs and wanted to give no excuse for violence. I tugged her along behind me into the outside hall. He leaned after us, saying, "How do you like my beard, Harold?"

"Makes you look religious."

"You think I'm not religious?"

"I mean it's a nice religious beard."

"Say what you mean, Harold. I hate innuendo. I'm not religious. I'm Satan, right? What should I do, Harold?"

He was yelling as we went through the lobby, then out to the street. She squeezed my hand, pressed to my side. He pressed to my other side, yelling, "A moralist like you knows about people. I'd like to be like you and keep my principles intact, but I'm weak, Harold. I lack integrity. I haven't the courage to commit suicide, Harold."

He laughed, nudged my ribs with a big fist. His meat angered and there were suddenly two of him: Laughing and Angry. I snickered and looked up the street for a cab. She whispered, "Ignore him," and I whispered, "Good idea." I saw a cab, waved. It started toward us. She got right in, but he had my arm now.

"Wait one minute, Harold. I want your opinion about a moral problem."

He pushed his face at mine and tapped his beard, grinning and winking. "Which way is better, pointed or rounded?"

"How about growing it into your mouth?"

He let go of me and stepped back.

"That would kill our conversation, Harold. And you know when people stop talking they start fighting. For instance, if I stopped talking right now I might kick you in the nuts."

He stopped talking, dropped his hands lightly on his hips, spread his legs. I kicked him in the nuts.

"Ooch."

I leaped into the cab, slammed the door, slammed the lock, and his face smeared the window as I rolled it up. His eyes glazed, his upper lip shriveled, spit came bubbling between his teeth. His fingers clawed then whipped across the glass as the cab shot away. I turned to her. She was staring at me with big lights in her eyes, quivering. She dropped her eyes. I inhaled, rubbed my hands together to keep them from shaking and from touching her.

"That look on his face," I said.

"And his penis."

"That, too."

"It was so biblical."

"Old Testament."

She touched me, then took my hand. Going across town we talked about the people, what they looked like, what they said, who did what, and so on. We talked in my apartment, listened to our voices, boats in the river, planes in the sky, and it was impossible to say when it happened or who laid whom and we fell asleep too soon afterward to think about it. Not that I would have thought about it. I'm not a poet, I'm Phillip. And then I awoke as if from a nightmare and it was brilliant morning. She was standing like a stork on one leg, pulling a stocking up the other. She said, "Hello," and her voice was full of welcome, but I saw she was too much in motion, already someplace else. Her eyes were pleasant, but they looked through mine as if mine weren't eyes, just tunnels that zoomed out the back of my head.

"Leaving?"

"I'll call you later. What's your number?"

"Leaving?"

I stared at her. She finished dressing, then sat stiffly on the bed to say goodbye. We kissed. It was external for her. I seized her arms, kissed harder, deeper. She was all surface despite me, despite the way she felt to me. I released her.

"Look," I said, "you can't leave."

"Please, Phillip. It's been nice, very nice."

She stared at a wall.

"Is something the matter?"

"No."

A toilet flushed next door, water retched in pipes. I got out of bed and went naked to my desk. I found a pen, returned, and pushed her backward onto the bed.

"I'm all dressed, Phillip."

I shook her hands off, lifted her dress, and scribbled across her belly: PHILLIP'S. On her thighs: PHILLIP'S, PHILLIP'S.

She sat up, considered herself, then me. As she rehooked her stockings she said, "Why do that?"

"I don't know."

"You must have something in mind."

"What can I say? I'm aware the couple is a lousy idea. I read books. I go to the flicks. I'm hip. I live in New York. But I want you to come back. Will you come back?"

"I have a date."

"A what?"

"Can't I have a date? I made it before we met."

"Break it."

"No."

"Will you come back?"

"I'll try."

"Today?"

"I'll try," she said, straightened her dress, went to the door, out, and down the steps. D'gook, d'gook. The street door opened. She was gone. I was empty.

I flopped on the bed, picked up the phone, and called my date for the afternoon. A man answered.

"Yeah?"

"May I speak to Genevieve?"

"Hey, baby, the telephone."

His voice was heavy, slow, rotten with satisfaction. Heels clacked to the phone. A bracelet clicked, a cigarette sizzled, she exhaled, "Thanks, Max," then, "Hello."

"This is Phillip."

"Phillip? Phillip, hello. I'm so happy you called. What time are you coming for me?"

"Never, bitch."

I dropped the phone, g'choonk.

I flopped on the bed, empty, listening to the phone ringing, ringing, and fell asleep before it stopped. There was no moment of silence, no dreaming, nothing but the sound of her footsteps going down, then coming up, a knock at the door and I awoke. It was early afternoon. She leaned over me.

"Phillip."

I caught her hand, dragged her down like a subaqueous evil scaly. We kissed. She kissed me. I bit her ear. We kissed and there was no outside except for the phone ringing again. I let it. We had D. H. Lawrence, Norman Mailer, *triste*.

I lighted cigarettes and put the ashtray on her belly. Even tired, groggy, *triste*, I could see we were a great team. Smoke bloomed, light failed, I savored the world. Before the room became dark I turned on my side to examine her belly and thighs. The PHILLIP'S were in each of the places. All about them like angry birds were: MAX'S, FRANK'S, HUGO'S, SIMON'S.

"For God's sake," I said.

I looked into her eyes, she mine. She put out her cigarette, gave me the ashtray, and turned her back to me. I was about to yell, but was stopped by writing down her spine: YOYO'S, MONKEY'S, HOMER'S, THE EIGHTY-SEVENTH STREET SOCIAL AND ATHLETIC CLUB'S.

My voice trickled.

"All right, we'll do this properly. Get to know one another. I see you're difficult. Good. Difficulty is an excellent instructor, just the one I need. It'll extend the reach of my original impressions. I misjudged you, but I appreciate you. I'll study you like a course. Turn around. Let me kiss you, all right?"

She turned around. I kissed her. She kissed me. We had Henry Miller.

In the shower I scrubbed everyone off front and back and asked her name.

"Cecily," she said.

"I'm Phillip," I said, "but you knew that. Cecily? Of course, Cecily."

I couldn't have stopped the tears unless I'd chopped out my ducts with an adze. She giggled, stamped her feet, clapped her hands with glee.

mildred

MILDRED WAS AT THE MIRROR ALL MORNING, cutting and shaping her hair. Then, every hour or so, she came up to me with her head tipped like this, like that, cheeks sucked in, a shine licked across her lips. I said, "Very nice," and finally I said, "Very, very nice."

"I'm not pretty."

"Yes; you're pretty."

"I know I'm attractive in a way, but basically I'm ugly."

"Your hair is very nice."

"Basically, I hate my type. When I was little I used to wish my name were Terry. Do you like my hair?"

"Your hair is very nice."

"I think you're stupid-looking."

"That's life."

"You're the only stupid-looking boyfriend I ever had. I've had stupid boyfriends, but none of them looked stupid. You look stupid."

"I like your looks."

"You're also incompetent, indifferent, a liar, a crook, and a coward."

"I like your looks."

"I was told that except for my nose my face is perfect. It's true."

"What's wrong with your nose?"

"I don't have to say it, Miller."

"What's wrong with it?"

"My nose, I've been told, is a millimeter too long. Isn't it?"

"I like your nose."

"Coward. I can forgive you for some things, but cowardice is unforgivable. And I'll get you for this, Miller. I'll make you cry."

"I like your legs."

"You're the only boyfriend I've ever had who was a coward. It's easy to like my legs."

"They're beautiful. I like both of them."

"Ha. Ha. What about my nose?"

"I'm crazy about your big nose."

"You dirty, fuck'n aardvark. What about yours, Miller? Tell me . . ."

The phone rang.

"His master's voice," she said, and snatched it away from me. "Me, this time. Hello." She smacked it down.

"What was that about?"

"A man."

"What did he say?"

"Disgusting."

"What did he say?"

"He asked how much I charged . . . I don't care to talk about it."

"To what?"

"It was disgusting. I don't care to talk about it, understand. Answer the fuck'n phone yourself next time."

She dropped onto the bed. "Hideous."

"Did you recognize the voice?"

"I was humiliated."

"Tell me what he said."

"It must have been one of your stinking friends. I'm going to rip that phone out of the wall. Just hideous, hideous."

I lay down beside her.

"He asked how much I charged to suck assholes."

I shut my eyes.

"Did you hear what I said, Miller?"

"Big deal."

"I was humiliated."

"You can't stand intimacy."

"I'll rip out the phone if it happens once more. You can make your calls across the street in the bar."

"He was trying to say he loves you."

She thrashed into one position, then another, then another. I opened my eyes and said, "Let's play our game."

"No; I want to sleep."

"All right, lie still. I want to sleep, too."

"Then sleep."

I shut my eyes.

"I'll play once. You send."

"Never mind. Let me sleep."

"You suggested it."

"I've changed my mind."

"Son of a bitch. Always the same damn shit."

"I'm sending. Go on."

"Do you see it clearly?"

"Yes."

"I see a triangle."

I didn't say anything.

"A triangle, that's all. I see a triangle, Miller. What are you sending?"

"Jesus Christ. Jee-zuss Chrice. I've got chills everywhere."

"Tell me what you were sending."

"A diamond. First a sailboat with a white, triangular sail, then a diamond. I sent the diamond."

I turned. Her eyes were waiting for me.

"You and me," I whispered.

"We're the same, Miller. Aren't we?"

I kissed her on the mouth. "If you want to change your mind, say so."

"I am you," she whispered, kissing me. "Let's play more."

"I'll call Max and tell him not to come."

"He isn't coming, anyway. Let's play more."

"I'm sleepy."

"It's my turn to send."

"I'm very sleepy."

"You are a son of a bitch."

"Enough. I haven't slept for days."

"What about me? Don't you ever think about me? I warn you, Miller, don't go to sleep. I'll do something."

"I want to sleep."

"Miller, I see something. Quick. Please."

"A flower."

"You see a flower?"

"It's red."

"What kind of flower? I was sending a parachute."

"That's it, Mildred. A parachute flower."

"Fuck you, Miller."

"You, too. Let me sleep."

"Miller, I still see something. Hurry. Try again."

I lay still, eyes shut. Nothing came to me except a knock at the door, so quiet I imagined I hadn't heard it. She said, "Was that a knock?"

I sat up and listened, then got out of bed and went to the door. It was Max and Sleek. Max nodded hello. Sleek stepped backward, but a smile moved in his pallor. I said, "Hi." I heard Mildred rushing to the kitchen sink and held them at the door. "Only one room and a kitchen," I said. Max nodded again. The smile faded slowly in Sleek's pale, flat face. Water crashed, then she was shooting to the closet, jamming into heels, scrambling a blouse on her back. A light went on. She slashed her mouth with lipstick. "Come in, come in."

They came in.

"Please sit down."

Max sat down in his coat, looked into the folds across his lap, and began to roll a cigarette. Sleek sat down in his coat, too, watching Max. Both of them glanced once at Mildred, at each other. I said, then Max said. Sleek laughed feebly as if suppressing a cough. Then they both stared at her. Max offered her the first drag on the cigarette. She said quickly, but in a soft voice, cool, shy. They looked at one another, Max and Sleek, and agreed with their eyes: she was a smart little girl. I sat down. I told them she might be pregnant. We were thinking about getting married, I said. I was going to look for a new job. Everyone laughed at something. Max said, Sleek said. They took off their coats. She was now shining awake, feeling herself, being looked at.

"Do you want some coffee?" She tossed her hair slightly with the question.

Max said, "Do you have milk?"

Sleek said, "Coffee."

She curled tightly in her chair, legs underneath, making knees, shins, ankles to look at. They looked. I stood up and went into the kitchen for the coffee and milk. Max was saying and Sleek added. She was quick again, laughing, doing all right for herself. I took my time, then came back in with the coffee and milk. I asked what they were into lately, imports, exports, hustlers, what. Sleek sucked the cigarette. Max rolled another and was looking at Mildred. He asked if she had considered an abortion. She smiled. Sleek said I was an old friend. He would get us a discount. They wouldn't take their cut until I had a new job. They shook their heads. No cut. Max mentioned a doctor in Jersey, a chiropractor on Seventy-second Street. He said his own girl had had an abortion and died. Almost drove him nuts. He drank like a pleeb. You have to get a clean doctor. Otherwise it can be discouraging. His stable was clean. Sleek nodded shrewdly, something tight in his face, as if he knew. "Of course," he said. "Of course." He opened his hand and showed Mildred some pills. She raised an eyebrow, shrugged, looked at me. I was grinning, almost blind.

"Do what you like."

She took a pill. I took a pill, too. Max talked about the eggbeater they use and what comes out, little fingers, little feet. Mildred squirmed, showed a line of thigh, feel of hip, ankles shaped like fire.

"Abortions are safe," I said, and waved a hand.

"Right," said Max. He tossed a pill into his mouth.

Sleek said he had a new kind of pill. Mildred asked shyly with her eyes. He offered immediately. She took it. "The whole country shoves pills up itself," he said. "My mother takes stoppies at night and goies in the morning." He gleamed, sucked the cigarette, and sat back as if something had been achieved.

Max frowned, mentioned his dead girl, and said it hadn't been his baby. He shook his head, grinding pity, and said, "Discouraging."

"Your mother?" asked Mildred.

Sleek said she lived in Brooklyn. I nodded as if to confirm that he had a mother. He whispered, "The womb is resilient. Always recovers." Max said, "Made of steel." "Of course," said Sleek, "chicks are tough." Mildred agreed, sat up, showed us her womb. Max took it, squeezed, passed it to Sleek. He suppressed a laugh, then glanced at me.

"Squeeze, squeeze," I said.

He said, "Tough number. Like steel."

I said it looked edible. Sleek stared at Mildred. She got up and took her womb to the stove. I had a bite. Max munched and let his eyelids fall to show his pleasure. Sleek took a sharp little bite and made a smacking noise in his mouth. I felt embarrassed, happy. Mildred seemed happy, seeing us eat. I noticed her grope furtively for something else to eat. But it was late now. Rain banged like hammers, no traffic moved in the street. They waited for a few more minutes, then Max yawned, belched, stood up. "We'll get a cab on Sixth Avenue," he said to Sleek. I said we would decide, then get in touch with him right away. We thanked them for the visit. I apologized for not being more definite. Max shrugged. They were in the neighborhood, anyway. Sleek said take a couple of days to think about it. Gay things were said at the door. Max said, Sleek said, Mildred laughed goodbye. Their voices and feet went down the stairs.

Mildred kicked off her shoes. I turned out the light. We kissed. I put my hand between her legs. She began to cry.

"You may not love me, Miller, but you'll cry when I'm gone."

"Stop it," I said.

She cried. I made fists and pummeled my head. She cried. I pummeled until my head slipped into my neck. She stopped crying. I smashed my mouth with my knee. She smiled a little.

"Do it again."

I started eating my face. She watched, then her eyes grew lazy, lids like gulls, sailing down. She lay back and spread underneath like a parachute. I lay beside her and looked at the window. It was black and shining with rain. I said, "I like your hair, Mildred, your eyes, your nose, your legs. I love your voice." She breathed plateaus and shallow, ragged gullies. She slept on her back, mouth open, hands at her sides, turned up. Rain drilled the window. Thunder burdened the air.

fingers and toes

I SCRIBBLED A HASTY NOTE, REGRETFUL, TO THE POINT. Fourteen pages, sharp as knives. I refuse. I don't feel good. The date is inconvenient. Sorry. Sorry. Sorry. Then I stopped and sat rigid as a sphinx. Henry was my dearest friend. It was brutal not to mitigate such severity. Not many people count in one's life. A fool slams doors. Who knows, given the vicissitudes, where a man has to grovel tomorrow? I sprang forward and said as much. I told him his company was more precious to me than my own. I'd love to come to your dinner party, I said. Nothing short of atomic holocaust can prevent it. You're a man of genius and personality. You give life to my life. But refuse I must. To be frank, Henry, it's impossible for me to come. You are a person who doesn't like me. Why? I could say this or that, but who knows his own deficiencies? Who? We know each other too well these days, but who, who among us knows what the others know? The mystery of self lies here, Henry. There in the hearts of others. Consider how often we've laughed at a mutual friend and said, That's just like him, or, You know Ahab would do that sort of thing. Yet the man himself, Henry, does he say these things? No. He goes his way, grinning, tipping his hat, waving to friends on every side. He goes ass out in the eyes of the world. I flew to the mirror, ripped down my pants. I flew back and said, Henry, I read books, I go to the movies, I look constantly in mirrors both literal and figurative. But do I see anything? How could I? I'm not my friend. I'm not Henry. I'm Phillip, Henry. Your friend. I could say things about you that would make your nipples pucker. As for your invitation let me say I am delighted to accept it. I reread the note, chucked up laughs like the clap of big buttocks, and flushed it down the bowl. The one I sent was a stream of polite, innocuous drivel. Twenty-five pages. Pleasing to hear from him, I said. I confessed that I loved to get letters, especially invitations. For just that alone I was grateful to him. I wished so much I could come to his dinner party. Nothing I'd rather, but I had stomach cancer and had to pass it up. Some future date perhaps when they cut out my stomach, etc., etc. I was sitting beside the phone nibbling Dexedrine when he called.

"I just read your letter, Phillip. Woo, what a letter. I'm sorry you're sick."

"My feet are like seashells, Henry."

"No."

"Seashells. Curled, hard, I walk bonky, bonky."

"Phillip, you're not the only one. Every time I lose touch with a friend something terrible happens to him. I could go on and on. I hate letters."

"Mine was impulsive. I'll never write you again."

"I hate to walk in the street, Phillip. I might meet some friend about to kill himself. I sneak everywhere. I wanted to talk to you, by the way, about our dinner party. And now look. I intended to say a few words to make you change your mind. This is what I get."

"Months of silence, Henry. Things happen."

"I couldn't leave well enough alone. Besides, Marjorie insisted. 'Call Phillip. Call Phillip,' she said. Such a trivial matter, one night, a dinner party. The truth is, Phillip, there aren't many people in one's life who count. I could ask seventy or eighty people for that night, but how many of them would be you?"

"I was going to kill myself that night."

"Are you saying you won't come?"

"But I'll come."

"I knew you would. I know you so well, Phillip. You have no convictions."

I laughed. He did, too. Nee, nee, nee. Behind him somewhere Marjorie clapped her mouth. Nee, nee filtered through, female, insidious. Henry snarled. I did, too. Footsteps hurried away and I knew there was going to be trouble. From a distance Marjorie screamed, "I laugh, I pee, and I don't care who knows it." Henry said, "I'll call you back, Phillip." "Just tell him to come," she screamed.

I quivered all over. It was excruciating to bear such knowledge. The private life of a friend is to be dreamed about, never known. I went to the bathroom and stepped under a hot shower. Wax coiled out of my ears like snakes. The phone rang again. "Henry," I said, "didn't you call earlier?" I picked up the phone. "Henry," I said, and he said, "Then we'll expect you, Phillip."

"Of course."

"It wasn't of course a little while ago."

His voice was hard and mean. I remembered he could be that way and shook my head.

"You know me, Henry."

"Of course, of course, but I'd as soon you stayed in your rathole downtown if you don't feel like coming."

"Just tell me when."

"Next Wednesday. Six-thirty. Perhaps you can't make it at such a wild hour?"

"It's perfect. One of the best times. It gives me pleasure just to think about it."

"You ought to hang up the phone and masturbate."

"Don't be silly. I'll just open the window."

Nee, nee, we laughed. I grinned and shook my head. I remembered how witty he could be.

"And another thing, Phillip. It's not crucial, but I want to say it."

"Please."

"I know about you and Marjorie, Phillip."

"Don't say it."

"Makes no difference. We're civilized people, not Victorians. What's finished is finished, no more, void. What remains is friendship. Our friendship. Even stronger than before. I hope you feel the same way. That's how Marjorie feels."

"That's how I feel, too, Henry."

"Then there isn't anything more to be said about that. Am I right?"

"You're right."

"Are you absolutely sure? I don't like to leave things unsaid, Phillip. They always come out one way or another."

"I know, I know. Henry, I get boils on my neck when I leave things unsaid."

"Good, then you understand me. Next Wednesday, Phillip. Six-thirty."

"Right."

Nee, nee we laughed and said goodbye.

———

Dinner with them was out. Furthermore I wouldn't eat a thing. Not that night and not until that night. The idea just came to me. I didn't struggle to establish thesis and antithesis. It came BOOMBA. Real ideas strike like eagles. A man who loves premises and conclusions loves a whore. I wouldn't eat that night and not until that night. That's how well he knew me. Not at all.

I ran about my room until I got sleepy and then spent the night whirling in bed shrieking curses. At dawn I was sitting up with two fists of hair, cool as a Buddha. Dinner with them was out. The idea gave me shivers. Fat ran off. Bones lifted under the skin. I went and leaned against the refrigerator door. Hours passed, the day, the night. I leaned with the insouciance of a hoodlum or a whore. I gazed down at my feet. Gaunt, sharp as chicken feet. The objective principles on which I stood. The first line of a poem came to me: "Bitter, proud metatarsals." I smelled chicken salad and cream cheese, but didn't move until I ripped open the refrigerator door, grabbed handfuls of salad and cheese, and flung them out the window. "Ya, ya," I shouted, "food is out." My hand seized a frozen steak and flung it into my mouth. I swallowed. Instantly, I became depressed. The steak was in. Like a virgin deflowering I sank to the floor. The steak worked grimly inside. I wanted to make it stop. My stomach churned like the back of a garbage truck. Arteries sucked. I had the steak in my neck, thighs, fingers, toes. But all right, I thought. I'll journey to the end of the night like Saint Augustine and the Marquis de Sade. The more things are different the more they are the same. Immoral is moral.

I went to the nearest restaurant, a fish house. It made no difference. I ate a cow, I'd eat a fish. I ordered lobster Leningrad and a plate of mixed crawlers, flung everything inside, and chewed in a deliberate way. In my mind I said, "Yum." The waiter refilled my bread basket. I grunted, "Thanks." People like me, he said, made his job meaningful. I told him I understood food. He nodded.

"May I watch?"

"Please," I said.

He stood beside my chair and put his hand discreetly on my shoulder. His mouth moved with mine. When I finished he smiled and asked if I enjoyed the meal. I rubbed my stomach and winked. He nodded in an appreciative way. I leaped from my chair. We embraced. "My name is

Phillip," I said. He said he could tell. I squeezed money into his hand. He protested. I refused to listen, squeezed more, snapped up the menu and shoved it down into my crotch.

Days passed. The dinner party was only hours away. As it drew closer I couldn't repress what Henry had said. He knew I was going to come. He knew me so well. "But you were very wrong," I said. However wrong I could indulge the idea that he was right. I indulged it: "You were right." The idea gave me pleasure. The pleasure of an infant. Something turned, poked, smelled, very known. I bobbled out into the street and walked among strangers to intensify the pleasure. None of them knew me. I went to a liquor store and bought wine, red and white, to express my contempt for Henry's dinner. A bottle of Armenian raki was on sale. I bought it, too, then left and bought flowers. Around midnight I stood outside Henry's door. It was open, welcoming the night. There were seventy or eighty people in the house. I knocked. Henry came running. "Someone's at the door," he yelled. "Phillip. What a surprise."

I leaped backward into the darkness. He leaped after me and caught my arm. "Come in, come in." He took my wine and flowers and flung them into a closet. "We had a little dinner party."

"I already had dinner. Thanks for inviting me in, Henry. I can't stay."

"Why not?"

"I'd rather not talk about it. It's nothing personal."

"But, Phillip, I want to talk to you."

"Let me continue for a moment. Then I'm going back to my rathole. I appreciate your invitation more than I can tell you. You believe me?"

"Of course."

"Don't say of course. I really mean it."

"I do, too, of course."

"Don't say of course, Henry. You mean a great deal to me. You're my dearest friend, the only one I have. It kills me not to come to your dinner party. But I can't. Let's not talk about it, all right? I don't ask a lot of favors of you."

"Will you have a drink?"

"Bourbon."

"Ice? Water?"

"No. In fact, look, don't even pour it into the glass."

I snapped up the bottle and swallowed. People were everywhere, standing, sitting, talking, smoking, drinking. It was a brilliant crowd. The women had nice legs. The men looked as if it didn't matter. I felt a bit out of place because I didn't know any of them. Henry touched my elbow. He spoke very quietly, very slowly, and as if we were the only ones there.

"Phillip, I do want to talk to you."

I was thrilled by the intensity of his voice.

"There's nothing to talk about at a party," I said.

He shrugged. "You're right, Phillip."

"What do you want to talk about?"

He shrugged again. It was very like him to do that when he had a lot on his mind. "About? You're hungry for topics? I want more than to talk about. I want dialogue, Phillip, not topics. I don't want to talk about a thing. Things crap up talk."

"I agree. Now I'm going, Henry."

"Go."

"But I'll listen for a minute if you like."

"Can you listen for a minute? Don't say yes if you can't."

"I'll listen for a minute."

"Phillip, I'm going out of my mind."

"Why?"

"I couldn't tell you in a million years."

"It's been good talking to you, Henry."

"Wait, Phillip. I want to tell you a story. Not a story, a parable."

"Oh."

"It represents my connection with the elemental life. Nothing else. Not art, not politics, not history, not anything but the elemental life. The truth is, Phillip, I don't give a damn about anything else. I'm talking about love."

"I know. I can tell."

"Of course. Phillip, listen. The first time Marjorie and I went out we went to a movie. I don't remember what was playing. At any rate, I put my arm around her and my hand fell on her breast. She didn't say anything. She trembled. At first, Phillip, I didn't notice where my hand had fallen. Then I felt her trembling and I noticed. I trembled. I was a hand. She was a breast. I don't have to tell you what a trembling breast feels like."

"Don't tell me."

"I've gone too far now to stop."

"No more about the breast."

"If I stop I'll be like Satan floating in space or Macbeth on his way to stab Duncan. Imagine if they had stopped. They would have felt like creeps. It's the kind of thing, Phillip, you have to get over with."

"Get it over with. You trembled, she trembled."

"I was a hand. She was a breast. One day, not much later, I touched her you know where and said, 'You tremble.' I told her I noticed and wondered if she noticed. More than that, I wondered if she noticed that I noticed. Never in my life was I so sincerely concerned about anything. It was a feeling. Do you follow me, Phillip? I knew immediately it was a feeling. Clear, authentic, like you standing here this minute. You're standing here, right? Nothing less. That's how this was. Nothing less."

"I see. What happened?"

"Phillip, I could spring up on her like an Irish setter and she wouldn't notice unless I called it to her attention."

"I don't know what to say."

"Say what you think. Say whatever you think."

"You lost your connection with the elemental life, is that it?"

"You could say that."

"At least you have dialogue, Henry. Where's Marjorie, by the way? I don't see her anywhere."

"Do you see that door? Go through it, you'll find her."

I looked at the door. It had a quality of shutness. I looked at Henry's face. It had the same quality, something vertical and shut, like the face of a mountain. Impassive, forbidding, beckoning, irresistible. Susceptibilities in my hands and feet became agitated.

"I won't go through any doors, Henry."

"I wouldn't have talked about this with anyone but you, Phillip."

"I'm flattered, but not another word, please."

"In that room, Phillip, in the dark, in a corner . . ."

"I'm leaving now."

I glanced away. He glanced after me. He arrived, I was gone. I turned back and looked him directly around the eyes, a swimming look. He tried to pierce it but wallowed. His eyes flailed for a grip but I widened my focus. "Phillip," he cried, "go speak to her. Tell her my love."

"Ech," I said. "I knew it would come to this. Tell her yourself. I'm going."

"Go. You have no right to go, but go. I've told you everything. Take it. Throw it in a sewer someplace."

"Be reasonable. What can I say to her?"

"Don't play stupid. You and she had plenty to say to each other before I came along. Say anything, just make her come out or let me come in."

"Henry."

"You owe me this. I'll never feel it's over between you unless you do it. Make her call me in there."

"What if I can't?"

"Then I'll know what it means and I'll kill you. To me the connection between love and death is very close."

"Henry."

His hand clutched my elbow like the claw of an angry bird. He walked me to the door.

"Henry, what can I do?"

"You know what."

He opened the door and shoved me through it. The door shut and I was in such darkness that I staggered and swayed. The sound of clinking glasses and talking trickled in after me, but I felt no relation to it. I was steeped, immobilized, wrapped up tight as a mummy. I was without head or arms or feet and my brain was suspended like a cloud. "Marjorie," I said. My voice whooshed away. No answer came. I crooned, "Marjorie, it's Phillip." A hiss cut the dark and there was a rough scratching like scales on rocks. "Marjorie," I crooned again, bending slowly until my hands touched the floor. "It's Phillip. I know you're there." I was on my hands and knees, whispering, urgent and conspiratorial. I leaned forward and put out my hand, letting it drift into the blackness like a little boat. I heard breathing. My hand drifted into it. My eyes bulged. I leaned after my hand, saw nothing, but smelled her very close and felt her heat on my face. The hiss came again. My hand drifted farther into the darkness, my fingertips quivering, quickening to the shape, the texture, the person of Marjorie. There was a slash. My hand snapped back.

"Don't try that again, jackass," she said.

"My hand is bleeding."

"Good."

"Henry has a lot of friends out there, Marjorie. Why don't you step outside for a moment and slash them up?"

"Give me your hand."

"Fat chance."

"Give it to me. I didn't mean to hurt you."

My hand drifted forward. She took it in both of hers and licked it.

"Better?"

"Feels all right."

I started to draw my hand back again. She hissed, clutched it tightly. I dragged. She wrapped herself around it, shimmied up my arm and hung from my shoulder like a bunch of bananas. She whimpered in my ear, "Phillip, I'm miserable."

I patted her knee with my free hand. She tightened her grip with her legs and pressed her face into my neck.

"It's not me they'll meet if I go out there. Not the me I am."

I felt sexual irritation and started patting her harder.

"I know what you mean."

"Phillip, when I woke up this morning there was something lying right beside me. You know what?"

"What?" I said, patting, patting. "Henry?"

"Me. Stretched out right beside me and staring at me in such a sad way."

"It's the *Zeitgeist*, Marjorie."

Blood stopped flowing in my arm. I tried to move it. She squeezed.

"Me," she said. "I want me, me, me."

I tried to shrug her off but it was like trying to shrug off a big wart. I smeared her against the floor, got up, and smeared her against a wall. She clung like my head on my neck, my foot on my leg. I rolled, rammed into tables and chairs. She clung. I leaped up and came down on her. She clung. She gnawed my neck, nibbled, licked, squeezed. I stopped and lay still. I tried to think, but darkness seeped into my ideas, clogged the parts and connections with heavy, impenetrable scum. Her fingers and toes worked into me like worms, coiling around tendons and bones. I could tell she was nervous and said, "Marjorie, as long as I'm here why don't you tell me what's wrong. I'll listen. Something wrong between you and Henry, for example?"

"There's nothing wrong."

"Is it this party? Don't you like this party?"

"I love it."

"But there is something wrong?"

"Nothing."

Instinctively, I wanted to punch her in the head. I said, "Marjorie, for all I care you can fester in here. Let me go."

She licked and squeezed.

"If you don't let go I'll punch you in the head."

She plunged her tongue into my ear. I breathed hard. Glaciers streamed down my face. Suddenly we heard footsteps approach the door and both of us lay still.

"You ask me what's modern," said a man. "No one feels anymore. That's modern."

Earrings tinkled as if a head were being shaken violently. A necklace rattled. "But I feel you can't say that," cried a girl. "I feel there are a lot of feelings today, feelings we feel deeply and that's why it feels as if we don't. I couldn't dance otherwise. How could I dance if I didn't? Answer that."

For a moment there was silence. Then the man spoke again, his voice dismal and pinched as if he had a finger in one nostril.

"Feel shmeel."

Marjorie whispered, "You feel, don't you?"

"I feel," I said, "but this is life. Who feels?" I thrashed. She clutched and bit. I collapsed and lay still. There was a bump against the door, hard rubbing, then a kick.

"Don't touch me," said a girl. "Look what you did to my dress. I think you suffer from jugular peacocks."

Others came by, stopped.

"Miss Genitalia, I'd like you to meet Miss Gapegunda."

"I'm sure she'll come back, Max. It's not like her to run out. She doesn't have carfare."

"If she comes back I'll spit in her face."

Marjorie was breathing as if she were asleep. I listened to her and to the people who came by and stopped outside the door.

"What you said, Irma, makes a lot of sense," said a man.

"I was just talking."

"But very intelligently."

"You can't mean that. I was talking, that's all. If you don't talk at these parties they think you're a fool."

"I do mean it. I'd like you to write it all up and submit it to my journal. Do you write German?"

Another man wheezed.

"Shut up, sweetheart. All right? Just once you shut up, all right? It's not so much to ask, is it? I say yes, you say no. I say no, you say yes. Why don't you write a book and shut up? Write one of mine in reverse. Where I say no you say yes."

"Fuck you, Ned."

Marjorie was asleep, wrapped around my arm like ten snakes. I moved a little. She constricted and said, "Nya, nya."

I lay still again and gaped into the darkness. It was important to think. I had a sense of the problematic towering above me in the darkness like a Gothic cathedral. Complex, violent, full of contradictions like the hairdo of a madwoman. I fell asleep. In my sleep I heard a knock at the door. It came drifting over waters like Noah's dove, little gray wings knocking through fog. It came closer, closer. I cried, "Here, little dovey." It went by, knocking dimly away into the fog.

"Phillip," said Henry.

I yelled in my dream, "Henureee."

Marjorie woke up, hissed, "Don't answer."

I tried to wake up.

"Phillip, you there? Who's there?"

Marjorie began moving all over me. She ripped open my shirt. She scraped off my shoes with her toes. I woke up as my zipper went down like a slashed throat. She wrenched under me. I said, "Love." She yelled and pummeled my back as if sending messages to friends across the veldt. "What's wrong?" I said.

"I like it, I like it," she yelled.

"Like what?" I said.

"Who's in there?" said Henry.

"Don't come in," I said.

His footsteps went away.

Marjorie went limp, her arms outflopped, languid as lily stalks.

"Finish," she said.

Her legs fell apart as if cleaved by an ax.

"Hurry," she said.

I hurried. Footsteps came back to the door. There was a knock.

"Marjorie," said Henry. "Was that you in there?"

I hurried.

"Wait for me," she said. "Slow down."

"Of course," said Henry. "You know I will."

I slowed down.

"Do it," she said.

"I won't move an inchy winchy until you tell me to." He made a kissing against the door.

"Up and down, up and down," she said.

"Ha, ha," said Henry. He jumped up and down, up and down. "Like this?"

"Yeah, yeah."

Nee, nee, nee he laughed. "Here I go up and down, up and down," he sang. "I'm skipping rope."

"Now," she yelled.

"Now?" said Henry. "Di oo say now now?"

"Wow, wow," she said.

"Marjorie," I said.

"Henry," she screamed.

He flung open the door. I was behind it. He laughed nee, nee, jumped up and down, and came skipping into the room. I flew out. His knees struck the floor like cannonballs.

"Marjorie," he said.

"Love."

I got my flowers and wine and slipped out into the night. It was moonless and cold. I slipped into it nose first. It nosed into me. I twitched like a fish and went quivering through dingy dingles, from blackness to blackness to blackness to blackness.

isaac

TALMUDIC SCHOLAR, MASTER OF CABALA, Isaac felt vulnerable to a
thousand misfortunes in New York, slipped on an icy street, lay on his
back, and wouldn't reach for his hat. People walked, traffic screamed,
freezing damp sucked through his clothes. He let his eyes fall shut—no
hat, no freezing, no slip, no street, no New York, no Isaac—and got a
knock against the soles of his shoes. It shook his teeth. His eyes flashed
open, darkness spread above him like a predatory tree, a dozen buttons
glared, and a sentence flew out, beak and claws, with a quality of moral
sophistication indistinguishable from hatred: "What's-a-matta, fuckhead,
too much vino?" He'd never heard of vino, but had a feeling for syntax—
fuckhead was himself. He said, "Eat pig shit," the cop detected language,
me-it became I-thou and the air between them a warm, viable medium.
He risked English: "I falled on dot ice, tenk you."

The man in the next bed wasn't alive. Gray as a stone, hanging over
the edge of the mattress, the head was grim to consider. But only a fool
points out the obvious; Isaac wouldn't tell a nurse. Even so, he couldn't
dismiss a head upside down, staring at him, and found himself crying. He
had traveled thousands of miles to fall down like a fuckhead and lie beside
a corpse. Crying loosened muscles. His shoulders began moving. Shoulders moving, he discovered arms moving, and if arms, why not legs? In
his left leg moved thunder and lightning. But he sat up and shouted,
"Sitting!" A nurse ripped open his pajamas and shoved in a bedpan. "I
appreciate," he said, and defecated.

Before dawn he had dressed himself and was in the street. Stumbling,
pressing into the dark as if pursued by dogs. More and more he tilted left
and thus, beneath horrible pain, felt horrible geometry. His left leg was

shorter than his right. He pressed into a phone booth. His sister screamed when she heard his voice. He told her what happened and she screamed, "Don't move." He sat in the booth, fell asleep, there was a knock and his eyes opened. She looked through the glass. "Katya," he said, "like a coffin." She wouldn't discuss the idea. Neither would Chaim, her husband, or Fagel, her husband's sister, or hunchback Yankel, the peddler, who asked where Isaac felt pain. In the back? In the leg? He remembered a fall in which he hurt his knee. Did Isaac's knee hurt? No? Very strange. How did a scholar, he wondered, fall in the street like an animal; but then what's one leg shorter compared to a brain concussion with blood bulging from the eyes? No comparison. Lucky Isaac. Isaac winked, made a little lucky nod, and collapsed. Fagel screamed. Katya screamed. Chaim gave Isaac his umbrella. Isaac pressed it with one hand. The other pressed his sister's arm. They went down the street together—Isaac, Katya, Fagel, Chaim, Yankel. Cracow, the chiropractor, had an office nearby.

To keep his mind off his stumbling torture, Katya told Isaac about Moisse, who wasn't lucky. He came to New York sponsored by a diamond merchant, friend of politicians, bon vivant, famous for witty exegeses of the Talmud. "So?" So as a condition of sponsorship, Moisse promised never to abandon, in New York, any tradition of the faith. He imagined no circumstances in which he might, but married, opened a dry-goods store, and had a son. Circumstances arose in doctor bills. He had to do business on Saturdays. Isaac licked his lips. Chaim punched his chest. Yankel shrugged his hunch. "So?" So it followed like the manifestation in the garden, that the merchant's beard hung in the door one Saturday. —You know what day this is, Moisse? What could he say? Isaac said, "Nothing. What could he say?" Chaim punched, Yankel shrugged. The beard nodded. The mouth hacked up a spittle, the spittle smacked the floor, and the baby son was discovered on the prostrate body of his mother, shrieking like a demon while he ate the second nipple. Now Moisse doesn't do business on Saturday. His worst enemies won't say he isn't a saint.

"You got another story?"

"It's the only story I know."

"Tell me again," said Isaac.

Before she finished they were inside an old brownstone, looking up a high, narrow stairway. She tugged at the umbrella, but Isaac only looked, as if they were stairs in a dream. To be looked at, nothing else. What can you do in a dream? She tugged. He fell against a wall. She went up alone

and came down with, "Dr. Cracow says." Isaac must walk up and lie face-
down on the chiropractor table. Otherwise go away and shrivel. In a week
his leg would be a raisin. He could look forward to carrying it in his
armpit. Fagel screamed, Chaim punched. They walked up.

Cracow stood suddenly erect, as if, the instant before, he had touched
his toes. His fingers were stiff, quivering like the prongs of a rake. He nodded to the table. Isaac dropped onto it as if into an abyss and Cracow
pummeled him from neck to tail, humming: *Muss es sein. Es muss sein,*
then said, "Get up." With dreamlike speed they were at the brink of the
stairs. A thing whooshed by, cracked, clattered to the landing. "Get it," said
Cracow.

Isaac shook his head.

"Isaac, get it," said Katya. Chaim said, "Get it." Yankel said, "Get it,
get it."

The umbrella was a streak of wood and cloth in another world. Isaac
shook his head at the possibility of getting it. Beyond that, not getting it.
Shaking his head, he started down. Not with delicate caution, like a man
just crippled, but mechanical exactitude, like a man long crippled. Even in
the bones of former incarnations, crippled, resigned to a thousand stric-
tures. Cracow hummed, Isaac descended. Every step an accident succeed-
ing an accident in a realm where perfection was grotesque. Cracow said,
"No pain?"

Isaac stopped, gazed out; then, carefully, into his own center. Pain? His
whole being was a question. It trembled toward yes or no and, like music,
yes, very slightly, yes, he felt himself lift and fly above the stairs. Then he
settled like dust. Cracow's voice shot through the air: "Six dollars, please."
Isaac turned to fly up to him. With four wings clapping he was struck by
stairs, smacked by walls, stopped by the ultimate, unyielding floor. He lay
on his back. His eyes fell shut. Thumps accumulated down the stairs. Katya
screamed. Yankel shrugged, Chaim whispered, "Dead?" Fagel screamed,
Cracow said, "Could be dead." Chaim said, "Dead?" Fagel screamed,
Katya screamed. "Dead? Dead?" said Yankel. Chaim said, "Not alive," and
Yankel said, "Dead." Fagel screamed, screamed, screamed, screamed,
screamed.

a green thought

I YELLED; SHE RAN IN; I POINTED. "WHY IS IT GREEN?" She clapped her mouth; I shrieked, "Why is it green?" She answered . . . I shrieked, "Vatchinol infection!" She whispered . . . "Green medicine!" I wouldn't let her mitigate; shoved her aside. "No mitigations!" She picked up a washcloth. I wouldn't let her wash it. "No washing it!" I lunged into my clothes, laughed ironically, slammed out . . . Subway steps, downtown express, eighty miles an hour. Hot, cold, nauseated. Nevertheless, nevertheless, nevertheless. Not like the last time, fighting, fighting, collapse: leetlekissywissysuckyfucky. I checked my fly. Light tight. But I sensed the green, looked away. No one noticed. Good fly. Develop photos inside. A lady sucked her teeth. Suck. Suck. The man beside me did a crossword puzzle, picked his nose. Suck. Pick. Everyone busy. New Yorkers in the raging underground. Sensuous. Insular. Discreet. All buried in noise. I vomited. Quick. No one noticed. Used my shoe; slipped foot back in; looked up coolly at the ads: have a lot of fun; worry about communism; smoke; drink. They made a sense of community. Lot of fun all around. The lady sucked her teeth, the man did his puzzle, picked his nose. Train full of pleasure. Involvement. I liked the mood. I philosophized: What does this mean to ride downtown? eighty miles an hour? three o'clock in the morning? shoe full of vomit? I noticed a girl leaning against her date. A marine. She had frog eyes; motionless, dreaming of flies. Looked something like a moron. It all meant nothing. I had slammed, certain it meant something. I'd laughed ironically. She opened the door. I waited ironically for the elevator. I felt her stare, gray, foggy, rotten with guilt. She said, "Your face, Phillip." I whirled. "Gimme carfare." A flash of white ass, of blond. She vanished, returned, wrist-deep-crap clicking in her purse. She

struggled, naked, shameless. I was cool. She pulled out a dollar. Green. I
was sick, getting sicker. Rocking, banging, rocking, banging. But this was
the last time. I sang it to the mambo of the wheels: "The last time, the last
time. Chunga cha-chunga. Green green." I'd soon have to walk. Deserted
buildings, warehouses, alleys, cats, rats, drunks, unpredictable figments of
the municipal dark. City at night, full of wonders, mysteries. Like a god. I
could hardly wait to get home, lock the door, lie down, sleep. But I might
run into neighborhood kids, get robbed, chopped up, set on fire, pissed
on, stuck in a garbage can. That would mean the city hated me. I appreciated its hatred, shared it, wanted to fling out to the speeding tunnel. But I
looked at the marine and his girl: both pale, tight in the face, yet healthy.
I'd seen him before. On toilet walls. Her, too, waiting for him, cock and
balls. It might have been us: Mr. and Miss Subway. No such luck. Cecily
had a high I.Q., degree from Barnard. I giggled a lot. The moron leaned
on the marine. I looked for a moral. They swayed against the rocking iron
tumultuous rush as . . . they would sway against the buffets of life. I was
envious; felt ashamed: my insularity, my self-pitying. I wanted to shove
them off the train. I wanted to go back, pound on her door. She would
open it. I'd giggle. But I knew the rules. It was her move. Love is not
enough. Hell with her. Blond hair, gray eyes, white skin, green crotch.
Every conceivable virtue. Happens to be festering in the vagina. Take
good with bad. I giggled ironically. The man covered his puzzle. Inched
away, erasing. Made me self-conscious, creepy feeling. I wanted to strangle him. I yelled, "No one can solve the puzzle!" He gave me a look as if
that hadn't occurred to him before. I shrugged. He changed his seat. I
sprawled like a vulgar swine, yawned, scratched my ass, studied the marine
and his girl, objects, paragons. My mother used to say, "Why don't you be
like Kenneth? . . . like Bernard? . . . like Schmuckhead? Why don't you
do the right thing, Phillip?" Why don't I be like that marine? No side-
burns to catch filth, unbalance his head. Just a haze of needles prickling at
the top. And her hair: thick, red, bulging around her ears like meat. Such
radical difference: Mr. Prickles and Miss Meat. What could their relationship consist in? "None of that rooting in my horn, Marie. Try it, I'll kick
your twat off." She melts. He upchucks like a tilted jug. Take that, that.
Spilling marines. Moral. But I was moral, too. I had slammed out. Exquisite dinner, wines, dessert in bed. Naked, satisfied, peeing hard into the
roaring center and the whole toilet echoing to a tinkling consonant with
the force that through the green fuse drives beyond right things, wrong

things, and "CECILY," I yelled, the train retching past Bloomingdale's. She did it on purpose. The train stopped. A man entered carrying a newspaper. PLANE CRASH. Green crotch strikes again. I didn't read another word. It all just came to me: fifteen hundred returning from a soccer game, team, coaches, cheering squad. Usual bunch. People shake their heads, tsk, tsk, but oneself isn't dead. Ten cents to find out one isn't dead. Cost me nothing, a glance, a second of subway lucubration. I was alive, aware of it, more than alive. I wanted to do kneebends, pushups, jog a couple of laps. Maybe the marine would join me. "Hey, schmuck, how about a little P.T. before the next stop?" He would really grin. So would his moron. But it was the next stop. Mine. I was up, striding out, step, splash, step, splash, hut-hut! I was alone. Now I could think. I shut my eyes, squeezed. I thought: Think! I couldn't think. It proved I was social. No lonely thinker, no Thoreau, this Phillip. Which way to the pond? Let me see; I remember that pile of bird shit from yesterday. Take years just to get from shack to pond. "Simplify," said Thoreau. Really see what life is about. Indeed, just come back, that's all: here's old Phillip, schmutz and fleas; no book; maybe a little map. "See, X is the shack. Dig? The circle is the pond." What do you mean open the door, fall into the pond? I was nervous. I needed another voice. All right. "Say something." What? "Say an important, sober, meaningful phrase." I said, "Ludwig Wittgenstein," snapped double, rolled, screeched, "What a dingleberry," rolled into a phone booth. Numbers scratched into the walls. Names. Recommendations. The city was social; how could I ever live anywhere else? "Call Carla for a first-rate toe job." I wiggled my toes. Seemed all right. I memorized her number, left the booth, ran. What I expected: deserted buildings, alleys, cats. My apartment. I had to phone someone. Green crotch was out. I grabbed the phone, dialed Henry. It was very late, but he was my friend. Marjorie answered: "Your name first, wise ass."

"Marjorie, this is Phillip. Tell Henry I'm sick."

"O.K."

She hung up.

I sat on the bed, chuckling. How silly of her to have done that. Now she had the rest of her life to wonder about what form my revenge would take. I chuckled, "Kill, kill, kill." The phone rang. I grabbed it. Henry's voice said, "Phillip? Phillip?"

"Phillip. Phillip."

"Don't tell me you're sick."

"Of course not."

I cracked the receiver against the wall, let it crash to the floor.

He piped: "Pheeleep, Pheeleep . . . Sometheen hapeen tee Pheeleep, Marjoreep."

I pushed over a chest of drawers.

"Pheeeep, Pheeeep."

I sang, "La, la," and vomited on the receiver.

"Pheeweep, wa dee mawee? . . . dee oo ha fie wee Ceceeweep?"

I felt better, hung up, undressed. I lay down, shut my eyes, began screwing Ceceeweep, but everyone was jumping, shouting, except the marine and me. There had been a crash. He nodded in my direction. I nodded back, very pleased to have been recognized by a person like him, with his moral haircut. The man dropped his crossword puzzle, yelled, "Breakdown. There's been a serious breakdown." He started to masturbate, but the train wouldn't move and suddenly, pop, he ripped his prick off. I screamed and a girl said, "Phillip, what's wrong?"

"Who?"

"A succubus."

I tried to smile. "You come back later, baby. I'm a tad indisposed."

She stood beside the bed, didn't move. I heard her breathing.

"Don't stand in the vomit, sweets."

"Shit!"

"You stood in it, eh?"

"Never mind. I see you're wearing a shoe, Phillip. Do you always sleep with a shoe?"

"Get up to leak, hop right to the bowl. Saves fuss."

"Phillip, don't you want to look at me?"

"I'm sick."

"A man is the sum of his actions."

"I didn't do anything."

"I believe you, Phillip, though some would say I'm mad."

"You good succubus, baby."

"Open your eyes. I'll take my clothes off, too."

"It's cold."

A coat and trousers dropped on me. A hat, shirts, ties, laundry bag, suitcase, something heavy. I smelled it.

"Good idea."

"Do you have another rug?"

"That's the only rug."

"May I get under it with you?"

"Gimme a cigarette."

I tried to sit, but there was too much weight on my chest. She put a cigarette against my lips. I dragged.

"Light it."

"Sorry."

"Light it."

"The answer is nopey nopey."

"Get under."

I smoked. She put a leg across mine, a hand on my belly. She said, "I want to ask you something."

"Ask."

"When a man is as sick as you, inhibitions vanish, right? He'll say anything, right?"

Her lips were in my ear.

"Ask, ask."

"What do you think . . . I can't. See that. Ha, ha. I'll never get another chance like this."

"Oh, Cecily, ask, ask."

I crushed the cigarette against the wall.

"I want to ask what you think of me. What do you think of me, Phillip?"

She seized my prick.

"I like your style," I screamed.

"What else?"

"There's nothing else."

She flung my prick down.

"I didn't have to come here, Phillip. I didn't have to chase out screaming for a taxi. You talk to me, you. I asked a question. What do you think of me, Phillip?"

"There's general agreement."

"That so?"

"Pretty general fucking agreement."

"What, what do people say?"

"They say you're an asshole."

"Is that what *you* feel? Is that what *you're* telling me?"

"I'm too sick to make qualifications."

"Goodbye, Phillip. This is the last time."

I grabbed her wrist. Things hit the floor. The rug scratched everywhere. She twisted, kicked, thrashed.

"Bastard. Take a shower. You wanted to infect me."

"No one else."

"You don't love me. Say it. I want to hear you say it."

"No one else."

"You swear?"

She kissed me. I pushed down on her head.

"I'm tired, Phillip."

I pushed, pushed.

"Say you love me, Phillip."

I pushed, pushed.

"Merm," she said.

"No teeth," I yelled. "Watch the teeth."

"Mumumu."

"All right," I said.

I felt all right. All right.

finn

FINN, LATELY FEIN, RAN INTO SLOTSKY and mentioned the change.

"By the way?"

"I agree. It goes without saying. Changing one's name isn't by the way. Neither are the harsh realities. The business world. You know what I mean, Slotsky? I was a little cavalier in my announcement. Nevertheless . . ."

"Call me Slot."

A smile wormed in Finn's lips. "That's very amusing, Snotsky."

To show Finn his smile, a smile wormed in Slotsky's lips. Reinforced by his speedy, ugly face, it was particularly revolting. But Finn, thumb hooked to alligator belt, stood six two, two hundred fifteen pounds. Imperturbable. Besides, against the big sharkskin curve of his can, he had a letter admitting him to graduate school in business administration. He also had a date that evening with Millicent Coyle at the Kappa house; darkish girl, but in manner and sisterhood fished out of the right gene pool. Black Slotsky, now, was chancy matter in the street; dog flop. Brilliant student, but pale, skinny, cross-eyed, irascible, contentious, a walking criticism of life, and a left-wing communist. In every way he seemed to beg for death. One felt his begging; also his contempt for one's reluctance to kill him on the spot. He sneered, "I thought your old name was fine."

Finn repeated, "That's very amusing, Snotsky."

"I'm still doing business under the same name."

Finn answered gently, sailing toward the Kappa house and business administration. "Granted, Slotsky. Your name is Slotsky. Mine is Finn. All right?" And he made concessions in a shrug. Two shrugs.

"Didn't it used to be Flynn?"

Finn waved bye-bye.

"Flynn, Finley . . . didn't you used to be Flanagan the rabbi?"

Finn was three, four, five steps into the evening, the life. Just up ahead there, Finn beckoned. To him, Finn.

"So long, Ferguson."

He tossed harbingers of love on his bed—trousers, shirt, tie, socks—but couldn't decide on a jacket to wear that evening. He wandered naked in his indecision, lit a cigar, then considered less the jacket than his indecision. Immediately, he discovered Slotsky in it, shimmering like fumes. Two years ago they had been roommates. People used to say, "You room with Slotsky?" Because Slotsky was famous. He wrote a column in the school paper, noticing films, plays, any little change in the campus ambience—Muzak in the administration building, yellow plastic chairs in the library, new pom-poms adopted by the basketball cheering squad. He was famous for screaming revulsion and his column's title, "Foaming at the Mouth," was a description of himself in the throes of a criticism. Otherwise he restricted his humor to sneering irony, never directed at himself, never humorous. Finn explained him to the world by saying, "He wants love. Anyhow, he has brain cancer." It would have been easy to be more cruel, but Slotsky helped him with chemistry and French—Finn's reason for rooming with him in the first place. Finn never said anything more about Slotsky. Anything more might have suggested there was more than an apartment between them. There was. It started one night before end terms. Finn heard himself pleading: "I read the books, Slotsky. I took notes in class. But I can't write it. I tried all week, but I've got nothing to say about the New Deal. Do I think it was good? Bad? I think I hate poly sci, that's all. It isn't fair not to be able to drop a course in the last week. Sometimes you can't tell until the last week that you want to drop it. What am I going to do? I need the B.A. I don't want to fail. My average won't support a failure in poly sci. I'll be thrown out of here. That'll be the end of everything for Bruce J. Fein. Everything."

"What a pity."

"I'm sorry I told you about it."

"You make me a little sick, Fein."

"I make myself sick. I can't stand the sound of my voice. I'm disgusting."

He went to the bathroom, stuck three fingers into his mouth, vomited, then slept all night in his clothes. Came morning, he opened eyes full of prayer. For what, he didn't ask himself. He dragged to the kitchen, sat down at the table. It was the first time since they had been living together Slotsky hadn't gotten up ahead of him to make breakfast. Finn looked toward the next room where Slotsky slept, then looked at his hand. It lay on a pile of paper. Eighteen pages, in fact: stapled, nicely typed with double spaces, wide margins, signed Bruce J. Fein under the title "The New Deal: Good and Bad." How could he not have felt contempt? In the next room Slotsky snored with miserable exhaustion, like a man scratching at the sides of his grave. He felt contempt bloom into hatred, bloat, blur into pity, and then, on his way to poly sci, he gradually felt something different, something new, in regard to Slotsky. He stopped for coffee. While reading through the paper, he coiled inward to catch it. He caught it in a word: he and Slotsky had "relationship." As for the paper, not bad. Not bad at all. Worth a B, maybe B+. He scratched out one phrase and scrawled his own above it. However brilliant, it was true, after all, Slotsky had never taken a course in poly sci. The correction made Finn feel as if the paper were a little bit his own. Two days later it was returned with an A++. Beneath the grade the professor had written: "Please, Fein, become a political science major, as a favor to the world." Beside his correction, Finn saw: "I will accept this because of the rest of the paper, but it is badly expressed and adds nothing to your argument." In a daze of gratitude so thrilling it reminded him of fear, Finn rushed back to the apartment, pulled a jacket out of his closet, and hung it in Slotsky's. Thus, among dull, shapeless gabardines, glowed a smoky tweed, a sensuous texture, a weight of life. Simply to have said, "Thank you, Slotsky, for saving my life," seemed impossible. Not that it wasn't sufficient return, but he couldn't say those words to Slotsky. Some element in their relationship would become too obvious, even grotesquely sentimental. Nevertheless, relationship, reciprocity: Finn was big, rich, good-looking, and he had girls; Slotsky, in relation and return, was his roommate—he wasn't living alone with himself and the walls; Finn had the paper; Slotsky, the jacket; Finn, Slotsky; Slotsky, Finn.

On his one date that year Slotsky wore the jacket. He also wore it at a president's tea for honor students, and at an address before a learned society, he appeared in the jacket. Big on him, but, if one knew nothing else about Slotsky, one knew he owned a fine jacket. Finer than anything else he owned. One knew that because he wore it with creaseless, flapping trousers that piled at the cuffs over patent-leather, busboy shoes. He didn't seem to think the owner of such a jacket might want to wear it with trousers a bit snappier. But Finn knew Slotsky wore no jacket at all. Only an idea of a jacket—Finn's jacket—beautiful in the eyes of mankind, spilling a superflux of beauty over anything Slotsky wore with it, even those trousers and shoes. Over Slotsky himself, wallowing in it. Finn was gratified. The paper, the jacket, the vision of Slotsky standing and walking in it—reciprocity, relationship. Until this moment.

Naked before the open door of his closet, where a harem of fifteen jackets languished—mute, lovely receptacles of his arms and torso—Finn was struck by the powerful idea: HIS. Then the powerful corollary: he hadn't given any jacket to Slotsky forever. When they split up he should have taken that jacket back, but he had thought Slotsky was already too disturbed by the loss of his roommate. He had been very foolish: no jacket in his closet had the drape, cut at the wrist, lapel, and haunch, or texture, tone, and quality of material that that particular jacket had. The one he loaned to Slotsky. Half an hour later, sitting on the bed in Slotsky's one room, in an odor of socks, underwear, and Slotsky, Finn had the feeling his seat would stick to the army blanket when he stood up. Slotsky said for the third time, "You want one of my jackets? Help yourself, roomie. I've got a dozen classy numbers."

"*My* jacket, Slotsky."

"Take a jacket."

"I didn't give it to you forever."

"There's the closet."

"You're being difficult. You don't have the right attitude. Not about anything."

"Toward anything. You think I stole your jacket."

"Never mind what I think. I want it back."

"Take, take, Fein."

"Finn."

Slotsky smacked his forehead, then adjusted his glasses. "That's right. How could I forget? You're Finn."

"This is very disappointing. I expected more from you."

"I've got a lot of work to do, roomie."

Finn walked to the closet. "This one."

"*That* one?"

"Mine!"

"I wouldn't use it for toilet paper."

"Ha, ha."

"I used to wear it because I pitied you."

"Ha, ha."

Finn was out the door.

Millicent Coyle had brown hair, blue eyes, a slender body, and she made an impression of cleanliness and optimism. Finn talked most of the evening about Slotsky. He told her about his filthy habits, his obnoxious political beliefs, and, striking at the essential man, told her Slotsky was neurotically sensitive about being a Jew and yet never went to all-campus Yom Kippur services or any others held at the Concert and Dance Theater or the Hillel Center, which had been designed by Miyoshi and cost several million dollars. Not once. He explained that Yom Kippur was an important holy day for Jewish people; at least that was Finn's understanding. They were parked in the lot outside the Kappa house. When Millicent didn't seem about to say anything in regard to Slotsky, he began to suspect she was waiting for a chance to scramble out of the car and just say good night. Suddenly she said, "I'll bet you think we're all alike at the Kappas'."

"Of course I don't think that. Everyone is different."

"I'll bet you do. I'll bet, for instance, you think we're all prudes."

Finn sighed. He would have found some answer to her accusation, but she didn't quite seem to be talking to him; to have sensed, that is, a particular subject in the air between them for the past several hours.

"Do you like to ski?" she asked.

"I've never skied, but I've thought about it. Up the mountain, down the mountain. Groovy."

She grinned. She knew he was making a joke. "Well it also gives you a chance to wear your après-ski outfits, you know. You could learn in a minute. I know a guy who has a car like this."

"Pontiac? I rented it for the evening."

"I love Pontiacs. His is a Mercedes."

Almost impetuously, Finn said, "You know when I called you last week I was afraid . . ."

"My roommate took the message."

"Really?" It seemed relevant. Finn considered. Nothing relevant occurred to him. He plunged on. "I'd been thinking about calling you for a long time."

The confession made silence. He felt sweat blossom in his palms and armpits.

"For months I've wanted you to call," she whispered, leaving the silence intact. "Months."

Finn's heart pumped into the silence. His hand, like an independent caterpillar, pushed softly down the top of the seat and touched her cashmere. He looked at her eyes. Her eyes looked. He held his breath, bent toward her, and her eyes shut. Their lips touched. On her breast he felt murmur. They kissed, slowly drawing closer, pressing more and more of themselves against one another. Beneath her skirt, along smooth tubes, he felt white, touched silky. "I wanted you to call months and months an' muns-ago." She crumbled in his ear. "Millicent," he whispered, shoving against her hand, her hard, fused tubes.

"Fein," she whispered.

"Finn," he said.

She pulled free. "I think I need a cigarette. I mean I really need a cigarette, but I'd like to talk a little."

Minutes later Finn was tapping the steering wheel with his fingernails. "I'm the only one who knows you're Jewish?"

"Well, actually, my mother converted years and years ago."

Finn drove to Slotsky's place and knocked until the door opened on Slotsky in underwear, his face deranged behind fingers shoving glasses against his eyes. "For Christ's sake. What the hell do you want?"

Finn shrugged, mumbled. Slotsky stared. The hall light made him look papery. Without a word Finn took off his jacket, then handed it to Slotsky. Slotsky frowned and shook his head.

"Take," said Finn.

"I don't want it."

"Take."

"No."

Shaking his head, Slotsky backed into the room. Finn shuffled after him, jacket stiff-armed at Slotsky's chest.

"Take it."

"I don't want it."

"Yes."

"Screw you. Get out of here, creep."

"Take it or I'll jam it down your throat."

"Screw you, Fein."

Finn lunged, stabbed the jacket against Slotsky's chest. Slotsky fell, smacking the floor with both palms, and Finn threw the jacket at his head. It caught over his head and chest like a lamp shade. Beneath it Slotsky screamed for help. Finn slammed the door. Slotsky shut up.

Alone and tired, Finn drove around town, the night droning, crowding into the car, pressing at the borders of his brain. He checked the dashboard again and again . . . twenty-five miles an hour . . . three-thirty . . . twenty-eight miles an hour . . . a quarter past four . . . less than half a tank of gas . . . ten past five . . .

And then Finn had a little waking dream in which he saw himself in Slotsky's glasses and Slotsky in his jacket, and Slotsky took his hand and he put his arm around Slotsky and they danced in the headlights, big Finn, black Slotsky, like ballroom champions, gracefully mutual, dancing for the delectation of millions until Finn hit the gas and crushed them into rushing blacktop.

going places

BECKMAN, A DAY OUT OF THE HOSPITAL, barely strong enough to walk the streets for a job, carrying a ruined face that wouldn't heal for weeks and probably never look the same, was shocked to find himself hired at the first place he tried, as assistant to a paint contractor, and thought to tell his parents and write his girl to come back from Chicago and marry him, but, recalling disappointments with jobs in the past, decided to wait, not say anything, and see how things went; to see if they continued to be real as the hard, substantial hand which had enveloped and strongly shaken his hand, less rough and hairy, but masculine, calloused by the wheel and stick of his trade, and a substantial hand, too; if not in muscle and bone, certainly in spirit, for in that shake Beckman was welcomed to the end of a successful interview and a life made wretched by rattling kidneys, the stench of gasoline, of cigarettes, of perfume and alcohol and vomit, the end of surly toughs, drunken women, whoring soldiers, vagrant blacks and whites, all the streaming, fearsome, pathetic riffraff refuse of the city's dark going places, though places in hell, while he, Beckman, driver of the cab, went merely everyplace, anyplace, until the sun returned the day and he stopped, parked, dropped his head against the seat, and lay mindless, cramped, chilled in a damp sweater and mucky underwear, lay seized by the leather seat, debauched by the night's long, winding, resonant passage and the abuse of a thousand streets.

Everyplace Beckman, anyplace Beckman, he went noplace until two figures in misty, dismal twilight hailed his cab—a man with a pencil mustache; a woman with big, slick, black eyes, orange lipstick, and Indian cheekbones—got in and beat him up while he begged, shrieking, "Take my money." They did, and they left him for dead.

They left him for dead, Beckman, who revived in a hospital and asked for a newspaper with his first deliberate words, and read want ads and thought about his life, so nearly his death, with a powerful, urgent thrust of mind entirely unlike the vague motions it had been given to while drifting through the dark streets of the city.

Something dreadful—running over a drunk, a collision with another car—might have happened sooner or later, but the beating, the beating, was precisely what he deserved, what he needed after years scouring the avenues like a dog, waiting for change to come into his life as if it might hail him from a corner like another fare. Indeed it had. Deserved, too, because he, Beckman, unlike the average *misérable*, could understand his own experience, and not without pride, he acknowledged the deity which had hailed him in the shape of twilight creatures and presented his face to their fists—as an omen, as a reminder of who he was—Beckman, son of good people who, when he pulled up before their two-story house in Riverdale on his monthly visit, became literally sick.

They were happy of course to see their son, but Beckman, winner of second place in an all-city essay contest celebrating fire prevention week, open to every child in New York, Beckman, the college graduate, history and economics major, risking life with strangers, ruining health in a filthy machine, it literally made them sick.

Laughing, telling stories, even a bit cocky, Beckman would finger the badge with his taxi number on it while his mother's eyes, with unblinking persistence, told him he was miserable, and his father, puffing a cigar against doctor's orders, sat quietly, politely killing himself, nodding, chuckling at the stories until Beckman left and he could stagger out of the room and grope down the wall to his bed. Behind the wheel, Beckman flicked the ignition key, squinted his mind's eye, and saw his father prostrate with a headache, and Beckman gunned the motor, gunned house and street, his mother's eyes and father's rotten heart and headache.

There had been omens in his life not so damaging, if hair loss, shortness of breath, and wrinkles around the eyes and mouth were omens, but death had never been so close and tangible, and Beckman had never thought, I am going to die, as he had, sprawled begging, writhing on the floor of his cab. Oh, he had felt the proximity of annihilation just passing a strange man on a dark street or making love to his girl, but the thrill of imminent nothing always came to nothing, gone before he might study it, leaving him merely angry or vacant and low. But now, like Pascal emerging from the carriage after nearly falling from it to his death, like Dostoevsky collapsed against the wall scribbling notes as the firing squad, dissolved by the witty czar, walked off giggling, like Lazarus rising, Beckman was revived, forever qualified and so profoundly reminded of himself he felt like someone else.

Hitting him, the woman cried, "Hey, hey, Beckman," a series of words chanted with the flat exuberance and dull inertia of a work song, repeated without change in pitch or intensity while fists rocked his skull and Beckman thrashed in the darkness, flapped his hands, and begged them to take his money and continued begging as they dragged him by his hair over the front seat and onto the floor in back where the mat reeked of whiskey, stale butts, the corruption of lungs, and a million yards of bowel. "Hell your lousy money, Beckman," said the woman, her spikes in his face and ribs as the man, squealing with effort, pummeled straight down into Beckman's groin. But the punches and kicks were heralds, however brutal, bearing oracles of his genius, the bludgeoning shapers of himself if properly understood. Years ago he should have had this job with the paint contractor, a steady salary, and his nights to sleep in.

He would write his girl this first day after work, thought Beckman, a letter of impressions, feelings, hopes, and the specific promise of their future, for now he wanted to get married, and his small gray eyes saw themselves reading that line as he leaned toward the mirror and shaved around the welts and scabs. His brows showed the puffed ridges of a pug's discolored, brutalized flesh where a billion capillaries had been mashed and meat-hammered to the consistency of stone. Ugly, but not meaningless, and Beckman could even feel glad there had been nothing worse, no brain damage, no broken eardrum, no blindness, and could indeed see qualities that pleased him in the petrified, moiled meat, Hardness and Danger, not in his face or in his soul before the beating, but there now as in the faces of junkies, whores, bums, pimps, and bar fighters, the city's most deeply kicked, stabbed, and slashed, whom he had carried to and fro in his cab; memento mori twisted into living flesh reflected in his rearview mirror, reflected now in his bathroom mirror, like the rock formations of aboriginal desert and plateau where snakes, lizards, and eagles subsist and life is true and bleak, where all things move in pure, deep knowledge of right and wrong or else they die. Beckman whispered, "They die," and the ruined flesh gave substance to the cocky twist of his head, his manner of speaking out of the side of his mouth and twisting his head as though whoever he addressed lived on his hip, though he himself was a few inches less than average height. The sense of his small hands flapped suddenly in his mind as the furies dragged him over the seat like a dumb, insentient bag, though he shrieked take his money, which they would take anyway, and his body refused to yield its hideous residue of consciousness even as they mercilessly refused to grant it any. He couldn't remember when he had passed out or ceased to feel pain or his voice had stopped, but thought now that he had continued screaming after he had stopped thinking or moving, and that they had continued beating him until his undeliberate, importunate voice stopped of its own. They couldn't have been human and so persisted, but had to have been sublime things which had seized Beckman as the spirit seizes the prophet, twists his bones, and makes him bleed in agonies of knowledge. Beckman, so gifted, saw himself like the Trojan Cassandra, battered, raped on the rowing benches by Agamemnon's men, and she was Apollo's thing. But then he looked into the mirror, looked at the lumps above his eyes and at the flesh burned green and blue around his mouth. Not a shaman's face. He pulled his tongue through space once filled by an eyetooth and molar, licked sheer, delicate gum.

Enough, this was another Beckman. In truth, no prophet, but neither a bag scrunched into leather, glass, and steel, commanded by anyone to stop, go, ache, count change out of nasty fingers, breathe gas, and hear youth ticked away in nickels. This was Beckman among painters, learning the business, gallon can in each hand, surveying the great hollow vault of the factory which he and the men were come to paint. High brick walls seemed not to restrict but merely to pose theoretical demarcations in all the space now his. He and the gang of painters trudged with cans, brushes, and ropes up a wall toward the sky and the factory's clangor dropped beneath them to a dull, general boom like a distant sea. The light they rose toward grew sharper and whiter as they entered it climbing the narrow stairway that shivered beneath their feet. Paint cans knocked the sides of Beckman's legs, the loops cut thin channels into his palms. At the top of the factory, against the white, skylighted morning, they settled their equipment on a steel platform. The men stirred cans of paint, attached ropes to the pipes that ran along beneath the skylight, and moved out on swings into the voluminous air. Beckman stood back on the platform trying to look shrewdly into the nature of these things and feel his relevance. The sun drifted toward the vertical and blazed through the skylight. It drilled the top of his head as he concentrated on a painter swinging ten feet out from the edge of the platform, his arm and trunk like a heavy appendage dangling from his hand. His feet jerked in vast nothing. His swing was suspended from a pipe running beside the one he painted, and as he moved farther from the platform he left yards of gleaming orange behind him. Beckman felt his breathing quicken as he leaned after the long smack and drag of the painter's brush. Repeated, overlapped, and soon, between Beckman and the painter, burned thirty feet of the hot, brilliant color. Beckman yearned to participate, confront unpainted steel, paint it, see it become a fresh, different thing as he dissolved in the ritual of strokes. The painter stopped working and looked at him. A vein split the man's temple down the center and forked like the root of a tree. Flecks of orange dazzled on his cheeks. He pointed with his brush to a can near the edge of the platform and Beckman snapped it up, stepped to the edge, and held it out into the air toward the painter. Thus, delivering the can, he delivered himself, grabbed life in the loop and hoisted it like a gallon of his own blood, swinging it out like a mighty bowler into the future. Concrete floor, towering walls, steeping light hosannaed while Beckman's arm stiffened and shuddered from wrist to mooring tendons in his neck as he held the stance, leaned with the heavy can like an allegorical statue: Man Reaching. The painter grinned, shook his head, and Beckman saw in a flash blinding blindness that his effort to reach thirty feet was imbecilic. His head wrenched back for the cocky vantage of height and relieved his stance of allegory. He shuffled backward with a self-mocking shrug and set down the can as if lifting it in the first place had been a mistake. The painter's grin became a smile and he tapped the pipe to which his swing was attached. Beckman understood—deliver the can by crawling down the pipe. Aggravation ripped his heart. A sense of his life constituted of moments like this, inept and freakish, when spirit, muscle, and bone failed to levels less than thing, a black lump of time, flew out of his occipital cup like a flung clod and went streaming down the inside of his skull with the creepy feel of slapstick spills, twitches, flops, and farts of the mind. But the painter had resumed his good work and Beckman, relieved and gratified, was instantly himself again, immune to himself, and snapped up the can. At the edge of the platform he stooped, laid his free hand on the pipe, then straddled the pipe. He clutched the loop in his right hand, shoved off the platform, tipped forward and dragged with his knees, thighs, and elbows down toward the painter. His feet dangled, his eyes dug into the pipe, and he pushed. He dragged like a worm and didn't think or feel what he did. Fifteen feet from the edge of the platform he stopped to adjust his grip on the can, heavier now and swinging enough to make him feel uneasy about his right side and make him tighten his grip on the left so hard he pitched left. The can jerked up, both legs squeezed the pipe, and a tremor set into his calves and shanks, moving toward his buttocks and lower back.

Beckman squeezed the pipe with his legs and arms and slipped his left hand gradually under the pipe to cup its belly. His right hand, clutching the loop of the can, hung straight down, and Beckman leaned his chin against the pipe and listened to his shirt buttons rasp against steel. He breathed slowly to minimize the rasping and gaped down the pipe at the hard, curved flare of morning light. His knees felt through cloth to steel and the pipe's belly was slick in his palm. The tremor, in his shoulders now, moved up toward the muscles of his neck. Against his mouth he smelled, then tasted, steel as it turned rancid with sweat and spit. He felt water pour slowly, beyond his will, into his pants as it had when they hit him and hit him for no reason and he twisted and shrieked on the floor of his cab. He felt the impulse to move and did not want to look around into the vacuous air, nor to imagine the beating or the possibility that the tremor in his chin and lips would become a long, fine scream spinning out the thread of his life as he dropped toward the machines and the concrete floor. He felt the impulse to move and he could remember how motion felt gathering in his body to move his body, how it felt gathering, droning in the motor of his cab, to move him through the dark avenues of the city. He stared down the pipe, clung to it, and saw the painter stop working to look at him, looking at him with surprise, saying as if only with lips, slowly, again and again, "Hold on, Beckman." He clung to the pipe, squeezed life against his chest, and would neither let go nor drag toward the painter. He heard men shout from the platform, "Don't let go, Beckman." He did not let go. The tremor passed into muscle as rigid as the steel it squeezed.

i would have saved them if i could
(1975)

murderers

WHEN MY UNCLE MOE dropped dead of a heart attack I became expert in the subway system. With a nickel I'd get to Queens, twist and zoom to Coney Island, twist again toward the George Washington Bridge—beyond which was darkness. I wanted proximity to darkness, strangeness. Who doesn't? The poor in spirit, the ignorant and frightened. My family came from Poland, then never went anyplace until they had heart attacks. The consummation of years in one neighborhood: a black Cadillac, corpse inside. We should have buried Uncle Moe where he shuffled away his life, in the kitchen or toilet, under the linoleum, near the coffeepot. Anyhow, they were dropping on Henry Street and Cherry Street. Blue lips. The previous winter it was cousin Charlie, forty-five years old. Moe, Charlie, Sam, Adele—family meant a punch in the chest, fire in the arm. I didn't want to wait for it. I went to Harlem, the Polo Grounds, Far Rockaway, thousands of miles on nickels, mainly underground. Tenements watched me go, day after day, fingering nickels. One afternoon I stopped to grind my heel against the curb. Melvin and Arnold Bloom appeared, then Harold Cohen. Melvin said, "You step in dog shit?" Grinding was my answer. Harold Cohen said, "The rabbi is home. I saw him on Market Street. He was walking fast." Oily Arnold, eleven years old, began to urge: "Let's go up to our roof." The decision waited for me. I considered the roof, the view of industrial Brooklyn, the Battery, ships in the river, bridges, towers, and the rabbi's apartment. "All right," I said. We didn't giggle or look to one another for moral signals. We were running.

The blinds were up and curtains pulled, giving sunlight, wind, birds to the rabbi's apartment—a magnificent metropolitan view. The rabbi and his wife never took it, but in the light and air of summer afternoons, in the eye of gull and pigeon, they were joyous. A bearded young man, and his young pink wife, sacramentally bald. Beard and Baldy, with everything to see, looked at each other. From a water tank on the opposite roof, higher than their windows, we looked at them. In psychoanalysis this is "The Primal Scene." To achieve the primal scene we crossed a ledge six inches wide. A half-inch indentation in the brick gave us fingerholds. We dragged bellies and groins against the brick face to a steel ladder. It went up the side of the building, bolted into brick, and up the side of the water tank to a slanted tin roof which caught the afternoon sun. We sat on that roof like angels, shot through with light, derealized in brilliance. Our sneakers sucked hot slanted metal. Palms and fingers pressed to bone on nailheads.

The Brooklyn Navy Yard with destroyers and aircraft carriers, the Statue of Liberty putting the sky to the torch, the dull remote skyscrapers of Wall Street, and the Empire State Building were among the wonders we dominated. Our view of the holy man and his wife, on their living-room couch and floor, on the bed in their bedroom, could not be improved. Unless we got closer. But fifty feet across the air was right. We heard their phonograph and watched them dancing. We couldn't hear the gratifications or see pimples. We smelled nothing. We didn't want to touch.

For a while I watched them. Then I gazed beyond into shimmering nullity, gray, blue, and green murmuring over rooftops and towers. I had watched them before. I could tantalize myself with this brief ocular perversion, the general cleansing nihil of a view. This was the beginning of philosophy. I indulged in ambience, in space like eons. So what if my uncle Moe was dead? I was philosophical and luxurious. I didn't even have to look at the rabbi and his wife. After all, how many times had we dissolved stickball games when the rabbi came home? How many times had we risked shameful discovery, scrambling up the ladder, exposed to their windows—if they looked. We risked life itself to achieve this eminence. I looked at the rabbi and his wife.

Today she was a blonde. Bald didn't mean no wigs. She had ten wigs, ten colors, fifty styles. She looked different, the same, and very good. A human theme in which nothing begat anything and was gorgeous. To me she was the world's lesson. Aryan yellow slipped through pins about her ears. An olive complexion mediated yellow hair and Arabic black eyes. Could one care what she really looked like? What was *really*? The minute you wondered, she looked like something else, in another wig, another style. Without the wigs she was a baldy-bean lady. Today she was a blonde. Not blonde. *A* blonde. The phonograph blared and her deep loops flowed Tommy Dorsey, Benny Goodman, and then the thing itself, Choo-Choo Lopez. Rumba! One, two-three. One, two-three. The rabbi stepped away to delight in blond imagination. Twirling and individual, he stepped away snapping fingers, going high and light on his toes. A short bearded man, balls afling, cock shuddering like a springboard. Rumba! One, two-three. *Olé! Vaya*, Choo-choo!

> *I was on my way to spend some time in Cuba.*
> *Stopped off at Miami Beach, la-la.*
> *Oh, what a rumba they teach, la-la.*
> *Way down in Miami Beach,*
> *Oh, what a chroombah they teach, la-la.*
> *Way-down-in-Miami-Beach.*

She, on the other hand, was somewhat reserved. A shift in one lush hip was total rumba. He was Mr. Life. She was dancing. He was a naked man. She was what she was in the garment of her soft, essential self. He was snapping, clapping, hopping to the beat. The beat lived in her visible music, her lovely self. Except for the wig. Also a watchband that desecrated her wrist. But it gave her a bit of the whorish. She never took it off.

Harold Cohen began a cocktail-mixer motion, masturbating with two fists. Seeing him at such hard futile work, braced only by sneakers, was terrifying. But I grinned. Out of terror, I twisted an encouraging face. Melvin Bloom kept one hand on the tin. The other knuckled the rumba numbers into the back of my head. Nodding like a defective, little Arnold Bloom chewed his lip and squealed as the rabbi and his wife smacked together. The rabbi clapped her buttocks, fingers buried in the cleft. They stood only on his legs. His back arched, knees bent, thighs thick with thrust, up, up, up. Her legs wrapped his hips, ankles crossed, hooked for constriction. "Oi, oi, oi," she cried, wig flashing left, right, tossing the Brooklyn Navy Yard, the Statue of Liberty, and the Empire State Building to hell. Arnold squealed oi, squealing rubber. His sneaker heels stabbed tin to stop his slide. Melvin said, "Idiot." Arnold's ring hooked a nailhead and the ring and ring finger remained. The hand, the arm, the rest of him, were gone.

We rumbled down the ladder. "Oi, oi, oi," she yelled. In a freak of ecstasy her eyes had rolled and caught us. The rabbi drilled to her quick and she had us. "OI, OI," she yelled above congas going clop, doom-doom, clop, doom-doom on the way to Cuba. The rabbi flew to the window, a red mouth opening in his beard: "Murderers." He couldn't know what he said. Melvin Bloom was crying. My fingers were tearing, bleeding into brick. Harold Cohen, like an adding machine, gibbered the name of God. We moved down the ledge quickly as we dared. Bongos went tocka-ti-tocka, tocka-ti-tocka. The rabbi screamed, "MELVIN BLOOM, PHILLIP LIEBOWITZ, HAROLD COHEN, MELVIN BLOOM," as if our names, screamed this way, naming us where we hung, smashed us into brick.

Nothing was discussed.

The rabbi used his connections, arrangements were made. We were sent to a camp in New Jersey. We hiked and played volleyball. One day, apropos of nothing, Melvin came to me and said little Arnold had been made of gold and he, Melvin, of shit. I appreciated the sentiment, but to my mind they were both made of shit. Harold Cohen never again spoke to either of us. The counselors in the camp were World War II veterans, introspective men. Some carried shrapnel in their bodies. One had a metal plate in his head. Whatever you said to them they seemed to be thinking of something else, even when they answered. But step out of line and a plastic lanyard whistled burning notice across your ass.

At night, lying in the bunkhouse, I listened to owls. I'd never before heard that sound, the sound of darkness, blooming, opening inside you like a mouth.

eating out

BASKETBALL PLAYER

I was the most dedicated basketball player. I don't say the best. In my mind I was terrifically good. In fact I was simply the most dedicated basketball player in the world. I say this because I played continuously, from the time I discovered the meaning of the game at the age of ten, until my mid-twenties. I played outdoors on cement, indoors on wood. I played in heat, wind, and rain. I played in chilly gymnasiums. Walking home I played some more. I played during dinner, in my sleep, in movies, in automobiles and buses, and at stool. I played for over a decade, taking every conceivable shot, with either hand, from every direction. Masses cheered my performance. No intermission, no food, no other human concern, year after year they cheered me on. In living rooms, subways, movies, and schoolyards I heard them. During actual basketball games I also played basketball. I played games within games. When I lost my virginity I eluded my opponent and sank a running hook. Masses saw it happen. I lost my virginity and my girl lost hers. The game had been won. I pulled up my trousers. She snapped her garter belt. I took a jump shot from the corner and another game was under way. I scored in a blind drive from the foul line. We kissed good night. The effect was epileptic. Masses thrashed in their seats, loud holes in their faces. I acknowledged with an automatic nod and hurried down the street, dribbling. A fall-away jumper from the top of the key. It hung in the air. Then, as if sucked down suddenly, it zipped through the hoop. Despite the speed and angle of my shots, I never missed.

PLEASURE

My mother was taking me to the movies. We were walking fast. I didn't know what movie it would be. Neither did my mother. She couldn't read. We were defenseless people. I was ten years old. My mother was five foot nothing. We walked with fast little steps, hands in our pockets, faces down. The school week had ended. I was five days closer to the M.D. My reward for good grades was a movie—black, brilliant pleasure. Encouragement to persist. We walked in a filthy, freezing, blazing wind for half a mile. The pleasure I'll never forget. A girl is struck by a speeding car. A beautiful girl who speaks first-class English—but she is struck down. Blinded, broken, paralyzed. The driver of the car is a handsome doctor. My mother whispers, "*Na*," the Polish word that stimulates free-associational capacities in children. Mind-spring, this to that. The doctor operates on the girl in a theater of lights, masks, and knives. She has no choice in this matter. Blind and broken. Paralyzed. Lucky for her, she recovers. Her feeling of recovery is thrilling love for the doctor. He has this feeling, too. It spreads from them to everywhere, like the hot, vibrant, glowing moo of a tremendous cow, liquefying distinctions. The world is feeling. Feeling is the deadly car, the broken girl and blinding doctor, the masks, knives, and kisses. Finally there is a sunset. It returns me with smeared and glistening cheeks to the blazing wind. I glance at my mother. She whispers, "*Na?*" Intelligence springs through my mind like a monkey, seizing the bars, shaking them. We walk fast, with little steps, our hands in our pockets; but my face is lifted to the wind. It shrieks, "Emmmmmdeee." My call.

SOMETHING EVIL

I said, "Ikstein stands outside the door for a long time before he knocks. Did you suspect that? Did you suspect that he stands there listening to what we say before he knocks?" She said, "Did you know you're crazy?" I said, "I'm not crazy. The expression on his face, when I open the door, is giddy and squirmy. As if he'd been doing something evil, like listening outside our door before he knocked." She said, "That's Ikstein's expression. Why do you invite him here? Leave the door open. He won't be able to listen to us. You won't make yourself crazy imagining it." I said, "Brilliant, but he isn't due for an hour and I won't sit here with the door open." She said, "I hate to listen to you talk this way. I won't be involved in your lunatic friendships." She opened the door. Ikstein stood there, giddy and squirmy.

ANSWERS

I began two hundred hours of continuous reading in the twelve hours that remained before examinations. Melvin Bloom, my roommate, flipped the pages of his textbook in a sweet continuous trance. Reviewing the term's work was his pleasure. He went to sleep early. While he slept I bent into the night, reading, eating Benzedrine, smoking cigarettes. Shrieking dwarfs charged across my notes. Crabs asked me questions. Melvin flipped a page, blinked, flipped another. He effected the same flipping and blinking, with no textbook, during examinations. For every question, answers marched down his optical nerve, neck, arm, and out onto his paper where they stopped in impeccable parade. I'd look at my paper, oily, scratched by ratlike misery, and I'd think of Melvin Bloom. I would think, Oh God, what is going to happen to me.

MACKEREL

She didn't want to move in because there had been a rape on the third floor. I said, "The guy was a wounded veteran, under observation at Bellevue. We'll live on the fifth floor." It was a Victorian office building, converted to apartments. Seven stories, skinny, gray, filigreed face. No elevators. We climbed an iron stairway. "Wounded veteran," I said. "Predictable." My voice echoed in dingy halls. Linoleum cracked as we walked. Beneath the linoleum was older, drier linoleum. The apartments had wooden office doors with smoked-glass windows. The hall toilets were padlocked; through gaps we could see the bowl, overhead tank, bare bulb dangling. "That stairway is good for the heart and legs," I said. She said, "Disgusting, dangerous building." I said, "You do smell piss in the halls and there has been a rape. The janitor admitted it. But people live here, couples, singles, every sex and race. Irish, Italian, Puerto Rican families. Kids run up and down the stairway. A mackerel-crowded iron stream. Radios, TVs, whining day and night. Not only a piss smell, but pasta, peppers, incense, marijuana. The building is full of life. It's life. Close to the subways, restaurants, movies." She said, "Rapes." I said, "One rape. A wounded man with a steel plate in his head, embittered, driven by undifferentiated needs. The rent is forty dollars a month. To find this place, you understand, I appealed to strangers. From aluminum phone booths, baby, I dialed with ice-blue fingers. It's January in Manhattan. Howling winds come from the rivers." "The rape," she said. I said, "A special and extremely peculiar case. Be logical." Before we finished unpacking, the janitor was stabbed in the head. I said, "A junkie did it. A natural force, a hurricane." She said, "Something is wrong with you. I always felt it instinctively." I said, "I believe I'm not perfect. What do you think is wrong with me?" She said, "It makes me miserable." I said, "No matter how miserable it makes you, say it." She said, "It embarrasses me." I said, "Even if it embarrasses you, say it, be frank. This is America. I'll write it down. Maybe we can sell it and move to a better place." She said, "There's too much." I said, "I'll make a list. Go ahead, leave out nothing. I have a pencil." She said, "Then what?" I said, "Then I'll go to a psychiatrist." She said, "You'll give a distorted account." I said, "I'll make an exact, complete list. See this pencil. It's for making lists. Tell me what to write." She said, "No use." I said, "A junkie did it. Listen to me, bitch, a junkie did it."

EATING OUT

Four men were at the table next to mine. Their collars were open, their ties loose, and their jackets hung on the wall. One man poured dressing on the salad, another tossed the leaves. Another filled the plates and served. One tore bread, another poured wine, another ladled soup. The table was small and square. The men were cramped, but efficient nonetheless, apparently practiced at eating here, this way, hunched over food, heads striking to suck at spoons, tear at forks, then pulling back into studious, invincible mastication. Their lower faces slid and chopped; they didn't talk once. All their eyes, like birds on a wire, perched on a horizontal line above the action. Swallowing muscles flickered in jaws and necks. Had I touched a shoulder and asked for the time, there would have been snarling, a flash of teeth.

WHAT'S NEW

My mother said, "So? What's new?" I said, "Something happened." She said, "I knew it. I had a feeling. I could tell. Why did I ask? Sure, something happened. Why couldn't I sit still? Did I have to ask? I had a feeling. I knew, I knew. What happened?"

THE BURGLAR

I dialed. The burglar answered and said Ikstein wasn't home. I said tell him I called. The burglar laughed. I said, "What's funny?" The burglar said, "This is a coincidence. When you called I was reading a passage in Ikstein's diary which is about you." I said, "Tell me what it says." The burglar snorted: "Your request is compromising. Just hearing it is compromising." I said, "I'm in the apartment below Ikstein's. We can easily meet and have a little talk about my request. I'll bring something to drink. Do you like marijuana? I know where Ikstein hides his marijuana. I have money with me, also a TV set and a Japanese camera. It's no trouble for me to carry everything up there. One trip." He said if I came upstairs he would kill me.

LIKE IRONY

He pried me open and disappeared inside, made me urinate, defecate, and screech, then slapped my dossier shut, stuck it in his cabinet, slammed drawer, swallowed key. "Well," he said, "how have you been?" I said, "Actually, that's what I'm here to find out." He said, "People have feelings. They do their best. Some of us say things to people—such as you—in a way that is like irony, but it isn't irony. It's good breeding, manners, tact— we have delicate intentions." I apologized. "So," he said, "tell me your plans." I said, "Now that I know?" "That's right," he said, "I'm delighted that you aren't very stupid."

ONE THING

Ikstein played harpsichord music on the phonograph and opened a bottle of wine. I said, "Let's be frank, Ikstein. There's too much crap in this world." He said, "Sure." The harpsichord was raving ravished Bach. Windows were open. The breeze smelled of reasons to live. I told him I didn't care for love. Only women, only their bodies. Talk, dance, conversation— I could do it—but I cared about one thing only. When it was finished, I had to go. Anyhow, I said, generally speaking, women can't stand themselves. Generally speaking, I thought they were right. "How about you, Ikstein?" He made a pleased mouth and said, "I love women, the way they look, talk, dress, and think. I love their hips, necks, breasts, and ankles. But I hate cunts." He stamped the floor. I raised my glass. He raised his. "To life," I said.

MALE

She was asleep. I wondered if I ought to read a newspaper. Nobody phoned. I wanted to run around the block until I dropped dead, but I was afraid of the muggers. I picked up the phone, dialed Ikstein, decided to hang up, but he answered: "This is Ikstein." I said, "Can I come up?" He said nothing. I said, "Ikstein, it's very late, but I can hear your TV." He said, "When I turn it off, I'll throw you out." I grabbed my cigarettes. His door was open. He didn't say hello. We watched a movie, drank beer, smoked. Side by side, hissing gases, insular and simpatico. It was male. I farted. He scratched his scalp, belched, tipped back in his chair with his legs forked out. His bathrobe fell apart, showing the vascular stump. It became a shivering mushroom, then a moon tree waving in the milky flicker. He said, "Well, look who wants to watch the movie." I said, "Hang a shoe on it." He refolded his robe and flicked off the TV. "If you decide to come out," he said, "let me be the first to know. Now go away." I went downstairs, sat on the bed, and put my hand on her belly. She whimpered, belly falling under my palm. She was asleep. I felt like a crazy man.

DIXIE

"Richard Ikstein" was printed on his mailbox. His nighttime visitors called him "Dixie." In every accent, American and foreign, sometimes laughing, sometimes grim. When he fell our ceiling shuddered. Flakes of paint drifted down onto our bed. She hugged me and tried to make conversation: "They're the last romantics." He was pleading for help. "If you like romance so much," I said, "why don't you become a whore." I twisted away, snapped on the radio, found a voice, and made it loud enough to interfere with his pleading. We couldn't hear his words, only sobs and whimpers. By the time he stopped falling, our bed was gritty with paint and plaster dust. We were too tired to get up and slap the sheets clean. In the morning I saw blood on our pillows. "It's on your face, too," she said. "You slept on your back." I was for liberation of every kind, but I dressed in silent, tight-ass fury and ran upstairs. "Look at my face, Ikstein," I shouted, banging at his door. It opened. The police were dragging him to a stretcher. I showed them my stained ceiling and bloody pillows. Obvious, but I had to explain. I told them about Ikstein's visitors, how he pleaded and sobbed. The police took notes. She cried when they left. She cried all morning. "The state is the greatest human achievement," I said. "Hegel is right. The state is the only human achievement." She said, "If you like the state so much, why don't you become a cop."

CRABS

My mother didn't mention the way things looked and said there was going to be a bar mitzvah. If I came to it, the relatives "could see" and I could meet her old friends from Miami. Their daughter was a college graduate, beautiful, money up the sunny gazoo. Moreover, it was a double-rabbi affair, one for the Hebrew, one for English. "Very classy," she said. I had been to such affairs. A paragraph of Hebrew is followed by a paragraph of English. The Hebrew sounds like an interruption. Like jungle talk. I hated the organ music, the hidden choirs, the opulent halls. Besides, I had the crabs. I wasn't in the mood for a Miami bitch who probably had gonorrhea. I said, "No." She said, "Where are your values?"

SMILE

In memoriam I recalled his smile, speedy and horizontal, the corners fleeing one another as if to meet in the back of his head. It suggested pain,
great difficulties, failure, gleaming life rot. A smile of "Nevertheless."
Sometimes we met on the stairs. He'd smile, yet seem to want to dash the
other way, slide into the wall, creep by with no hello. But he smiled.
"Nevertheless," he smiled. I would try to seem calm, innocuous, nearly
dead. That made him more nevertheless. I would tell him something
unfortunate about myself—how I'd overdrawn my checking account, lost
my wallet, discovered a boil on my balls—and I would laugh at his self-
consciously self-conscious, funny remarks. He nodded gratefully, but he
didn't believe I thought he was funny. He didn't believe he was funny. I
thought about the murder of complex persons. I thought about his smile,
bleeding, beaten to death.

RIGHT NUMBER

A girl lived in the apartment below. We became friends. I'd go there any
time, early or late. She opened the door and didn't turn on the light. I undressed in darkness, slid in beside her, made a spoon, and she slid into my
spoon. She had no work, nothing she had to do, no one expected her to
be anyplace. Money came to her in the mail. She had a body like Goya's
whore and a Botticelli face. She was tall, pale, blond, and wavy. I knocked,
she let me in. No questions. We talked fast and moved about from bed to
chairs to floor. Sometimes I'd pinch her thigh. Once she knocked a coffee cup into my lap. Finally we had sexual intercourse. We made a lot of
jokes and she was on her back. I tried to be gentle. She thrashed in a complimentary way and moaned. Later she said to guess how many men she'd
had. I said ten. She said fifteen. How does that sound? It sounds more
depraved than I feel. After the Turk, she understood the Ottoman Empire.
She said people thought of her as manic-depressive. But it wasn't true. She
had good reasons for what she feels. Germans are friskier than you'd
imagine. The right number is seven or eight. It sounds like a lot, yet it
isn't depraved. It's believable. A girl shouldn't say seven or eight, then
describe twenty. What if I said more than ten, less than twenty? How does

that sound? Six came in one weekend. They count as one. How old do you think I am? Twenty-eight? I'm only twenty-two. With A, it is a way of making something out of nothing. With B, it is a form of conversation. With C, it is letting him believe something about himself. With D, it is a mistake. I've had seventeen. People think I've had fifty or a hundred. Do I want fifty or a hundred? No. I want twenty-five. Twenty-five or thirty. Do you remember what my face is like? I think it looks sluttish. Indians are the nicest. Blacks don't talk to you afterward. I was raped when I was a kid. Then I rode my bicycle around and around the block and talked to myself in a loud voice. All my life I've tried to keep things from getting out of hand, but I get out of hand. Nothing works. Nothing works. I like you very very much, I said, let's try again. I was gentle. She thrashed in a complimentary way and moaned. The next day she knocked at my door, wearing a handsome gray wool suit and high heels. Her hair had been washed and combed into a style. She looked neat, intelligent, and extremely beautiful. She said she was going to a job interview to have something to do. We hugged for good luck and kissed. Somehow she was on her back. We had sexual intercourse. I wasn't gentle. She whipped in the pelvis and screamed murder. Me, too.

ANIMALS

Her skin was made of animals, exceedingly tiny, compressed like a billion paps in a breathing sponge. Caressing her, my palm was caressed by the smooth resilient motion in her skin. Awake or asleep, angry, bored, loving, made no difference. Her skin was superior to attitudes or words. It implied the most beautiful girl. And the core of my pleasure ached for her, the one she implied.

GOD

My mother said, "What's new?" I said, "Nothing." She said, "What? You can tell me. Tell me what's new." I said, "Something happened." She said, "I had a feeling. I could tell. What happened?" I said, "Nothing happened." She said, "Thank God."

HIS CERTAIN WAY

Ikstein had a certain way of picking up a spoon, asking for the time, getting down the street from here to there. He would pick up his spoon in his certain way, stick it in the soup, lift it to his mouth, stop, then whisper, "Eat, eat, little Ikily." Everything he did was in his certain way. He made an impression of making an impression. I remembered it. I remembered Ikstein. It was no different to remember than to see the living Ikstein, in his certain little ways. For me, he never died. He lived where he always lived, in my impression of Ikstein. I could bring him back any time, essentially, for me. "Eat, eat, little Ikily." When he did his work—he was a book and movie reviewer—he always made himself a "nice" bowl of soup. It sat beside his typewriter. He typed a sentence, stopped, said, "Now I'll have a tasty sip of soup." Essentially, for me, Ikstein had no other life. If he had in fact another life, it was never available for me. I could not pretend to regret it was no longer available for him. "Oh, poor Ikstein" would mean "Oh, poor me, what I have lost. The sights and sound of Ikstein." I lost nothing. His loss, I couldn't appreciate. Neither could he. So I remembered Ikstein and felt no sorrow. I mentioned somebody who had married for the second time. "His second wife looks like the first," I said. "As if he were pursuing something." In his certain way, Ikstein said, "Or as if it were pursuing him." Thus, even his mind lived. I said, "My intention was modest, a bit of chitchat, a germ of sense. I wasn't hoping, when I have a headache and feel sick and unable to think, to illuminate the depths. Must you be such a prick, Ikstein?"

MOURNFUL GIRLS

Busy naked heels, a rush of silky things, elastic snaps, clicks, a rattle of beads, hangers clinking, humming, her quick consistent breathing as the mattress dipped. Lips touched mine. Paper cracked flat near my head. Wooden heel shafts knocked in the hallway. I opened my eyes. A ten-dollar bill lay on the pillow. I got up, dressed, stuck the bill in my pocket, went to the apartment below, and asked, "Do you want anything?" She said no. She lay on the bed. On the way back I picked up her mail. "Some letters," I said, and dropped them beside her. She lay on the bed, skirt twisted about her hips and belly, blouse open, bra unhooked to ease the spill. Her blanket was smooth. I whispered, "Mona, Melanie, Mildred, Sarah, Nora, Dora, Sadie." She whispered, "Mournful girls." I lost the beginning of the next sentence before I heard the end. She heard as much, glanced at me, quit talking. We undressed. I tugged her off the bed to the mirror. I looked at her. She looked at me. Our arms slipped around them. All had sexual intercourse. I was upstairs when she returned from work. She asked, "Why didn't you go to the grocery?" I said, "It will take five minutes," and dashed out. The street was dark, figures appeared and jerked by. In the grocery I couldn't find the ten-dollar bill. It wasn't in my pockets. It wasn't on the floor. I ran back along the street, neck bent like a dog's, inspecting the flux of cigarette butts, candy wrappers, spittle plops, dog piss, beer cans, broken glass, granular pavement—then remembered—and ran upstairs quietly. She lay on the bed. The milk and meat were warm, butter loose and greasy. Everything except the cream cheese was in the bag beside her bed. She lay on the bed, gnawing cream cheese through the foil. "You should have put the bag in the refrigerator," I said. She gnawed. "It would have been simple to put the bag in the refrigerator," I said. "Shut your hole," she said. I shoved her hand. Cream cheese smeared her nostrils. She lay in the bed, slack, still, breathing through her mouth, as if she wouldn't cry and was not crying. I took the bag of groceries and went upstairs. The table was set. She was sweeping the kitchen floor, crying.

THE HAND

I smacked my little boy. My anger was powerful. Like justice. Then I discovered no feeling in the hand. I said, "Listen, I want to explain the complexities to you." I spoke with seriousness and care, particularly of fathers. He asked, when I finished, if I wanted him to forgive me. I said yes. He said no. Like trumps.

ALL RIGHT

"I don't mind variations," she said, "but this feels wrong." I said, "It feels all right to me." She said, "To you, wrong is right." I said, "I didn't say right, I said all right." "Big difference," she said. I said, "Yes, I'm critical. My mind never stops. To me almost everything is always wrong. My standard is pleasure. To me, this is all right." She said, "To me it stinks." I said, "What do you like?" She said, "Like I don't like. I'm not interested in being superior to my sensations. I won't live long enough for all right."

MA

I said, "Ma, do you know what happened?" She said, "Oh my God."

NAKED

Ugly or plain she would have had fewer difficulties cultivating an attractive personality or restricting sex to cortex, but she was so nearly physically perfect as to appear, more than anything, not perfect. Not ugly, not plain, then strikingly not perfect made her also not handsome and not at all sentimentally appealing. In brief, what she was she wasn't, a quality salient in adumbration, unpossessed. She lived a bad metaphor, like the Devil, unable to assimilate paradox to personal life, being no artist and not a religious, suffering spasms of self-loathing in the lonely, moral night. Finally, she smacked a Coke bottle on the rim of the bathtub, mutilated her wrist, then phoned the cops. So clumsy, yet her dinner parties were splendid, prepared at unbelievable speed. She hated to cook. Chewing gum, cigarettes, candy, drugs, alcohol, and taxicabs took her from Monday to Friday. The ambulance attendant—big ironical black man in baggy white trousers—flipped open the medicine cabinet and yelled, "See those barbiturates. You didn't have to make a mess." He dragged her out of the tub by the hair, naked, bleeding. She considered all that impressive, but if I responded to her with a look or tone, she detected my feelings before I did and made them manifest, like a trout slapped out of water by a bear. "You admire my eyes? How about my ass?" I thrilled to her acuity. But exactly then she'd become a stupid girl loosening into sexual mood, and then, then, if I touched her she offered total sprawl, whimpering, "Call me dirty names." I tried to think of her as a homosexual person, not a faggot. She begged me to wear her underpants and walk on my knees. When I demurred, she pissed on the sheets. "You don't love me," she said. "What a waste getting involved with you." Always playing with her flashy, raglike scar, sliding it along the tendons like a watchband.

BETTER

I phoned and said, "I feel good, even wonderful. Everything is great. It's been this way for months and it's getting better. Better, better, better. How are you, Ma?" She said, "Me?" I said, "Yes, how are you?" "Me?" she said. "Don't make me laugh."

getting lucky

LIEBOWITZ MAKES his head out of cigarettes and coffee, goes to the West Side subway, stands in a screaming iron box, and begins to drift between shores of small personal misery and fantastic sex, but this morning he felt fingers and, immediately, the flow of his internal life forked into dialogue between himself—standing man who lived too much blind from the chest down—and the other, a soft inquisitive spider pinching the tongue of his zipper, dragging it toward the iron floor that boomed in the bones of his rooted feet, boomed in his legs, and boomed through his unzipped fly. Thus, with no how-do-you-do, Liebowitz was in the hand of an invisible stranger. Forty-second Street, the next stop, was minutes away. Liebowitz tried to look around. Was everyone groping everyone else? Fads in Manhattan spread to millions. Liebowitz didn't care to make a fuss, distinguish himself with a cranky, strictly personal statement. He tried to be objective, to look around, see what's what in the IRT. On his left, he saw a Negro woman with a tired sullen profile and a fat neck the color of liver. Directly ahead he saw a white man's pale earlobe dangling amid the ravages of a mastoid operation, behind the tension lines of an incipient scowl; his sentiment of being. Against Liebowitz's back were the pillars of indeterminate architecture; palpable and democratic weight. On his right, steeped in a miasma of deodorants and odorants, stood a high school girl. Thick white makeup, black eyeliner, and lipstick-blotched mouth, which, in the sticky puddle of surrounding skin, seemed to suck and drink her face. Her hair, bleached scraggle, hung. She stared up at an advertisement for suntan lotion, reading and reading and reading, as if it were a letter from God. Telling her perhaps, thought Liebowitz, to wash the crap off her face. Her blotch hung open. She breathed through eight little teeth.

There were others to consider, but Liebowitz decided communications issued from the girl stinking perfume, dreaming of the sun. He didn't look down. He didn't look at her directly. Why not? He was ashamed. Is that any way to feel? It is the way he felt. Besides, Liebowitz thought a direct look might seem aggressive, even threatening, and he didn't want her to stop. Of course, not looking down, he couldn't be sure who was doing it. But whoever it was perhaps couldn't be sure to whom it was being done. Did this make a difference? Yes, thought Liebowitz. A difference between debauchery and election. Unsought, unanticipated, unearned. Not sullied by selfish, inadmissible need. He didn't think, Filthy need. He made a bland face. It felt good. Some might call this "a beautiful experience."

In effect, 8:30 a.m., going to work, crushed, breathing poison in a screaming iron box, Liebowitz was having a beautiful experience. People paid money for this. He could think of no reason not to give it a try. Liebowitz was a native New Yorker, with an invulnerable core of sophistication. He realized suddenly that he felt—beyond pleasure—hip. After so many years in the subway without feeling, or feeling he wasn't feeling, he felt. Getting and spending, he thought. And now he had gotten lucky. He believed he had done nothing to account for it, which was the way it had to be if the experience was miraculous, beautiful, warm, and good. Like the unaccountable sun shining in the advertisement. Or, for that matter, in the sky. Lucky, thrilled, beatified. All of it was assumed with silent, immobilized dignity. He got lucky and floated half blind, delicious, cool, proud to be a New Yorker. He floated above a naked ferocity which, he knew, he couldn't call his own. The emblem and foundation of his ethical domain—wife, child, responsibility of feeding them, the "Mr." on his tax forms—and yet, had someone said, "Who belongs to this hard-on?" Liebowitz himself would have led the search. Despite denials and scruples, Liebowitz had a general, friendly hard-on. Even without an object, his sensations were like love.

He came.

Fingers squeezed goodbye, replaced him, zipped up, slipped away. The train stopped at Forty-second Street, doors opened, the crowd dissolved, shuffling huggermugger hugely to the platform. The man with the incipient scowl stepped away. A garden of camellias flashed down his pants leg. Liebowitz looked elsewhere. Bleary, ringing with a chill apocalyptic sense, he was pressed loose and dopey into the crowd's motions. Moving, he began to move himself, popping up on his toes, peering over heads. The girl with the deathly hair had disappeared. On the platform now, amid figures going left, right, and shoving past him toward the train, Liebowitz was seized in a confusion of vectors, but, gathering deep internal force, his direction, himself, he thrust to the right, on his toes, and saw it—limp, ghoulish scraggle flying away like a ghostly light. Exhilaration building, beating in him like hawks, he felt his good luck the second time that morning. To let things end in the dingy, dirty, booming abyss of the Forty-second Street subway station would be a desecration of feelings and a mystery forever, he thought, chasing amid gum machines, benches, kiosks, trash cans, and innumerable indifferent faces. She went up a flight of stairs, quickly, quickly, and—painful to Liebowitz—as if she didn't care to know he was chasing her. Was there nothing between them? That's what he wanted to know. He needed psychological consummation. He was a serious human being. He needed it now and here, in subway light, under low ceilings, in the pressure of heavy moving crowds. He caught her. Against the door of a ladies' room, the instant she pressed it, he caught her arm, a thin bolt, and stopped her flight. "Miss," he said, staring, beginning to say, "You know me, don't you?" A weightless, overwrought rag of girl reeked in his close, tight grip. It whispered, "Get the claw off me, motherfucker, or I'll kick your balls." Whispering fire, writhing, murderous. Not a girl. Liebowitz let go.

The boy twisted into the ladies' room. A dozen faces bloomed in peripheral vision, like vegetables of his mind. A lady in a hat said, "Creep." Beneath the hat, her small shrill eyes recognized Liebowitz. She said "Creep" as if it were his name. "Mister Creep," he muttered, pushing away through the liquid of gathering attention. He didn't run. But he was ready, if anyone moved toward him, to run.

In the brilliant windy street, Liebowitz hailed a cab. Before it stopped, he had the door open. The meter began ticking. Ticking with remorseless, giddy indifference to his personal being and yet, somehow, consonant with himself. Not his heart, not the beat of his viscera, and yet his ticking self, his time, quickly and mercifully growing shorter. I'll be dead soon, he thought. Tick-tick-tick.

The driver said, "*Where*, mister?"

"Nowhere," said Liebowitz from the creaks and shadows in back.

"You can sit in the park for free. This is costing you."

To Liebowitz, the smug, annoyed superiority of the driver's tone was Manhattan's theme. He ignored it, lit a cigarette, breathed in the consolations of technology, and said, "I want to pay. Shut up."

storytellers, liars, and bores

I'D WORK AT A STORY until it was imperative to quit and go read it aloud. My friend would listen, then say, "I feel so embarrassed for you." I'd tear up the story. I'd work at a new one until it was imperative to quit and read aloud. My new friend would listen, but wouldn't say good, no good, or not bad. I'd tear up the story.

Meanwhile, I turned to relatives and friends for help. My uncle Zev told me about his years in a concentration camp. "Write it," he said. "You'll make a million bucks." My friend Tony Icona gave me lessons in breaking and entering. Zev's stories I couldn't use. Tony's lessons were good as gold. Criminal life was intermittent and quick. It left me time to work at stories and learn about tearing them up.

One evening, while I was reading to my new friend, she yawned. It was the fifth time I had read this story to her. The hour was late. She had to get up at dawn to leave for work. But I had rewritten the story and had to read it aloud, start to finish. I watched her eyes go fluid, her mouth enlarge. I saw fillings in her teeth and the ciliations of her tongue. By the time she completed her yawn, our friendship had ended.

After I understood so much about stories and friendship, it was easier to write stories and more difficult not to tear them up. There was bad tension between my new friend and me when I tore up a story she liked, but I did it for her sake and mine. Even as she beamed and clapped with delight, I tore it up and stepped on it.

My appeals to Tony Icona for lessons in quick, remunerative work became more frequent. I told him how hard it was to write stories without being a liar or a bore, and there was nothing, nothing, I was unwilling to do for time. He listened, picked his nose, then said if I ended up in the slam doing time, I'd kill myself. He said one person wanted money and power; the other had ideals. Both got money and power. As for himself, he liked walking on the beach in a tight bathing suit and lifting dumbbells in the sun. "That's purity, right?"

When my newest friend said the story was good, but I knew otherwise, I'd be angry and she would begin to cry. She couldn't ignore the solicitous mother in my voice, offering encouragement and music while the story did nothing for itself. She'd let the voice tell her lies, darken her understanding, weaken her will, and incline her toward evil. To make her know it, I broke her nose. Then I couldn't write. "Don't you want to read anything to me?" she'd ask, fingering her nose. "It will never be the same, you know."

When I started again, reading to my newest friend, she'd say, "That reminds me of what happened at work. Can I tell you?" I'd say, "Tell me." She was an astonishing bore. Listening to her, I tore up all my stories, never wrote stories, broke into cars, climbed through windows, and poisoned dogs. She told me what happened to her at work. I made myself ugly, lonely, and miserable.

I explained my condition to Tony Icona, a man to whom I could speak in a theoretical way. He said, "I can't sympathize. You got one leg shorter than the other and you're walking in a circle. But I'll give you a job in my delicatessen. Fifty bucks a week and you keep your tips. If the customers like you, you'll do all right. If they don't, you'll starve and be known as a dope."

The delicatessen, called Horses, was a giant hall with a long bar, mirrors on the walls and ceiling, and a hundred tables. It rang plates and cutlery; twenty chefs boiled at the steam counters and the floor thundered with speeding waiters in black tie, jacket, and shoes. I thundered among them, a napkin slapped across my forearm. At my shoulder a trayload of relishes, bread, and meat. Ladies snatched my elbow and said, "Please, darling. Could you be so wonderful as to bring me a lean pastrami and a piece of cheesecake?" They'd cling and whimper, lips speckled with anticipatory saliva, pleading for complicity in the desire to eat. Then they'd say,

"Was it too much to ask, darling? A lean pastrami?" I felt guilty of revolting gristle and the miseries that brought them to Horses. I'd swear there is no such thing as a lean pastrami, pleading for complicity in truth. My tips were small. I was known as a dope. But I studied other waiters and learned to say, "Here, sweetie, just for you—a lean pastrami. Enjoy." My pleasure in their pleasure was their pleasure. My tips were tremendous. When next I learned to say, "Eat, bitch. Stop when you get to the plate," my tips were fantastic.

Sometimes I'd slip into the back of the delicatessen, hide in the meat locker, smoking a cigarette in blood-rancid air, flayed animal tonnage hooked and blazing about my head, and I'd think, There is no such thing as lean pastrami.

After work I'd see my newest friend, the one who told me boring stories. Her name was Memory. She'd take off my shoes and socks, then wash my feet. A swinish indulgence, but I had the corns of Odysseus and ancient sentiments. Besides, she had needs in her knees, and it was her way of making me uncritical when she told a story. So much like a lie. Always a bore.

Telling what happened to her at work, she began by saying what time she got up that morning, what the weather was like, and how it differed from the weather report she'd heard the evening before. The last thing she wanted to hear before shutting her eyes was what tomorrow would be like. She had fears of discontinuity. A city girl, nine to five in an office. The days didn't return to her bound each to each by daisies. The weather report was her connection between Monday and Tuesday. One night the man said, "Tomorrow it will not rain." But it rained. Gusty, slapping rain. She said, "Isn't that strange?" She told me what bus she took in the rain, to get the bus that took her near enough to walk, in the rain, to her office. As always, she bought a newspaper to read during coffee break. The newspaper, the coffee break—with Memory I had mortal fears. I hated her story. I wanted her to go on and on. She told me what her boss said before lunch, and what he said after lunch when they chanced to meet in the hallway outside her office as she returned from the ladies' room. She told me that her boss—a married man with three kids—for the first time since she'd been working for him made sexual advances. That was the end of her story. She didn't stop talking or lift her glance to mine. She massaged my corns a bit harder.

I said, "Did you say broom closet?"

"Yes. Isn't that strange?"

Perhaps she'd been telling him a story and he nudged her and glanced significantly at the broom closet, and perhaps he worked her along subtly, as she told the story, sidling her in among brooms, mops, and cans of detergent, as she persisted in her story . . .

"You heard the weather report. You got up in the morning. You noticed the weather, rode a bus, and a married man with three kids made sexual advances in a broom closet."

"The kids weren't there."

I put on my socks.

"You didn't like my story, did you? That's how it is with me. I thrash in a murk of days. But look. Have pity. Take off your socks. I'm skinny and nervous and finicky. I can't tell you stories. I have problems with sublimity. I'm not Kafka."

That night, in a dream, I met Kafka.

A ship had gone down. In one of its rooms, where barnacles were biting the walls, I was reading a story aloud. Sentences issuing from my mouth took the shape of eels and went sliding away among the faces in the room, like elegant metals, slithering in subtleties, which invited and despised attention. When I finished, my uncle Zev rose among the faces, shoving eels aside. He came to me and said nothing about my story, but only that his teeth had been knocked out in the concentration camp. "Write it. Sell it to the movies. Don't be a schmuck. You could entertain people, make a million bucks. They also killed my mother." Tony Icona was there. He said, "Starting next week, you write my menus." With his thumbs he hooked the elastic of his bathing suit and tugged up, molding the genital bulge. The room was full of light, difficult as a headache. It poured through plankton, a glaring diffusion, appropriate to the eyes of a fish. Broken nose appeared, swimming through the palpable light, her mouth a zero. She said, "Have you been introduced to Kafka? He's here, you know." I followed her and was introduced. He shook my hand, then wiped his fingers on his tie.

in the fifties

IN THE FIFTIES I learned to drive a car. I was frequently in love. I had more friends than now.

When Khrushchev denounced Stalin my roommate shit blood, turned yellow, and lost most of his hair.

I attended the lectures of the excellent E. B. Burgum until Senator McCarthy ended his tenure. I imagined N.Y.U. would burn. Miserable students, drifting in the halls, looked at one another.

In less than a month, working day and night, I wrote a bad novel.

I went to school—N.Y.U., Michigan, Berkeley—much of the time.

I had witty, giddy conversation, four or five nights a week, in a homosexual bar in Ann Arbor.

I read literary reviews the way people suck candy.

Personal relationships were more important to me than anything else.

I had a fight with a powerful fat man who fell on my face and was immovable.

I had personal relationships with football players, jazz musicians, assbandits, nymphomaniacs, non-specialized degenerates, and numerous Jewish premedical students.

I had personal relationships with thirty-five rhesus monkeys in an experiment on monkey addiction to morphine. They knew me as one who shot reeking crap out of cages with a hose.

With four other students I lived in the home of a chiropractor named Leo.

I met a man in Detroit who owned a submachine gun; he claimed to have hit Dutch Schultz. I saw a gangster movie that disproved his claim.

I knew two girls who had brains, talent, health, good looks, plenty to eat, and hanged themselves.

I heard of parties in Ann Arbor where everyone made it with everyone else, including the cat.

I knew card sharks and con men. I liked marginal types because they seemed original and aristocratic, living for an ideal or obliged to live it. Ordinary types seemed fundamentally unserious. These distinctions belong to a romantic fop. I didn't think that way too much.

I worked for an evil vanity publisher in Manhattan.

I worked in a fish-packing plant in Massachusetts, on the line with a sincere Jewish poet from Harvard and three lesbians; one was beautiful, one grim; both loved the other, who was intelligent. I loved her, too. I dreamed of violating her purity. They talked among themselves, in creepy whispers, always about Jung. In a dark corner, away from our line, old Portuguese men slit fish into open flaps, flicking out the bones. I could see only their eyes and knives. I'd arrive early every morning to dash in and out until the stench became bearable. After work I'd go to bed and pluck fish scales out of my skin.

I was a teaching assistant in two English departments. I graded thousands of freshman themes. One began like this: "Karl Marx, for that was his name . . ." Another began like this: "In Jonathan Swift's famous letter to the Pope . . ." I wrote edifying comments in the margins. Later I began to scribble "Awkward" beside everything, even spelling errors.

I got A's and F's as a graduate student. A professor of English said my attitude wasn't professional. He said that he always read a "good book" after dinner.

A girl from Indiana said this of me on a teacher-evaluation form: "It is bad enough to go to an English class at eight in the morning, but to be instructed by a shabby man is horrible."

I made enemies on the East Coast, the West Coast, and in the Middle West. All now dead, sick, or out of luck.

I was arrested, photographed, and fingerprinted. In a soundproof room two detectives lectured me on the American way of life, and I was charged with the crime of nothing. A New York cop told me that detectives were called "defectives."

I had an automobile accident. I did the mambo. I had urethritis and mononucleosis.

In Ann Arbor, a few years before the advent of Malcolm X, a lot of my friends were black. After Malcolm X, almost all my friends were white. They admired John F. Kennedy.

In the fifties I smoked marijuana, hash, and opium. Once I drank absinthe. Once I swallowed twenty glycerine caps of peyote. The social effects of "drugs," unless sexual, always seemed tedious. But I liked people who inclined the drug way. Especially if they didn't proselytize. I listened to long conversations about the phenomenological weirdness of familiar reality and the great spiritual questions this entailed—for example, "Do you think Wallace Stevens is a head?"

I witnessed an abortion.

I was godless, but I thought the fashion of intellectual religiosity more despicable. I wished that I could live in a culture rather than study life among the cultured.

I drove a Chevy Bel Air eighty-five miles per hour on a two-lane blacktop. It was nighttime. Intermittent thick white fog made the headlights feeble and diffuse. Four others in the car sat with the strict silent rectitude of catatonics. If one of them didn't admit to being frightened, we were dead. A Cadillac, doing a hundred miles per hour, passed us and was obliterated in the fog. I slowed down.

I drank Old Fashioneds in the apartment of my friend Julian. We talked about Worringer and Spengler. We gossiped about friends. Then we left to meet our dates. There was more drinking. We all climbed trees, crawled in the street, and went to a church. Julian walked into an elm, smashed his glasses, vomited on a lawn, and returned home to memorize Anglo-Saxon grammatical forms. I ended on my knees, vomiting into a toilet bowl, repeatedly flushing the water to hide my noises. Later I phoned New York so that I could listen to the voices of my parents, their Yiddish, their English, their logics.

I knew a professor of English who wrote impassioned sonnets in honor of Henry Ford.

I played freshman varsity basketball at N.Y.U. and received a dollar an hour for practice sessions and double that for games. It was called "meal money." I played badly, too psychological, too worried about not studying, too short. If pushed or elbowed during a practice game, I was ready to kill. The coach liked my attitude. In his day, he said, practice ended when there was blood on the boards. I ran back and forth, in urgent sneakers, through my freshman year. Near the end I came down with pleurisy, quit basketball, started smoking more.

I took classes in comparative anatomy and chemistry. I took classes in Old English, Middle English, and modern literature. I took classes and classes.

I fired a twelve-gauge shotgun down the hallway of a railroad flat into a couch pillow.

My roommate bought the shotgun because of his gambling debts. He expected murderous thugs to come for him. I'd wake in the middle of the night listening for a knock, a cough, a footstep, wondering how to identify myself as not him when they broke through our door.

My roommate was an expensively dressed kid from a Chicago suburb. Though very intelligent, he suffered in school. He suffered with girls though he was handsome and witty. He suffered with boys though he was heterosexual. He slept on three mattresses and used a sun lamp all winter. He bathed, oiled, and perfumed his body daily. He wanted soft, sweet joys in every part, but when some whore asked if he'd like to be beaten with a garrison belt he said yes. He suffered with food, eating from morning to night, loading his pockets with fried pumpkin seeds when he left for class, smearing caviar paste on his filet mignons, eating himself into a monumental face of eating because he was eating. Then he killed himself.

A lot of young, gifted people I knew in the fifties killed themselves. Only a few of them continue walking around.

I wrote literary essays in the turgid, tumescent manner of darkest Blackmur.

I used to think that someday I would write a fictional version of my stupid life in the fifties.

I was a waiter in a Catskill hotel. The captain of the waiters ordered us to dance with the female guests who appeared in the casino without escorts and, as much as possible, fuck them. A professional *tummler* walked the grounds. Wherever he saw a group of people merely chatting, he thrust in quickly and created a tumult.

I heard the Budapest String Quartet, Dylan Thomas, Lester Young and Billie Holiday together, and I saw Pearl Primus dance, in a Village nightclub, in a space two yards square, accompanied by an African drummer about seventy years old. His hands moved in spasms of mathematical complexity at invisible speed. People left their tables to press close to

Primus and see the expression in her face, the sweat, the muscles, the way her naked feet seized and released the floor.

Eventually I had friends in New York, Ann Arbor, Chicago, Berkeley, and Los Angeles.

I did the cha-cha, wearing a tux, at a New Year's party in Hollywood, and sat at a table with Steve McQueen. He'd become famous in a TV series about a cowboy with a rifle. He said he didn't know which he liked best, acting or driving a racing car. I thought he was a silly person and then realized he thought I was. I met a few other famous people who said something. One night, in a yellow Porsche, I circled Manhattan with Jack Kerouac. He recited passages, perfectly remembered from his book reviews, to the sky. His manner was ironical, sweet, and depressing.

I had a friend named Chicky who drove his chopped, blocked, stripped, dual-exhaust Ford convertible, while vomiting out the fly window, into a telephone pole. He survived, lit a match to see if the engine was all right, and it blew up in his face. I saw him in the hospital. Through his bandages he said that ever since high school he'd been trying to kill himself. Because his girlfriend wasn't good-looking enough. He was crying and laughing while he pleaded with me to believe that he really had been trying to kill himself because his girlfriend wasn't good-looking enough. I told him that I was going out with a certain girl and he told me that he had fucked her once but it didn't matter because I could take her away and live somewhere else. He was a Sicilian kid with a face like Caravaggio's angels of debauch. He'd been educated by priests and nuns. When his hair grew back and his face healed, his mind healed. He broke up with his girlfriend. He wasn't nearly as narcissistic as other men I knew in the fifties.

I knew one who, before picking up his dates, ironed his dollar bills and powdered his testicles. And another who referred to women as "cockless wonders" and used only their family names—for example, "I'm going to meet Goldberg, the cockless wonder." Many women thought he was extremely attractive and became his sexual slaves. Men didn't like him.

I had a friend who was dragged down a courthouse stairway, in San Francisco, by her hair. She'd wanted to attend the House Un-American hearings. The next morning I crossed the Bay Bridge to join my first protest demonstration. I felt frightened and embarrassed. I was bitter about what had happened to her and the others she'd been with. I expected to see thirty or forty people like me, carrying hysterical placards around the courthouse until the cops bludgeoned us into the pavement. About two thousand people were there. I marched beside a little kid who had a bag of marbles to throw under the hoofs of the horse cops. His mother kept saying, "Not yet, not yet." We marched all day. That was the end of the fifties.

reflections of a wild kid

MANDELL ASKED if she had ever been celebrated.

"Celebrated?"

"I mean your body, has your body ever been celebrated?" Then, as if to refine the question: "I mean, like, has your body, like, been celebrated?"

"My body has never been celebrated."

She laughed politely. A laugh qualified by her sense of Liebowitz in the bedroom. She was polite to both of them and good to neither. Certainly not to Liebowitz, who, after all, wanted Mandell out of the apartment. Did she care what he wanted? He was her past, a whimsical recrudescence, trapped in her bedroom. He'd waited in there for an hour. He could wait another hour. As far as she knew, he had cigarettes. But, in that hour, as he smoked his cigarettes, his bladder had begun to feel like a cantaloupe. He strained to lift the window. The more he strained, the more he felt his cantaloupe.

"I mean really celebrated," said Mandell, as if she'd answered nothing.

Perhaps, somehow, she urged Mandell to go on. Perhaps she wanted Liebowitz to hear Mandell's witty questions, his lovemaking. Liebowitz didn't care what she wanted. His last cigarette had been smoked. He wanted to piss. He drew the point of a nail file down the sides of the window, trailing a thin peel, a tiny scream in the paint. Again he strained to lift the window. It wouldn't budge. At that moment he noticed wall-to-wall carpeting. Why did he notice? Because he couldn't piss on it. Amazing, he thought, how we perceive the world. Stand on a mountain and you think it's remarkable that you can't jump off.

"My body," said Mandell, "has been celebrated."

Had that been his object all along? Liebowitz wondered why Mandell hadn't been more direct, ripping off his shirt, flashing nipples in her face: "Let's celebrate." She was going to marry a feeb. But that wasn't Liebowitz's business. He had to piss. He had no other business.

"I mean, you know, like my body, like, has been celebrated," said Mandell, again refining his idea. Despite his pain, it was impossible for Liebowitz not to listen—the sniveling syntax, the whining diction—he tasted every phrase. In that hour, as increasingly he had to piss, he came to know Mandell, through the wall, palpably to know him. Some smell, some look, even something about the way he combed his hair, reached Liebowitz through the wall. Bad blood, thought Liebowitz.

He remembered Nietzsche's autobiographical remark: "I once sensed the proximity of a herd of cows . . . merely because milder and more philanthropic thoughts came back to me." How true. Thoughts can be affected by invisible animals. Liebowitz had never even seen Mandell. As for Joyce, a shoe lying on its side, in the middle of her carpet—scuffed, bent, softened by the stride of her uncelebrated body—suffused the bedroom with her presence, the walking foot, strong well-shaped ankle, peasant hips rocking with motive power, elegant neck, fleshy boneless Semitic face. A warm receptive face until she spoke. Then she had personality. That made her seem taller, slightly forbidding, even robust. She was robust—heavy bones, big head, dense yellow-brown hair—and her voice, a flying bird of personality. Years had passed. Seeing the hair again and Joyce still fallow beneath it saddened Liebowitz. But here was Mandell. She had time.

"Has it been five years?" asked Liebowitz, figuring seven. "You sound wonderful, Joyce." She said he sounded "good." He regretted "wonderful," but noticed no other reserve in her voice, and just as he remembered, she seemed still to love the telephone, coming at him right through the machine, much the thing, no later than this minute. When his other phone range he didn't reach for it, thus letting her hear and understand how complete was his attention. She understood. She went on directly about some restaurant, insisting let's eat there. He didn't even consider not. She'd said, almost immediately, she was getting married to Mandell, a professor.

Did Liebowitz feel jealousy? He didn't ask professor of what or where does he teach. Perhaps he felt jealousy; but, listening to her and nodding compliments at the wall, he listened less to what she said than to how she spoke in echoes. Not of former times, but approximately these things, in approximately the same way, he felt, had been said in grand rooms, by wonderful people. Joyce brought him the authority of echoes. And she delivered herself, too, a hundred thirty-five pounds of shank and dazzle, even in her questions: "Have you seen . . . ?" "Have you heard . . . ?" About plays, movies, restaurants, Jacqueline Kennedy. Nothing about his wife, child, job. Was she indifferent? embarrassed? hostile? In any case, he liked her impetuosity; she poked, checked his senses. He liked her. Joyce Wolf, on the telephone. He remembered that cabbies and waiters liked her. She could make fast personal jokes with policemen and bellhops. She tipped big. A hundred nobodies knew her name, her style. Always *en passant*, very much here and not here at all. He liked her tremendously, he felt revived. Not reliving a memory, but right now, on the telephone, living again a moment of his former life. For the first time, as it were, that he didn't have to live it. She has magic, he thought; art. Merely in her voice, she was an event. She called him back, through time, to herself. Despite his grip on the phone, knees under the desk, feet on the floor, he felt like a man slipping from a height, deliciously. He said he would meet her uptown in forty minutes. Did he once live this way? Liebowitz shook his head; smirked. He was a wild kid once.

On his desk lay a manuscript that had to be edited, and a contract he had to work on. There was also an appointment with an author . . . but, in the toilet with electric razor and toothbrush, Liebowitz purged his face of the working day and, shortly thereafter, walked into a chic Hungarian restaurant on the Upper East Side. She arrived twenty minutes later; late; but in a black sleeveless dress. Very smart. It gave her a look that seized the day, the feeling and idea of it. She hadn't just come to meet him; she described their moment and meaning, in a garment. She appeared. Late; but who, granted such knowledge, could complain? Liebowitz felt flattered and grateful. He took her hands. She squeezed his hands. He kissed her cheek. "Joyce." The hair, white smile, hips—he remembered, he looked, looked. "It was good of you to call me." He looked at her. He looked into his head. She was there, too, this minute's Joyce Wolf, who once got them to the front of lines, to seats when the show was sold out, to tables, tables near windows, to parties. Sold out, you say? At the box office, in her name, two tickets were waiting. Then Liebowitz remembered, once, for a ballet, she had failed to do better than standing room. He hadn't wanted to go. He certainly hadn't wanted to stand. Neither had she. But tickets had been sold out to this ballet. Thousands wanted to go. Liebowitz remembered how she began making phone calls, scratching at the numbers till her fingernail tore. That evening, pelvises pressed to a velvet rope, they stood amid hundreds of ballet lovers jammed into a narrow aisle. The effluvia of alimentary canals hung about their heads. Blindfolded, required to guess, Liebowitz would have said they were in a delicatessen. Lights dimmed. There was a thrilling hush. Joyce whispered, "How in God's name can anyone live outside New York?" She nudged him and pointed at a figure seated in the audience. Liebowitz looked, thrusting his head forward to show appreciation of her excitement, her talent for recognizing anyone in New York in almost total darkness. "See! See!" Liebowitz nodded greedily. His soul poured toward a glint of skull floating amid a thousand skulls. He begged, "Who? Who is it?" He wasn't sure that he looked at the correct glint of skull, yet he felt on the verge of extraordinary illumination. Then a voice wailed into his back, "I can't see." Liebowitz twisted about, glanced down. A short lady, staring up at him, pleaded with her whole face. "I can't see." He twisted forward and said, "Move a little, Joyce. Let her up against the rope." Joyce whispered, "This is the jungle, schmuck. Tell her to grow another head." He was impressed. During the ballet he stood with the velvet rope in his fists, the woman's face between his shoulder blades, and now, as he went uptown in the cab, his mouth was so dry he couldn't smoke. After all these years, still impressed. Joyce got them tickets. She knew. She got. Him, for example—virtually a bum in those days, but nice-looking, moody, a complement to her, he supposed. Perhaps a girl with so much needed someone like him—a misery. Not that she was without misery. She worked as private secretary to an investment broker, a shrewd, ugly Russian with a hunchback and a limp. "Hey, collich girl, make me a phone call." After work she used to meet Liebowitz, hunching, dragging a foot, and she would shout, "Hey, collich. Hey, collich girl, kiss my ass." They'd laugh with relief and malice; but sometimes she met Liebowitz in tears. Once the Russian even hit her. "In a Longchamps, during lunch hour," she said. "He knocked me on the floor in front of all those people eating lunch." Liebowitz remembered her screaming at him: "Even if there had been a reason." He stopped trying to justify the horror. It got to him. "Gratuitous sadism!" Liebowitz raged. He'd go next morning and punch the Russian in the mouth. The next morning, in Italian sunglasses, Joyce left for the office. Alone. Five foot seven, she walked seven foot five, a Jewish girl passing for Jewish in tough financial circles. Liebowitz smoked a cigarette, punched his hand. Liebowitz remembered:

The sunglasses—tough, tragic, fantastically clever—looked terrific. She knew what to wear, precisely the item that said it. Those sunglasses were twenty punches in the mouth. She'd wear them all day, even at the typewriter. The Russian would feel, between himself and the college girl, an immensity. He'd know what he was, compared to her in those black, estranging glasses. Liebowitz felt an intellectual pang; his reflections had gone schmuckway. Beginning again:

Joyce made two hundred and fifty dollars a week. With insults and slaps, the Russian gave tips on the market. The year she lived with Liebowitz, Joyce made over a hundred thousand dollars. Liebowitz, then a salesman in a shoe store, made eighty dollars a week hunkering over corns. He had rotten moods, no tips on anything; he had a lapsed candidacy for the Ph.D. in philosophy and a girl with access to the pleasures of Manhattan. Her chief pleasure—moody Liebowitz. In truth, he never hated the Russian. He pitied Joyce; for a hundred thousand dollars she ate shit. The sunglasses symbolized shame. Liebowitz remembered:

Twenty-four years old, a virgin when she met Liebowitz, who took her on their first date. "I don't know how it happened," she said. "Two minutes ago I had some idea of myself." Liebowitz replied, "Normal." She'd been surprised, overwhelmed by his intensity. She'd never met a man so hungry. Now he was cool, like a hoodlum. "Where's your shower?" He wondered if he hadn't been worse to her than the Russian. Hidden in the bedroom, crouched in pain, Liebowitz made big eyes and held out his hands, palms up, like a man begging for apples. He'd had certain needs. She'd been good to him—the tickets, the parties, and calling now to announce her forthcoming marriage; invite him to dinner. It was touching. Liebowitz had to piss. He remembered that, walking into the restaurant, he'd had an erection. Perhaps that explained the past; also the present, running to meet her as if today were yesterday. Then they strolled in the park. Then they went to her apartment for a drink. Life is mystery, thought Liebowitz. He wondered if he dared, after all these years, after she'd just told him she was getting married, put his hand on her knee; her thigh; under the black dress where time, surrendering to truth, ceased to be itself. The doorbell.

"Don't answer," said Liebowitz.

"Maybe it's someone else," she said, her voice as frightened as his.

It wasn't somebody else. Liebowitz opted for the bedroom. Then he was tearing at the window, wild to piss.

"Didn't you say you were going to work this evening?"

"Did I say that?"

Mandell had had a whimsy impulse. Here he was, body freak, father of Joyce's unborn children. She could have done better, thought Liebowitz. Consider himself, Liebowitz. But seven years had passed since he'd put his hand on her thigh. A woman begins to feel desperate. Still—Joyce Wolf, her style, her hips—she could have done better than Mandell, thought Liebowitz, despite her conviction—her boast—that Mandell wasn't just any professor of rhetoric and communication art. "He loves teaching— speech, creative writing, anything—and every summer at Fire Island he writes a novel of ideas. None are published yet, but he doesn't care about publication. People say his novels are very good. I couldn't say, but he talks about his writing all the time. He really cares."

Liebowitz could see Mandell curled over his typewriter. Forehead presses the keys. Sweat fills his bathing-suit jock. It's summertime on Fire Island. Mandell is having an idea to stick in one of his novels. "You know, of course, my firm only does textbooks." Joyce said she knew, yet looked surprised, changed the subject. Liebowitz felt ashamed. Of course she knew. Why had he been crude? Did he suppose that she hadn't really wanted to telephone him, that she was using him as a source of tickets? What difference? He had an erection, a purpose; she had Mandell, novel- ist of ideas, celebrated for his body. "He is terribly jealous of you," she said. "It was long ago, I was a kid, and he wasn't even in the picture. But he's jealous. He's the kind who wonders about a girl's former lovers. Not that he's weird or anything, just social. He's terrific in bed. I'll bet you two could be friends."

"Does he know I'm seeing you tonight?" Liebowitz's hand had ached for her knee. Her voice had begun to cause brain damage and had to be stopped. It was getting late, there was nothing more to say. She laughed again. Marvelous sound, thought Liebowitz, almost like laughter. He was nearly convinced now that she deserved Mandell. But why didn't she send him away or suggest they go out? Was it because Liebowitz's firm didn't do novels? Was he supposed to listen? burn with jealousy? He burned to piss.

"Is something wrong, Joycie?"

Mandell didn't understand. Did she seem slightly cool, too polite? Did she laugh too much?

"I wanted to talk to you about my writing, but really, Joycie, is something, like, wrong?"

"What do you mean? There's nothing wrong. I just thought you'd be working tonight."

Mandell was embarrassed, a little hurt, unable to leave. Of course. How could he leave with her behaving that polite way? Mandell was just as trapped as Liebowitz, who, bent and drooling, gaped at a shoe, a dressing table, combs, brushes, cosmetics, a roll of insulation tape . . . and, before he knew what he had in mind, Liebowitz seized the tape. He laid two strips, in an X, across a windowpane, punched the nail file into the heart of the X, and gently pulled away the tape with sections of broken glass. Like Robinson Crusoe. Trapped, isolated—yet he could make himself comfortable. Liebowitz felt proud. Mainly, he felt searing release. Liebowitz pissed.

Through the hole in the windowpane, across an echoing air shaft, a long shining line—burning, arcing, resonant—as he listened to Mandell. "I have a friend who says my novels are *like* writing, but not real writing, you get it?" Liebowitz shook his head, thinking, Some friend, as he splashed brick wall and a window on the other side of the air shaft and, though he heard yelling, heard nothing relevant to Robinson Crusoe and, though he saw a man's face, continued pissing on that face, yelling from the window, on the other side of the air shaft.

A good neighborhood, thought Liebowitz. The police won't take long. He wondered what to say, how to say it, and zipped up hurriedly. In the dressing-table mirror he saw another face, his own, bloated by pressure, trying not to cry. According to that face, he thought, a life is at stake. His life was at stake and he couldn't grab a cab. Mandell was still there, whining about his writing. Joyce couldn't interrupt and say go home. Writers are touchy. He might get mad and call off the marriage. Liebowitz had no choice but to prepare a statement. "My name, Officers, is Liebowitz." Thus he planned to begin. Not brilliant. Appropriate. He'd chuckle in a jolly, personable way. A regular fellow, not a drunk or a maniac. Mandell was shrill and peevish: "Look here, look here. My name is Mandell. I'm a professor of rhetoric and communication art at a college. And a novelist. This is ironic, but it is only a matter of circumstances and I have no idea what it means."

A strange voice said, "Don't worry, Professor, we'll explain later."

Joyce said, "This is a silly mistake. I'm sure you chaps have a lot to do—"

Mandell cut in: "Take your hands off me. And you shut up, Joyce. I've had enough of this crap. Like, show me the lousy warrant or, like, get the hell out. No Nazi cops push me around. Joyce, call someone. I'm not without friends. Call someone."

The strange voice said, "Hold the creep."

With hatred Mandell was screaming, "No, no, don't come with me. I don't want you to come with me, you stupid bitch. Call someone. Get help." The hall door shut. The bedroom door opened. Joyce was staring at Liebowitz. "You hear what happened? How can you sit there and stare at me? I've never felt this way in my life. Look at you. Lepers could be screwing at your feet. Do you realize what happened?"

Liebowitz shrugged yes mixed a little with no.

"I see," she said. "I see. You're furious because you had to sit in here. What could I do? What could I say? You're furious as hell, aren't you?"

Liebowitz didn't answer. He felt a bitter strength in his position. Joyce began pinching her thighs to express suffering. Unable to deal with herself across the room from him, she came closer to where he sat on the bed. Liebowitz said, "The cops took the putz away." His tone revealed no anger and let her sit down beside him. "It's horrible. It's humiliating," she said. "They think he pissed out the window. He called me a stupid bitch." Liebowitz said, "You might be a stupid bitch, but you look as good to me now as years ago. In some ways, better." His hand was on her knee. It seemed to him a big hand, full of genius and power. He felt proud to consider how these qualities converged in himself. Joyce's mouth and eyes grew slow, as if the girl behind them had stopped jumping. She glanced at his hand. "I must make a phone call," she said softly, a little urgently, and started to rise. Liebowitz pressed down. She sat. "It wouldn't be right," she said, and then, imploringly, "Would you like to smoke a joint?"

"No."

She has middle-class habits, he thought.

"It wouldn't be right," she said, as if to remind him of something, not to insist on it. But what's right, what's wrong to a genius? Liebowitz, forty years old, screwed her like a nineteen-year-old genius.

downers

BEYOND ORGASM

She didn't like me. So I phoned her every day. I announced the new movies, concerts, art exhibits. I talked them up, excitements out there, claiming them in my voice. Not to like me was not to like the world. Then I asked her out. Impossible to say no. I appeared at her door in a witty hat, a crazy tie. Sometimes I changed my hairstyle. I was various, talking, dancing, waving my arms. I was the world. But she didn't like me. If she weren't so sweet, if she had will power, if she didn't miss the other guy so much, she'd have said, "Beat it, you're irrelevant." But she was in pain, confused about herself. The other guy had dumped her. I owed him a debt. It took the form of hatred, although, if not for him, she wouldn't have needed me. Not that she did. She needed my effort, not me. Me, she didn't like. Discouraged, sad, thinking I'd overdone this bad act and maybe I didn't like her all that much, I said, "Let's go to the restaurant next door, have dinner, say goodbye." She seemed reluctant, even frightened. I wondered if, in such decisive gestures, there was hope. She said, "Not there." I wondered if it was his hangout, or a restaurant she used to enjoy with him. I insisted. "Please," she said, "any other restaurant." But I needed this concession. She'd never given me anything else. For two men I'd talked and danced, even in bed. I insisted. Adamant. Shaking. "Only that restaurant." She took my arm. We walked briskly in appreciation of my feelings. As we entered the restaurant, she pulled back. I recognized him—alone, sitting at a table. Him. The other guy. My soul flew into the shape of his face. He yawned. Nothing justifies hate like animal simplicity. "Look. He's yawning. What a swine." Was it a show of casual vulnerability? Contempt? She pulled my arm. I didn't budge. I stared. His eyes squeezed to dashes. I heard the mock whimper of yawns. He began scratching the tablecloth.

Two waiters ran to his side with questions of concern. His yawn was half his face. Batlike whimpers issued from it. Jawbones had locked, fiercely, absolutely. He needed help. My fist was ready. She cried, begging, dragging me away. I let her. That night was our beginning. Whenever I yawned at her, she'd laugh and plead, "Stop it." Her admiration of me extended to orgasm. Even beyond. It was not unmixed with fear.

THE PINCH

Night came. I went to the window. My mother said, "What are you looking at?" I looked. She stood beside me and touched my arm. "What are you looking at?" Swinging through the windy blackness were spooky whites. My mother looked. She said, "Sheets. Sheets on a line." I saw pale neurasthenics licking bodies of the air. She said, "You don't believe me? Put on your coat." She took me to the alley and held my hand. We stood beneath the sheets. I heard a dull spasmodic flap as the wind released them. We went home. I stood at the window. "Sheets on a line," she said. I was crying. She pinched my arm. "I pinched your arm," she said. Her face came closer to mine, as if to bring my face closer to mine, pleading, "I will pinch your arm."

LEFTY-RIGHTY

Running in a fast game, I was pushed and went running off the court into a brick wall. My palm flattened against brick, driving shock into my wrist. The city wasn't big enough for that pain. Other players left the game to watch me. Buildings grumbled in their roots. In tiny grains of concrete I saw recriminations. I rolled onto my back. A circle of faces looked down. I looked at the sky and didn't scream. I might have broken my nose, my cheek, my left wrist. Why had it been the right? Then someone replaced me in the game. It resumed before I left the playground. I was abolished by tenements. For six weeks I wore a plaster cast. It itched in warm rooms. The left hand held forks and spoons, combed my hair, buttoned shirts. It could soon knot a tie. But it took passes like a wooden claw. It threw them like a catapult, not a hand. Broken this way, a wild animal would have been noticed, killed, got out of sight. I appeared daily, lingering on the sidelines, shuffling in among the healthy when they formed teams. Not saying a word, I begged: "Choose me." Nobody looked in my direction, but being there gave me a right. Begrudged, but a right. Sooner or later, at least once a day, I'd be chosen. Any team I played on lost. Before and after games, alone, I practiced running to my left, dribbling lefty, shooting lefty. I became less bad. The left hand became a hand. In a tough, fast game, a few days after the cast was removed, my opponent said, "Hey, man, you a lefty or a righty?" I mumbled, "Lefty-righty." My team won easily. He came up to me and whispered, "How do you wipe your ass?" Out of noblesse oblige, I laughed. He grinned like a grateful ape, then offered me a cigarette, which I declined.

ANGRY

I heard that he had come to town. He hadn't called me. I supposed he was angry. I became angry, too. I wouldn't call him. When he called I was polite and agreed to go to his place. Dinner was pleasant. We talked for hours. When I yawned he raised new subjects, offered more cognac. His wife offered more to eat. I lighted another cigarette. His child, a two-year-old boy, came into the room. It seemed appropriate, delightful. But something was wrong with him. A distortion, quite serious, impossible not to notice. He was told to say hello, then sent back to bed. The air resisted words. We became flat and opaque. I put out my cigarette. They didn't try to detain me. We shook hands at the door.

WHAT YOU HAVEN'T DONE

Wildly piled, pinned black hair. A face of busyness interrupted.

"Ever think of anyone but yourself?"

"You."

"Bullshit."

I shut the door, waited. Nothing changed. Bullshit banged my head.

"I haven't cleaned my apartment or done my shopping. My cat has to go to the vet. My mother will phone in twenty minutes."

I rushed forward, hugged her, kissed her neck—deep—as if to plug a hole. She hung in my arms. I quit kissing. She looked at me with fatigue, an expression like apology but distinct from it. Then she touched my hand.

"Take off your clothes," I said.

"So much to do."

"Everything off."

Her face flashed through spaces in her black wool sweater. Her skirt dropped. She walked away naked, rapid, matter-of-fact, and sat on the bed.

"I want to know something," I said. "What have you never done with another man?" I sat beside her.

"This," she groaned, then plucked out hairpins.

"A man used to ask a woman if she's a virgin. Now I ask you a question of the heart."

"What do you want to know, exactly?"

"What you haven't done . . ."

She smacked her fists to her ears. "Cleaned my apartment. Expect a phone call. Cat has to go to the vet."

THE BROKEN LEG

My aunt tapped the spot and described the pain. Big Doctor sneered, "Nothing is wrong with your knee." She tapped again. Described the pain. Big Doctor slapped his own knee and said, "Nothing is wrong." She said, "Just give me a prescription." He refused to prescribe even an aspirin. My aunt said, "My knee is sick. My knee is in pain. That pleases you." He glanced at his calendar, set a date for the knife. My aunt went home. She read books on diet and health and started doing yoga exercises. Her knee felt better. There was no pain. She dressed and hurried out to see Big Doctor—blue-tinted hair, maroon lipstick, necklace, bracelets, rings, girdle, stockings, high heels—running down Broadway, singing, "Big Doctor, my knee is better," running, running . . .

PORNOGRAPHIC

The girl had Oriental eyes with blue pupils in a round, white Oriental face. Blue pupils beneath epicanthic folds in the innocent emptiness of a round face. Her mouth was heavy and long and linear. Beautifully curled. The camera identified it with the genitals of her colleagues, perhaps a dozen males bearing temperamentally stiff or floppy pricks. Opposed to her mouth, not beautiful; but problematic or hysterical. Relieved of this or that prick, her mouth smiled. Personal light went unpricked, smiling along abdominal walls to their owners, reassuring them: "We are actors in a pornographic movie. Nothing is at stake." Then it recurred quickly to cinematic obligations—to suck and lick with conviction. The camera adhered to it, lucid, neutral, ubiquitous. The camera's look. Nearly like her mouth, assimilating advertisements of the male, but only in its totalitarian looking. The camera's invincible distance. The look of looking.

BEING MORAL

"I've got a problem," she said. "I'm obsessed by trivial reflections. When I brush my teeth, I think people are starving. Yet I'm determined to brush my teeth because it's moral. But brushing makes me hungry. Eat, brush, eat, brush. I'm afraid someone will have to put a bullet in my head to save me from myself. Being moral is a luxury, isn't it? No, it's asking the question. That's why I spend my time stealing, fucking, and taking dope."

LISTENING

Every seat was taken. Students sat on the floor and window ledges. They barely moved. Nobody smoked. He took off his raincoat, laid it on the desk. At the end of the hour he'd look for his hat. Which was on his head. He arrived with a handkerchief pressed to his lips, wiping away his breakfast. Zipping his fly. He ground fingers into his ears, as if digging for insects. Then, putting his hands in his trouser pockets, he tumbled his prunes. We watched. His loneliness made revelations. Dirty fingernails, nicotine stains, one shoelace a clot of knots. Students followed him to his office. Papers on his desk, piled level with his chest, smelled of rotting food. They defeated conversation. He'd invite you to sit. The chair looked greasy. The floor was splotched with coffee, dried oils, trapped grit. No walls, only book pressure, with small gaps in the volumes for shaving equipment, mirror, hairbrush, and toothbrush. "Please sit." They never stayed long. They rushed to his classes. Girls with long hair, shampooed five times a week, gave him feeling looks, accumulating knees and ankles in the front row. His life in a pool of eyeballs. He didn't know he was there. He'd begin. The silence was awesome, as if subsequent to a boom. Nobody had been talking, yet a space cleared, a hole blown out of nothing for his voice. It was like a blues piano rumbling in the abyss; meditations in pursuit of meditations. His course, "Philosophy 999: Great Issues," was also called "Introduction to Thought" and "History of Consciousness." He taught one course. He'd blow his nose. The handkerchief still in his hand, he, too, observed a silence. Listening. To listen was to think. We listened to him listening. World gathered into mind. Sometimes the hour ended that way, in silence, then spontaneous applause. His authenticity was insuperable. He scratched his buttocks, looked out the window. Once he said, "Winter." A girl cried, "January," eager for dialogue. Toward the end, he sat in a chair, elbows on knees, and shut one eye. Through the other, with heavy head cocked, he squinted at the ceiling, as if a last point were up there. After taking his course, students couldn't speak without shutting one eye, addressing the ceiling. At a party I saw a girl shut one eye and scratch her buttocks. That was in Chicago, years later, after he was dead. I went up to her, shut one eye, and asked, "Can you tell me one thing, any particular thing he said? He never published a book, not even a book review." She looked at me as if at moral scum.

THE CONVERSATION

We twisted up together in New York. Intimacy was insult; love could hate. Then I went away. Years passed. He came to visit. It wasn't easy to talk. Finally I mentioned a pornographic movie. He said, "Which pornographic movie?" I said, "You distinguish carefully among them?" He didn't smile. As if to spare my feelings, he began talking about New York. The complexities, the intensities. I listened with humble attention, trying to remember the title of the pornographic movie. Naked bodies came to mind, agitating to the impulses of community. If I'd remembered the title, I'd have screamed it. But I couldn't remember. He went on, the Metropolis of Total Excitement flying out of his mouth. Later, I asked him to see the other rooms in my house. It was a corny gesture. But he stood right up and made an urbane shrug, suggesting revulsion or eagerness. I led him out of the foyer. When we came to my study I pushed the windows wide. "Trees, birds," I said. He grinned a mellow hook and didn't glance at the view. He said, "Do you know about Sartre's study?" I said, "No; so what." He said, "Jean-Paul Sartre's study gives out upon great Parisian avenues. They converge in his desk. Endless human traffic converges in Jean-Paul Sartre's desk." I said, "Actually, I hate trees and birds. They make me sick." He giggled, poked my arm, told me to go fuck myself. "Why?" I asked. He said, "Because you're deficient in social hormones." I laughed, "That's the title of the pornographic movie. *Social Hormones*." I laughed, but his remark felt incisive; I couldn't be sure what he meant. In the foyer again, I shook his hand, slapped his back. He was rattling goodbyes, edging out the door, looking at me with exhilaration.

THE SNAKE

The road, crowded by woods on either side, turned whimsically as a line of smoke, taking its own peculiar way, unpredictable, inevitable as fate, but I continued driving hard, pressing it until I'd go too fast and have to slow suddenly, holding the turn until I could press again, fast, faster. It was like that for hours. Me against it. I was tired. She was bored, nervous, giddy. Whenever I said anything, she'd say, "Awfully Jewish of you." She giggled, tried to read a magazine, brushed her hair. I smoked cigarettes, attacked the road, and stopped talking to her. She played with the radio knobs, pulled up her skirt, stroked her legs. Then I noticed a brown snake. I stopped the car. "Drive over it," she said. "Don't you leave this car." I left the car. She moaned, "Please." The snake was thicker than my foot. Blinkless eyes; medals of mud against its sides; tiny sticks of grass embedded in the mud. Ants crawled across the scales. She said, "Please." Her voice was bright, meaningless, far away. I crouched and reached slowly— toward the neck—a necessity. It would fill my fist; whip; hiss. She yelled, "My mother was bitten by a brown snake like that, you New York asshole." I grabbed it. I screamed. She tumbled out of the car. I lifted the snake. It hung. It was a dead snake. We got back into the car and sat there quietly. Then I asked her to marry me. She said, "O.K." We laughed and fucked until dark.

LIVER

"Everything is fine," I said. My mother said, "I hope so." I said, "It is, it is." My mother said, "I hope so." I said, "Everything is wonderful. Couldn't be better. How do you feel?" My mother said, "Like a knife is pulling out of my liver."

trotsky's garden

TROTSKY IS WRITING. He will mention his love of life and his unquali-
fied faith in dialectical materialism. He will mention Natasha, the strip of
green outside his window, his invincible atheism, and he will contemplate
his death. It is morning. Trotsky sits at his wooden desk. He looks at letters
and a blotter. The Mexican sun burns in the green outside his window, just
opened by Natasha. Trotsky notices. Natasha and the green slide into his
writing. A man will strike Trotsky in the head with a pickax. Trotsky's
sons—murdered—are mentioned in the writing. From Russia to Mexico,
friends, secretaries, and bodyguards—murdered—are mentioned in the
writing. In Berlin, where he sent her for psychoanalysis, his daughter
killed herself. The pen does not cease or grovel in individuals. Trotsky will
mention his faith in dialectical materialism, his faith in meaning. His
mother suffered difficulties in reading; she crouched over novels and said,
"Beta, alpha . . ." Trotsky says:

> If I could begin all over, I would try to avoid this or that mistake, but the
> main course of my life would remain unchanged. I shall die a proletarian
> revolutionist, a Marxist, a dialectical materialist.

Dialectical materialism, in the heat of the day, draws a pickax from its
raincoat. Some say "rusty ax." Others say "ice pick." Trotsky himself
noticed nothing—it descended from behind—but he will bite the assassin's hand. He is writing that if he lived again, he would avoid mistakes.
The sun, as it did yesterday and will tomorrow, is shining. Trotsky loves
the green outside his window and flourishes it in his writing. We shout,
"O.K., Trotsky, no time for poems." He cannot hear us. His poem is a

march of corpses, the din is terrific. Feet are beating in his writing. The
sun is in the green in his writing. Sedova, the aristocrat, lifts her elbow for
photographers. "See? A bullet made that ugly scratch. My old man isn't
nobody. Yesterday they machine-gunned our bedroom." She means, From
revolution to Mexico, Trotsky is pursued by his inventions. Trotsky himself says that he put the idea of exile into the ear of Stalin's spy; hence, into
the mind of Stalin. In effect, Trotsky exiled Trotsky and machine-gunned
his bedroom. Now, writing that one cannot be reborn until one is dead—
and look: it sits beside him with a raincoat and pickax. It makes nervous
conversation about alphabetical materialism. Suddenly Trotsky is fighting,
not writing. Blood runs into his eyes. Nevertheless, he catches the personal fact. Who said Lenin is morally repulsive, and Stalin is a savage who
hates ideas, and Parvus is a fat, fleshy bulldog head? Trotsky said these
things. Now the assassin's hand is in his teeth. With fury of intimacy,
Trotsky bites. This hand wanted to remind him of something. But what?
On the wall outside, the guards carry rifles and binoculars. They are gos-
siping in the sun when Trotsky screams. They see him standing in the
window, bleeding and blind, a figure of history. "What?" he screams. The
assassin is behind him, bent, sobbing like a child as he sucks his mutilated
hand. The guards are running on the wall with their rifles and binoculars.
Freud lights a cigar and contemplates this tableau. He says, "Trotsky and I
were neighbors in Vienna." Trotsky admired Freud. He sent him his best
daughter. Now Trotsky shouts in the window: "What does it mean? Such
heat. In such heat a raincoat . . ." Trotsky flings toward his wooden desk.
He needs only seconds to write: "On hot days in Mexico beware of
raincoats."

annabella's hat

1

The butler says, "Lord Byron jumped out of the carriage and walked away." Annabella appeared next. The butler says, "The bride alighted, and came up the steps alone, her countenance and frame agonized and listless with evident horror and despair." A scarf, twisted about her head, was bunched up in imitation of a hat. Others report the arrival, among them Lord Byron. His memoirs were burned. One who read them claims Lord Byron took Annabella before dinner. They withdrew after dinner and lay in a four-poster bed near a fireplace. The crimson curtains of the bed, quickened by firelight, made flickering blood-colored walls. Lord Byron imagined himself within the membranes of a giant stomach. "I am in hell," he screamed. Annabella crept downstairs, hid in the kitchen, and later begged medical advice. Assured that Lord Byron was mysterious, not mad, she hired investigative agents. A year passes. The incontinent Lord Byron flees to the Continent. His affair with his sister, consummated before the marriage, is being noised about. People cut him at parties. He flees; soon thereafter, dies in Greece. Annabella's agents rush into the room. Lord Byron's servant—a bad-tempered man named Fletcher—draws his sabre but they beat him unconscious and rip the boot from Lord Byron's crippled foot. They saw a hoof of great beauty, subtly united with the fetlock. The memoirs—where Lord Byron mentioned it—were burned at Annabella's insistence. Now, sufficient to say, in the mass of Byroniana—letters, scholarship, gossip—no extended reference to his hoof exists.

2

Lord Byron published amazing poems. He had sexual union with his sister. Then came the wedding. Afterward, with Annabella and her maid, he rode forty miles from Seaham Church to Halnaby Hall, where he honeymooned. It is said the day was cold and Lord Byron despised the cold, but nothing is reported as to where he sat in the carriage—beside Annabella or beside the maid, or if Annabella sat between, with the meat and bags and wine opposed. Fletcher, a sullen lout, refused to say a word. He galloped behind the carriage. It isn't known if the maid was acquainted with Lord Byron, or if they sat as strangers pressed, he by she, at turns in the road. Reported then, as here reported, Lord Byron was cold. Annabella's head, round as an Esquimau's, was conservative of temperature. It is known that Lord Byron's head, examined the previous year by the craniologist Spurzheim, was a structure of antithetical dispositions. The rest is inevitable. Indifferent to cold or hot—by nature, virtuous—the Annabella head through intimate contiguity with the crippled, incestuous bisexual caused him to feel dialectically cold, Satanic, probably squashed by the maid. It is rumored that he began shrieking, then stamping the carriage floor viciously with his hoof.

i would have saved them if i could

GIVING NOTICE

A few days prior to the event, my cousin said, "I'm not going through with it. Call off the bar mitzvah." My uncle said, "You're crazy." My aunt said, "I think so." He'd already reserved the banquet hall, said my uncle, with a big deposit; already paid the rabbis, the caterers, the orchestra. Flying in from everywhere in the Americas and Canada were relatives and friends. My aunt said, "Deposit. Relatives." My cousin said, "Do I know the meaning of even ten Hebrew words? Is the bar mitzvah a Jewish ceremony? Do I believe in God?" My aunt said, "Get serious." My uncle said, "Shut up. The crazy is talking to me." My aunt said, "You, too, must be crazy." My cousin said, "Call it off." My uncle said, "I listened. Now you listen. When the anti-Semites come to kill your mother, will it be nice to say you aren't a bar mitzvah? Don't you want to be counted?" My cousin pulled open his shirt. "Look," he cried. My aunt said, "I can't talk so I can't look." "Look," he screamed. Green, iridescent Stars of David had grown from his nipples. My uncle collapsed on the wall-to-wall carpet. Looking, my aunt said, "I can't talk so I refuse to look at your crazy tits." That night my uncle sent telegrams throughout the Western Hemisphere. He explained, with regrets, that his son didn't believe in God, so the bar mitzvah was canceled. Then he pulled my cousin's five-hundred-dollar racing bike into the driveway, mangled the handlebars, kicked out the spokes, and left it for the neighborhood to notice.

A SUSPECTED JEW

Jaromir Hladík is suspected of being a Jew, imprisoned by the Gestapo, sentenced to death. In his prison cell, despite terror and confusion, he becomes ecstatic, then indistinguishable from his ecstasy. He is, in short, an ecstasy—the incarnation of a metaphysical state. Borges wrote this story. He calls it "The Secret Miracle." Whatever you call it, says Gramsci, it exemplifies the ideological hegemony of the ruling class. In the mediating figure Jaromir Hladík, absolute misery translates into the consolations of redemptive esthesis. It follows, then, the Gestapo, an organization of death, gives birth to "The Ecstatic Hladík"—or, to be precise, "The Secret Miracle." Borges, master of controlled estrangement, makes it impossible to feel that Jaromir Hladík—say, a suspected Jew of average height, with bad teeth, gray hair, nervous cough, tinted spectacles, delicate fingers, gentle musical voice—physically and exactly disintegrates (as intimated in the final sentences) between a hard stone wall and the impact of specific bullets.

THE SUBJECT AT THE VANISHING POINT

My grandfather—less than average height—had bad teeth, gray hair, nervous cough, tinted spectacles, delicate fingers, and a gentle musical voice. To appear confident and authentic, worthy of attention by clerks in the visa office, he memorized the required information—his mother's maiden name, the addresses of relatives in America—and, walking down the street, he felt constantly in his coat pockets to be sure that he had photos of himself, wife, daughter, enough money for the required bribes, and the necessary papers—documents from America, passports, birth certificates, and an essay by himself in praise of Poland—when a pogrom started. Doors and windows slammed shut. The robots were coming. Alone in a strange street, he couldn't tell which way to go. At every corner was death. Suddenly—for good or ill isn't known—somebody flung him into a cellar. Others died. He, bleeding and semiconscious, hidden in a cellar, survived the pogrom. That day he didn't get a visa to leave Poland. He was a tailor—short, thin-boned. Even in a winter coat, easy to fling. He crawled amid rats and dirt, collecting his papers. When night came and Poland lay snoring in the street, he climbed out of the cellar and ran home. Wife and daughter ministered to his wounds. All thanked God that he was alive. But it was too late to get a visa. The Nazis came with the meaning of history—what flings you into a cellar saves you for bullets. I don't say, in the historical dialectic, individual life reduces to hideous idiocy. I'm talking about my grandfather, my grandmother, and my aunt. It seems to me, in the dialectic, individual life reduces not even to hideous idiocy.

MATERIAL CIRCUMSTANCES

His idea about labor power came to him while he strode back and forth in his room in Paris and smoked cigarettes. Indeed, striding back and forth, he smoked cigarettes, but striding, smoking, whistling, etc., are contingent activities. What *matters* is the stage of development in the class struggle when it is possible for a person to think seriously—to have an idea—about labor power. Certainly, in Paris, Karl Marx strode, for example, smoking cigarettes. Now and then, he strode to the window, pushed it open to free the room of smoke and listen for developments. But the precisely particular determinants of consciousness, within the class struggle, are material circumstances. Intuitively, perhaps, Karl Marx felt the burden of determined consciousness in the black, thick hair thrusting from the top of his head like implications and slithering down his chest and back to converge at his crotch, like a conclusion. But, even scrutinizing the hair beneath his fingernails (very like the historical grain in wood), he detected nothing beyond mute, inexorable flux until—striding, smoking—he pushed open his window and noticed Monsieur Grandbouche, his landlord, a figure of bourgeois pieties, who shouted, "When will you pay the rent, my hairball?" Karl Marx strode back and forth and smoked. *La question* Grandbouche burned in his roots, like the residue of a summer rainstorm, quickening the dialectical material of his struggling circumstances. Hair twisted from his ears and whistling nostrils. Angry messages. An idea was occurring. Indeterminable millions would die. Indeterminable millions would eat. Thus, a Parisian landlord, frightened by a smoky blotch in the window, shouted a pathetic joke in the spirit of nervous conviviality, and as a result, his descendants would be torn to pieces, for he'd epitomized material circumstances by shouting—across generations of Grandbouche—an idea, intensified by repercussions, echoed in concussions of Marxian canons, tearing fascist ligament even in the jungles of the East. *Voilà*, implicit in a landlord's shout is the death rattle of his children's children.

BUSINESS LIFE

My uncle invested his money in a beauty parlor, began to make a little profit—and the union representative came. My uncle promised to hire union workers soon as the mortgage was paid. Pickets arrived. Back and forth with their signs in front of the beauty parlor. My uncle brought them coffee. They talked about their troubles. A picketer didn't have a soft job. Long apprenticeship; pay wasn't good; and morning to evening, march, march, march, screaming insults at my uncle's customers. The signs didn't look heavy, but try to carry one all day. My uncle agreed: a sign is heavy. Anyhow, business improved. After a while the union bombed the beauty parlor, set fire to my uncle's car, and beat up my aunt. This was reported in the newspaper. Business became much better. My uncle negotiated for a second beauty parlor. One afternoon a picketer leaned against the window of the beauty parlor and lit a cigarette. My uncle started to phone the union, but he hadn't forgotten his life in Russia, his hatred of informers. He put down the phone. The image of that man—slouched against the window, smoking, not carrying the picket sign so that people could read it—seethed in my uncle like moral poison. He soon developed a chronic stomach disturbance. Next came ulcers, doctors, hospitals—all the miseries of a life in business.

LITERARY CRITICISM

Photographs of suspected Jews—men, women, children with hair, teeth, etc.—are available in great sufficiency. If you demand one, either you hate, or do not understand, Borges's critical point, which is that any reader knows stories of this exquisitely general kind. Besides, Borges made his story not from photographable reality—your Polish relatives whose undernourished kosher height never exceeded five feet six inches—but from a stupid story called "An Occurrence at Owl Creek Bridge." My aunt, a schoolgirl, was bleeding on the ground with her mother and father in Brest Litovsk.

SHRUBLESS CRAGS

The Prisoner of Chillon, by Lord Byron, isn't essentially different from "The Secret Miracle." It, too, is about a condemned prisoner who becomes ecstatic. Suddenly, after years in a dungeon, Bonnivard transcends his mortality:

> *What next befell me then and there*
>   *I know not well—I never knew—*
> *First came the loss of light, and air,*
>   *And then of darkness too:*
> *I had no thought, no feeling—none—*
> *Among the stones I stood a stone,*
> *And was, scarce conscious what I wist,*
> *As shrubless crags within the mist;*
> *For all was blank, and bleak, and grey;*
> *It was not night—it was not day;*
> *It was not even the dungeon-light,*
> *So hateful to my heavy sight,*
> *But vacancy absorbing space,*
> *And fixedness—without a place.*

Like Hladík, in a state of intensified absence, he is a presence.

SONG

Byronic romanticism entered the Russian soul, at the deepest level, as evidenced in the beloved folk song "Oi yoi, the shrubless crags."

BLOSSOMS

Metaphysical possibilities—Hladík, Bonnivard—as inherent in the world, are appreciated by Wordsworth when he focuses on shrubless crags and imagines them spiritual entities, theoretical men who neither live nor die. They hover in the mist of universal mind, or the moods of finitude. In a snowstorm outside Smolensk, fighting the Nazis, my uncle was hit in the head by shrapnel, carried to a hospital, and dropped in the dead ward. That night a Jewish woman, who was a surgeon and colonel in the Russian army, discovered him when she left the operating room and, to smoke a cigarette, retreated to the dead ward. A vague moan, "Mama," reached her from shadowy rows of corpses. She ordered a search. Nurses running down the rows, pressing back eyelids, listening at mouth holes, located my uncle. The body wasn't dead; more you couldn't say. The surgeon stepped on her cigarette. "I'll operate." My uncle lived, a hero of the people, guaranteed every right of Russian citizenship. At his first opportunity he fled, walking from Russia to Italy through the confusion of ruined cities; stealing by night across the borders of Poland, Czechoslovakia, Romania, and Austria; starving, pursued by dogs and police, and always repeating to himself the address of his sister in lower Manhattan. When he got to America he struggled for years, with little English and great anxiety, to make money. Today he owns racetracks and a chain of beauty parlors. He drives a Lincoln Continental. Though he speaks six languages, he isn't much of a conversationalist, but likes a good joke, especially if it comes from life—how, for example, during a Chinese dinner, his brother-in-law's appendix ruptured. Both his sons are doctors and drive Jaguars. He reminds them that his life was saved by a woman less than five feet tall who, during the battle of Smolensk, performed miraculous surgery while standing on ammunition boxes. It could seem, now that he's a big shot, he gives lessons in humility. But how else to defend himself against happiness? He sees terrifying vulnerability in the blossoms of *nachas*.

THE SCREAMS OF CHILDREN

The New Testament is the best condemned-prisoner story. Jesus, a "suspected" Jew, sublimates at the deadly moment. In two ways, then, he is like Jaromir Hladík. Insofar as the Gestapo gives birth to the ecstatic Hladík, he and Jesus are similar in yet another way. Both are victims of parental ambivalence, which tends to give birth to death. One could savor distinctions here, but the prophetic Kafka hurries me away: humanity, he says, is the growth of death force. For reasons of discretion the trains rolled before dawn, routed through the outskirts of Prague. Nevertheless, you could hear the screams of children.

BLACK BREAD, BUTTER, ONION

The black bread should be Pechter's, but the firm went out of business, so substitute bialys from the bakery on Grand Street, between Essex and Clinton, on the right heading toward the river, not SoHo. With your thumb, gouge and tear bialys open along the circumference. Butter bialys. Insert onion slices. Do this about 3:00 a.m., at the glass-topped table in my parents' dining room, after a heavy date in Greenwich Village. My parents should be asleep in their bedroom, twenty feet away. Since my father is dead, imagine him. He snores. He cries out against murderous assailants. I could never catch his exact words. Think what scares you most, then eat, eat. *The New York Times*, purchased minutes ago at the kiosk in Sheridan Square, is fresh; it lies beside the plate of bialys. As you eat, you read. Light a cigarette. Coffee, in the gray pot, waits on the stove. Don't let it boil. Occasional street noises—sirens, cats—should penetrate the Venetian blinds and thick, deeply pleated drapes of the living-room windows. The tender, powdery surface of the bialys is dented by your fingertips, which bear odors of sex; also butter, onion, dough, tobacco, newsprint, and coffee. The whole city is in your nose, but go outside and eat the last bialy while strolling on Cherry Street. The neighborhood is Mafia-controlled; completely safe. You will be seen from tenement windows and recognized. Smoke another cigarette. Take your time. Your father cries out in his sleep, but he was born in Europe. For a native American kid, there is nothing to worry about. Even if you eat half a dozen bialys, with an onion and coffee, you will sleep like a baby.

ALIENATION

In his essay "On the Jewish Question," written in exile, Karl Marx—an alienated Jew assuming the voice of a Hegelienated Jew—says, "Money is the jealous god of Israel." He means, by this oblique smear, the Virgin is a prostitute, her child is capitalism. Hence, it is Jesus—not the exiled Karl Marx—who objectifies alienation. And why not? The life of Jesus, described early and late by the absence of his father, is nothing less than the negation of negation. Marx never gives the least attention to the journey of the Magi, the mystery on the bestial floor, or the ultimate figure of Jesus in the excruciating pictorial epitome. For an execution Roman-style—with three prisoners and ritual paraphernalia—there is Lord Byron's letter.

LORD BYRON'S LETTER

"The day before I left Rome I saw three robbers guillotined. The ceremony—including the *masqued* priests; the half-naked executioners; the bandaged criminals; the black Christ and his banner; the scaffold; the soldiery; the slow procession, and the quick rattle and heavy fall of the axe; the splash of the blood, and the ghastliness of the exposed heads—is altogether more impressive than the vulgar and ungentlemanly dirty 'new drop' and dog-like agony of infliction upon the sufferers of the English sentence. Two of these men behaved calmly enough, but the first of the three died with great terror and reluctance. What was very horrible, he would not lie down; then his neck was too large for the aperture, and the priest was obliged to drown his exclamations by still louder exhortations. The head was off before the eye could trace the blow; but from an attempt to draw back the head, notwithstanding it was held forward by the hair, the first head was cut off close to the ears: the other two were taken off more cleanly. It is better than the oriental way, and (I should think) than the axe of our ancestors. The pain seems little, and yet the effect to the spectator, and the preparation to the criminal, is very striking and chilling. The first turned me quite hot and thirsty, and made me shake so that I could hardly hold the opera-glass (I was close, but was determined to see, as one should see every thing, once, with attention); the second and third (which shows how dreadfully soon things grow indifferent), I am ashamed to say, had no effect on me as a horror, though I would have saved them if I could."

SPECIES BEING

Casual precision, lucidity, complexity of nuance, smooth coherent speed. I admire the phrase "great terror and reluctance." It makes the prisoner's interior reality and his exterior—or social—reality simultaneous. Surely he felt more than reluctance. But the word stands in contrast to "great terror" and thus acquires the specifically social quality of great terror suffered by an individual at the center of public drama. He could collapse and dissolve into his great terror, but doesn't. Nor does he become ecstatic. Instead, sensitive to the crowd, he tries to join it by conveying an idea of himself—as also watching, like the crowd, a man who is about to get his head chopped off, who is in great terror and who—reluctantly—is himself. He owes the crowd his head. He knows the crowd will have his head. The crowd didn't go to the trouble of gathering itself around him for nothing. He wants to indicate that he is not the sort who is indifferent to what the crowd wants, but after all, it is his head it wants. Of course he is in no position not to provide it. The crowd sees that he has brought it with him. He would like, just the same, to suggest that he is "reluctant" to do so. At the last instant, he loses poise and pulls back. The result is a messy chop, a bad show. Ethics and aesthetics are inextricable. All this, and much more, is intimated in Byron's letter. Though it is infected, slightly, by ironical preciosity, the letter was written to somebody; therefore, like the prisoner, it participates in a consciousness other than its own; by attitudinizing, it suggests that it sees itself. This is Byron's concession to society; it is justified by his honesty—the childlike, high-spirited allegiance to the facts of the occasion inside and outside *his* head. Compared to the sneering, sarcastic, bludgeoning verbosity of Karl Marx, who walked in Paris, it isn't easy to believe the latter's idea of humanity as social essence is either witty or attractive.

DOSTOEVSKY

In Dostoevsky's story, a condemned prisoner—at the penultimate instant before a firing squad—is reprieved by the czar. Dostoevsky says it was his own experience. The reprieve was announced, he says, and the firing squad—not the prisoner Dostoevsky—sublimated. What follows? In life and art at once, the czar is a champion of imaginative forms. For condemned prisoners—which is all of us—the czar, a true aristocrat, is godlike in his manifestations. Astonishing, arbitrary, inscrutable. More evil than good—but thus are we saved. From above! Of course, in historical fact the czar and his family were slaughtered. Trotsky considered this "action" indispensable. Stalin's considerations, regarding Trotsky and his family, were identical. It is impossible to live with or without fictions.

THE NIGHT I BECAME A MARXIST

I heard a voice, turned, saw nobody, walked on, heard the voice again, but didn't turn. Nobody would be there. Or somebody would. In either case—very frightened—I walked faster, stiffened back and neck, expecting a blow, anxious to swivel about, but not doing it until I could no longer, and, walking quickly, stiffly, swiveling to look back, walk on, I noticed street lamps were smashed, blackness took sections of everything, signs were unreadable, windows glossy blotches, doorways like sighs issuing from unimaginable interiors. I felt absolutely outside, savage, and I'd have begun running, but there was the park, the streets beyond. I continued to walk, swivel, walk, saving power, holding self—and then, hearing it, whirled, dropped into a crouch, legs wide, fists raised. I'd have seen nothing, nobody, but—crouched low—realized, suddenly, I was face to face with it, shorter than a midget, speaking mouth, teeth like knives: "Always having fun, aren't you? Night after night, dancing, drinking, fucking. Fun, fun, fun."

CONCLUSION

Long before ruling-class, ideological superstructures, there were myths describing ecstasies like those of Jaromir Hladík and Jesus. Nymphs and beautiful boys, fleeing murderous gods, were always sublimating into flowers, trees, rivers, heavenly constellations, etc. The earliest stories, then, already convey an exhilarating apprehension of the world as incessantly created of incessant death. Nothing changes. Stories, myths, ideologies, flowers, rivers, heavenly constellations are the phonemes of a mysterious logos; and the lights of our cultural memory, as upon the surface of black primeval water, flicker and slide into innumerable qualifications. But Jaromir Hladík, among substantial millions, is dead. From a certain point of view, none of this shit matters anymore.

hello jack

JACK PHONED.

I said hello Jack.

He said he was going to the hospital.

I said all right I'll go with you.

I asked if I should phone his wife. They weren't living together.

He said he wanted me to know where he was. He didn't want me to do anything.

I said you're the boss. What's wrong? I made my voice little.

He yelled let's not talk about it. I'm in the hospital.

I said you said that you had to go to the hospital. Little words. Cheepee cheepee cheepee. His wife couldn't stand him. I knew plenty.

I said hello Jack and rushed to the hospital.

I had a bad foot. Every step was a wolf bite.

But Jack was in the hospital. He was the boss.

Jack phoned so I said hello taxicab. He'd do the same for me. We were old friends from Novgorod. Nothing to think about.

Taxi. Taxi.

In the hospital I noticed everyone was dead. Then a nurse was walking. I yelled rooms rooms rooms.

She said she personally didn't build the hospital.

I said so where's Jack?

She said he was in a room with another man.

In a hall I was running.

I saw Jack. Compared to the other man, Jack was Mr. Universe. What the Mongolians did to one grandmother the Germans did to the other.

They made a big blond Chinese Jew. His wife hated him. She was from Budapest. I didn't say anything.

What's with that man I said. I limped to a chair and took the shoe off my bad foot. The other man was blankets up to a face the color of chicken fat. His eyes were sticking out like swords.

Jack said the man was recovering from pneumonia. I didn't say anything.

If you ask me that man finished recovering I said. I put my shoe on Jack's bed.

Jack said what's the matter with your foot?

Nothing I said.

The man heard us. He said virus.

My foot was sweating.

Jack said virus is different from plain pneumonia.

I rubbed my foot. Poo I said. Open a window.

Jack said don't do anything. It's not important.

I said how much are they paying you to stay here? Stinks is not important?

I hopped to the window in one shoe and asked the virus I'm opening the window.

His eyes didn't move. They looked like a sign: BE QUIET. BE QUIET. Two killers, shining, pushing. He said virus.

I asked him again I'm opening this window so it will stop stinking.

He said virus.

A little snow came in. You couldn't notice. Like feathers. Nothing. It melted on the radiator. The virus didn't complain. Only a maniac would complain. The virus looked at the ceiling as if a movie was playing there. I looked too. I knew there was no movie on the ceiling but I looked. I was right. Jack was happier with the window open. Why not? He was a man with a friend. He began a speech why he was in the hospital.

He couldn't eat, he couldn't sleep. This. That. He fell down at work. In his stomach a pain. So his union sent him to the hospital.

Talk talk talk. I knew plenty.

I said I'm glad you want to talk.

He said is it wrong to talk?

I said tell me if what you have is serious and forgive me for laughing. A friend can laugh.

He said you think it's not serious?

I said to you serious is to the world ridiculous. Sure an enemy wouldn't laugh. He doesn't care so he can care. You have no sense of proportion. I rubbed my foot.

The other man said virus.

Jack said nobody told him not to talk.

I said maybe you would like to sing.

He began to sing. Ya–ya–ya.

The man said virus.

Me too. Ya–ya–ya.

All of a sudden the virus pushes his blankets on the floor and gets out of bed. His gown was pinched in his behind. His legs were bones, his face green. Like a tomato. I thought he was a tomato not a virus. He walked out of the room.

We stopped singing.

I said he went to the toilet.

Jack said a toilet is behind the door over there. He didn't go to the toilet.

I said how do you know? Maybe he doesn't like that toilet.

Jack said he didn't go to the toilet.

I said he'll be back in a minute. He went to another toilet because he didn't want us to hear him make a tinkle.

Jack said he didn't go to any toilet.

I said all right. Then he recovered. Why should he pay another penny? He recovered. Stop the clock. A motel is cheaper. I noticed I had a headache.

Jack gave me a face like Genghis Khan. A rock with eye slits. I could see the tomato was my fault. I could see it in the rock.

I said I know how it is Jack. You come in with trouble and they put you with a virus. Look at my foot. Is that sweat Jack? It's sweat believe me. Jack's wife hated him. A small skinny from night school. Hair and pimples.

She used to read to him from Goethe. He couldn't understand a word so they got married. When Jack had a hard-on she would vomit. He called her The Stomach. He used to say I'm going home now to The Stomach. I knew plenty. I said what do you say about my foot?

He said he phoned me so I would walk on my rotten foot. Then he grabbed my shoe and went to the window. A guy like him makes life meaningless.

Jack I said it was a shoe. You should throw Goethe out the window. Maybe you're in the Mongolian mood to throw my other shoe out the window? I slapped it on his bed.

He threw it out the window.

How about this lamp I said.

Out the window.

These blankets you want to keep?

Out the window.

I said this is too big don't even look at it.

For a Chinese Jew the mattress was no trouble.

A nurse came in when I was pulling Jack's bed toward the window. She started hitting and scratching me. Jack knocked her down with a punch. I jumped on her face. Jack put his tongue in her wallet, then me, then we pushed the bed out the window.

We were singing ya-ya-ya when nurses and doctors from all over the hospital came in. Why not? How often do schmucks see a friendship?

I walked home without a shoe. Not one shoe. I begged myself to take a taxi. It's cold. It's snowing. Take a taxi. But I refused. No taxi. For proof I yelled taxi taxi. It stopped. Drive into a wall I said.

The driver looked at me. I made a Jack face. He picked up a wrench. I could see he was a maniac. I was standing without shoes and a maniac was coming with a wrench. He could hit me in the foot. When he pushed open the door another taxi knocked it off.

It figures I yelled. But he was hitting the other driver with the wrench. In the snow I ran away. You'll get pneumonia I said.

I said I hope it's a virus.

Then I saw a phone booth and called Jack's wife.

She said hello.

I recognized her voice because it was so little and quiet. That's how she talked. Like a one-year-old.

I said hello Jack's wife?

She said yeah Jack's wife.

I said Jack is dead.

She said what who?

I said you're no good believe me. East Side hospital.

She was screaming with her little voice what who?

I didn't say anything. I said I'm hanging up. You think my foot isn't killing me? What do you care?

She screamed wait wait.

I said Jack's wife?

She screamed yeah yeah Jack's wife.

I said Jack's wife from Goethe?

She screamed yeah Jack's wife.

I said listen. Let another person talk sometimes.

She stopped screaming.

Are you listening I said.

She whispered yes yes.

Gloonk I hung up.

That night Genghis Khan and The Stomach were together. I didn't say anything. I went home and put my foot in the toilet bowl and flushed the water. Who needs a hospital? Or a small skinny from Budapest? Not for me. A friend calls and I said hello Jack. I also have a toilet bowl. It sucks my foot and soon it feels better. At night I knock over the garbage bag under the sink so in the dark I listen to them eat. The rats are happy. I'm happy. I yell sleep. It comes like a taxicab.

some laughed

T. T. MANDELL locked his office door, then read letters from experts advising the press against publishing his book, *The Enduring Southey*. One letter was insulting, another expressed hatred. All agreed *The Enduring Southey*—"an examination of the life and writing of Robert Southey"—should not be published. Every letter was exceedingly personal and impeccably anonymous. Mandell, an assistant professor of rhetoric and communication art at Bronx Community State Extension, had hoped to win a permanent position at the college. But no published book, no job. In effect, the experts said T. T. Mandell should be fired. But in every negative lives a positive. Mandell could read the letters; Mandell could revise *The Enduring Southey*. Where he'd previously said "yes" or "no," he now said "perhaps yes," "perhaps no." Miss Nugent, the department secretary, retyped the manuscript, then mailed it to another press. It was rejected.

T. T. Mandell locked his office door, then read the letters. All different, yet one conclusion: *The Enduring Southey* must not be published. Again there were insults: "To publish this book would represent an attack on the mind." Mandell wasn't troubled by insults. His life had been shaped by them. Two criticisms, however, were troubling:

The introductory chapter is full of errors of fact and judgment, and the prose is like that of a foreigner who has no feeling for English and probably not much more for his indigenous bush tongue.

The other:

The introductory chapter, where Mandell says he approaches Southey from the inside, is bad. The rest of the manuscript falls below its level.

Mandell realized, considering these criticisms, "Even experts can't agree." More important, a contradiction implied intellectual space. He could perhaps shoot *The Enduring Southey* through that space into publication. He corrected facts wherever he sensed them. With commas he jerked his style toward elegance. Because an expert had said the introductory chapter was best, Mandell put it last. Miss Nugent retyped, then mailed *The Enduring Southey* to another press. It was rejected.

T. T. Mandell locked his office door and thought: I went to required schools, received required degrees, made changes required by experts. What then do they want? It struck him: A man can't be rejected. He can only reject himself. Thus he recovered will and, to the new criticisms, responded with vigorous compliance. He eradicated paragraphs and pages as if they contained nothing. Though he worried about leaving breaks in his argument, time was short. He could not say, when required to state his achievements, that for a long while he had been rewriting a book that he had been rewriting. Anyone could say that. Even a moron. The manuscript—retyped, mailed to a scholarly press called Injured Merit—was returned with a letter from an editor: "Chop Southey in half. Put in pictures."

T. T. Mandell locked his office door, removed his clothes; silently, he rolled on the floor.

To colleagues he showed the letter—not with pride but by the way, as if unsure of its tone. They said it urged, without committing the editor to a promise of publication, that Mandell rewrite and resubmit. He frowned, puckered, and said, "Hmmm." His colleagues stared. He himself wondered, fleetingly, if he wasn't a prick.

Mandell cut *The Enduring Southey* in half and inserted a photo of the library in the Bronx where he'd done research. Below the photo he wrote, "Thanks." It occurred to him to insert a photo of himself. That might seem presumptuous, but he remembered scholarly books where the author's photo appeared—an old book on Southey, for example. In the library he found that book again, but no photo, only a drawing, and not of the author but Southey. Mandell nearly cried. Instead, he laughed and told people. Some laughed.

The Enduring Southey was not resubmitted to Injured Merit. It had become too good. Miss Nugent mailed it to a university press. It was rejected.

T. T. Mandell locked his office door, then telephoned a number he had prepared for this eventuality. A moment later he spoke to a lawyer who specialized in outrage. Mandell told the lawyer what degrees he held and where he had been teaching, as an assistant professor, for several years, while he tried to fulfill the publication requirements of a scholar as well as the general institution of requirements as such. He spoke of his faith in the system. He said he wasn't a troublemaker or a critic of prevailing values but the author of a proper book rewritten according to the criticism of experts. There had been a time, Mandell said, when he wore sneakers to class, but upon noticing that no other faculty members wore sneakers, he quit doing so. There were other things of this nature, but, Mandell believed, the lawyer had the picture. The lawyer then explained: "Professor, there's no action in this crap." Mandell read the letters, revised the manuscript, threw out the photo. Miss Nugent retyped, mailed. *The Enduring Southey* was rejected.

T. T. Mandell locked his office door. As if from the abyss of authenticity, a voice came: "It doesn't matter if you're a nice guy." Mandell listened. The voice continued: "I made the whale." Mandell felt depressed—or deepened. In this mood, he made revisions.

Miss Nugent now wore glasses and walked faster. Leaving her typewriter to go pee, she always glanced at her wristwatch as if to confirm her need. She retyped *The Enduring Southey*, mailed it away again, then again. Mandell's face had a greasy, dissatisfied quality now, impossible to wash or shave away, and his manner had gained spasmodic vigor. Once he interrupted a conversation between two colleagues, rushing up to their lunch table, driving a bread knife into the Formica top, and shouting, "You were talking about *Moby Dick*, right?"

The Enduring Southey had been mailed away for the last time. To Stuttgart. Miss Nugent believed the finest scholarly books were published there. Mandell could afford no more rejections, certainly none that might take long in coming, but Miss Nugent felt *The Enduring Southey* was hers as much as his. She wanted the last rejection to come from the best. *The Enduring Southey* was accepted.

A VW mechanic in Mandell's neighborhood translated the letter for him. Mandell waved it at Miss Nugent and flung into a dance before her typewriter. She pummeled the keys and hissed, "Don't let them have it. Tell them to screw off." He gave her a look of terror and fled.

Der andauernde Southey was published. Mandell was given permanency. He mastered the ho-ho style of laughter and, at department meetings, said things like "What fun." Discussing the book with students who, someday, would write one like it, he said it wrote itself. Nasty reviews appeared, but they were in German. Mandell was considered an expert and received manuscripts from university presses with requests for his opinion. His letters were always written with uncompromising and incisive hatred.

the captain

HE SMILED AT HER. She smiled at him and ate dessert, her pinky so nicely hooked it tore my heart. Dessert was pear under chocolate and flaming brandy. It slipped from spoon to blubbery dissolution. When I tried to taste, I swallowed. Then came a flickering city of liqueurs. Then marijuana, a language green and gold popping around the table from mouth to mouth. Nothing went by me unlipped. Nothing tasted. From course to course I'd swallowed textures, not tastes, like a cat gobbling kill. I'd eaten; I wanted to eat. Other guests flashed marvels achieved, readiness to die. Music from the drawing room—black, full of drum—summoned us to further pleasure. Actual blacks, stationed around the table, stiff and smug in tuxedos, gleamed consummation. I assumed they'd pissed in our soup. Stanger smiled at Mildred. She at him. Above glass, silver, flowers, candles, and the ministrations of swift black hands, everyone at the table had smiled for the last two hours. Servants are the price elegance pays to pain. Alone, the Stangers couldn't have made this occasion for forty guests; not without threatening every institution upon which society stands. To that sentiment, I drank piss. A ritual initiation. I'd never been to such a dinner party, but I could tell it was first-rate. Teeth stabbed out of my ass to eat the chair. However, the meal was over. Stanger rose. His hand claimed my wife's lower back. They strolled to the drawing room, a sight flattering to me, the lovely valley of her back appreciated in his munificent hand. Yet it gave me a feeling I couldn't understand, act upon, or use. Like Hamlet's feeling in Elsinore. But this was no dingy, boozy castle in barbaric Denmark. This was Now Town, Sutton Place. Windows triangulated, above the East River, north to Welfare Island, south to the Statue of Liberty. I couldn't make a speech or kill. I did what I could. I tried not to look at them, not to see. I joined the other guests, wondering what brought them here. Did they all want jobs? During our interview, Stanger said, "Come to dinner, Mr. Liebowitz. On Bastille Day. We'll chat some more about the job." I arrived. He nodded at me, took Mildred's arm, then talked to her, no one else, and here I was, his dinner in my gut, his grass in my brain, talking to myself, thinking grass. How did you play this game? Like a delegate to my thinking, Mrs. Stanger swept boldly through the grass. "So, Mr. Liebowitz, you're interested in publishing," and she led me to a chair opposite hers. "You'll make a lovely publisher." Her shoes were gold, her dress was white material through which I couldn't tell if I couldn't see. Intimations of symmetry seesawed her voice. Slowly, precisely, she crossed her legs, sliding white skin beneath white, translucent membrane. Her shoe began winding in the air. I looked.

"You can have the shoe, Mr. Liebowitz. Are you a man who wants things?"

"Everyone must want your things, Mrs. Stanger."

And that's what I thought. Yet I had to beg Mildred to dress for this party, comb her hair, show me good girl in the aspect of sullen bitch:

"Do you *want* to walk so quickly, Phillip? Do you *want* to suppose Stanger won't give you the job if we're two minutes late? Is it thrilling to have people think you're out with some whore? Is that what you *want*? Take my arm, you bastard, or I don't go another step."

A savage ride on the IRT, then worse in the crosstown cab.

"Two bucks for a lousy cab. But if I need, really need, a pair of shoes, you throw a fit. Tomorrow, I buy shoes. Hear me?"

She hadn't wanted to go. I had wanted to rush. Stanger had nodded at me, taken her arm, and la-la—I looked—his hand was on her knee. Wanting not to go, she had a moral advantage. She could now blow him and lift a virtuous face: "Don't give me that jealous crap."

Mrs. Stanger, apparently, wanted symmetry. A social lady with a Viking face, symmetrical by instinct. The ghost of long bone figure, unexorcised by a life of such occasions, still fighting, giving good as it got. Perfect for Stanger. Why not for me? One thinks meat or languishes.

Her eyes were tiger-bronze. They looked at me; not across the room at them. She seemed to be saying, "Do you really want the job, Mr. Liebowitz?" And she was. Winding her shoe, stirring a golden pool of time. I had five seconds, perhaps, to seem not stupid. The mathematics of her face demanded speed and precision, answers in kind, not self-analysis. I clicked on the smarts:

Stanger wanted Mildred. His missus wanted me. I wanted the job. The question was, then: What could I get? The answer answered everything. If I couldn't get only what I wanted, I had to want what I could get, to get what I wanted. Things equal to the same equal one another.

"Do you really want the job, Mr. Liebowitz?"

I said, "Let's fuck."

She blinked and shook her head. She sighed.

I had been too quick, too smart. I shrugged like a man with nothing more to say, and looked across the room at them, sitting close together on a couch, talking. To express life's failure, I lifted a cigarette. Mrs. Stanger knocked it out of my mouth. "That's a social disease, Mr. Liebowitz." She stood up in a blur of dancing and a storm of jazz, turned, pushed through shuddering couples, and went around a corner, disappeared. Reappeared. Frowning at me. To my feet I leaped.

Down a hall in pursuit of her gliding back, feeling concentrated in crotch, monolithic shark with blood in its nose and no appetite for analysis. I'd read that eating is the final extension of touch and believed it. I also believed the reverse. Paintings, etchings, Chinese jugs, chairs, tables, sculptured metals whispered as they flashed by, "Beast, beast, beast." Right. Psychology and art were dead. I didn't understand my motives, but that didn't prove I had any. Does the moon have a motive? Aristotle says, "Love." All right, love. Later, with nothing at stake, I'd return to this hall and contemplate a jug, make excuses for love, recall the meal, the hideous smiling, how he didn't talk to me, how Mildred did. I'd argue, Between me and Mildred had loomed the shape of a foreign penis. His moon. My motive. I'd recall the job, my own penis, and I'd raise the distinction between men and women. Men do what they have to do. A woman can do anything a man can do, but does she have to? Mrs. Stanger didn't have to open the door. I stepped through it into another world. The enemy of Freud, the son of Marx, Phillip Liebowitz. Plunging beyond analysis in the wake of a shark.

The walls bore guns, horsewhips, heads of gazelle, buffalo, giraffe, and photos of Stanger amid naked blacks and guns. Dead animals lay at his feet. Mrs. Stanger locked the door and turned with her shoes kicked off, standing shorter, flat-footed, loose in arm and shoulder, chin up to give me a level glance from slits. Her expression, face and body, said, "Go on, look, Mr. Liebowitz. I'm without my shoes and no less terrific." There was a dull lamp in a corner of the room. Its light mixed delicate oils for metal and a breath of leather. She advanced in it slowly, face darkening, slits shining. "Don't you dare fuck me." We used the back of a brown bear. Her face beneath mine, in a field of bristle, opened as she opened and opened. Her hands slid up my spine, then away, up through her hair. Rings clicked on bear teeth. She fingered the fangs until they were bloody, then lay still, silent, perfectly flat, showing the indifference to my glance and the perfect ease of a woman who is proud of her body. I dressed. When I stood over her, she said, "Poor me. See the boo-boo. Lick the boo-boo, Mr. Liebowitz." I kneeled. She fed me fingers. I licked. The mute choir of staring animals, fifty Mr. Stangers, naked blacks, instruments of pain and annihilation, dull light intimating the circles of her breasts and white shield of belly, thickening of hair and shadow at the conflation of thighs and greater labia, were in my mouth. I swallowed.

The party had mounted to its preclimactic moment, music booming, blacks winding about wheeling carts of ice, glasses, and bottles. I felt the general tension that precedes both success and failure. All could decline into scattered, desultory chitchat or fly toward community. Two men, stripped to the waist, were fighting in a corner. Some guests made a circle about them. Most were dancing, or talking in groups. I returned to the chair I had been sitting in. Black hands fixed me a bourbon; yellow; kickling ice. Through it I watched Stanger and Mildred, the intense, wishy-washy figures of an erotic urn, evoking the prick of perpetuity. Blows, grunts, incoherent curses, spiced with squeals from spectators, filled gaps in the music. The ambience was dense, rude, various flow. Blacks in tuxedos; hard black rock; whites chatting, slugging, dancing the inventions of black kids in ghettos. To think was impossible. I couldn't have added two and two unless driven by hatred or an equivalent passion. I couldn't have read a paragraph of Austen or James unless I shrieked each word. Mrs. Stanger remained behind to wash. I had nothing to do but sit, feel the life, watch Stanger and Mildred, drink my bourbon. Then a big wild lady plopped into Mrs. Stanger's chair. Her dress was channeled to discover tits, her talk was electrified by topics of slick magazines—decadent New York, divorce, the problems so many had these days with kids. She mentioned grass raps, politics, syphilis, runaways, and said, "I used to play kissing games, but today a kid spots a hair on his crotch and runs out to fuck." She waited for my comment. I grinned agreement. Between her tits the stream of little hair was bleached. Her own kid, she said, making a bomb, had blown out his eye. "Blew it out," she sneered, as if amazed at his incompetence. My head shook sympathetically while inside—along with the tiger haunted by former ass and thigh—I added first-class eats, marijuana, servants, and the job, say twenty thousand. "Blew it out," she repeated, encouraging me to respond. I tried for a sexual-philosophical tone. "There is nothing left not to do, is there?" She looked puzzled and annoyed, as if, despite blatant tits and endless mouth, she hated double messages. "I mean, you know, make bombs. Fuck. What have you." The men fighting had begun to shout. One claimed the other had kicked him in the balls, which was against the rules. Then the blows were thicker and louder. Tits laughed, slapped her hand lightly on my face, and gave it a little push, the way one treats a naughty child. Affectionate repudiation. "You're a gas," she said, her hand lingering on my lips, but sensing a prior claim, she withdrew it. Mrs. Stanger had appeared and stood looking down at us. I tried to keep the tits sitting by turning my back slightly to Mrs. Stanger. But the tits, unnerved, rose from the chair and turned her ass to me, as though displaying another pair of tits in departure. Mrs. Stanger reassumed her chair. I leaned toward her in humble admiration and squeezed her thigh. "I wanna marijuana, Mrs. Stanger."

"You can begin calling me Nell. Why do you want a marijuana? Didn't you like fucking me?"

Her expression was imperious. Her voice was irascible.

"I see no connection."

"There is one. Answer my question, Phillip. Didn't you like it?"

"I didn't like it, Nell."

"Are you being moral?"

"My only luxury."

"A luxury of poor, sad, uneducated people. I liked it very much. Perhaps you're more fussy than moral."

She made an amused eyebrow and leaned back in the theater of great class.

"I'm sure my husband may give you the job."

I forgot that she wheezed and didn't sweat right. She saw that in my
face. Fresh color leaped into her bronze, as if to meet some gift I held. She
was ready again. So was I, but I didn't move. I couldn't predict tomorrow's
feelings if I allowed no forbearance. A man needn't be immoral to know
that. He feels things. Her hand on mine. We stood up together. Pretending to dance, we drifted toward the zoo, both of us quivering with the
nastiness of our exchange. Sobs issued from the corner. Blows persisted.
She said, "One of those chaps is a plastic surgeon."

"Which?"

I asked the question in a quiet, natural voice, like hers, to seem as
ready as she for anything, even conversational drivel. And I turned her
slightly to face the corner. "Which one?"

"The bigger one. His name is Swoon. I'll introduce you, if you like.
I've never seen him at a party where he doesn't fight."

"You've invited him here before?"

"God, yes. About fifty times. You and your wife are the only ones
never here before. He killed a man in that corner. February. Yes, it was
February."

"Curious name."

"Silly. I mean he killed him in February."

She kissed my cheek. Stanger and Mildred receded through hair,
vapors of perfume, alcohol, and cigarettes, immobilized figures on the
couch, begging for trouble. In the zoo I buggered Nell. She noticed
smears, said, "Shit," and ran off to change.

Nothing definite had been said about the job, but I was doing all right.
Swoon, on the other hand, was down, spinning on his back while the
other man, with pointed shoes, kicked him in the face, skipped away,
stopped, kicked him in the face again, and skipped away. A lady with
bulging eyes and tendons scoring her neck shouted, "Get up, Jack, get up.
Get up, you fairy." Beyond the fight, through agitations of dancing couples, I saw his hand on her thigh. She offered semiparted lips, lick of bare
leg, pure neck and arm, and inflexible attention to him. She was lovely
all in all. To me, a stranger. I'd have fucked her myself, though the idea
seemed unnatural. She was mother of my child, not lady of this glory.
However unnatural, I wanted her and envied her. I wondered how long
before I was homosexual by circumstance. "Didn't you want me to do it,

Phillip?" That they hadn't once left the couch was proof they felt some-thing. "I did it for your job."

"No lies. Just tell me if you liked it."

"He was revolting. An old man."

"That means you liked it."

Swoon suddenly seized the dancer's crotch and dragged himself up through seven or eight punches in the face. The move was brilliant and courageous. I found myself shouting, "Go, baby. Kill. Kill. Kill." A voice hissed into my ear, "Devil." In another dress, another degree of fresher, whiter person, Nell smiled, then pinched at my kidney, screwing the flesh until I thrust an elbow into her abdomen. I giggled and tried not to look at the fight or across the room at dirty Mildred. To my giggles, shifting, and lack of focus, Nell said, "The toilet is that way." I said, "Thanks," won-dering if I had to piss. She smiled, and her smile deepened, taking knowl-edge of her devil into places she'd taken the man. She knew him, this devil: he had to piss. In fact he didn't, but he smiled, too, at her periodon-tal plastic, pink, low in the gleaming tooth. As I started away she grabbed my elbow.

"Tell me one thing."

The fighting and the music were loud. I gave her a steady, deaf look.

"I want you to tell me one thing before you go." She didn't stop smiling.

"It was all right, Nell."

"But?"

I waited to see what she made of nothing.

Her smile strained as if tugged by waters. "You'd like to beat me, wouldn't you? I think you'd like to beat me."

I winked.

The other man went down. Swoon was grinding a heel into his neck. People were cheering, calling his name. "Jack. Jack." That was love, waves of love. Nell clasped her hands on her breast and jumped up and down. "Oh, kill, kill," she said. "Make him be dead."

Like a child, a little girl. Yet her exquisite jumping epitomized the party, spoke for the fighting men, and the others, too, even the servants. They served, danced, fought for the lady in white and gold, of the symmetrical face. The spot where she pinched me seemed to burn a message into my kidney. Her crowd wasn't made of phonies. Between desire and action they interposed no mask. Impulse didn't twist into perversion, into games. They were whole, straight, noble creatures, slave and master. To me, the challenge they represented left no alternatives. Maybe Stanger and Mildred had seen to that, but I was glad that I'd made the first deadly stroke, going to the zoo with Nell, killing Mildred as surely as Stanger killed giraffes. I imagined him on the veldt, amid naked blacks who hand him gun after gun, begging him to shoot straight as the giraffe charges. Great, but I'd buggered his wife. I'd wanted the job. Now, I could not *not* have it. Something definite would be said tonight. Yes or no. Either answer would be a comment on myself. Before the evening was over I'd be purged of irony. Made clean. Hired. Or a simple schmuck. I'd walked off in the direction indicated by Nell. My step was light. Too light, nearly wraithlike in the spacious, winding substance of this apartment. It made me feel weak and sick, the apartment, the creepy trivial way I walked in it. Like a man looking for his own pathetic step on a huge ship at sea. A man who has never seen or felt a high sea, never learned to walk its long surge, its remorseless drag and lunge. I needed this moment away from the blazing, loud incoherence of the crowded land, alone, out of sight, to practice walking. And my feelings, while practicing, were like those of a young captain in a novel by Conrad. First opportunity to command. He is alone, pacing the deck, getting a sense of himself. A storm is rising on the horizon. Members of the crew try to call it to his attention, but he has already noticed it, and seen through it to himself. He is sympathetic to their fears, yet more sympathetic to his own. Could I get at that sense of myself required by this storm? I notice it's a moral storm. The worst kind. The ship is fraught with goods meant for the best people. Could I bring it home intact? Was I the captain? I tried to walk right. One, two, three, six, fifteen . . . It wasn't easy to walk right. No prerequisite of honor is easy. I was afraid I might kick a jug, scratch a painting, the way I walked, like a crazy, spastic, stoned, drunken gawk. Not a captain. I might even fall off the whole fucking ship. But then I felt it begin: one, two, three, four . . . I was walking, and all right. I was the captain.

A hallway led to hallways, to rooms opening into rooms, a labyrinth, a weight of money, accumulating in vistas of paintings, etchings, hanging rugs, pewter, throbbing lacquers, silver, gold. Touch these good things, I thought. Let sublimation steel you. Touch. Let lech. Love any hole that feels. I smacked a door, hands flat to spare me a broken nose, and fell through onto my face. I looked up moments later and saw a girl at a dressing table. Her back was to me. She was brushing long brown hair, like the household genie of serene indifference. She didn't seem to know or care that I lay behind her on the floor, watching. She spoke:

"Please don't apologize for being late and slamming through my door like the offensive pig you happen to be. I much prefer your silence. Any apology will make me exceedingly furious. I'm not exceedingly furious now, Colin. So keep your mouth shut. I suppose you haven't shaved, have you? I won't hear your apologies. I won't hear your voice."

She clapped the brush down. Her legs lashed by my face, negligee flying, to the bed. Books and papers were knocked off the bed. I stood. She flung onto the bed, twisted onto her back, eyes shut, forehead writhing with contradiction. She gave a blind, shrill order to the ceiling:

"Go on, Colin, you know what I want."

Lest he'd forgotten, her legs struck out, stiff, isoscelean. I saw voluted conch in wire tangle, the picture of her mind. The Colin in me rose, perked up like a rat, snout quivering, pointing at the answer to a question never asked. Life is this epitome. Red, tidal maw. Yawn. Aching exfoliant. Hole. I flicked light, shut door, three steps, and I straddled her neck. "Smells," she cried, and muddy flux dragged me, gripping my head, churning circles into the circles of her need, the cherished head which she recognized—"Who you?"—as not the right head. A good one nonetheless, already thinking how to apologize. She screeched and kicked. I pressed on to suggest the suction of feeling, but, thinking, thinking, I felt only ideas, tones, and tropes rise upon one another like waves, curling, crashing, failing to hold, sliding faster, faster down the beach to the seething, shapeless inane. Remember the job, I thought, and a hairy hemp ripped from my liver to my throat. I came at both ends simultaneously. Apology was impossible. I opted for vigor. "Fantastic," I cried, hoping thus to distract her with vigor. Also oblique flattery. She said, "Eeee," scrambling to one end of the bed, and me to the other, pleading, "Don't scream. I'm turning on the light." It discovered her biting the sheet. "Woo woo woo," she said. I bent, pleading in the harmless posture of a dog at stool. "Didn't you like it?" She twisted about to slap the night table. I expected a gun. She twisted back, glasses on her face, big eyes, the tigerish mother apparent. "Say, you're Nell Stanger's kid, aren't you?" My voice was eager, genial. She screamed. I fled.

Streaming chair, rug, jug, I whipped into the last hall, kicked into high for the heart-bursting straightaway, and a person—shortish, bald, bow tie, drink in chubby grip—was there, like the eternal child who plays in the road before the speeding Ferrari, or the peasant lifting slow, clotted, laborious face to a thunder of horses and hounds, but this particular incarnation of the common denominator leaned toward a painting, touching, smelling, wallowing in the color and texture of converging neural streams which filled the airy delta between himself and better life on the wall, and was unaware of me, running, whole man running, legs, arms, head running, stomach, knees, balls running, and he still savored the painted dream as he looked up into the oncoming real, the drink warm in his forgotten fist, all of him big, bigger in my eyes, looking up with no intention, no expectation, and before his eyebrows fully elevated, eyes fully opened, and pulpy sluggish lip curled fully away from stained teeth, my hands struck his neck. Behind me was a faint thud. Empty rumble of a rolling glass.

I reentered the drawing room with expanded lungs. Heat in my eyes. Couples were still dancing, others sprawled. Nobody watched Swoon and the other man, lugubrious with exhaustion, flailing in slow arcs, rarely hitting. Rancid breath lay in the torpid, festering air. Screams came from the distance. No cigarette was put out or drink lowered. Between me and the couch, where Stanger and Mildred sat necking, there was a forest of shifting fashions, the black tuxedos and the clothing of the guests, pinks, greens, blues, and yellows crying out for pleasures of middle age. It hummed everywhere, omnivorous conversation of a dying party that insisted on living. Nell stepped out of it. "Let's dance." Her voice was grim, as if dancing were war, but it had an undercurrent of something more particular. Instantly, I became a dancing fool. She danced me off to the zoo and said it.

"Undress."

Her clothes were a heap of white, pink, and gold. She sprawled on the bear, its fangs encrusted, shining blood. Her limbs cast out in the languid shape of her mood, suggesting nets. Her voice was soft, yet coarse in tone. "Get it, Phillip. On the shelf in the closet."

Still in my shirt and tie I trotted to the closet to get it, whatever it was. On a shelf about chest high lay three hundred sausages, coiled in convoluted complications, a monster brain. A long gray iron chain. The prospect of such appetite suffused me with feelings of poverty, no education, and moral shock, but in one clean movement of self-disgust I laid on hands like he who knows. The chain chuckled as my fingers pierced its holes. I pulled. It came slowly, heavily, as each link stirred from sleep, and then too heavily, gaining speed, personal will, clamor, a raging snake of cannonballs pouring through my hands to bury my feet, shins, knees. Writhing, arms out, I was half man, half bonsai tree with impoverished roots, strangled in its springs, sucking denial. "I hate pain," I screamed. Nell bobbled up off the bear. She seized the chain, tugged. I pummeled the top of her head. For real, not in a sexual way. She said, "Quit that." I shouted sincerely, "I hate pain. I'll beat your head off," pummeling. She lugged; steady, patient strength; the motion of serious, honest work. In different conditions, I'd have considered it beautiful; her naked, multidimpled back, rippling, heaving spine against iron. I beat the measure of her lugging into her head and shouted my refrain. At last I fell free and could properly convulse. She rolled onto me, tried to soothe me with mothery tongue, breasts, and holes, but something had happened to make me unreceptive, inconsolable, as if my body, in trauma, had shaken free of my mind, and now my eyes, my flesh in every place retreated, fleeing toward the murdered buffalo, gazelle, and giraffe. "That," I gasped, "rub with that." She, too, seemed unselved, brained. She rose, stumbling across the room to grab the giraffe by the nostrils and tear it off the wall. She returned, kneeled, rubbed its eyes and great slop of lip carefully, gently, against my face and neck, then back and forth between my legs until I felt better. I dressed rapidly. She stared, sitting on the floor beside the giraffe, a limp, naked, stupid woman. I let myself think of her that way. "Get dressed, woman." She crawled to the heap of clothing and clawed out her underpants. I left for the drawing room. Not once had I struck her in a deliberate and evil way. I thought of that as I limped down the hall. I felt myself ringing like a bell that calls men from this world. For the first time that evening, if not in my life, doing nothing, I'd done tremendously. Though nothing definite had been said, I knew the job was mine. It was inconceivable that it wasn't mine. I hadn't hit her. I hadn't even wanted to.

In the force of not wanting, I'd made the job mine. This wasn't magical thinking. This was true; or the world was chaos and less than hell. Nevertheless, I was prepared to accept a word, a strong hint. I didn't need legal forms, a ten-page contract, sixteen carbons. I would approach Stanger now. The confrontation would be his chance to talk, not mine. I had the job. He had only, for his salvation, to confirm it, suggest an idea of wages per annum. My limp deepened. I deepened it. Hard, good lunge. Dragging foot. An arm hooked back for balance, for the feel of bad damage swinging itself, dragging, lunging down the hall. What rough beast? What rough beast, indeed.

Suddenly the hallway didn't look familiar. I'd taken a wrong turn, perhaps two, but there was a door. It had no knob, a swinging door. I shoved it wide. Something registered. Just as quickly, it was gone, wiped out, retrogressively unseen. I was back in the hall again, the door was shut. I was about to continue lunging on to the next door, the next turn, when I realized I'd fallen into my old ways, protecting myself, letting myself believe there were things one mustn't see. I'd been through that, I'd seen, transcended. I could see anything now, see it squarely, name it with exactitude and indifference. I shoved the door again. It opened on a brilliant kitchen, a long counter with a tall, steel coffee urn. I'd seen that. The black servant stood on the counter beside the urn. That, too. Pissing into the urn. Yes, yes; that, too. He wore sunglasses as if to shield his eyes against the glare of his yam. "That's offensive," I said, naming it. He shook his last drops into the urn, hopped off the counter, zipped up, and began putting cups and saucers on a tray. When he finished he turned to me and said, "We're born offensive, brother." He stepped toward me, hand extended, palm up. "Give me some skin, brother." The flat, gleaming opacity of his sunglasses seemed menacing, but I lunged to meet him and drew my palm down his. We locked thumbs, pressed forearms and elbows together. He was all right, but boiling in me now was a phrase for Mildred: "Don't drink the coffee." I returned to the drawing room with it, and in the weariness of this crowd, I felt it dissolve into the quiet voice of a Britisher, like head boy at a school for supersadists, fashioning managerial scum for the colonies: "Mildred, get your coat." Terribly mild, yet the pitch of majestic will. She and Stanger were locked, pretzeled together, still necking, his hand was plunged beneath her dress, but she wiggled hard, slapped knees together, sprang up. Suddenly my wife! He sprang up behind her. There were people everywhere, some standing behind their couch, others sprawled at their feet, and yet only I could invade their privacy, only I had the power of invasion attributed ordinarily to voyeurs and God. The power against which society makes laws, or out of which it claims to draw them. Now there was stir all about the room. My power had spread, initiating small spasms, like a wind seen in the motion of trees. And Nell appeared, the hostess again, cooing good-nights and so-good-yous. She smiled at me in a frowning, quizzical, sad, not miserable way. I read her lips: "Coffee?" Thus encouraging me to stay a bit after the others. I smiled regrets and waved lyrical goodbye. From the depths, dimly, mechanically, came "*Eeee*." Some of the guests who seemed to hear it tried to look worried.

We left the apartment with Dr. and Mrs. Swoon. Stanger walked us out to the elevator. Dr. Swoon was in his clothes again. Mrs. Swoon, it turned out, was the lady with the bulging eyes and violent neck. Swoon's face was splotched with pimiento color and torn. Somewhere behind it he seemed to have withdrawn into a severe dignity. Mrs. Swoon chattered as if it had been she who'd done the fighting and could find no way of containing its momentum. "You should have gone for the eyes, Jack. Your plan was no good. It never is when you don't listen to people. I mean, you use diagnosticians, don't you, before you operate?" She turned to me. "Two of them. Jack has two young doctors who see the patient and tell Jack what to do. Awfully clever, but their hands are made of shit, you know what I mean? Jack operates. Of course, without them, he couldn't tell the difference between an asshole and an elbow. I mean, he'd have to consult the nurses to find out which was which. But once he knows, look out, look out, that's Jack Swoon, king of fingers. Never uses a knife on nose jobs. Do you, Jack?" He shook his head no. "Does them with fingers and the heels of his palms. This is the heel. See, this part. Gets it smack up against the nares and grinds. Makes nice little ski jumps every time. 'I make the whole world Gentile,' says Jack. Personally, I think it leaves the holes too big, but that's what folks want." Stanger chuckled and raised a voice to obscure hers, and also the screaming, which followed us out to the elevator. "Didn't somehow find a chance to talk to you, Phillip, and get to know you. But I haven't forgotten our interview." His thumb ground the elevator button as if it were an eyeball. "We'll get together soon. You must promise me that." Sufficient, I thought. Enough said. He had dark, penetrating eyes and a feeble mouth. His expression was over-bred, full of difficulties, as if something in his chemical history wasn't finished. An animal, perhaps, still to shoot. His handshake was tentative, trying to close on a good-humored assurance. Mine was a quick, up-down fuck-you. "I promise. Good night. Thanks." He nodded to Mildred and they said good night as the elevator door opened. Then he shook hands with the Swoons. We stepped into the elevator. As the door slid shut he turned away. The door stuck, by the grace of *deus ex machina*, just for an instant, to show Stanger with the right buttock in his fist, pulled away from its brother. An abstracted, habitual gesture, expressing long famil-iarity with pressures of his body. He released slow, thoughtful gas, a final good night to his guests in the elevator. The door shut. Mrs. Swoon stared at it. Dr. Swoon's fiery face ripped into a great smile. I glanced at Mildred. She pinched her nose. Even thus, beautiful. The door opened, we said good night to the Swoons. She took my arm. We walked wildly, bumping hips. "I was bored, bored, bored," she cried. "Do you hear me? Bored. The screaming was worth it, maybe, but I was bored. I hope you're happy about the job. You'd have gotten it even if we stayed home. Probably a better salary, too. Did you know a man was almost beaten to death and another had a stroke while looking at a picture? I wish I'd seen that picture. Must have been very dirty, don't you think?"

"He named a figure?"

"You imagine I asked?"

"Of course you asked."

"Eleven and a half to start."

"Bullshit. How much?"

"He said his daughter, Naomi, wants to be an actress. He calls her Nimi. Maybe it was Ninny screaming, rehearsing some part."

"How much? Don't prattle."

"He said she has a neurological problem. Theater is so good for her. 'So good for Nimi,' he said. He meant she's a crazy loony, right?"

"Who cares? How much?"

"The wife is very good-looking, but sort of a dopey slut, wouldn't you say? Wouldn't you say that, Phillip? He's a weakling. I'm sure you'll like the job, Phillip. You know what he told me?"

"What did he tell you?"

"He told me he hates the sound of eating, even the sound he makes. So he has these big dinner parties, see? Are you limping, Phillip?"

"Yeah."

"And he's got a scheme for buying property on the moon. Because of the blacks, not to make money. He's in lumber and publishing. He doesn't need money. There's a family place in Connecticut, to which we've been invited, and another one in California. But the moon, man, is where it's really at. 'Nowhere else to go,' he said. 'What do you think NASA is all about? Space agency? No, sir. Surreal estate agency.' No blacks on the moon, Phillip. He thinks New York is finished. Phones don't work. Blacks everywhere. But he hires black servants. What do you think that means, Phillip? He wants to keep an eye on them? Please stop that limping and walk more quickly."

"What the hell does he mean by eleven and a half? I'm no typist."

"Stop crying. I can't stand the sight of you crying."

"I'm not crying."

"Yes, you are. I'm tired. Let's take a cab all the way home. We can afford it. He said twenty-five. With his paw on my ass, he says twenty-five. 'Twenty-five, dear.' Jealous? Mrs. Stanger digs you. You should fuck her or something, if you haven't already. I hate you."

"You acted badly."

"I'm sorry I acted badly. There's a cab. Kiss me. Tomorrow I'll buy three pairs of shoes."

I kissed her in the cab, then asked, "Did you like Stanger's paw on your ass?"

"I liked the way you told me to get my coat in front of everybody. But if you ever do that when we're with human beings, Phillip, I'll do something you won't forget. Twenty-five. Hee-hee."

"Yeah."

The cab went west to Third Avenue, then north, then west through Central Park. The trees, lacerated by lights, seemed to fly into the cab and about our heads. Mildred leaned back, giving herself to the trees and to me. Her pants tangled at the ankle, but I couldn't get it out of mind and up again for naked traffic until she whispered, sliding down to the floor, whispering "Twenty-five" into my crotch. "Kootchie-kootchie." At our place the driver waited, a head on a leather jacket, smoke sliding and twining up like hair from his invisible cigarette, and the whole cab shuddering in idle. His photo looked down at us in the back, smiling; Nunzio Salazar, machismo–fascismo mustache, number 999327, approves of it. Mildred's legs seemed to lift from my ribs like wings. She said, "Oh," and came. I was satisfied. A sentimental man prefers happiness to truth. I did prefer it. Her dear, lovely cheek on my shoulder as I fingered sticky leaves, peeling away singles for the fare, twice as many for the tip. Mildred jerked. "Don't be a fool. We live in this town." Half as many for the tip.

from
shuffle
(1990)

journal

THE WOMAN SAID THAT HER HUSBAND phoned her at her lover's apartment. She had to ask him to repeat himself.

"I want you to come home and collect your clothes."

She'd been conscious of his pain before then, but in a general way. She'd have said, if you asked, "He doesn't feel good. He cries." He was sobbing like a child on the telephone. To her lover, she'd confessed, "I feel guilty for not feeling guilty." She could virtually see her dresses and shoes in the bedroom closet. She hurried home. Her husband locked the door and beat her up. "Did you do it with him in the toilet?" he said, and forced her to do it there with him, too. The same for every room in the house. "It really happened," she said, laughing at herself. "Saved my marriage. You'd think I could write about that. Not moral. Just a story."

We reviewed the events. "You told your husband about the other man and named him?" Already, to my mind, a failed marriage. Her husband should have known her body, guessed there was another man. Smells change. Besides, her love affair should have reached him in how she gave herself. "Where did you learn to do that?" He never asked.

He made nothing of her luminous moods or impatience with him. "How many times have I told you to put the cap back on the toothpaste tube?" Even her revulsion at the shape of his feet didn't strike him as a curious development. She imitated him muttering, shaking his head: "That's how they always looked." He made nothing of his own malaise. Simply didn't know why he'd become that way. Never supposed it was because his wife had a lover. He'd had to be told about him. The poor man's suffering exceeded his understanding. He beat her up. He didn't know what else to do. He couldn't do nothing.

"But it really happened," she said again, laughing moronically at herself. "Maybe I'll try to write it as a poem."

Another woman at the literary conference, drawn forth by the story, said her husband accused her of sleeping with his best friend. The accusations began at breakfast and resumed at night when he returned from work. He ruined her nicest dinners. He ruined her sleep. All her efforts to make them happy—she "really tried"—were turned ugly by his suspiciousness. She insisted on seeing a marriage counselor. He didn't want to, but she said the marriage was over if he didn't agree to counseling. Marriage counseling did no good. Her husband wouldn't discuss "real problems."

"Were you?" I asked.

"What?"

"You know. Were you fucking his friend?"

"Yes, but that's not the point."

She lifted her hands, fingers bent to suggest hard labor.

"I cleaned. I cooked. I washed his filthy hairs out of the bathtub."

There was nothing anyone could say. The point was she cleaned and cooked. She washed the bathtub.

In the emptiness, I remembered how I used to meet a woman, on Sunday mornings, behind her church. I waited in my car, in the shade of a low-hanging willow, until the service was over. Then she would appear, striking across the steamy asphalt of the parking lot in her high heels and dark blue churchgoing suit, a white flower in the lapel. She looked magnificent, yet my car was good enough; all we needed. When she talked of God, her cloud of hair floated in a blonder light. Once, she surprised me, her voice reproachful, "Same damn thing all the time," as if I'd done something bad. But it was her fiancé, not me. She said he'd made a gruesome scene, shrieking at her in a crowded oyster bar, "You sucked another man's cock."

I started to kiss her. She thrust me back, making me see how pity mixed with pain in her eyes. "Can you believe he said that to me? All those people sitting there eating oysters. Can you imagine how I felt?" I nodded yes, yes, needing to kiss her, but she wanted me to wait, to let the sacred fullness of her sorrow sink into me. She wanted me to feed on her immensely beseeching stare, prim blue suit, little flower in the lapel. I pressed her backward. She tucked up her skirt and her thighs flashed in the shady car. The pretty church danced beyond the willow. Her fiancé, far away, suffering . . . It should matter, but in the pitch of things there is no should.

"You're greedy," she said.

I asked her to marry me.

Her lips moved against my cheek, as if I were a deaf child, each word a touching pressure. "You know," she whispered, "I've never gotten a speeding ticket. The cop looks at me and can't seem to write it. When they start writing me tickets, ask again."

She saved me from myself, but why did I want her? She was only ten years older than my son. He'd have started smoking dope; run away.

"Can you believe my fiancé said that to me?"

Her question passed like the shadow of a bird through my heart.

Beard wrote to me saying he'd heard there was "bad blood" between us. We'd met only two or three times. As far as I knew, there was hardly anything between us. But I answered his letter, impelled by guilt, though I could imagine nothing to feel guilty about. I didn't dislike the man. I felt nothing, had no opinions, yet I was now going about mysteriously oppressed, concerned for his feelings and also burdened by weird apprehensions. You couldn't simply live your life in society. No, others noticed you. Others demanded that you notice them, welcome them in your life somehow. Simply to breathe incurred responsibilities. Then, after my letter arrived, came the phone calls. We tried to make a date for lunch. Beard didn't want to come to Berkeley. I didn't want to go to San Francisco. He said if he came to Berkeley, I'd pay for lunch. If I came to San Francisco, he'd pay. Again guilt. Which did he prefer? Which do I prefer? I said I'd go to him. It was difficult to find a place to park, then I had to walk five blocks to his apartment house. I felt I was surely paying for something, though I didn't know what. He answered the door with a letter in his hand. For an instant, I supposed it was a letter for me. He asked if I'd like something to drink. I said, "No, let's go to lunch." On our way out to lunch, he said that he'd written a letter of condolence to the wife of a friend, a famous writer who had just died. He said it was easy for him to write the letter, having had to write so many of them lately. He flipped it into a mailbox. We ate in a local restaurant. Since he was paying, I ordered only soup, salad, and a glass of wine. That would seem enough like lunch without seeming expensive. He left the table several times before and after the food arrived to talk to women at other tables and the bar. Walking back to his apartment, he told me about a time when he didn't write a letter of condolence to a certain wife. He didn't like her, he said. This woman's husband had been a good friend and also a famous writer. She'd been sexually unfaithful to him with his friends. She taunted him with it, made him feel despised and lonely. Finally he died. Beard didn't write to her. Soon afterward, she phoned Beard and asked why he hadn't writen her a letter, or at least called her. It was the middle of the night. She was drunk. She raved about the many letters of condolence she had received. Everybody of importance in the literary world, publishers, editors, writers, had written her. Why not Beard? I thought it was a good story and asked if I could have it. He looked puzzled. He hadn't thought the story was anything special. Now he wondered. He was reluctant to say I could have it. Again guilt: I had enjoyed the story too much, I felt I understood something more than he intended. As he spoke, I'd seen the woman raving drunkenly into the phone at Beard. I could almost hear her voice. I supposed Beard had fucked her, but that wasn't interesting. I was seeing her pain. At his apartment, he asked if I'd like coffee or wine. I chose wine. I noticed, as he poured the wine, that the glass was caked at the bottom with black dregs and there was a smear of lipstick on the rim. I supposed, when he handed me the wine in the filthy glass, he intended nothing hostile, because the whole apartment seemed never to have been cleaned. The fabric of his couch and chairs carried a greasy film, the windows were dull and blurry with greasiness, and the air smelled of dust mixed with the sweetness of decaying fruit. Something else, a faint yet penetrating sour smell, like what rises from the neglected litter box of cats. I saw no cats, but there was cat hair on the rug. Later, as we stood together in the narrow hallway to his door, saying goodbye, assuring each other there was no bad blood, he farted. The tight space became noxiously suffocating. Eager to get out, I said for perhaps the third time, "There is no bad blood," which was the thing "between us" we'd not once mentioned, though it was the reason for my visit. He said, as though it hadn't ever really mattered, "A puff of smoke."

Jimmy sits at his typewriter high on cocaine, smiling, shaking his head. He says, "I'm so good I don't even have to write." He's six foot three and charcoal brown, the color of a Burmese cat. His chest is high and wide.

From neck to belt he is a hard, flat wall. No hips. Apple ass. Long legs. Long hands and feet. He looks as good in clothes as he looks naked. In two senses, clothes *become* his body. A woman said he is so clearly a man he could wear a dress. He sits at his typewriter, smiling, shaking his head, his long, beautiful hands turned up, lying open and loose in his lap. There is nothing wrong with him. He doesn't even have to write.

Evelyn had something to tell me, needed my opinion, I must come right away. She said she had met a famous writer. "He got the Pulitzer Prize." I say that's nice, so what? She says he asked her to do something. I say what? She can't say. Oh, come on. Really, what? I know you want to tell me, so tell me. "Please," she begs. "Please don't do this to me. You're my friend. I feel soiled. It was so disgusting." She drops her head, takes her hair in her fists. I say what? what? what? She just can't say it. Suddenly she screams, "I mean I was flattered, but he's over seventy. He told me to phone him when I go East this Christmas, he's in the National Academy, the Hall of Fame, everything, but what should I do? How can I phone him? I can't."

"Tell him you're pregnant."

"Tell him I'm pregnant? I'll say, 'Your friendship means more to me than anything, but I'm pregnant, so I can't do it, I want to do it, but I'm liable to vomit. I can't even look at a pizza.'"

Kafka imagines a man who has a hole in the back of his head. The sun shines into this hole. The man himself is denied a glimpse of it. Kafka might as well be talking about the man's face. Others "look into it." The most public, promiscuous part of his body is invisible to himself. How obvious. Still, it takes a genius to say that the face, the thing that kisses, sneezes, whistles, and moans is a hole more private than our privates. You retreat from this dreadful hole into quotidian blindness, the blindness of your face to itself. You want to light a cigarette or fix yourself a drink. You want to make a phone call. To whom? You don't know. Of course you don't. You want to phone your face. The one you've never met. Who you are.

Jimmy says he met a woman at a literary conference in Miami. They spent the night talking and smoking marijuana in his hotel room. They read their stories to each other. He says he had a great time. Never touched once. The talk was so good. Later it came to him—he doesn't know why—that was no woman. That was a man. He saw her the next day. He wanted to ask but he couldn't think how to put it. "Hey, man, are you a man?" Either way, her feelings would be hurt. He snaps his fingers, claps, says, "That is the trouble with women, you dig?"

Plato says the face is a picture of the soul. Could this be true? I thought how noses, teeth, ears, and eyes—in the faces of Evelyn's ancestors—flowing through the centuries, had combined to make the picture of her soul. But then she had her teeth fixed and her ears pinned back. A face is more like a word than like a picture. It has a sort of etymology. Ancient meanings, drawn from the experience of races, from geography and weather, from flora and fauna, collect in a face just as meanings collect in a word. In Evelyn's face, I saw the travels of Marco Polo, the fall of Constantinople, the irredentist yearnings of Hungaro-Romanians. How many ancestors vanished when Evelyn had her teeth fixed? In Evelyn's face I saw the hordes of Genghis Khan invading Poland. Among them was a yellow brute, with a long mustache flowing away from his nostrils like black ribbons. He raped Evelyn's great-great-great-grandmother with his fierce prick, thereby giving a distinctly slanted plane to Evelyn's cheekbones, her nicest feature.

I'm in Boris's living room. He fixed me a drink. We sit in chairs facing each other. His girlfriend prepares dinner. I'm grateful for the comfort, the prospect of dinner with them. I've brought a bottle of wine, but it's hardly enough. I must give of myself, something personal, something real. None of us has long enough to live for yet another civilized conversation. Boris waits, enjoying the wine. He looks peaceful. Perhaps the book he is writing is going well, but I don't ask. A book is a tremendous project of excruciating difficulty; sacred business. Thomas Mann lit candles before he began to write. Kafka imagined huge spikes below his desktop which would drive into his knees. To ask Boris if his book is going well would be like asking if he writes with a pencil or a pen. I tell Boris I'm still working on the screenplay. I hope that makes him feel good, superior to me. A screenplay is a low order of writing, nothing compared to a book.

He says, "Don't be ashamed. Movies are the most important art form of our day." As always, he's brilliantly penetrating. I am embarrassed, confused. I wanted to say something real, but offered a species of fraudulence. He saw through it. I can't stop now. I tell him the work is torture, hours and hours of typing, though it is relieved by flights to New York and L.A., fine hotels and good restaurants, the company of celebrities, actors, whores.

Boris says, "I don't want to hear about it."

The pleasant noise from the kitchen, where his girlfriend cooks, comes to a stop. She overheard us. Women have superb ears. In the deepest sleep, they can hear a baby crying. She appears in the living room, saying, "We're going to have the most delicious crab that ever lived."

I say, "What do you mean you don't want to hear about it?"

She says, "Boris only means . . ." but he raises his hand, cuts her short. Then he says, "I just don't want to hear about it, that's all. Fuck it."

I'm yelling now, "Well, what the fuck do you want to hear about?"

"How about my book?" he shouts. "You never fucking ask about my book."

The woman started doing it again, scratching at her neck. It was difficult to ignore. Her neck was reddish near the collar, almost bloody. I tried to look elsewhere, but I lectured in confusion and finally dismissed the class early. Amid the rush of students, I stopped her.

"Miss Toiler, do you notice how students chew gum and writhe in their seats?"

"You must see everything."

"I do," I said, pressing her with my look, urging her silently to understand, to leap from the general to the particular. I stood close to her, too close, but she appeared comfortable, receptive. Her blue eyes were light as her hair, the pupils dark and flat. Her hair was exceptionally fine, several shades below blond. Something in me relaxed, grew still, gazing, desiring nothing. It didn't matter, suddenly, that she scratched at her neck. She was in her late twenties, older than most of my students. They were gone now, the hallway empty. I could speak to the point. Nobody would overhear.

"You're not from California, are you?"

Thus, no point. I had changed the subject I never raised, and then I asked if she'd like to have coffee.

"We arrived this summer," she said. "My husband took a job with an engineering firm in Palo Alto."

Her gray wool suit and black shoes were wrong for the hot September morning. Her creamy silk blouse, also too warm, was sealed high on her neck by a cameo, obscuring scratches she had inflicted on herself. She looked correct in an East Coast way, insulated by propriety.

"Stanton is a geologist and an engineer."

I imagined a tall Stanton, then no—average height, or maybe a short man with a lust for power, or, like her black shoes, officious and priestly. I knew nothing. My mind swung around the periphery of concern, like my spoon in the coffee cup.

"Do you have children?"

"I have horses." Smiling, lips together, showing no teeth. Her horses were special, delicious. She blushed, an emotional phenomenon long vanished from this world. It embarrassed me. She said she loved to ride in the hills after dinner. She'd once seen a bobcat. Her voice lifted. The memory excited her. I smiled consciously, trying to seem pleased.

"In Palo Alto?"

She giggled. "We live far from any town."

She didn't scratch at her neck, but occasionally pushed her knuckles at her nose. She had long, tapering, spiritual fingers. Her skirt, tight-fitting, showed the line of her thigh, good athletic legs. I guessed that she played tennis in Palo Alto.

"I should tell you that I'll be missing some classes. I have to go to doctors' appointments."

"Nothing serious, I hope."

"I might have a tropical parasite. Nigerian fluke. We lived in Africa for a year while Stanton worked for an oil company." She smiled again in the prissy way. The smile was self-mocking and embarrassed. Telling about the fluke presumed too much. "It's probably an allergy. All the new grasses and flowers. The Bay Area is a hotbed of allergies. Stanton loved Africa. He doesn't blame me for ruining things. I had a persistent fever. Poor Stanton quit the job because of me. He's so good. Very healthy. He lifts weights." She grinned, shrugged. "I go on too much."

"Not at all. I'm interested."

At the south gate, we said goodbye. I went to my office. There was a knock, then Henry peeked in. "Busy?" He carried an unlit cigarette. I waved him inside. He sat; lit his cigarette. His head, fixed high on a skinny neck, was eagle-like; critical. "What's new?" he said.

"I have a student who tears at her neck while I lecture. What should I do?"

"I never thought of you as squeamish."

"I'm not squeamish."

"I would like to tell you about an extremely offensive student, but you won't believe me."

"Yes, I will."

"If you repeat it, I'll say it's a lie. There's a gentleman in my class—a Mr. Woo—who has a mandarin fingernail."

"No shit."

"On the little finger of his left hand, the nail is ten inches long. It's a symbol of his leisurely life."

"You find his fingernail extremely offensive?"

"Why should I care about his fingernail?"

"I didn't say you cared."

"His face is a mass of pus pimples and he grins at me throughout the hour, as if everything I say is intended for him."

"He's in love with you."

"I want to throw a knife through his face."

"You do?"

"There's a pilot in my class who is an alcoholic. All pilots, surgeons, and judges are drunks. You know this is true?"

"Everyone knows."

Henry stood, turned to the door. "Let's have lunch next week," he said.

"O.K. Tuesday."

"Impossible."

"Thursday."

"No."

"You tell me what day."

"I will." He left.

After the next class, Toiler waited outside the room, leaning against a wall, pretending to read her notes. She wore the same suit with a white shirt and a thin black tie. She looked boyish, ascetic, pretty.

"Would you like to have coffee? I'll buy it this time."

I couldn't remember saying yes.

As we talked, she didn't touch her face or neck. Had I cured her by seeming flirtatious? Sexual juices have healing power. I'd intended nothing, but the human face, with its probing looks and receptive smiles, is a sexual organ. I wondered if Toiler, scratching at her neck, yearned only to be touched.

She said, "I won't be able to meet you after class next time. I go to my doctor."

I hadn't asked her to meet me.

She missed the next class and the next and the next.

Maybe I was glad not to see her, but I didn't wonder. I simply forgot her. Over the years whole classes go from memory, as if you'd been lecturing to nobody, hallucinating in the flow of academic seasons. Thales, the first philosopher, said everything is water. I remembered Thales as I stared out my office window at the black-green trees of the Berkeley hills and the glaring blue of a cloudless sky. A hawk circled. There was some bird or mouse, generating flirtatious signals, calling to the hawk.

The term was half over when I found Toiler waiting outside my office. "I must talk about dropping the class," she said.

I ushered her inside, gesturing toward the chair. She wore a new suit, summery cotton, lavender with a dull sheen. Its vitality suggested compromise with California. The dark green silk of her blouse had the lush solemnity of a rain forest. It lay open negligently, not casually, revealing a bra strap and scratches on her neck, like spears of thin red grass slanted this way and that by an uncertain wind. She wasn't cured.

"I thought you'd dropped the class."

"It's the doctors' appointments. They can't tell me anything. All they do is give me different drugs. Can I take the class independently? I'll make up the work, do the reading on my own, and write a paper."

A breeze, from the slightly open window behind her, pressed the back of her neck. She shivered.

"Are you uncomfortable? Move away from the window."

"I'm fine," she said.

"Independent study means conferences. Driving back and forth. Hours on the highway."

"I want to do it." She was resigned to the highway, resigned to sit shivering. I felt irrationally annoyed. She'd asked for only a small privilege, a chance to do the classwork.

The spasms became stronger. Her torn neck demanded attention. Was it a plea for help? Students in my office sometimes cried over disaffected boyfriends, alcoholic parents, suicidal roommates. I stood up and said, "I'll shut the window." I stepped to the window, knowing I wanted only to shut her blouse. The window was built in an old, luxurious style, plenty of oak and glass. I pulled. It moved a little, then stuck, fused in its runners.

"Please don't bother," she said.

Her face, close to my right hip, looked dismayed and apologetic, with sweet pre-Raphaelite melancholy, otherworldly, faintly morbid. Her husband didn't blame her for ruining things. I could see why. Dreamy hair, eyes of a snow leopard, lacerated neck. I felt pity, not blame; frustration more than pity. The window wouldn't move. Then her fingers slid beneath the sash. To pull from the bottom. Ethereal fingers vanished as sixty pounds of wood and glass rushed down. Smashed them. She gasped. I lunged, shoving the window back up, the strength of gorillas suddenly in my arms. "I'm so sorry," I said, backing away. She whispered, "My fault, my fault," her eyes lit by weird, apologetic glee. "I did it. It's my own fault."

Her hands lay palms up in her lap, fingers greenish-blue. They looked dead, a memory of hands. I sat, waiting for it to end. Turgid feeling, like the walls of a tomb, enclosed us. I said, "Drop the course. Take it independently. Do it any way you like."

She whispered, "Don't you care what I do?"

"What do you mean?"

"You know."

"I do?"

"You started this."

"This?"

"Yes, this."

"What? You sit there shivering in front of me. I go to the window. You stick your hands under it . . ."

She leaned forward and kicked me in the shin. Her green blouse, with its open collar, looked more dissolute than negligent; the torn neck fierce. Her posture stiffened, as if she carried a bowl of indignation within. Abruptly she reached to her purse, snapping it open. She removed a pearly comb and pulled it through her hair swiftly. Her hands were all right. She stopped, glanced at me, startled, remembering where she was.

"May I?" she said.

"Go ahead."

Long, gleaming tears flowed from her eyes, in the way of a child too deeply hurt to make a sound. She combed her hair. I watched. She finished, put the comb back into her purse, snapped it shut, and walked to the door in three brisk steps, as if she had somewhere to go. Books and papers lay on my desk in a meaningless clutter. I put them in order as the office darkened.

The next day I received a note on heavy beige paper, in a fine, small, careful handwriting. It said she'd dropped all classes, apologized for wasting my time, and thanked me for being patient. Squeezed into the right corner was a phone number. I read the note twice, looking for more than it said. The clear script, with its even pressure, said nothing inadvertently. I folded it, put it into my pocket, then picked up the phone. I was about to do something I'd regret. I shouldn't phone her, I thought. My concern will be misinterpreted. After dialing I listened only to ringing, monotonous ringing. I phoned her from my office, gas stations, drug-stores, restaurants . . .

One afternoon, on the way out to lunch with Henry, I said, "A student of mine who lived in Africa came back with a parasite. She calls it Nigerian fluke. Have you heard of it?"

"Nigerian fluke is fatal in every case. I've had many students who were diseased . . ."

"She dropped out."

"See?" Henry seized my elbow and stopped me, grinning as if pleased, yet frightened. "But I'm not a doctor," he said. "And I've never been right about anything. She's dead?"

"Dropped out. That's all I know."

As we left the building, he asked, "Were you smitten by her?"

The daylight was so pure there seemed nothing to say. Like creatures sliding into a lake without disturbing the surface, we entered it.

I visited a monastery in the wilderness. The monks had carved every stone by hand. It took years to complete. They were content, but their work was so ugly it seemed to comment on their faith. I wandered in halls and courtyard looking for a redeeming touch. There was none. In works of self-abnegating faith is there necessary ugliness?

In the American South, it's said of a medical student, "He is going to make a doctor." For writers there is no comparable expression, no diploma, no conclusive evidence that anything real has been made of himself or herself.

I go to the movies. The hero's girlfriend, about twenty years younger than he, tells him that he is made stupid by his closeness to realities such as work, debts, domestic life. He sees too clearly the little daily facts. He lacks historical understanding, the perspective required for political action. She berates him because he doesn't assassinate the President, blow up a department store, change the world. He sits stolidly in his tweed jacket and dark knit tie. The seriousness of his expression tells me that he suffers, like a European intellectual, the moral weight of thought. He has no choice. The scriptwriter gave him nothing to say in defense of himself. I want to shout at his girlfriend for him, "What do you know, you narcissistic bitch with your bullshit Marxism and five-hundred-dollar shoes from Paris," etc. But she is good-looking. I grow quiet inside and try to take in her whole meaning. I wonder, if she were plain, would I put up with her for a minute? The hero wants to be a good man, think the right thoughts, do the right things. I believe he wants more to shove his face between her legs. The scriptwriter is no fool. Why should he give the hero anything to say? It's enough to sustain a serious expression. This is like life, but I think I can't stand it another minute, when suddenly she puts her face in her hands, collapses beneath a weight of feeling, and says she wants his baby; that is, she wants him to give her a baby. They lie down on a narrow couch, still wearing their clothes, him in his oppressive tweed jacket, which probably stinks of cigarettes. He is presumably giving her a baby as the scene fades. Is this also like life? Oh, come off it. The question is, When did I last do it with my clothes on? My senior year in high school? No, I remember a hard, cold, dirty floor, papers strewn about, and a shock of hot wet flesh through clothing, wintry light in the windows, the radiator banging, a draft from beneath the door sliding across my ass, the telephone ringing, voices outside saying, "He isn't here." "Knock." "I knocked, he isn't here." And the indifference to all that in her eyes, their yellowish-brown gaze taking me into her feelings. She said, "Wait for me.

I have to go to the bathroom." How real that seemed, its sensational banality. My hands trembled, making the flame jerk when I tried to light my cigarette. Why did I light it? Was it a way of collecting the minutes we'd lost? She straightened her skirt, and then, with a quick wiggle, hoisted her pants. Odd not to have straightened her skirt last, but like her. "What are you laughing at, you?" she said.

Ortega says men are public, women are private. Montaigne says if you want to know all about me, read my book. "My book has made me," says Montaigne, "as much as I made it." In the same spirit, a man writes a letter, then decides not to mail it. He thinks it's himself, a great letter, too good for just one person. It should be published. One of Byron's letters was made into a poem. Real intimacy is for the world, not a friend.

The woman wakes beside me and tells me her dream. She might forget otherwise. Nothing is easier to forget than a dream, or more difficult to remember. Her voice—I'm half asleep—twists into my skull, trailing a residue of strange events. This is always irritating, but I wake, listen, urge her to see more, see the whole dream. Frightening, sad, funny, her voice remains neutral, as if it mustn't interfere with what she sees. The secret of writing.

Writers die twice, first their bodies, then their works, but they produce book after book, like peacocks spreading their tails, a gorgeous flare of color soon shlepped through the dust.

I phoned my mother. She said, "You sound happy. What's the matter?"

They say "Hi" and kiss my cheek as if nothing terrible happened yesterday. Perhaps they have no memory of anything besides money or sex, so they harbor no grudges and live only for action. "What's up?" Just pleasure, distractions from anxiety and boredom. Impossible to sustain conversation with them for more than forty seconds. The attention span of dogs. Everything must be up. They say you look great when you look near death. They laugh at jokes you didn't make. They say you're brilliant when you're confused and stupid.

I phoned Boris. He's sick. He gets tired quickly, can't think, can't work. I asked if he'd like to take a walk in the sun. He cries, "It's a nice day out there. I know it, believe me."

Feelings come for no reason. I'm tyrannized by them. I see in terms of them until they go away. Also for no reason.

Bodega Bay. Want to write, but I sit for hours looking at the dune grass. It is yellow-green and sun-bleached. It sparkles and changes hue with the changing light. It is more hue than color, like the whole northern coast. Now the dune grass has the sheen of fur. I need to be blind. Only the blind can write.

Anything you say to a writer is in danger of becoming writing.

The poets reading their poems.
    The critics reading their criticism.
    The him reading his me.
    The Cedar River, the woods, the fields.
    I prefer the houses and barns of Iowa to what *knows* it prefers.

Boris tells me, apropos of nothing, that he has been rereading certain novels and poems. It's as if he is talking to himself, yet he is curious to hear my opinion. He says the novels and poems mean different things whenever he returns to them. As he talks, he picks up a small lacquered bowl which he brought back from Japan. It is very old, very good. It has the aura of a museum object whose value has emerged over time and declared itself absolutely, but he studies it with a worried, skeptical, suspicious eye.

———

Dinner party. Mrs. R. kept asking Z how her son got into Harvard, as if it had nothing to do with his gifts. Z laughed, virtually apologizing, though she's very proud of her son, who is a good kid and also a genius, which I tried to suggest, but Mrs. R. wouldn't hear it because her son didn't get into Harvard and she was too miserable or drunk merely to agree that Z's son would be welcome at any university. Mr. R. left the table, went to the piano, and started banging Haydn on the keys so nobody could hear his wife raving about Harvard, but she raised her voice and talked about her glorious days in graduate school when she took seminars with Heidegger and then she asked Z, "When exactly did you stop loving *your* kids?" Instead of saying never, and never would, whether or not they got into Harvard, Z sat there laughing in the sophisticated style of Mrs. R. and feeling compromised and phony and intimidated. Mr. R.'s Haydn got louder, the sweetness torn by anguish and humiliation.

Natural light passes through murky glass windows in the office doors and sinks into the brown linoleum floor. It is scuffed, heel-pocked, and burned where students ground out cigarettes while waiting to speak to their professors. The halls are long and wide, and have gloomy brown seriousness, dull grandeur. You hardly ever hear people laughing in them. The air is too heavy with significance. Behind the doors, professors are bent over student papers, writing in the margins B+, A−.

Henry comes to my office. "Free for lunch?" I jump up and say, "Give me a minute." He glances at his watch. I run to the men's room, start pissing, want to hurry. The door opens. It's Henry. Also wants to piss. He begins. I finish. Seconds go by and then a whole minute as he pisses with the force of a horse. He would have gone to lunch with me, carrying that pressure.

Boris asks my opinion of a certain movie that has been highly praised. I know it isn't any good, but I'm unwilling to say so. He'll ask why I think it isn't any good. I'd have to tell him, which would mean telling him about myself, becoming another object of endless, skeptical examination. I prefer to disappoint him immediately and not wait for the negative judgment, the disapproval and rejection, like one of his women who never know, from day to day, whether they are adored or despised. I confess, finally, that I disliked the movie, but I understand why many others loved it. The woman I live with has seen it several times. He laughs. He approves. I feel a rush of anxiety, as though I've said too much. I'll be haunted later by my remark, wondering what I told him inadvertently.

Boris had been very successful in Hollywood, but he didn't have one good thing to say about the industry or his colleagues. Producers were conniving, directors were bullies, stars were narcissistic imbeciles. Given his talent and brains, a little contempt for his colleagues was understandable, but he was bitter, he was seething. He went on and on, as if to prove that an emotion perpetuates itself, and then he told a story which I promised not to repeat, but I don't feel bound. Others heard him. He'd been invited to L.A. to meet a group of wealthy people who wanted him to write a movie on a loathsome subject. This was neither here nor there. Any subject, he said, can be made worthwhile. What matters is the way it's rendered. I disagreed, but he became impatient, he didn't want to discuss "art." He was too upset by life. He'd been offered for writing the movie a stupendous sum, endless cocaine, and a famous beautiful woman. "They treated me like an animal."

"What did you say?"

"What do you think? I took the next plane home." Looking sullen, he said, "You think I'm a schmuck?"

"You're lying. Who was the woman?"

"I can't tell you. She's famous. You've heard of her, believe me. Everyone has heard of her."

"Tell me."

"It would be wrong."

"If that's how you feel, don't tell me. I'd rather not know."

"Marilyn."

"She's dead."

"I knew you'd say that."

"Well, she's dead, isn't she?"

"It was Marilyn. I saw her."

"Amazing. What did you do?"

"We did everything. You hate me now."

Annette didn't want to go to Danny's. I followed her from room to room, cajoling, arguing. Not to go was not to live. It wasn't her idea of living. She didn't want to go, but she bought a few yards of silk and began to make herself a dress, working on it at night after the kids were in bed. None of her dresses was good enough. What about the dress she wore last week, the green dress, or what about the black dress? Anyhow, look, I've known Danny since we were kids. We played basketball together in the neighborhood. His mother knows my mother. It makes no difference that he's prospered and everyone at his party is likely to be rich except us. Who'll care about your dress? It's a dinner party, not a fashion show. More to the point, who will be as beautiful as you?

I didn't say anything like that. She didn't want to go, let alone talk about it. She was making a dress. That was a sign. She hadn't actually said she was going, but why else would she make a dress? So I phoned the babysitter. She didn't tell me not to phone the babysitter. Saturday came. She hadn't said she was going, but she moved more slowly than usual. That was a sign. I didn't ask if she was going. She might have felt challenged and said no. She took much longer than usual with dinner for the kids, much longer putting them to bed. I helped, but nothing I did seemed to speed the process. She was moving slowly, as if with weighty business on her mind. I couldn't just say, "If we're going, let's move a little quickly, all right?" The babysitter arrived, a cheery girl, not too stupid. I read to the kids, then shut the lights and said good night, and went to our room and saw that she had put on the dress she made. Rose-colored silk. Extremely simple sheath. I looked at her looking at herself. She could tell what I felt, since there is every sort of silence. My voice asked, "How does it feel to look like you?" She said, "It's all right."

I imagined seeing myself like that. The surprise; the little delirium. It must be frightening, pleasing. She'd never admit she liked it. Me, I looked all right, but not good enough for her. I wasn't rich enough either. If I were rich, or an older man, we might connect better. We'd have moral pathos; delicate binding sorrow. I said, "Are you ready?"

We drove to Danny's place, from flats to hills, from sycamores to Monterey pines. She didn't say a word, but she was in the car. She didn't have to talk. What did she owe the world? The evidence was in. Like a flower or a painting, her existence was enough. I wished she'd talk, just the same. I'd have been happier even if she complained, or if she were happier. But this was a lot. I didn't need more; except maybe a cigarette. She never objected to my smoking, but she was doing something for me. I could forgo.

There were twelve people at Danny's party. We knew some of them. Sooner or later, I'd slide up beside her and whisper, "What's that guy's name, the bald guy with the mustache?" She'd whisper it to me. She was talking to Danny's wife, doing fine, even if she was uncomfortable. She looked better than anyone in the room. Or California. Or the planet. I'd have whispered that to her, but she'd get annoyed, the way she got annoyed in bed. I had the wrong effect. I liked her too much. Always a mistake. You can't expect a woman to want you to like her too much.

The things I'd done in my frustration. I never dared think about that. I'd have denied it under torture. It wasn't a question of getting laid, only how. The ferocity. Could one live without it? Or with it? How was everyone living, anyway? It was a secret. *The secret.*

She seemed to be having a good time. I always had a good time, being cruder stuff. Later in the car, still high, I'd say something like "Well, didn't you have a good time?" She'd say, "No. Neither did anyone else." All the people laughing and talking, they'd been miserable. They didn't know it, but they'd had a truly lousy time. I'd want to scream and pummel the steering wheel, but I just drove more quickly. She'd say, "You'll hit a dog. Then you'll be sorry." I never hit anything, but I'd feel as if I hit a dog. It was lying in the street behind me, blood sliding from its mouth like an endless tongue. I was a good driver, fifty times better than she, but I slowed down. She slowed me down.

I was having a splendid time, drinking and eating like a king, feeling free to enjoy myself. A completely bullshit feeling, but it refused to be questioned. She seemed to be doing better than all right, sitting obliquely opposite me at the dinner table between a lawyer and a gay stockbroker, new friends of Danny's. I was his only old friend in the room. He wanted me to see his crowd, enjoy his new life. I was proud of him, happy for him. She turned to the lawyer, then to the stockbroker, whom I could see she preferred. No sexual tension. They could talk easily. She was a column of rose silk rising toward gray eyes. I'd have made a pass at her, the girl at the party, the one I was still dying to meet.

After coffee and dessert, somebody lit a marijuana. I was surprised, then figured it was the right touch. There was a Republican judge from San Diego at the table. A marijuana couldn't be more inappropriate, more licentious, but this was Berkeley. We were The People, finishing off a two-thousand-dollar dinner party with a joint. Danny knew how to make a statement.

The marijuana was moving around the table, everyone taking a drag, even the judge, consolidating our little community in crime. It would soon reach her. What would she do? She didn't even smoke. I tried not to stare, make her nervous. She took it with no sense of the thing in her fingers, as if it were a pencil, and tried to pass it straight on to the stockbroker. He urged her to take a drag. She looked from him to the lawyer. He, too, offered friendly encouragement. She lifted it to her lips and sipped a little, not to any effect, not really taking a drag. The ash was long and needed to be tapped off, or it might fall of its own, which it did. She jumped up, slapped at her lap. There was a black hole, the size of a penny, in the rose silk. The ash had burned through instantly, ruined her dress. Now the drive home, my speeding car, the bleeding dog.

That quick efficient feeling in the hands, plucking the shaft free of the pack, dashing a match head to perfection. Fat, seething fire. You pull the point of heat against tobacco leaf and a globe of gas rolls into the tongue's valley, like a personal planet. Then the consummation, the slithering hairy smoke. Its danger meets the danger we live with in the average street, our lethal food, poisoned air, imminent bomb. In Morocco and Berlin, in Honolulu's sunshine or the black Siberian night, in the cruel salons of urban literati, in the phantasmagoria of brothels, in rain forests full of or-chids and wild pigs where women bleed to phases of the moon and men hunt what they eat, in the excremental reek of prison cells, or crouched be-side a window with a gun in your lap, or sitting in your car studying a map, or listening to a lecture at the Sorbonne, or waiting for a bus or a phone call, or just trying to be reasonable, or staying up late, or after a meal in some classy restaurant, hands repeat their ceremony. The shock of fire. The pungent smoke. Disconnection slides across the yellowing eye. True, it's very like but morally superior to masturbation; and you look better, more dignified. We need this pleasing gas. Some of us can claim no possession the way a cigarette is claimed. What wonderful exclusiveness. In company a cigarette strikes the individual note. If it's also public suicide, it's yours. Or in the intenser moment after sexual disintegration, when the old regret, like a carrion bird, finds you naked, leaking into the night, a cigarette re-deems the deep being, reintegrates a person's privacy. White wine goes with lobster. What goes with bad news so well as a cigarette? Imagine a common deprivation—say, a long spell of no sex—without a cigarette. Life isn't good enough for no cigarette. It doesn't make you godlike, only a lit-tle priest of fire and smoke. All those sensations yours, like mystical money. Such a shame they kill. With no regard for who it is.

Boris said that his first wife was a virgin. She came the first time they had sex. Worse, he says, she came every time after that. He watches my eyes to see if I understand why he had to divorce her.

The pain you inflict merely trying to get through the day. Pavese talks about this great problem. He had a woman in mind. Pavese does his work he kills her . . . Pavese reads a newspaper he kills her . . . Pavese makes an appointment to see an old friend . . . Finally, he killed himself. Sartre says to kill another is to kill yourself. He spent hours in coffee shops and bars. He liked to carry money in his pocket, lots of money. He compared it to his glasses and cigarette lighter. So many companions. He'd never have killed himself.

Self-pity is a corrupt version of honesty.

I tell Boris my grief. He says, "I know I'm supposed to have a human response, but I'm hungry."

Annette claimed Dr. Feller "worked hard" during their sessions. "I trusted him," she says. "So many therapists sleep with their patients." As if it were entirely up to him. That hurt my feelings. Later we met his girlfriend at a party. I was friendly, as usual, but Annette was furious, confused, depressed. I asked, "What's the matter?" She wouldn't answer, but then, in bed, unable to sleep, she announced, "I will confront him, tell him off." I ask, "Why?" She hisses, "I trusted him." I begin to wonder if I'm crazy. Dr. Feller took a fifth of my income. I feel a spasm of anger, but fall asleep anyway, imagining myself taking a three-point shot from the sideline with no time on the clock. The ball feels good as it leaves my hand.

I meet Eddie for lunch. He wants to talk, but is too agitated, doesn't know how to begin. We order this and that. He starts, tells me that his wife came to his office and made a scene. There were patients in the waiting room. He had to beg her to shut up till they got out in the street. It wasn't better in the street. She berated him, threatened to ruin his life. His eyes begin to glisten and now I can't eat. I imagine her yelling at him in front of his patients. I hear myself groan with sympathy. Then he says, "I bought a radio car. It's about this big." He raises his hands, holding them a foot and a half apart. "It's fast, too."

I was talking to Eddie about difficulties with my wife's lawyer. He cuts me off, very excited, nearly manic, shouting about difficulties with his wife's lawyer. "She snarls at me in legal letters, like I might forget this is war. I get very upset. I write back long angry letters. I tear them up, then write angrier letters and tear them up, too. Today I decided I can't write. I must phone and tell her what I think of her fucking letters. So I phoned. Soon as I say my name, her voice becomes high and warm. Like she is delighted to hear from me. I thought maybe I dialed the wrong number, reached her cunt. But you know what? I responded very warmly. Like a prick."

Women are tough. They know what they want. Men know more or less what they need, which is only what they like, not even what they need. King Lear wails, "But, for true need . . ." then can't define it. That's a real man.

My neighbor is building his patio, laying bricks meticulously. The sun beats on him. Heat rises off the bricks into his face. I'm in here writing. He'll have built a patio. I'll be punished.

X tells Y. Y repeats it to W and thus betrays X. The moment of telling, for X, felt like prayer, almost sanctified. He thinks the betrayal was evil, but evil lay in the telling, in daring to assume one could.

Spoke to her on the phone. She cried. Said she missed me. I feel like a ghoul wandering in the darkness.

The secretary said a long goodbye. A minuscule flake of mucus, like a fish scale, trembled in her right nostril. Her face shone with cosmetic oils, as in feverish sweating. I thought she loved me, and I was reluctant to meet her eyes. I could have kissed her, perhaps changed her life, made her a great pianist, or poet, or tennis star, kissing her every day.

Eddie says he wanted to run out into the street, grab the first person he saw, and tell that person everything. He wanted to tell everything to any-body. But he picked up the phone and dialed his girlfriend. When she said hello, the sweetness of her voice, which had always pleased him, enraged him. He spoke with strenuously deliberate slowness, as if to a very stupid person, as he told her about the burning sensation he felt that morning when he pissed. She made no comment, asked no question. She under-stood what he was getting at. With the same slowness, he continued to speak to her, now offering an analysis of her character, saying things she would never forget, frightening even to him when he thought later about what he'd said. She said, when he let her speak, "You didn't get it from me." He heard the pressure of feeling in her voice, and he knew that she wanted to say much more, but she could only manage to repeat, "You didn't get it from me." Then she hung up. Eddie phoned her again imme-diately, still angry but already regretful, and no less wretched, probably, than she. She wouldn't pick up the receiver. This struck him as unjust, but what could he do? He went into the next room. His wife, sitting at her desk, was writing a letter. She looked so much involved in her letter that Eddie was reluctant to say anything to her, but he couldn't be silent. The very sound of his voice, as he began, struck him as criminal, a violation of their peaceful domestic order. He was deeply ashamed as he said, "I have an infection." He was about to tell her about his girlfriend, but she thrust herself away from her desk, rushed toward him, sank to her knees, and clutched his legs. "I betrayed you," she said. "I betrayed you in every possible way." Eddie says it wasn't simply her confession that appalled him. It was the strangeness of her emotion and the way she begged, "Forgive me, forgive me." The words came from far away, like sounds in the night, as though he and she had nothing in common, only the darkness, and there couldn't even be anything to forgive.

His neck was as thick as his head, and he had long heavy arms. His hands were stained black in the creases and in the cusp of his fingernails. Beside him stood a pale girl about nine years old. Too clean and pretty to be his daughter, but they had the same flat, grim expression and whenever he moved she moved. She was his daughter. They didn't talk to each other, didn't look at each other. He finished his business at the counter and turned to go. She turned to go. She walked step by step beside him out the door and into the parking lot. They looked sad. A brutalized man; a pale girl. As I watched them through the glass windows of the door, the man whirled suddenly, sweeping up the girl in his tremendous arms. She screamed. My heart bulged, as though I had to act quickly to save her, but her scream changed from terror to delight. My heart dissolved. That man would die for her. She hugged his monstrous neck. Would she find such love again?

Eddie invited his soon-to-be-former wife and her lover, a guy with two kids, over to his place for dinner. He cooked a duck, prepared a garden salad, and built a fire. They sat watching it after dinner, sipping cognac. His wife and her lover stayed the night. Eddie's house is big, lots of extra rooms. He says they talked for hours, but something was wrong. He keeps thinking about it. "I don't know," he says, "something was wrong." I laugh. He laughs, too, but I can tell he doesn't know what's funny.

I talk to Annette only on the phone. Afraid we might touch.

———

Henry is talking and eating a turkey sandwich. A piece of turkey falls out of his sandwich onto the floor. My life stops. What will he do? Something told me that he will go on talking as he picks it up and pops it into his mouth. He did exactly that. I felt we knew each other. At his funeral, I thought, I will cry.

I asked Boris to read my screenplay. Then I sat in his living room. He stood and spoke in complete sentences, built paragraphs, obliged me to read him. He wanted revenge for having done me a favor. I responded to him with laughter, dismay, surprise, assent, always appropriate and quick, feeling insulted by his concern for my edification. Other friends read it and said it isn't good; others said it is. One said, "The best screenplay in the world can be made into a lousy movie." Was the reverse also true? There was no truth.

Only desire and luck prevail in this world. If my screenplay isn't good, could it be bad enough to succeed?

Boris tells me he *really* loves Y and he REALLY wants to fuck X. Montaigne says there is more wildness in thinking than in lust.

Whatever was wrong was wrong from the instant we met, but like kids with big eyes we plunged into eating. Later she said, "I knew it instinctively. I could feel it was wrong." Even then she reached me, her voice speaking—beyond the words—of her. I must have the heart of a dog. I live beneath meaning.

I eat standing up, leaning over the sink. I wouldn't eat like this if anyone could see me.

Her voice is flat and coolly distant, so I imagine things aren't over between us.

From the woe that is in marriage has come the *Iliad* and ten thousand novels, but nothing from me. I missed her voice too much. After talking to her on the telephone, I turn on the radio loud.

The distance between us is neither long nor short, merely imperishable, like the sentiment in an old song.

A huge fellow with the face of a powerful dullard stood behind the counter. He turned for items on the shelf and I saw that his pants had slipped below his hips, where he was chopped sheer from lower back to legs. No ass to hold up his pants. His bulk pushed forward and heaved up into his chest. He had a hanging mouth and little eyes with a birdlike shine. I bought salami and oranges from him, though I no longer felt any desire to eat.

Eddie said he ran into his former wife in the street in New York, and they talked. They talked as if neither of them knew how to say nice to see you, I'm expected somewhere, goodbye, goodbye. They went to a restaurant and ate and talked some more, and they went to her apartment, and they made love. Then she said, "So why did we get divorced?" Eddie smiled at me and said, "See?" as if he were the idiot of circumstances, shlepped into pain and confusion by his cock. "You know how long I was divorced before I remarried?" he asked. "Not three days," he said. I was sad for him and for her, and her, and her. The feeling widened like circles about a leaf fallen onto the surface of a pond.

We left Berkeley on December 14, driving south on Route 5, straight, flat road policed by aircraft. Jesse, eleven years old, twisted the radio dial searching for rock music. Ethan, fourteen, in the backseat with the luggage, was reading. For no reason, they'd begin to fight. Holding the wheel with one hand, I smacked at them with the other until they stopped. They were bored. There was nothing to see but the canal, a vein that leaked life out of Northern California into the agricultural empire of the Central Valley and beyond that into real estate from Los Angeles to Mexico.

At twilight we checked into a motel near Barstow. The boys chased each other about the room and began wrestling. I stepped outside and waited until they'd wrestled themselves into a stupor.

Early the next morning I woke them and said, "Shower and pack. We're going to the Grand Canyon. It's ten miles deep and full of snakes and panthers." They cheered. I left for the motel office. The sunlight was brassy, the air was cool. Big trucks running down the highway pulled at me. Get out in the energy. Go.

Behind the motel desk stood a woman about fifty, with a red loaf of hair, like body and blood mashed into her personal fashion statement. While figuring my bill she said, "Going home for the holidays?"

"I'm delivering my sons to their mother. We're divorced, passing them back and forth. I'm doing it for the first time." She looked up, startled. I was startled, too. I'd been babbling, as if I'd owed her a confession in exchange for what she offered in her hair. It got to me, bespeaking desire beyond consummation on this planet, bulging upward, packed and patted into shape, bursting with laborious and masturbatory satisfaction, like a bourgeois novel, the kind you live with for days or weeks, reading slowly, nourished by its erotic intimacies and the delicious anxieties of a plot, wishing it would never never end.

"I once drove my Labrador from Berkeley to Sacramento," I said, "and gave it to a family that could take better care of it than I could. Then I had to sit by the side of the road for half an hour, until I could stop crying and drive."

"You're talking about a dog?"

"Yes. A Labrador retriever. Now I'm going to New York."

"You're going a funny way to New York."

"We'll stop at the Grand Canyon and have some fun. I'm taking a southern route to avoid bad weather."

She stood very still, as my meaning sifted down and settled inside her like sediment in a wine bottle. I said again, "Bad weather." Her head dipped, the red dome a second head, making a slow double bludgeon of assent. "But it's better than none at all," she said.

"That's a fact."

"It is," she said. We smiled together. She was a nice lady. She had nice hair. I yearned to be within its fold. I yearned to be taken into her hair.

I returned to the room. The boys hadn't showered. Their clothes were flung about everywhere. They sprawled on the beds, gleaming with violence that had ceased when they heard the key in the lock. Like my opponents in a rough game, evil half smiles on their faces, they waited for my move. I thought of strangling them, but nothing in me wanted to move. It was plain they didn't give a shit about the Grand Canyon.

At a place called Truck Stop, I ate lunch. Truckers leaned toward each other, eating pills, coffee, and starch. They looked fat, vibrant, seething with bad health.

Checked into a motel in Manhattan, Kansas, and got the last room. Though it was midnight, people were still arriving. The highway was loud throughout the night. American refugees seek the road, the road.

Infinitely clear sky and prairie of Kansas. I felt vulnerable, easily seen, as in the eye of God.

A farmer came into the diner. He wore a baseball cap with a long bill. He was very tanned and dusty, and moved ponderously with the pain of this long day. His hands were much bigger than the coffee cup in front of him. He stared at it. In his eyes, no ideas, just questions. "What's this?" he asked. "A coffee cup," he told himself. "What do you do with it?" he asked. He told himself, "Pick it up." Between the first and second question, no words. No words even in the questions.

A young couple sat opposite of me. The woman was long and pale. Her husband was not as tall as she. His double-breasted suit and dark shiny tie were very ugly. He'd tried to dress impressively, perhaps for an official occasion. She wore a hand-knit gray sweater, setting off her lovely pale complexion. She could have improved her husband's taste, but was maybe indifferent to it. He had thin, colorless hair and red-rimmed, obedient eyes. They flicked nervously in her direction, hoping for a command. He suggested a

small-town bureaucrat whose every action is correct and never spontaneous, but he was in love with his wife and lived in agonizing confusion. He
looked to her for sympathy. She offered none. She had what she wanted in
life. It was this man, or such a man. She made him feel ashamed of himself,
his need of her, specifically her.

New York. Mother's apartment. Moritz visits, tells a story. One freezing
morning everybody had to go outside and watch a man be hanged. He'd
tried to escape the previous night. Beside Moritz stood a boy, the man's
brother. "His nose became red. It was so red," said Moritz. "That's what I
remember." Moritz's eyes enlarge and his voice becomes urgent, as if it
were happening again. His excitement isn't that of a storyteller. He can
recite passages from *Manfred* in Polish, but he isn't literary. The experience
is still too real to him. His memories are very dangerous. He fears another
heart attack, but he tells about the camps. It should be remembered as he
tells it. Freezing morning. The boy's red nose.

Alone, you hear yourself chewing and swallowing. You sound like an
animal. With company everyone eats, talk obscures the noises in your head,
and nobody looks at what your mouth is doing, or listens to it. In this high
blindness and deafness lives freedom. Would I think so if I hadn't left her?

She screamed and broke objects. Nevertheless, I refused to kill her.

Jimmy phones me after midnight. He's been living in Paris. I haven't
spoken to him for over a year, but I recognize his voice, and I recognize
the bar, too, the only one in Berkeley Jimmy likes. I hear the din of a
Friday-night crowd and a TV. I imagine Jimmy standing in the phone
booth, the folding door left open to let me know he doesn't want to make
conversation. He says he needs five hundred and seventy dollars for his
rent, which is due tomorrow. He wasted a month trying to find an apartment in Berkeley, and he'll lose it if he doesn't come up with five hundred and seventy dollars. He'll pay me back in a couple of days. I know he
won't. He never pays me back. He says, "I would go to your place, but I'm

hitting on some bitch. I just met her. I can't split." What about tomorrow morning? Impossible. "I don't know where I'll be," he says.

I get out of bed and put on my clothes. My hands tremble a little when I tie my shoelaces; I have to concentrate on the job like a kid who just learned how to do it. Then I drive across town to Brennan's, being careful to stop at stop signs. At night cops get lonely and need to have a word with you.

Brennan's is crowded and loud. I can't spot Jimmy, though he's the only black man in the room—if he's there. He is. He's waving to me from the bar. I must have been looking at him for a few seconds before I saw him, because he is laughing at me.

The woman on the stool beside him is wearing jeans and high heels. She's blond, like all his others. When I walk up, Jimmy turns his back to her, takes my hand. He doesn't introduce us. She looks away and begins watching the talk show on TV. I slip Jimmy the check I've written. He doesn't look at it as he folds it into his wallet and says, "Thanks, man. I'll pay you back. Have a drink." I tell him I'm not feeling good. I can't stay. But he has ordered an Irish whiskey for me. It's waiting on the bar beside his own.

He tells the guy next to him there's a free stool at the end of the bar. Would he mind? The guy picks up his beer and leaves. I take his stool and Jimmy hugs me, laughing at this accomplishment. The blonde, on his other side, glances at me and then back to the TV as if she doesn't expect to be introduced and is indifferent, anyway. I wonder if the Irish whiskey will be good for my flu. My hand trembles when I pick it up. I ask Jimmy how it was in Paris. He says, "Oh, man, you know. I get tired of them, even the finest ones." The blonde, I suppose, is also fine. What lasts is him and me. This idea is at the margins of my mind, fever occupies the middle like a valley of fog. I know for sure Jimmy has flattering ways. He says, "Look, man, do you really want to do this?" He's studying my glazed eyes. I think he's concerned about my illness, and then realize he means the money. "Didn't I?" I say, reaching into my shirt pocket before I remember that I gave him the check. Now I'm embarrassed. "Talk about something else, will you?" I say, though he wants me to ease the burden of gratitude. I get out of bed with fever to give him money . . . I don't finish the thought. The blonde turns, looks at me with cold blue intelligent eyes, but I see better than she does. I see that the connection to Jimmy is her fate. He's going to hurt her. She holds her martini as if she is invincible, and smokes her cigarette in a world-weary manner. I say, "I'm sick, man. Would I be here if I didn't want to be?" The blonde half-laughs, more a cough than a laughing sound. She wants me to leave and shows it by putting down her martini and heading for the ladies' room. Jimmy turns and watches. Her jeans are cut for trouble. The door shuts behind her and Jimmy says, "Her name is Gunnel. She's bad."

He laughs, unable to contain his excitement. Then he slaps my arm, surprised by how entertaining I am, though I've been very dull. I laugh, too, but I won't ever give him another cent, I think. That's what I always think. Then one night the phone rings and he says, "Hey, man," his voice low and personal, like there's nobody in the world but him and me.

Boris drove past me in his new car, speeding down Euclid Avenue, picking his nose. He didn't see me. He was watching the road, driving fast, obsessed with his nose. Each life, says Ortega, is a perspective on reality.

Boris laughs at his unexpressed jokes, then gives me a compassionate look for having missed the point known only to himself.

I found a modest place with only three main dishes on the menu, none over ten bucks. Not good; not terrible. In Oakland near the courthouse. Nobody I know is likely to walk in. I don't remember the name of the place, I never noticed. I was eating dinner and reading the legal papers, telling myself they're written in English, they will have a great effect on my life, so I should try to understand them, I must be calm and read slowly, when the door opens and lets in a draft with street noise and perfume. The noise hits me like a personal criticism, the perfume cuts through the steam coming off my plate. I look toward the door. I see a white linen blouse, pearls, and a face heavily made up, correct for the pearls but not for dinner in this place. Maybe the pearls are to suggest that she's meeting somebody here, but something tells me she is alone. Her green eye shadow is a touch sloppy, as if she wants to be beautiful, but she has troubles, agonies, who knows. Maybe she's a lawyer, works too hard, and wishes she'd had a child instead of a career. The green eye shadow, part of a mask, tells more than it hides. I look away to avoid her feelings. I don't know her. I'm

eating dinner. I'll soon finish, smoke a cigarette, and then go home to
sleep without a body against whose heat to press my complications. The
food tastes like pork or chicken, but not enough like either to create anxieties. I don't remember what I ordered, but it's boring. I like it.

I'm trying to eat and read, not to look at her, though she is garishly
depressed and sits five feet away. The waiter goes to her. It's his job. She
tells him she wants the fish, but without sauce, and she would like it
grilled, not poached. I look. He starts to ask what else she wants. She
interrupts, asks if the wine is dry. He says, "Yes." She says, "Very dry?" He
says, "I'll ask," and hustles away to the kitchen. I hear him consult the chef
in a foreign language, maybe Arabic. She calls from the table, "I don't want
it if it isn't very dry." He comes back, whispers, "It's very dry." She then
says that she'll have soup and salad, but no cream in the soup, and bring
the salad dressing on the side, then adds "Please" with a too strong voice
and a frightened stare, like a person who is basically shy, struggling to be
forthright. Instead of forthright, a kind of begging enters her tone, almost
sexual. She smiles, amused at having betrayed herself, and also as if the
waiter must be grateful for such a gift, which has now established a bond
between them. He smiles politely and hurries away, confused by messages.
She sits alone. As the waiter goes about his business at other tables, a light
inside her grows dim. She feels abandoned. I want to rise and go hug her,
or at least mess up her clothes, but you can't do anything for anybody.
"Oh, waiter," she cries, "could you please bring the bread now?" He starts
for the bread. "And I'd like a little water." He hurries to her with bread
and water, as if that's what she wants.

Every wildness plays with death. Washing your hands is a ritual to protect
against death, and so are all the small correct things you do every day.
Aren't there people who do nothing else? They pay their bills on time and
go to the doctor once a year. They have proper sentiments and beliefs.
They are nice people. I wanted to do dull ordinary chores all day. I wanted
to be like nice people only to forget death, only to feel how I'm still alive.

The waiter does everything quick, everything right—no sauce on the
fish, dry wine, salad dressing on the side. Then he bends over her and
whispers, "Why are you angry?"

She says, "I'm not angry."

He says, "I can see that you're angry."

"I'm not angry."

"Didn't I bring you everything you asked for?" His voice becomes bigger, self-pitying. "Fish, soup, bread, wine. Everything you asked for."

She says, "I shouldn't have to ask."

The waiter walks away rolling his eyes. He doesn't understand American women. I rise, go to her table, and say, "Do you mind if I join you?"

She says, "What took you so long?"

She pressed my leg with hers under the table. Conversation stopped. She continued pressing, then pulled away abruptly. Conversation resumed. She did it to excite herself, that's all. Her makeup was sloppy, her clothes were stylish. She'd start to say something, then laugh and say, "No." I'd never seen anyone more depressed. She said, "Driving to work I brush my teeth. I'm the invisible woman."

I said, "I locked myself out of my office and my car. I don't even exist."

She said, "I lost my checkbook and sunglasses. Nobody needs them."

"I forgot my appointment. Nobody wants to meet me."

She frowned. "You're trying and that's sweet. But I don't care."

Billy says, "Why don't you let me do it? Afraid you might like it?"

Billy phones, says, "Want to play?" I think about it, then say, "The traffic is heavy. It will take forever to get to your place. I can't stay long. I'd feel I'm using you. It's not right. I don't want to use you." She says, "But I want to be used." I drive to Billy's place. She opens the door naked, on her knees. We fuck. "Do you think I'm sick?" she says. I say, "No." "Good," she says, "I don't think you're sick either."

You know your feelings, so you mistrust them, as if they belonged to an unreliable stranger. He behaved badly in the past and is likely to do so again. But you can't believe that. You believe you've changed. Then it happens again and the same feelings surprise you. Now you're fearful of yourself because of what you can't not do.

If there are things I'd never tell a psychotherapist, I would waste time and money talking to one. It would feel like a lie. I need a priest.

Sex in one place. Feeling in another.

Afterward, afterward, it is more desolating than when a good movie ends or you finish a marvelous book. We should say "going," not "coming." Anyhow, the man should say, "Oh God, I'm going, I'm going."

Schiller says, "When the soul speaks, then—alas—it is no longer the soul that speaks." William Blake says, "Never seek to tell thy love/Love that never told can be." They mean the same as Miles Davis's version of "My Funny Valentine," so slowly played, excruciating, broken, tortured.

She wore baggy pants, a man's sweater, no makeup, and had strong opinions about everything, as if to show, despite her exceedingly beautiful face and body, she damn well had a mind. I felt sick with regret at having met her, ready to forgive every fault, half in love with a woman I won't ever see again.

The soul is known through intuitions, or forms without meaning—like fish, flowers, music . . . Certainly not a face.

"Do you think it's possible to have fifteen sincere relationships?"
    "Not even one," says Billy. "Let me tie you to the bed."
    "No."
    "Why not?"

"Because I don't want you to."

"I'll stop when you tell me. Just don't say 'stop.' That only excites me. Say 'tomato' or something."

Deborah wants to have her eyes fixed so they'll look like white eyes and she hates her landlady who gave her the Etna Street apartment, choosing her over 157 other applicants. Her landlady assumed Deborah is a good girl, clean and quiet. "A Japanese angel," says Deborah with a sneer. I was shocked by her racism. I hadn't imagined that she thought of herself as Japanese. She showed me photos of her family. Mother, father, brothers, sister—all Japanese, but I hadn't supposed she thought she was, too. What the hell did I imagine? Never to have to think of yourself as white is a luxury that makes you deeply stupid.

Deborah holds a new blouse up to her chin, tilts her head, and says, "Do you like this blouse?" I look at it and at her, how she's tilted her head so seriously, waiting for my opinion, but I can't speak. She sees what's happening and lowers the blouse. Her head remains tilted like an iris on the fine white stalk of her neck. She whispers, as if there were someone else in the room, "You're hopeless. You're like my girlfriend. I ask if she likes what I'm wearing and she says, 'You're beautiful.'"

Margaret says she went to Cesar's Latin Palace and stood at the bar until some guy asked her to dance, a handsome Jamaican. Great dancer. She says there's a divorced couple at Cesar's who will not have anything to do with each other, except when they show up Saturday night and dance together, drawn to the music in each other's body. When the number ends they separate instantly, without a word, and go to different tables. They'd rather drink with strangers. Then the great Francisco Aquabella starts slapping conga drums, driving the whole world to cha-cha-cha, and she feels the need for him, that one, the guy over there across the floor sitting with the white bitch, that one who is standing up and crossing the floor to her table, and she is standing up, too, even before he asks her to dance, feeling the music in his body. Don't talk to me about love. Talk about cha-cha-cha, and the way he touches her. His eyes are cold, yet full of approval. When they dance, they belong to each other and nothing else matters until the music ends.

Kittredge loves pretty women, but he is blind, can't pursue them. So I take him to a party and describe a woman in the room. He whispers, "Tell me about her neck." Eventually I introduce him to her. They leave the party together. Kittredge is always successful. Women think he listens differently from other men. In his blind hands they think pleasure is truth. Blind hands know deep particulars, what yearns in neck and knee. Women imagine themselves embracing Kittredge the way sunlight takes a tree. He says, "Talk about her hips." As I talk, his eyes slide with meanings, like eyes in a normal face except quicker, a snapping in them. Kittredge cannot see, cannot know if a woman is pretty. I say, "She has thick black hair." When they leave together I begin to sink. I envy the magnetic darkness of my friend. To envy him without desiring his condition is possible.

Evelyn told me that Sally, her dearest friend—"Don't ever repeat this!"— came down with the worst case of herpes the doctor had ever seen.

Evelyn's four-year-old son had a nightmare in which Evelyn appeared with a big knife stuck in her head. She has scheduled him for psychotherapy five days a week.

Margaret says she went back to Cesar's. The Jamaican asked her to dance again. She refused. She liked him, but she kept a closed face. If she showed interest, he'd think she was in the same mood as last time. They would dance, then go out to his car and make love. She said, "I have a Ph.D. I can do anything. I can even read fashion magazines. He's a nice guy, but he'd never understand me."

Deborah's dentist, a little Jewish man, talks incessantly and she can't say a word because her mouth is pried open, under investigation by steel instruments, and also hooked like a fish by a suction tube. Nevertheless, her dentist says things that require an answer, so she grunts and moans to say yes, no, really, how nice, too bad. Last time she saw him he carried on about Buddhism, which he studies with monks in a temple. He said, incidentally, that he'd learned to levitate. When he finished working, Deborah could talk. She asked if he meant "meditate" rather than "levitate." He said, "No. I meant levitate." She asked him to show her. He said, "No, no." She pleaded with him. He refused. She refused to leave. He said, "Just once." He turned his back to her, crouched slightly, and lifted off the floor. I waited for Deborah to continue, but that was the end. She had no more to say. I snapped at her, "He did not levitate." She said, truly astonished, "He didn't?"

Evelyn goes shopping Monday through Sunday. Clothes, jewelry, books, records, prints, paintings, ceramics. Her house of many things shrieks good taste. The latest dress style isn't always right for Evelyn, but she is the first in town to wear it. She believes her clothing and her automobile say something about her. After shopping, Evelyn feels she's done good. She must know she is too wide for a zebra-striped dress, but still, it's the most new thing, and it gives her moral sensations to wear it with bright red socks, her black pearl necklace, and a wide aluminum belt. All of it is hidden under her black cape, which she throws off in the restaurant, driving the women in the place mad with envy.

Margaret doesn't like oral sex because she was once forced to do it at gunpoint, in a car, in the parking lot next to the railroad tracks, outside the bar where the guy picked her up. I wish she hadn't told me. I hear freight trains. I see people coming out of the bar, laughing, drunk, going to their cars while she crouches in misery and fear, the gun at her head. How easy, if I had the gun at his head, to pull the trigger.

Eddie calls her Stop-and-Go. She's up early and moving, then collapses into hours of marijuana. It's like everything with her, he says. No degrees. Truth or lies, good or bad, stop or go. She criticizes Eddie constantly. He can't do anything right. He wants to break up, but plans to provoke her into doing it by hanging a picture she doesn't like in a place she finds disturbing. They've already argued about that. He took the picture down, but he plans now to put it up again. She'll see that he is saying the house is his. She'll go. He says she becomes affectionate after a fight. He finds her adorable then. He says she dislikes his father for his Jewish traits, and also dislikes Eddie for his. He says she doesn't even know what they are, then smiles in a silly way, as if he weren't really offended. Tomorrow her mood will be different. She'll forget what she said today. Her feelings aren't moored to anything, no important work, like his medical practice, for example. He is accomplished; successful. The woman is merely herself, except when she objects to him. He thinks it costs him nothing and it makes her feel real. He says, "Let me ask you something. You and me, we've had dinner together a couple of hundred times. Is there anything about how I eat that looks to you Jewish?"

"Is that what she thinks?"

"How I eat, how I dress, how I talk, how I fuck."

I laugh.

"O.K. She doesn't treat me well," he says. "She disapproves of me. Criticism is my daily bread. But I'm never lonely with her, never bored. I'm miserable. But this word 'miserable,' in my case, is not the end of the discussion. It's only the beginning. There are kinds of misery . . ."

Feelings swarm in Eddie's face, innumerable nameless nuances, like lights on the ocean beneath a sky of racing clouds. Eddie could have been a novelist or a poet. He has emotional abundance, fluency of self. He's shameless.

"Believe me, I'm not a faithful type. I've slept with a hundred women. More. But it's no use. She hits me, curses me. She says, 'I don't want to be touched. I don't want to be turned on.' No matter. It begins to happen. She relaxes, lets me disgrace myself. She tells me, 'Lick the insides of my legs while I make this phone call.' My father slaved six days a week, year after year, to put me through medical school. For me to do this, to lick this woman, he went to an early grave."

The paper was thick and creamy, textured like baby flesh. Every night she opened to a new page, wrote the date, then "Dear Diary," then thought for a minute, then quit. After a while it came to her that she had no internal life. Ortega says this is true of monkeys. But monkeys are known to dream. Evelyn says, "I never had a dream."

———

She was once making love and the bed collapsed on her cat, who was asleep underneath, and broke its back. Since then, she says, sex hasn't been the same for her. Then she dashes to the sink, grabs a knife, and looks back at me, her teeth shining, chilly as the steel, welcoming me to the wilderness.

Margaret tells me her lover is wonderful. "He makes me feel like a woman," she says, "without degrading me." I don't know what she means, but can't ask. What is it to feel like a woman? or to be made to feel that way?

I said to Margaret, "When we talk we make a small world of trust." Quickly she says, "There are men so loose of soul they talk even in their sleep." She laughs, surprised by her good memory and how wonderful Shakespeare is. She didn't get it right, but the point is that it no longer mattered what I was going to say. I said, "You didn't get it right." She was talking, didn't hear me.

I asked Deborah out to dinner. She said, "You looking for an exotic date or something?" Now she tells me that she went to an orgy in Berkeley. It was highly organized. On Wednesday, everyone met at the home of the couple, an engineer and his wife. People talked, got to know one another, then went home. They returned on Friday and took off their clothes. "But you didn't have to undress or do anything," said Deborah. "I only wanted to watch." But so many of them begged her to undress that she finally consented, except for her underwear. Then she lay on the floor. The engineer, his wife, and their friends, all of them naked, kneeling on either side of her, mauled her. She was being polite.

"A Japanese angel."

"I didn't behave like them," she said.

Sonny was my best friend. Then she says, "I met a man last night." My heart grew heavy. I couldn't count on her anymore for dinner, long talks on the telephone, serious attention to my problems, and she'd no longer tell me about herself, how well or ill she slept last night, and whether she dreamed, and what she did yesterday, and what people told her and she them. She said, "I don't know why, but I feel guilty toward you."

I said, "What's he like?" She said he is some kind of a psychotherapist, divorced, lives in Mill Valley. His former wife is Korean, a fashion model. She made him install a plate-glass window in their living room so birds would fly into it and break their necks. She had them stuffed.

"Oh, I know the guy," I said. "Women find him attractive."

"How do men find him?"

I was conscious of the danger.

"He dresses well. He likes classical music and hiking. He goes sailing. He's a good cook. Doesn't smoke."

"You think he's a prick."

Sonny was six years old when she went up on a roof with a boy. He pulled down his pants. She pulled down hers. They looked. Years later she still worried about what she'd done, thinking she could never be famous because the boy would tell everybody she'd pulled her pants down. She was a success in school and had innumerable boyfriends. None of that changed anything for her. At the age of six, in a thoughtless moment, she ruined her life.

Billy comes to my office, sits, looks me in the eye, and says, "Girls like to be spanked."

Sonny will see the man, sleep with him, then linger in regret to the end. If I said, "I know for certain he has leprosy," she would still see the man, etc. Nobody passes up romance.

Sonny says she dislikes being touched by doctors. I thought to remind her, but she said quickly, "He's different." With me—as if talking to herself—she needn't bother about little connections.

———

There was a message for me at the motel. I hoped it was Sonny, but it's from Evelyn. "Call immediately." I call. The crazy pitch of her hello means she bought something or she met a famous person. I'm wrong. She says, "I went to a garage sale in the Oakland hills. Are you listening? There was a Swedish dresser with glass pulls. Inside one drawer I see a piece of paper, like folded in half. I opened it. It's a sketch in red crayon. Old, but nice, not faded. I scrunched it quick into my purse. I also got a pewter dish and a pocket watch. I went home. No, first I met Sheila for coffee. I didn't tell her what I got. She's so jealous. Later I went home and took the sketch out of my purse. I smoothed it out. It's the head of a woman, signed by Raphael. I almost died. So I phoned Sheila—"

"You stole a Raphael?"

"Listen, I almost died. Sheila has a friend in the art department at Berkeley. I called him and went to his office. He almost died. He said it looks authentic, but he couldn't be positive. He told me to mail it to a man in England. The greatest living expert. So I mailed it to him."

"Insured?"

"Regular mail. Listen. Listen, the expert just phoned me. He says he almost died. It's authentic. But listen. Wait till you hear what else . . ."

Sonny tells me she will separate her emotional life from her sexual feelings. "In other words," she said, "I'll have an affair only if I can't become entangled with the man."

"In other words, you're already doing it."

"How embarrassing . . . I lied."

Byron says, "And, after all, what is a lie? 'Tis but the truth in masquerade."

Are some truths told only by lying?

You know why there is heaven and hell? It's to make the past real. Otherwise there is no past. There is only the present.

————

Eddie met the woman years ago, in another state, prior to her divorce, long before she changed her hairstyle and became a different person. His own hair, though beginning to gray, was much the same. He figures she recognized him immediately, but since he didn't recognize her, she didn't tell him they'd met before. Both acted as if neither was part of the other's past, even after they'd slept together again. Eddie imitated himself: "Oh, did you grow up in Michigan?" By then he knew she had. He remembered. Years earlier, he now remembered, the first time they made love, he'd asked, "How do you handle your feelings?" She had told him, in the tender darkness, that she loved her husband.

"Why are you doing this with me?"

"This is this," she said, "and that is that."

It would have been possible early on, with only a little embarrassment, to stop pretending.

"Don't you remember me?"

"Should I? Wait, oh no. Oh no. This can't be happening. You're not Eddie Finger, are you?"

But Eddie didn't, or couldn't, stop pretending. Naturally, then, she couldn't either. He told himself that she didn't want to be recognized. Why else would she have changed her look? She actually did look different. Time passed. Then it was too late. It was impossible to stop pretending. Too much was invested in the lie, the black hole of their romance into which everything was sucked. He thinks she knew he knew she knew he knew. He couldn't go on with it. There was too much not to say. He stopped seeing her. "She waits for me in hell," he says. "We'll discuss it then. But she'll have changed her hair, you know what I mean?"

Breakfast with Henry near campus. A strange woman joined us at the table. She smoked my cigarettes and took my change for her coffee. In her purse she had a fold of bills compressed by a hair clip. "My tuition fee," she said. Henry smiled and carried on as if she weren't there. He refused to be inhibited in our conversation. He said one of his colleagues felt happy when he turned fifty because he no longer desired the pretty coeds. He would concentrate on biochemistry, get a lot of work done, not waste time fucking his brains out. Henry laughed. He didn't believe in this lust for biochemistry. The woman, pretending to study for a German class, looked up from her grammar and said, "I will learn every word."

It was cold, windy, beginning to rain. Deborah was afraid she wouldn't find a taxi. She'd have to walk for blocks in the rain. She didn't want to go, but her psychotherapist wasn't charging her anything. A few months back, she told him she couldn't afford to continue. He lowered the rate to half. Even that became too much for her, so he lowered it to nothing. She stood, collected her things, and pulled on her coat like a kid taking orders from her mother, then fussed with her purse, her scarf, trying to be efficient but making dozens of extra little moves, rebuttoning, untying and retying her scarf, and then reopening her purse to be sure there was enough money for a taxi if she could find one. She wanted to stay, talk some more, but couldn't not go to her psychotherapist. She felt he really needed her.

Sonny says, "The woman can't understand any experience not her own. She's Irish." She didn't mean because she's Irish. She meant thin, practical, cold. She meant not like herself, dark and warm. She meant blond. In effect, the way people talk is what they mean. It is precise and clear—more than mathematics, legal language, or philosophy—and it is not only what they mean, but also all they mean. That's what it means to mean. Everything else is alienation, except poetry.

Sonny has green eyes. I can't not see them.

Sonny's teeth are crooked. I can't not desire to lick them.

I think of Sonny's terrible flaws. I love her flaws.

I'm so furious at Sonny I almost hate her.

———————

I told Sonny I love her. She said, "I'm a sucker for love."

Sonny strides toward me across the room holding something behind her back. Her face is expressionless. Then she raises her hand above her head and I see she is holding her high-heeled shoe. She brings it down, trying to spike the top of my head, but I grab her wrist, wrench her about, shove her away. She falls into the chair and sits as she fell, arms limp, legs sprawled apart. I go to her, drop to my knees, and hug her about the waist. She says, "Intimacy brings out the worst in us," and then whispers, "I want to pull your whole head into my cunt."

We made love all afternoon. Sonny said, "Was it good?" My speech was slurred: "Never in my life . . ." She said, "I should be compensated."

Sonny reads in the paper about a child who was sexually assaulted and murdered. She says quietly, as if to herself, "What are we going to do about sex?"

We made love all afternoon. Sonny asked, "Was it good?" I said, "Never in my life," etc. The irrelevance of words, the happiness of being free of all such clothing. I lie on my back. Dumb. Savoring dumbness. My mother said she found my father on his back on the bedroom floor, staring up at her with a dumb little smile on his face, as if it weren't bad being dead. He'd gone like himself, a sweet gentleman with fine nervous hands, not wanting her to feel distressed. It's a mystery how one learns to speak, the great achievement of a life. But when the soul speaks—alas—it is no longer the soul that speaks.

There used to be a desert here. Now there are banks, office buildings, shopping malls, and wide roads striking in all directions, rolling with cars—going away, going away—pressed by unresisting emptiness. Nothing says stay. Nothing speaks to you, except the statue of John Wayne. I waited in front of the terminal building, studying him. (Sonny was late.) Nine feet tall, cast in brownish metal, he wears a cowboy outfit—wide-brimmed hat, gun belt, boots, spurs. The big body, a smidgeon too big for the head, goes lumbering toward the traffic. Beneath his hat is the familiar sunlight-cutting squint and tight dry scowl. He sees no traffic, no concrete or asphalt. He sees the California desert of long ago, the desert of his mind. No woman was ever late for "Duke."

The afternoon sky was purest blue, without birds or clouds. It was perfect until planes appeared, flickering specks. I'd hear their engines as they descended. It seemed I'd heard dozens of them. I stopped looking at my watch, stopped waiting for her.

Light sank into bluer and bluer blue. Air moved in swift, thin currents, like ghostly fibers drawn across my cheeks. John Wayne's metal face had an underwater glare; eel-like menace. Cars pulled up. Travelers hurried to night flights. She'd been happy to hear from me. "Are you in town?" she cried. Her enthusiasm must have leaked away when she hung up the phone. Maybe she'd checked the mirror and seen something to discourage her; or she'd had an accident driving to the airport. I wasn't thinking about her when the apparition appeared. "I've been looking at you," it said, "standing right here looking at you." Sonny's hair, freshly washed and brushed, released airy strands of light. She shook her head, as if to deny what she couldn't help believing.

"You're very late," I said.

"You can beat me."

"My plane leaves soon."

"Miss your plane."

I already knew I would.

"I didn't come straight from my office," she said. "I had to go home first, shower and dress. Look, I'm here. Aren't you a little happy to see me?" She took my arm, squeezing it as she pressed against my side, saying, "I'm hungry," walking me away toward her car.

We ate in a restaurant near the ocean, then went to a bar. An old black man, wearing glasses, played sentimental songs on the piano.

Sonny said, her hand stroking mine, "Nothing is going to happen. I don't care how sad you look."

"I missed you."

"We never got along." She took a cigarette from my pack and shoved the matchbook toward me.

"I think about you every day."

"What do you think?"

"What do you suppose?"

"Nothing is going to happen. Tell me what you think."

"Making love to you."

"Tell me what you do to me."

"It's hard to say."

"Say it."

Strolling in the balmy night, we stopped and kissed, holding each other long after the urge subsided. The ocean raved in darkness.

"Don't feel me," she said.

"You feel good."

"Men don't turn anymore. I go by and that's all."

"Does it matter?"

"They used to say, 'Wow.' 'Mamma mia.' Of course it matters. It's a way of being."

"It's savage."

"Nothing else is real."

I heard the dull repeated crash along the beach. I smelled the ocean salt on Sonny's skin.

She stood at the bathroom mirror, making up her face. Tiny jars of cosmetics clanked against the sink, like stray notes of a wind chime. I sat on the edge of the tub.

"I hadn't planned to stay," I said.

She didn't answer at first. She unbuttoned her dress, letting the top fall about her hips, not to be soiled by makeup. She wore no bra. Leaning close to the mirror, she did her eyes, restoring shadows with brush and fingertip. I watched her rebuilding her look, perfecting it. She drew back, studying her work as she said, "I don't know why you phoned. Anyhow, I don't care."

"Must you say that?"

"Sad, isn't it? I used to get excited looking at you. But all you ever wanted was to fuck me. Admit it. Come on, be honest." She leaned toward the mirror again, speaking to herself. "It's hard work being beautiful. See this line?"

"What line?"

"This line. It wasn't there last week."

In a minute, she'd be out the door, gone. I imagined the empty motel room. I stood, pressed against her back, my cheek against hers in the mirror. I held her breasts. Her mirrored eyes remained blind to me. She said, "I knew you'd do that."

"I'll stay another day."

Her blind eyes widened, as if to see what I meant.

"I don't want to make you stay. You have your job, your family." Her tone was principled. She tugged up the top of her dress, buttoned it.

"It's what I want."

"I don't want you to do anything you don't want to do."

"We'll sleep late, then go someplace."

"Have a cigarette. We'll talk. You never really talked to me. Then I'll get out of here."

I held her hand, leading her from the mirror. She sat on the edge of the bed, her legs crossed, and watched me with no expression as I kneeled. I took off her shoes. She let me take off her dress—"No, don't . . ."—slowly. Her voice was slithery, labile silk sliding away as she lay back, eyes shut, hands resting on the pillow.

Ocean made its word.

Far far away, John Wayne endured the blaze of traffic.

"Talk," she whispered.

"About what?"

"Why did you phone me?"

"Why did you meet me?"

"What if I didn't love you anymore?"

"I'd die."

"I've been with another man. Are you dying?"

"Tell me."

"He was so handsome he scared me. Do you want to hear?"

"Yes."

"Does it turn you on?"

"I love your pleasure."

"Hold me," she whispered, then slept, her body fused along my side, breathing as I breathed.

Ocean fell along the beach.

I heard the god of night heaving a great sheet and hauling it back, and then heaving it again, trying to make his bed.

stories from
to feel these
things
(1993)
and a girl with a
monkey
(2000)

honeymoon

ONE SUMMER, at a honeymoon resort in the Catskill mountains, I saw a young woman named Sheila Kahn fall in love with her waiter. She had been married a few hours earlier in the city. This was her first night at dinner. The waiter bent beside her and asked if she wanted the steak or the chicken. She stared at him with big sick eyes. Her husband said, "Sheila?" Three other couples at the table, all just married, looked at Sheila as if waiting for the punch line of a joke. She sat like a dummy.

The waiter, Larry Starker, a tall fellow with Nordic cheekbones and an icy gray stare, was considered dangerously handsome. In fact, he'd modeled for the covers of cheap paperbacks, appearing as a Teutonic barbarian about to molest a semi-naked female who lay at his feet, manacled, writhing in terror-pleasure. He'd also appeared chained to a post, watching the approach of a whip-queen in leather regalia. But the real Larry Starker, twenty-two years old, didn't have a clue about exotic sex. He'd completed a year of dental school and hoped to have an office someday in Brighton Beach, where he'd grown up playing handball with the neighborhood guys. Like everyone else on the dining-room staff, he was working to make money for books and tuition.

I was eighteen years old, Larry's busboy. This was my first job in a good resort. The previous three summers, I'd worked in a schlock-house where, aside from heavy meals and a lake with a rowboat, there were few amenities, and the dining-room staff slept two to a bed. Husbands arrived on weekends, set a card table on the lawn, and played pinochle, ignoring the women and children they'd come to visit. My own family used to go to a place like that every summer, and my father was one of the men playing pinochle. He never once took me fishing or hunting, like an

American dad, but then he never went fishing or hunting. The only place he ever took me was to the stonecutter's, one Sunday afternoon, when he ordered his gravestone.

As Larry's busboy, I cleared away dishes, poured coffee, served desserts, then set the tables for the next meal. Between breakfast and lunch, we had an hour break and we all lay about dozing in the bunkhouse or sat on our narrow beds writing letters home. Between lunch and dinner, there was a two-and-a-half-hour break. Some of us slept through the afternoon heat, others spent the time reading, and others played cards, or handball, or basketball, or went swimming. After we worked dinner, nobody wanted to sleep. It was then about 9:00 p.m. We'd taken orders from strangers in the dining room, and chefs had screamed at us from behind a steam table. We should have been exhausted, but the nighttime air smelled good, the starry mountain skies were exhilarating, and we were young.

As we showered and dressed, the fine strain of a flute came through the darkness. It meant the Latin dance band was playing. In clean shirts and sport jackets, we left the bunkhouse, hurrying toward the lights of the casino, where we danced the mambo. Our partners were the young brides. When that became depressing, we took off for another resort and danced with free women, governesses, chambermaids, or guests who were unmarried or whose husbands were in the city.

There may have been waitresses in the Catskill resorts, but I never met one. Since women guests far outnumbered the men, waiters and busboys were universally hired to make up the shortage. At the honeymoon resort there was no shortage, but the dining-room staff was all men, anyway. I don't know why. Maybe the atmosphere of newly married bliss forbade hanky-panky among the help.

Latin music was the rage in the early fifties. You would hear the dining-room staff singing in Spanish: rumbas, mambos, cha-cha-chas. We understood the feeling in the words, not the words. We called Latin music "Jewish." The wailing melodies were reminiscent of Hebraic and Arabic chanting, but we only meant the music was exciting to us. A fusion music, conflating Europe and Africa. In mambo, Spanish passion throbs to Nigerian syncopation. In Yiddish, the German, Hebrew, Spanish, Polish, and English words are assimilated to a culture and a system of sound. The fox-trot and lindy hop we called "American." They had a touch of Nigeria, too, but compared to mambo or Yiddish, they felt like "Jingle Bells."

Handsome Larry Starker, with his straight dark-blond hair and long bones, danced the mambo as well as anyone at the Palladium in Manhattan, great hall of the conga drum, Machito, and Tito Puente. Other dancers made a space when Larry stepped onto the floor. The music welcomed him, horns became more brilliant, congas and *timbales* talked to his belly. He did no fancy steps, but in the least of his motions he was wonderful, displaying the woman who danced in his arms, turning her around and around for the world to see.

Larry gave me 40 percent of his tips, the customary waiter-busboy split. On Sundays after lunch, guests checked out and tipped the waiter six dollars, and the busboy four. Sometimes they put money directly in my hand, but more often they gave it to Larry. We shoved the money into the pockets of our black sweaty trousers. Later, in the bunkhouse, each of us went off alone and pulled out sticky wads by the fistful, peeling away bills, counting as they fluttered to the bed. At the end of the summer, having worked ten-to-fourteen-hour days, sometimes seven days a week, I expected to make between eight and twelve hundred dollars.

I'd have done a little better working with a waiter who didn't have icy eyes and a face like a cliff above the North Sea, beaten by freezing winds. Larry spoke Yiddish and was fluent in the mambo, but he looked like an SS officer. Not a good way to look after World War II, especially in the Catskills, where the shadow of death, extending from millions of corpses in Europe, darkened the consciousness of surviving millions in New York.

Comedians, called *tummlers*, who played the Catskills were even stranger in their effects than Larry. Masters of Jewish self-mockery, they filled casino theaters with a noise never previously heard in the human universe—to my ears, anyway—the happy shrieks of unghosted *yiddim*. "What does not destroy me makes me stronger," says Nietzsche. We laughed. We danced the mambo. Because we weren't dead, we lived.

Entertainers came streaming up from the city—actors, magicians, hypnotists, jugglers, acrobats, impersonators, singers. But with or without entertainment, there was always dancing. After the dancing, we sometimes drove to a late-night Chinese restaurant called Corey's, ate sweet-and-sour spareribs, and listened to a small Latin band. Piano, bass, horn, congas, and a black-haired Latina in a tight red dress who played maracas and sang so beautifully you wanted to die at the table, lips shining with grease, cigarette forgotten, burning your fingers. She played maracas as she sang and danced, taking small steps, her shoulders level, hips subtly swaying to intimate the grandeurs and devastations of love. Pleasure was in the air, day and night.

The newly married couple, Sheila and Morris Kahn, took meals in their honeymoon suite for two days after their embarrassment. Larry said, ironically, "I don't expect them to tip big." I thought they had checked out of the resort and we'd never see them again, but the evening of the third day, they returned to the dining room.

Wearing a bright blue dress and high heels, Sheila looked neat, cool, and invulnerable. She took her seat, greeted everyone at the table, plucked her napkin out of the water glass, where I'd propped it up like a tall white iris, and placed it in her lap. But she didn't make it past the soup. Larry set down her bowl. She stood up clutching the napkin and hurried away. Morris gaped after her, his ears like flames of shame, his cheeks pale. An urgent question struggled to shape his lips, then perished. The blue dress of happiness fled among the tables. Larry muttered, "I didn't do anything," and strode off to the kitchen to pick up the next course. I collected Sheila's soup bowl, contents untasted, and put it out of sight.

Morris lingered through the meal. I heard him talking, in a loud, officious voice, about Hitler. "According to my sources," said Morris, "Hitler isn't dead." Nobody disagreed with his sources. The flight of Sheila, the only subject, wasn't mentioned.

Larry read one book all summer, which was about the mechanics and pathology of the human mouth. Otherwise, he was dedicated to Latin dancing and handball. He took on challengers at handball every week— lifeguards, tennis instructors, waiters, and bellhops—first-class players who often came from resorts miles away. Some referred to him as "the Nazi," even to his face. Catskill resorts weren't polite society, and conversation could be blunt and cruel. To call Larry a Nazi wasn't fair, but he looked the way he looked. It had an alienating effect, despite his Yiddish, despite his being a Jew.

The hard black rubber ball, banging the backboard, sounded like gunfire as Larry annihilated challengers. I didn't root for Larry, because he always won anyway, and I felt sorry for the others. They wanted badly to beat him, as if more than a game and a couple of dollars were at stake. He knew what they felt, men with strength and speedy reflexes who had come from miles away to beat the Nazi. He beat them week after week.

There was another great handball player, "Hairy Murray," also known as "the maniac from Hackensack." He worked the resort circuit as a *tummler*.

He'd challenged Larry, and a date had been set for a game. The odds were usually around ten to one against the challenger, but against Hairy Murray there were no odds. People wanted to see these competitors in the flesh, the way people want to see horses before a race. I assumed Larry would win. He played like the God of Isaiah, an insatiable destroyer. Larry's dancing wasn't altogether different. He moved without a smile or the dopey rictus of ball-room professionals, his body seized by rhythms of the earth. I could live with his inhuman sublimity, and even his good looks, but I couldn't think that I'd ever have Larry's effect on a woman.

I felt envy, a primitive feeling. Also a sin. But go not feel it. According to Melanie Klein, envy is among the foundation stones of Brain House. Nobody is free of it. I believed envy is the chief principle of life: what one man has, another lacks. Sam is smart; hence, you are stupid. Joey is tall; hence, you are a midget. Kill Sam and Joey, you are smart and tall. Such sublogical thoughts applied also to eating. The first two bites satisfy a person's hunger. After that comes eating, which satisfies more than hunger. Seeing hundreds of people eat three times a day in the dining room brought to mind the Yiddish expression "Eating is nothing to sneeze at," which is no joke. Guests looked serious in the dining room, as if they had come to eat what life denied them—power, brains, beauty, love, wealth—in the form of borscht, boiled beef, chopped liver, sour cream, etc. In the bunkhouse at night, falling asleep, I saw hundreds of faces *geshtupt*, like chewing machines in a factory that ingests dreams.

I also saw Sheila's light brown curly hair and her appealing face, with its pointy lips and small, sweet chin, and her nice figure, today called a "body." Like a sculptor's vision, it was nearly palpable, an image in my hands. I remembered her agony, too, how she stood up clutching her napkin, how she seemed transfigured, going from mere appealingness to divinity. She got to me, though she wasn't my type, and I'd have felt nothing, maybe, if she hadn't been deranged by Larry.

The morning after she fled the dining room, Morris Kahn arrived for breakfast alone. He carried the *Times*. It was to suggest that he was an intelligent man, with interests beyond personal life. He opened the *Times* and began to read. Larry approached like a robot waiter, wordless. Not looking up, Morris said, "Scrambled eggs."

Larry spun away, returned with scrambled eggs.

Morris said, "These eggs are cold."

Larry took away the eggs.

Morris said, "Fuck eggs. Bring pancakes."

Larry quick-marched to the kitchen, reappeared with pancakes.

Morris let them get cold, then ordered more.

I stepped forward, took away cold pancakes.

Larry set down warm pancakes.

Morris read his newspaper, ate nothing. Larry's white rayon shirt, gray with sweat, sucked his chest. Hair, pressing up against the rayon, was a dark scribble of lines.

Morris, about thirty years old, maybe ten or twelve years older than Sheila, was almost completely bald, and he had a pink, youthful, placid face that showed no anguish. He ordered pancakes five times. He wanted to make a bad scene, but, like a round-headed dog, he was hopelessly affectionate and at a loss for an appropriate violence. Larry and I sped back and forth, rolling our eyes at each other as we passed, in opposite directions, through the swinging doors of the kitchen. At last Morris was content. He rose and walked out, the *Times* folded under his arm, like one who has completed important business and is at leisure to amble in the sunlight.

That morning, he checked out of the resort with Sheila. At the desk, he left an envelope with Larry's name scrawled across the front. It contained a thirty-five-dollar tip, much more than he'd have left if he'd stayed a week and never missed a meal. The tip was an apology. Had Morris been a Catskill gangster, Larry Starker would have disappeared, dumped in a mountain lake.

In the following weeks, Larry received phone calls from the city, sometimes in the middle of the night. It was no secret who was calling. He stayed long on the phone and never discussed the calls. Sheila had spent only a few days at the resort, and if she and Larry had found moments to talk, nobody noticed. Lovers are sly, making do in circumstances less convenient than the buildings and grounds of a resort in the Catskills.

One afternoon, in the break after lunch, I was lying in my bunk, groggy with fatigue and heat, unable to sleep or to sit up and finish reading *The Stranger*, in which Camus's hero mysteriously murders an Arab, on a blindingly sunny beach in Algiers, and feels no remorse, feels hardly anything else, and has no convictions. A modern believer, I supposed, different from the traditional kind, like Saint Teresa, who draws conviction from feeling. I thought the book couldn't have been written before the Holocaust.

Larry was lying in the bed next to mine. I heard his voice: "What do you say?"

"All right," I answered, hearing my own voice, as I sprawled in stuporous languor after lunch, a dairy meal, which was always the hardest of the day. Guests had to sample everything. Busboy trays became mountains of dirty dishes. The dining room was too warm. The kitchen was hot, and the wooden floors were soft and slick, dangerous when rushing with a heavy tray on your shoulder. The chefs, boiling behind the steam counter, screamed at you for no reason. In the middle of the meal, the dishwasher cut himself on broken glass. He couldn't stop working. More and more dishes were arriving, and there was blood everywhere.

"Then get up."

"Doing it," I said.

I'd agreed to play handball, surprised and flattered by Larry's invitation, never before offered, but my body got up reluctantly, lifting from the clutch of mud. I followed him out of the bunkhouse. He'd brought a ball and two gloves. "You lefty or righty?" he asked. I mumbled, "Righty," as if not sure. He said, "Here. Take both gloves." He didn't really need them, since he could hit killers with his iron-hard, naked hands. In the glare and stillness, the ball boomed off the backboard. As we warmed up, my body returned to itself. I hit a few good shots, then said, "I'm ready." We played one game. Larry beat me by eighteen points. It felt like an insult. He'd slammed the ball unnecessarily on every play. My palms were burning and swollen. Walking back to the bunkhouse, he said, "Sheila Kahn has a sister. Adele. Would you like a date with her? They live in Riverdale."

"Too far."

"I'm talking about later, in the city. Not now, not in the Catskills, moron. She's seventeen, goes to Barnard, a chemistry major. Sheila says Adele is pretty. You and Adele. Me and Sheila. A double date."

"Double-shmubble. I don't have wheels, and I don't want to sit in the subway for an hour and a half to meet a chemist."

"Ever hear of Glock Brothers Manufacturing?"

"No. Go alone."

"I'll pick you up on my way from Brooklyn. You never heard of Glock Manufacturing?"

"You think, if I go with you, it will be easier to face Sheila's parents. Since you ruined her life."

Larry said, "Don't *hock mir a chinek*," which means, "Don't bang me a teakettle," or, without the Yiddish compression, "Don't bug me with empty chatter." He continued: "You don't know shit. You'll never get anywhere."

"Fuck you. I don't like to be used."

"Sheila's father is Herschel Glock."

"Fuck him, too."

"Glock Manufacturing makes airplane parts for Boeing and McDonnell Douglas. Her father owns the company."

"So he's a rich man. So his daughters are rich girls. Big deal."

"I can't talk to you."

"You want to talk to me? Why didn't you tell me?"

To go out with Sheila's sister would have been kicks, but Larry let me score only three points and used me like a dog to retrieve the ball for him so he could hit it again too hard and fast for me. Besides, I had no car and didn't want charity. Who knows what the date would cost? Maybe twenty bucks. It took a week, serving a married couple, to make fifteen. I planned to go alone the next day to the courts and slam the ball till the pain was unbearable. It was near the end of the season, not enough time to improve much, and I'd never beat Larry anyway. But if I could win five points, I'd say I twisted my ankle, and quit in the middle of the game, and never play him again. He wouldn't know for sure if he could beat me. The sunlight was unbearable. And I was too mixed up with feeling to know what I wanted, but I could refuse to go out with Sheila's sister. That was a powerful response, disappointing to Larry and hurtful to me, because I wanted to go with Sheila's sister. In the bunkhouse we flopped on our beds, two feet apart, and lay shining with sweat. I reviewed the game in memory, making myself more depressed and angry. I couldn't stop thinking about it, couldn't relax. Larry said, "Is it raining?"

"It's the sunniest day on record," I said, and my hurt feelings grabbed my voice. "You want to know something, Larry. We're different. We don't look like each other. We don't think like each other. We don't nothing like each other. It's a miracle that we can even speak and understand what's said, either in English or Yiddish."

He groaned.

I glanced at him and saw eyes without pupils, showing only whites. A horrible face, as if he were tortured by my remarks or he'd remembered something extremely important that he hadn't done.

I sat up, saying, "You're making me sick, you freak," then realized he couldn't hear me. He was foaming at the corners of his mouth, and his body was thrashing like a live wire. Foam pinkish with blood streamed down his chin. I shouted for help. Nobody came. I heard voices in the next room. I ran into the next room. A bed was strewn with dollars and quarters and playing cards. Two guys sat on the adjacent bed to the left, facing three on the bed to the right. Nobody noticed me until I brought both fists down on the cards and dollars. Quarters flew up in the air. I shouted, "Larry is having a fit."

They rushed after me into my room. Larry, still thrashing, was sliding up the wall against his back, as if to escape a snake on his mattress. His face was blue. Bloody foam was running down his neck. Someone said, "He's swallowing his tongue. Do something." I saw a comb on the window ledge above Larry's bed and snatched it. Two guys seized Larry's arms and forced him down flat onto the bed. I straddled his chest and pried his mouth open with the edge of the comb, clenching it in my fists at either end. I said, "Open, open, open," as I forced the edge of the comb between his teeth, trying to press his tongue down. He went limp abruptly. The guys let go of his arms. I slid off his chest. We backed away. His head rolled to one side, then slowly to the other, as if to shake away the seizure. He opened his eyes, seeing, and said, "What?" The word was dim, from far away. I said, "Are you all right, Larry? You had a seizure."

"When?"

I took over his station at dinner, waiting his tables. Busboys came shooting from nearby stations to clear dishes, doing double work. We'd have done the same at breakfast, but he insisted on returning to his station. He made it through the day with no help. That night, in the casino bar, drinking beers, he said he felt fine. He didn't remember the seizure. I described it to him, feeling nervous and guilty, as if I shouldn't be telling him this about himself. He said it had happened before. Only his parents knew.

"I'm worried," he said.

"Of course."

"Hairy Murray the *tummler* is driving up to play handball tomorrow afternoon."

"You're worried about that? Call off the game."

"I'll rip his head off."

"Sure. But not tomorrow."

"I put money down."

"Forfeit. Tell him you're sick. Hairy Murray doesn't need your money. He'll let you keep it."

"He hangs out with hard guys. He won't let me keep one cent. It's a question of honor."

"It's a question of you being sick."

"I can play."

"You want to be king of the little black ball."

"Yeah."

We sat for a while in silence. Then I said, "Because of Sheila?"

"That's over."

"Yesterday you were fixing me up with her sister, the great chemist."

"I phoned Sheila last night. I told her what happened and said to stay out of my life."

"What did she say?"

"She was crying."

"I'm sorry. So why are you playing?"

"I want to win."

"You want to lose."

"If I need a psychiatrist, I'll give you a ring."

"Do that. I'll have you put in a straitjacket. You had a fit right in my face. *El gran mambo.*"

Hairy Murray arrived like a boxer, with an entourage. He was on the short side, with a thick neck, wide and deeply sloping shoulders, and short arms. He wore a white linen suit, white shoes, and sunglasses. He looked tropical. When he stepped out of his Cadillac, he began limping heavily toward the handball court, then, suddenly, he became a blind man, walking in the wrong direction. His entourage, five guys in flashy gabardine slacks, were laughing their heads off. The dining-room and kitchen staff were already in the stands, along with the musicians and a lot of the guests. When people arrived from other resorts, they sat on the grass. Everyone knew about Larry's seizure. It made the game more interesting.

Hairy Murray waved to the crowd, then began to strip. One of the gabardine men held his shorts and sneakers. It was another joke, changing in public. When Hairy Murray dropped his pants, he snapped them back up again instantly. He had no underwear. He pretended to be confused, shamed by his forgetfulness. Everyone had seen his big cock slop free of his pants. Men cheered and booed. Women stared wildly at each other, smiling with disgust. Hairy Murray's entourage, virtually in tears, was laughing as they made a circle around him, shielding him from view while he changed.

Larry ignored the spectacle and warmed up, serving the ball to himself, slamming righty, then lefty. He looked thoughtful, faintly slower. He wouldn't even glance at Hairy Murray, whose legs, arms, back, and neck were covered with black hair. A gold Star of David, on a fine gold chain, floated on the black sea of chest hair. I thought maybe he would beat Larry. A man couldn't have so much hair without being exceptionally gifted. His arms were stumpy but looked powerful. The question was, could he move fast? Larry's hope was to hit wide angles, make Hairy Murray chase the ball.

The coin was tossed. Larry called tails. It came down tails. Hairy Murray quit joking, took his position on the court, and braced to receive the first serve, a tremendous boom off the board, speeding back low and at a wide angle to the left sideline. Hairy Murray was after it with a blur of short steps. He sent the ball back with the least flick of his left wrist, a soft, high lob. Larry went drifting to the end line, where he returned hard, but no slam was possible. They played even for seventeen points. Neither was clearly superior. Then Hairy Murray served, won four straight points, and the game was over. There wasn't a sound from the stands and nobody moved to pay off bets. Hairy Murray said, "Double or nothing?"

Larry shrugged. "I don't think so."

"I'll spot you the four points you lost and triple the bet."

"Thanks, no."

"You don't have the cash?"

"Not today."

"You'll owe me."

"You want to play me that bad?"

"I want to kill you." He said this smiling.

Larry looked vague, as if he didn't remember he was a Teutonic barbarian, handball ace, mambo genius, future dentist, and the man Sheila Kahn had been smitten by so hard it ruined her life. I wanted to go to the bunkhouse, go to sleep. Seeing him like this was a kind of betrayal. Nameless, creepy feelings swarmed about my heart. I wished I could shoot him and put an end to my feelings. I wished he would say goodbye, go. He couldn't say anything, and couldn't go. He bounced the ball, caught it, bounced it. Hairy Murray put his hands on his hips, waiting, patience and contempt in his posture.

Then another man walked out on the court. A bald man, so much the opposite of Hairy Murray, he looked like his taller brother. It was Morris Kahn. I hadn't noticed him arrive. "Take the bet," he said. "I'll cover it." Morris looked haggard, with dark, puffy crescents under his eyes.

Hairy Murray said, "Hey, Starker, you hear this cat?"

"I don't want to lose your money," said Larry to Morris.

"So don't lose it." Morris's voice was quick and definitive. "Do you think I drove up here, two hours from the city, to see a loser?"

Hairy Murray, grinning, said, "Four points, kid. Beat me." He twitched faintly, enough to suggest epilepsy, then grinned, holding his hands out, palms up, to suggest no harm intended. Morris said, *"Chazzer fisl kosher,"* meaning, more or less, Hairy Murray is a pig showing us clean little feet. Hairy Murray laughed, exhibiting every tooth and a flare of crimson gums. In his thickness and vigor, he was pleased; didn't feel injured. Smiling at Larry, he said, "What's shaking, baby? You'll take a four-point spot?"

He looked at Morris; said nothing.

"A four-point spot is for losers," said Morris. "Larry plays even. Double or nothing." Morris reached into his pants pocket, came up with a quarter, tossed it high, and said, "Call, Larry." The coin hit the ground and rolled away too far to make out how it landed. Hairy Murray looked at Larry and said, "*Nu*, boychick, you call it, or I'll call it."

Larry said, "Tails." I heard a sort of keening in his voice, high and miserable. It came from neither fear nor defiance, but, like the wind of Golgotha, from desolation. In that instant, I knew the difference between winners and losers has no relation to talent or beauty or personal will, what athletes call "desire," but only to a will beyond ourselves. Larry had just established his connection to it. If I weren't exceedingly frugal, I'd have bet every cent I made that summer on Larry. He slipped off his wristwatch and T-shirt, handed them to me, then returned to the court. His eyes were lonely, remotely seeing, unlike the blind man a day ago, torso electrified and thrashing. Charged with cold control, he looked grim and invincible. I wasn't the only one who felt it. People were making new bets even before the first serve. Hairy Murray took in the change. He chuckled, as if he'd thought of something funny but decided not to say it. I think he felt fear. Between himself and Larry, the air had become glass. Hairy Murray would play against himself, his limits.

Morris went to the coin to see how it lay. He said, "Larry serves." Morris then picked up the coin and walked off the court, returning to the stands, where he'd left his newspaper. He began reading as he had that morning in the dining room. The moments of the game were of no concern.

Larry bent low to serve. His long naked arm swept back, then flashed forward. He slapped the ball, and it boomed off the wood face of the backboard. Hairy Murray returned boom for boom. Larry then hit a killer. Murray couldn't return it without tearing his knuckles on the concrete. He let it go. Larry served again, stronger, faster. Near the end of the game, Morris looked up from his newspaper. There was no excitement in his eyes and hardly much interest. He looked back at the newspaper, its bad news. From the way his shoulders slumped, I felt his resignation. Larry won by eleven points. People were counting money, passing it back and forth. Morris put the paper down. His expression was tired and neither pleased nor displeased. He rose and walked toward Larry.

What Morris and Sheila had said to each other can't be known, but I imagined fifty conversations, how Sheila called Morris after Larry told her to stay out of his life, how she cried. It was inconceivable that she had asked Morris to help her with Larry, but I knew she had. Morris must have loved her a lot. In his pain and disappointment, he drove up from the city to talk to Larry and heard about the game. Afterward, he and Larry walked away together. Morris's round, youthful face was turned toward Larry. Larry stared at the ground. Their conversation was brief. Morris extended his hand. Larry extended his. I didn't want to watch them and walked away to the bunkhouse, carrying Larry's T-shirt bunched up in my fist with the watch.

A few days later, the season ended, and the dining-room staff went home. I didn't go out on any double dates with Larry. I didn't see him again until three summers later. I'd been promoted to waiter at the honeymoon resort. Larry appeared in the casino bar one night, drinking alone. He wore a dark blue suit, white-on-white shirt with sapphire-studded cuff links, and a yellow silk tie. He looked elegant as a gangster. In his chest and face, he was slightly heavier. "Larry Starker," I said. He looked at me without a word as he shook my hand, offering only a little smile, as if he were remembering his opinion of me.

"Sigmund Freud, right?"

The hotel *tummler*, master of ceremonies at the resort, thrust between us before we could talk, slapping Larry on the shoulder, saying, "Let's go, Doctor. Where's the wife?" Walking away, Larry glanced at me and said, "Hang around. Come backstage later." Then the *tummler* was onstage, introducing a dance team. They had won a Latin dance contest in Brooklyn and were touring the Catskills. "Larry, the dentist, and beautiful Sheila. Give these kids a hand."

The first number, a triple mambo, was wild with congas, bongos, and *timbales*. Cowbells were clanging, gidong-gidong-gidong-dong. The beat could make dancers look frantic, but Larry and Sheila were smooth and cool. Him in his dark suit and yellow tie. She in spike heels and a black, supremely elegant cocktail dress. A moment ago, she might have been sipping an exquisitely dry martini. In the stage light, in this music, they were king and queen. I ached with admiration and primitive envy, and applauded madly. Afterward in a room backstage, I shook hands with Larry again, told him he and Sheila were fantastic, and reminded him that I'd once been his busboy.

He said, "I know."

"I'm waiting table now. Our old station."

To my own ears, I sounded a little false, pressing our connection too happily. My feelings were impure. I'd never actually been able to love him as a friend. He introduced me to Sheila, his wife, and said she was almost four months pregnant. It didn't show. She sat in a folding chair, legs crossed, smoking a cigarette.

I said, "Hi."

She said, "Hi."

I didn't feel invited to step closer and shake her hand, but she nodded to me with an empty smile, then looked at Larry. The moment was strangely awkward, nobody saying anything. I felt intrusive. Then Larry said he had his dental degree.

"Not everyone in my class made it. You need hand-eye coordination. Like a fighter pilot. You're always looking in a tiny mirror to see what your hands are doing—in reverse—inside somebody's mouth."

"Are you still playing handball?"

Sheila's father had bought him into an office in Brighton Beach, he said, walking distance to the handball courts, but he didn't play much. He was too busy, too tired at the end of the day. Then he talked about their dance routine.

"We're working a story into it. The man dances in place. He is almost motionless. The woman dances for his pleasure, like she is exhibiting herself. He watches, but still dancing in place. Suspense is building, building, until the woman can't hold back, can't stay away. She goes to him. It's a chase, but different."

He worked himself up as he talked, and began to clap out the clave rhythm—1, 2, 3—1, 2—doing the steps in place, carrying himself like a tall, smooth, arrogant seducer. Sheila, sitting in her chair, watched with no expression until she realized he was seriously involved in the routine and expected her to join him. She said, "Aw, Larry. Enough already. I just finished dancing my ass off."

Larry looked good, even when almost motionless; he had the music inside him. He ignored her protest, and kept dancing in place, clapping out the clave sharp and loud, and he raised an eyebrow the least degree, and faintly, he curled his lip. Barbarian lights flashed in his teeth. He said, "Dance, bitch."

Sheila sighed, dropped her cigarette on the floor, looked down, and stepped on it. She looked back up at him with the face of a sweet, pathetic dummy and whimpered, "No."

Larry kept on dancing, clapping out the beat, staring at her. The tension was unbearable. I wanted to say, "I'll see you two do it another time," or, "Leave her alone," but I didn't know if I was looking at a dance routine or real life. As if in a trance, Sheila was then rising from her chair, beginning to move toward Larry, tentatively, moving to the beat in a deliberately broken, mechanical way. She said, "No," once more, but was now very close to him, face to face, then leaning into him, pressing against his chest. He had stopped clapping, and they were pressed flat together from chest to thigh, dancing. There was silence in the room, except for the rhythm of their feet sliding along the floor, perfectly together.

As I watched, gooseflesh swept along my arms, like a breeze across the surface of a Catskill lake. At the bottom of the lake, in the shimmering murk, I made out Larry Starker, ankles chained to cinder blocks, straight blond hair streaming up, wavy in the water, slow as smoke. His arms were flailing at his sides. There was a bullet hole in his forehead.

a girl with a monkey

IN THE SPRING of the year following his divorce, while traveling alone in Germany, Beard fell in love with a young prostitute named Inger and canceled his plans for further travel. They spent two days together, mainly in Beard's room. He took her to restaurants for lunch and dinner. The third day Inger told Beard she needed a break. She had a life before Beard arrived. Now she had only Beard. She reminded him that the city was famous for its cathedral and zoo. "You should go look. There is more to see than Inger Stutz." Besides, she'd neglected her chores, and missed a dental appointment as well as classes in paper restoration at the local museum.

When she mentioned the classes, Beard thought to express interest, ask questions about paper restoration, but he wasn't interested. He said, "You could miss a few more." His tone was glum. He regretted it, but felt justified because she'd hurt his feelings. He'd spent a lot of money on Inger. He deserved better. He wasn't her life, but he'd canceled his plans, and he wouldn't be staying forever. She didn't have to remind him of the cathedral and zoo. Such things had been noted in his travel itinerary by the agent in San Francisco. He also had a travel guide.

Beard had in fact planned to do a lot of sightseeing, but moments after he checked into his hotel there was a knock at the door and he supposed it was a bellhop or chambermaid, and he saw the girl. She was very apologetic and apparently distressed. She'd come to the wrong room. Beard was charmed, not deceived. He invited her in.

Now, the evening of the third day, Beard said, "I don't want to hear about your chores or classes." He would double her fee.

Beard wasn't rich, but he'd inherited money and the court excluded his inheritance from the divorce settlement. It was enough money to let

him be expansive, if not extravagant. He'd quit his job in television production in San Francisco and gone to the travel agent. The trip cost
plenty, but having met Inger and fallen in love, he was certainly getting
value for his money until she said, "Please don't tell me what I could do
or could not do. And it isn't a question of money."

The remark was inconsistent with her profession, even if Inger was
still young, only a semi-pro, but it was the way she said "could," exactly as
Beard had said it, that bothered him. He detected hostility in her imitation, and he was afraid that he'd underestimated Inger, maybe provoked a
distaste for his character that was irredeemable.

He'd merely expressed his feelings, merely been sincere, yet somehow
offended her. Her reaction was unfair. He did not even know what he'd
said that was offensive. Worse yet, he was afraid that he'd established with
Inger the same relations he'd had with his ex-wife. In twenty-five years of
marriage, she'd had many fits of irrational hostility over his most trivial
remarks. Beard could never guess what he might say to make her angry.
Now in another country, in love with another woman—a prostitute, no
less—Beard was caught up in miseries he'd divorced.

The more things change, he thought, they don't.

Inger knew nothing about Beard's marriage, but she'd heard that
one's clients sometimes become attached, and it was hard to get free of
them. Beard was only her fifth client. What troubled her particularly was
that she'd upset Beard more than she might have expected. He sounded
deranged, shouting in the crowded restaurant, "I'll pay double," and slapping the table. How embarrassing. What had the waiter thought? She felt
slightly fearful. "You are a sweet man," she said. "Very generous. Many
women in Germany would be yours for nothing."

"I prefer to pay for you. Can't you understand?"

She understood but shook her head no, astonished and reproachful at
once. "I understand that you are self-indulgent. If I were like you, I would
soon become dissolute. My life would be irregular. I would feed my monkey table scraps instead of monkey food, because it gives me pleasure. She
would then beg every time I sit down at the dinner table. It would be no
good for her or for me."

"I'm not your monkey."

"You think you're more complicated."

Beard was about to smile, but he realized Inger wasn't making a joke.
Her statement was flat and profoundly simple. Beard wasn't sure what she

intended. Maybe she was asking a question. But it seemed she really saw in Beard what she saw in her monkey, as if all sentient beings were equivalent. She put him in mind of Saint Francis of Assisi.

As had happened several times during his acquaintance with Inger, he was overcome by a sort of mawkish adoration. His eyes glistened. He'd never felt this way about a woman. Spiritual love. At the same time, he had a powerful desire to ravish her. Of course he'd done that repeatedly in the hotel room, in the bed and on the floor, and each time his desire had been satisfied, yet it remained undiminished, unsatisfied.

"Well, what are you, then?" she asked softly.

Beard, surprising himself, said, "I'm a Jew." With a rush of strong and important feeling, it struck him that he was indeed a Jew.

Inger shrugged. "I might have Jewish blood. Who knows about such things?"

Beard had anticipated a more meaningful, more sensitive response. He saw instead, once again, the essential Inger. She was, in her peculiar way, as innocent as a monkey. She had no particular, cultivated sensibility. No idea of history. She was what she was, as if she'd dropped into the world yesterday. A purely objective angelic being. He had her number, he thought. Having her number didn't make him detached. His feelings were no less intense, no less wonderful, and—no other word for it—unsatisfied. She got to him like certain kinds of music. He thought of unaccompanied cello suites.

"Inger," he whispered, "have pity. I'm in love with you."

"Nonsense. I'm not very pretty."

"Yes, you are."

"If that's how you feel . . ."

"It is."

"You feel this now. Later, who knows."

"Could you feel something for me?"

"I'm not indifferent."

"That's all?"

"You may love me."

"Thanks."

"You're welcome. But I think . . ."

"I'm self-indulgent."

"It's a burden for me."

"I'll learn to be good."

"I applaud this decision."

"When can I see you again?"

"You will pay me what you promised?"

"Of course."

She studied his face, as if to absorb a new understanding, and then, with no reservations in her voice, said, "I will go home tonight. You may come for me tomorrow night. You may come upstairs and meet my roommate."

"Must you go home?"

"I dislike washing my underwear in a bathroom sink."

"I'll wash your underwear."

"I have chores, things I have to do at home. You are frightening me."

"I'll call a taxi."

"No. My bicycle is still at the hotel."

The next morning Beard went to a barbershop and then shopped for a new jacket. So much time remained before he could see Inger. In the afternoon he decided to visit the cathedral, a Gothic structure of dark stone. It thrust up suddenly, much taller than the surrounding houses, on a curved, narrow medieval street. Beard walked around the cathedral, looking at saintly figures carved into the stone. Among them he was surprised by a monkey, the small stone face hideously twisted, shrieking. He couldn't imagine what it was doing there, but the whole cathedral was strange, so solemn and alien amid the ordinary houses along the street.

Men in business suits, students in their school uniforms, and housewives carrying sacks of groceries walked by without glancing at the cathedral. None seemed to have any relation to it, but surely they felt otherwise. They lived in this city. The cathedral was an abiding feature of their landscape, stark and austere, yet complicated in its carvings. Beard walked inside. As he entered the nave, he felt reduced, awed by the space. Most of all, he felt lonely. He felt a good deal, but it struck him that he could never understand the power and meaning of the Christian religion. With a jealous and angry God, Jews didn't need such space for worship. A plain room would do. It would even be preferable to a cathedral, more appropriate to their intimate, domestic connection to the deity, someone they had been known to defy and even to fight until, like Jonah, they collapsed into personal innerness, in agonies and joys of sacred delirium.

Walking back to the hotel, he remembered that Inger had talked about her monkey. The memory stirred him, as he had been stirred in the restaurant, with sexual desire. Nothing could be more plain, more real. It thrust against the front of his trousers. He went into a café to sit for a while and pretend to read a newspaper.

That evening in the hotel room, with his fresh haircut and new jacket, he presented himself to the bathroom mirror. He had once been handsome. Qualities of handsomeness remained in his solid, leonine head, but there were dark sacks under his eyes that seemed to carry years of pain and philosophy. They made his expression vaguely lachrymose. "You are growing the face of a hound," he said to his reflection, but he was brave and didn't look away, and he decided he must compensate for his losses. He must buy Inger a present, something new and beautiful, a manifestation of his heart.

In a jewelry store window in the hotel lobby, he noticed a pair of gold earrings set with rubies like tiny globules of blood. Obviously expensive. Much too expensive for his travel budget, but he entered the store and asked what they cost, though he knew it was a mistake to ask. He was right. The price was even higher than he had guessed. It was nearly half of his inheritance. Those earrings plus the cost of the trip would leave him barely enough money to pay his rent in San Francisco, and he didn't have a job waiting for him when he returned.

He left the store and walked about the streets looking in other store windows. Every item that caught his attention was soon diminished by his memory of the swirl of gold and the impassioned red glob within.

Those earrings were too expensive. An infuriating price. It had been determined by a marketing demon, thought Beard, because the earrings now haunted him. He grew increasingly anxious as minutes passed and he continued walking the streets, pointlessly looking into shop windows, unable to forget the earrings.

He was determined not to return to the jewelry store, but then he let himself think: if he returned to the store only to look at the earrings—not to buy them—they would be gone. So it was too late to buy the earrings, he thought, as he hurried back to the store. To his relief, they were still there and more beautiful than he remembered.

The salesperson was a heavily made-up woman in her fifties who wore a black, finely pleated silk dress and gold-rimmed eyeglasses. She approached and stood opposite Beard at the glass counter. He looked down strictly at a necklace, not the earrings, though only a little while ago he'd asked her the price of the earrings. She wasn't fooled. She knew what he wanted. Without being asked, she withdrew the earrings from their case and put them on the counter. Beard considered this highly impertinent, but he didn't object. As if making a casual observation, she said, "I've never seen earrings like these before. I'm sure I'll never see any like these again."

"They're much too expensive."

"Do you think so?" She looked away toward the street, apparently uninterested in his opinion. It was late afternoon, nearly closing time. Her indifference to Beard's remark annoyed him.

"Too expensive," he said, as if he didn't really want the earrings but was inviting her to haggle.

"Should I put them away?" she asked.

Beard didn't answer.

"They are expensive, I suppose," she said. "But prices fluctuate. If you like, I'll keep your business card and phone you if the earrings aren't sold in a few weeks."

Beard heard contempt in her voice, as if she were saying the point of jewelry is to be expensive, even too expensive. He drew his wallet slowly from his jacket pocket, and then, with a thrill of suicidal exultation, he slapped his credit card, not his business card, on the glass beside the earrings. She plucked it up, stepped away, and ran the card through a machine. He signed the receipt quickly to disguise the tremor in his hand.

When he arrived at Inger's apartment house, his heart was beating powerfully. He felt liberated, exceedingly happy, and slightly sick. He planned to take Inger to a fine restaurant. He'd done so before. She'd seemed not the least impressed, but tonight, after dinner, he would give her the earrings. The quality of the light in the restaurant, the delicious food, the wine, the subtle ministrations of the staff—such things matter. The earrings would intensify the occasion. She would be impressed, even if she didn't think precisely like a whore. Besides, it would matter to Beard.

A woman in a short skirt opened the door. She was older than Inger and had cold violet eyes. Her black hair was cut level with her ears and across into severe, straight bangs, emphasizing her hard, thin-lipped expression. She looked somehow damaged and petrified by her beauty. Beard introduced himself. The woman said she was Greta Matti, Inger's roommate, then said, "Inger is gone."

"Impossible."

"It is possible," said Greta, her lips briefly, unpleasantly curled. Beard understood that Greta disliked being contradicted, but he didn't believe her. The woman was malicious.

"She took her monkey," she said. "Please go look for yourself. No clothes in her closet, no suitcase, no bicycle."

Greta turned back into the apartment. Beard entered behind her and looked where she gestured toward a room, and then followed her into it. Closets and drawers were empty. There was nothing, no sign of human presence. Stunned by the emptiness, Beard felt he himself had been emptied.

"You never know a person," said Greta. "She seemed so shy and studious, but she must have done something criminal. I was an idiot to let her move in, a girl with a monkey. Half the time it was I who fed the beast. The telephone never stopped ringing."

Beard followed Greta to the kitchen. A teapot had been set on a small table with a cup and saucer.

"Where did she go?" he said. He didn't expect a positive, useful answer. Who would disappear like that and leave an address? But what else could he say?

"You are not the first to ask. I don't know where she comes from or where she went. Would you like a cup of tea?"

Greta sat at the table and turned slightly toward Beard. She crossed her legs. It was clear that she didn't plan to stand up again to get another cup and saucer, and she seemed merely to assume Beard would stay. Her legs, he couldn't not notice, were long, naked, and strikingly attractive in high heels. He glanced at the white flesh of her inner thigh and felt humbled and uncomfortable.

Greta poured tea for herself without waiting for his answer, and took a sip. Did she think her legs gave him enough? He wanted to ask questions, perhaps learn something about Inger. He knew hardly anything about her.

"I'm sorry," said Greta, softening a little. "Her disappearance is very inconvenient for me. Perhaps it is worse for you."

Beard nodded. "Does Inger owe you money?"

"Technically, I owe her money. She paid a month in advance. I can make another cup of tea."

Beard was inclined to say yes. He needed company, but the whiteness of Greta's legs had become unbearable; repulsively carnal. He couldn't not look at them.

"Thank you," he said. "I must go."

Beard found a phone directory in a bar, looked up the address of the museum, and then hailed a taxi. He'd remembered that Inger took classes in paper restoration. They were given in the evening. At the museum, an administrator told him that Inger had quit the program. Beard next went to the restaurants where they had gone together. He didn't expect to find her in any of them. To his painful disappointment, it was just as he expected. He returned to the hotel. Inger's bicycle was no longer in the lobby, where it had been propped against a wall for two days. Its absence made him feel the bleakness of the marble floor, the sterility of the potted plants beside the desk, the loneliness of hotel lobbies.

In his room, Beard unwrapped the earrings and set them under the lamp on the night table. He studied the earrings with grim fascination, as if to penetrate their allure, the mystery of value. It came to him that, after creating the universe, God saw it was good. "So what is good about it?" Beard asked himself. He smoked cigarette after cigarette, and felt tired and miserable, a condition long associated with thought.

The earrings, shining on the night table, told him nothing. They looked worthless. But it was value—the value of anything aside from life itself—that Beard thought about. As for life itself, he assumed its value was unquestionable because he hadn't ever wanted to kill himself. Not even this minute when he felt so bad. Before he went to sleep, Beard read a train schedule and set the alarm on his travel clock.

At noon he checked out of his hotel, wearing his new jacket, and went to a restaurant where he ordered a grand lunch. He refused to suffer. He ate the lunch assiduously, though without pleasure, and then he took a taxi to the train station. The ticket he bought was first class, another luxurious expense, but he wanted—angrily—to pamper himself, or, as Inger would say, to be "self-indulgent."

As the train pulled out of the station, Beard slid the compartment door shut and settled beside the window with a collection of colorful, expensive magazines that he'd bought in the station. The magazines were full of advertisements for expensive things. Almost every page flared with brilliant color, and they crackled sensuously. They smelled good, too. He stared at pictures of nearly naked models and tried to feel desire. Exactly for what he couldn't say. It wasn't their bodies. Maybe it was for the future, more experience, more life. Then he reached into his jacket pocket to get his cigarettes and the earrings, intending to look at them again and resume his engagement with deep thought. He felt his cigarettes, but the earrings weren't in his pocket. Nor were they in any other pocket.

Beard knew instantly that he needn't bother to search his pockets, which he did repeatedly, because he remembered putting the earrings on the night table and he had no memory of picking them up. Because he hadn't picked them up. He knew. He knew.

As the train left the city and gained speed, he quit searching his pockets. Oh God, why had he bought the earrings? How could he have been so stupid? In an instant of emotional lunacy, he'd slapped his credit card down in the jewelry store and undone himself. The earrings were a curse, in some way even responsible for Inger's disappearance. He had to get hold of himself, think realistically, practically. He had to figure out what to do about retrieving them.

It was urgent that he communicate with the hotel. Perhaps he could send a telegram from the train, or from the next station. He would find a conductor. But really, as he thought further about it, he decided it wasn't urgent to communicate with the hotel. It was a good hotel. This was Germany, not America. Nobody would steal his earrings. They would soon follow him to his destination, another good hotel. They were not gone forever. He had nothing to worry about. This effort to reassure himself brought him almost to tears. He wanted desperately to retrieve the earrings. He stood up and went to the door. About to slide it open and look for a conductor, he heard a knock. He slid the door open with a delirious expectation. The conductor would be there, grinning, the earrings held forth in his open hand. Beard stared into the face of Inger.

"Hello," he said, in a gentle, reproachful voice.

She said, looking at his eyes, her expression bewildered and yet on the verge of recognition, "I'm so sorry. I must have the wrong—" and then she let go of her suitcase and said, *"Gott behüte!"* The suitcase hit the floor with a thud and bumped the side of her leg.

Beard said, "Inger," and he didn't think so much as feel, with an odd little sense of gratification, that she wasn't very pretty. There was a timeless, silent moment in which they stared at each other and his feelings collected. The moment gave Beard a chance to see Inger exactly as she was: a slender, pale girl with pensive gray eyes whose posture was exceptionally straight. She made an impression of neatness, correctness, and youth. In this access of plain reality, he felt no anger and no concern for the earrings. As he could now see, they would look absurd on the colorless Inger. He felt only that his heart was breaking, and there was nothing he could do about it.

With a slow, uncertain smile, Inger said, "How are you?"

Beard picked up her suitcase. "You always travel first class?"

"Not always."

"It depends on the gentleman who answers the door."

"I'm very pretty," she said, her tone sweet and tentative and faintly self-mocking.

"Also lucky."

"I don't think so."

"I'm sure of it."

He put her suitcase onto the seat strewn with magazines. Then he took her hand, drew her toward him, and slid the door shut behind her. She said, "Please. Do give me a moment," but she didn't resist when he pressed her to the floor, his knee between her thighs. Her gray eyes were noncommittal and vast as the world. Beard raised up on his knees to undo his trousers and then he removed Inger's sandals. He kissed her feet and proceeded to lick her legs and slide her skirt to her hips. Then he hooked the crotch of her underpants with an index finger and drew them to the side and he licked her until she seized his hair with her fists and pulled him up, needing him inside as much as he needed her. He whispered, "I love you," his mouth against her neck, and he shut his eyes in a trance of pleasure and thrust into her, in her clothes, as the train pressed steadily into a mute and darkening countryside.

tell me everything

CLAUDE RUE had a wide face with yellowish green eyes and a long aristocratic nose. The mouth was a line, pointed in the center, lifted slightly at the ends, curving in a faint smile, almost cruelly sensual. He dragged his right foot like a stone, and used a cane, digging it into the floor as he walked. His dark blue suit, cut in the French style, armholes up near the neck, made him look small in the shoulder, and made his head look too big. I liked nothing about the man that I could see.

"What a face," I whispered to Margaret. "Who would take anything he says seriously?"

She said, "Who wouldn't? Gorgeous. Just gorgeous. And the way he dresses. Such style."

After that, I didn't say much. I hadn't really wanted to go to the lecture in the first place.

Every seat in the auditorium was taken long before Rue appeared onstage. People must have come in from San Francisco, Oakland, Marin, and beyond. There were even sad creatures from the Berkeley streets, some loonies among them, in filthy clothes, open sores on their faces like badges. I supposed few in the audience knew that Claude Rue was a professor of Chinese history who taught at the Sorbonne, but everyone knew he'd written *The Mists of Shanghai*, a thousand-page, best-selling novel.

Onstage, Rue looked lonely and baffled. Did all these people actually care to hear his lecture on the loss of classical Chinese? He glanced about, as if there had been a mistake and he was searching for his replacement, the star of the show, the real Claude Rue. I approved of his modesty, and I might have enjoyed listening to him. But then, as if seized by an irrational impulse, Rue lifted the pages of his lecture for all to witness, and ripped them in half. "I will speak from my heart," he said.

The crowd gasped. I groaned. Margaret leaned toward him, straining, as if to pick up his odor. She squeezed my hand and checked my eyes to see whether I understood her feelings. She needed a reference point, a consciousness aside from her own to slow the rush of her being toward Rue.

"You're terrible," I said.

"Don't spoil my fantasy. Be quiet, O.K.?"

She then flattened her thigh against mine, holding me there while she joined him in her feelings, onstage, fifty feet away. Rue began his speech without pages or notes. The crowd grew still. Many who couldn't find seats stood in the aisles, some with bowed heads, staring at the floor as if they'd been beaten on the shoulders into penitential silence. For me it was also penitential. I work nights. I didn't like wasting a free evening in a crowded lecture hall when I could have been alone with Margaret.

I showed up at her loft an hour before the lecture. She said to her face in the bathroom mirror, "I can hardly wait to see the man. How do I look?"

"Chinese." I put the lid down on the toilet seat, sat on it.

"Answer me. Do I look all right, Herman?"

"You know what the ancient Greeks said about perfume?"

"I'm about to find out."

"To smell sweet is to stink."

"I use very little perfume. There's a reception afterward, a party. It's in honor of the novel. A thousand pages and I could have kept reading it for another week. I didn't want it to end. I'll tell you the story later."

"Maybe I'll read it, too," I said, trying not to sound the way I felt. "But why must you see what the man looks like? I couldn't care less."

"You won't go with me?" She turned from the mirror, as if, at last, I'd provoked her into full attention.

"I'm not saying I won't."

"What are you saying?"

"Nothing. I asked a question, that's all. It isn't important. Forget it."

"Don't slither. You have another plan for the evening? You'd rather go somewhere else?"

"I have no other plan. I'm asking why should anyone care what an author looks like."

"I'm interested. I have been for months."

"Why?"

"Why not? He made me feel something. His book was an experience. Everybody wants to see him. Besides, my sister met him in Beijing. She knows him. Didn't I read you her letter?"

"I still don't see why . . ."

"Herman, what do you want me to say? I'm interested, I'm curious. I'm going to his lecture. If you don't want to go, don't go."

That is, leave the bathroom. Shut the door. Get out of sight.

Margaret can be too abrupt, too decisive. It's her business style carried into personal life. She buys buildings, has them fixed up, then rents or sells, and buys again. She has supported herself this way since her divorce from Sloan Pierson, professor of linguistics. He told her about Claude Rue's lecture, invited her to the reception, and put my name on the guest list. Their divorce, compared to some, wasn't bad. No lingering bitterness. They have remained connected—not quite friends—through small courtesies, like the invitation; also, of course, through their daughter, Gracie, ten years old. She lives with Sloan except when Margaret wants her, which is often. Margaret's business doesn't allow a strict schedule. She appears at Sloan's door without notice. "I need her," she says. Gracie scampers to her room, collects schoolbooks for the next day, and packs a duffel bag with clothes and woolly animals.

Sloan sighs, shakes his head. "Really, Margaret. Gracie has needs, too. She needs a predictable daily life." Margaret says, "I'll phone you later. We'll discuss our needs."

She comes out of the house with Gracie. Sloan shouts, "Wait. Gracie's pills."

There's always one more word, one more thing to collect. "Goodbye. Wait." I wait. We all wait. Margaret and Gracie go back into the house, and I stand outside. I'm uncomfortable inside the house, around Sloan. He's friendly, but I know too much about him. I can't help thinking things, making judgments, and then I feel guilty. He's a fussy type, does everything right. If he'd only fight Margaret, not be so good, so correct. Sloan could make trouble about Margaret's unscheduled appearances, even go to court, but he thinks if Margaret doesn't have her way, Gracie will have no mother. Above all things, Sloan fears chaos. Gracie senses her daddy's fear, shares it. Margaret would die for Gracie, but it's a difficult love, measured by intensities. Would Margaret remember, in such love, about the pills?

Sloan finds the pills, brings them to the foyer, hands them to Margaret. There. He did another correct thing. She and Gracie leave the house. We start down the path to the sidewalk. Gracie hands me her books and duffel bag, gives me a kiss, and says, "Hi, Herman German. I have an ear infection. I have to take pills four times a day." She's instructing Margaret, indirectly.

Margaret glares at me to show that she's angry. Her ten-year-old giving her instructions. I pretend not to notice. Gracie is a little version of Margaret, not much like Sloan. Chinese chemistry is dominant. Sloan thinks Gracie is lucky. "That's what I call a face," he says. He thinks he looks like his name—much too white.

I say, "Hi, Gracie Spacey." We get into my Volvo. I drive us away.

Gracie sits back. Margaret, sitting beside me, stares straight ahead, silent, still pissed, but after a while she turns, looks at Gracie. Gracie reads her mind, gives her a hug. Margaret feels better, everyone feels better.

While Margaret's houses are being fixed up, she lives in one, part of which becomes her studio, where she does her painting. Years ago, at the university, studying with the wonderful painters Joan Brown and Elmer Bischoff, Margaret never discovered a serious commitment in herself. Later, when she married and had Gracie, and her time was limited, seriousness arrived. Then came the divorce, the real estate business, and she had even less time. She paints whenever she can, and she reads fifty or sixty novels a year; also what she calls "philosophy," which is religious literature. Her imagery in paintings comes from mythic, visionary works. From the Kumulipo, the Hawaiian cosmological chant, she took visions of land and sea, where creatures of the different realms are mysteriously related. Margaret doesn't own a television set or go to movies. She denies herself common entertainment for the same reason that Rilke refused to be analyzed by Freud. "I don't want my soul diluted," she says.

Sometimes, I sit with her in her loft in Emeryville—in a four-story brick building, her latest purchase—while she paints. "Are you bored?" she asks.

I'm never bored, I like being with her. I like the painting odors, the drag and scratch of brush against canvas. She applies color, I feel it in my eyes. Tingling starts along my forearms, hairs lift and stiffen. We don't talk. Sometimes not a word for hours, yet the time lacks nothing.

I say, "Let's get married."

She says, "We are married."

Another hour goes by.

She asks, "Is that a painting?"

I make a sound to suggest that it is.

"Is it good?"

She knows.

When one of her paintings, hanging in a corner of a New York gallery owned by a friend, sold—without a formal show, and without reviews—I became upset. She'll soon be famous, I thought.

"I'll lose you," I said.

She gave me nine paintings, all she had in the loft. "Take this one, this one, this one . . ."

"Why?"

"Take them, take them."

She wanted to prove, maybe, that our friendship was inviolable; she had no ambition to succeed, only to be good. I took the paintings grudgingly, as if I were doing her a favor. In fact, that's how I felt. I was doing her a favor. But I wanted the paintings. They were compensation for her future disappearance from my life. We're best friends, very close. I have no vocation. She owed me the paintings.

I quit graduate school twenty years ago, and began waiting tables at Gemma's, a San Francisco restaurant. From year to year, I expected to find other work or to write professionally. My one book, *Local Greens*, which is about salads, was published by a small press in San Francisco. Not a best-seller, but it made money. Margaret told me to invest in a condominium and she found one for me, the top floor of a brown-shingle house, architect unknown, in the Berkeley hills. I'd been living in Oakland, in a one-room apartment on Harrison Street, near the freeway. I have a sedentary nature. I'd never have moved out. Never really have known, if not for Margaret, that I could have a nicer place, be happier. "I'm happy," I said. "This place is fine." She said my room was squalid. She said the street was noisy and dangerous. She insisted that I talk to a realtor or check the newspapers for another place, exert myself, do something. Suddenly, it seemed, I had two bedrooms, living room, new kitchen, hardwood floors, a deck, a bay view, monthly payments—property.

It didn't seem. I actually lived in a new place, nicer than anything I'd ever known.

My partner, so to speak, lives downstairs. Eighty-year-old Belinda Forster. She gardens once a week by instructing Pilar, a silent Mexican woman who lives with Belinda, where to put the different new plants, where to prune the apple trees. Belinda also lunches with a church group, reviews her will, smokes cigarettes. She told me, if I find her unconscious in the garden, or in the driveway, or wherever, to do nothing to revive her. She looks not very shrunken, not extremely frail. Her eyes are beautifully clear. Her skin is without the soft, puffy surface you often see in old people.

Belinda's husband, a professor of plant pathology, died about fifteen years ago, shortly after his retirement. Belinda talks about his work, their travels in Asia, and his mother. Not a word about herself. She might consider that impolite, or boastful, claiming she, too, had a life, or a self. She has qualities of reserve, much out of style these days, that I admire greatly, but I become awkward talking to her. I don't quite feel that I say what I mean. Does she intend this effect? Is she protecting herself against the assertions, the assault, of younger energies?

Upstairs, from the deck of my apartment, I see sailboats tilted in the wind. Oil tankers go sliding slowly by Alcatraz Island. Hovering in the fuchsias there are hummingbirds. Squirrels fly through the black, light-streaked canopies of Monterey pines. If my temperament were religious, I'd believe there had to be a cause, a divinity in the fantastic theater of clouds above San Francisco Bay.

Rue spoke with urgency, his head and upper body lifting and settling to the rhythm of his sentences. His straight blond hair, combed straight back, fell toward his eyes. He swept it aside. It fell. He swept it aside, a bravely feminine gesture, vain, distracting. I sighed.

Margaret pinched my elbow. "I want to hear him, not your opinions."

"I only sighed."

"That's an opinion."

I sat quietly. Rue carried on. His subject was the loss to the Chinese people, and to the world, of the classical Chinese language. "I am saying that, after the revolution, the ancients, the great Chinese dead, were torn from their graves. I am saying they have been murdered word by word. And this in the name of nationhood, and a social justice which annihilates language, as well as justice, and anything the world has known as social."

End.

The image of ancient corpses, torn from their graves and murdered, aroused loonies in the audience. They whistled and cried out. Others applauded for a whole minute. Rue had said nothing subversive of America. Even so, Berkeley adored him. Really because of the novel, not the lecture. On the way to the lecture, Margaret talked about the novel, giving me the whole story, not merely the gist, as if to defend it against my negative opinion. She was also apologizing, I think, by talking so much, for having been angry and abrupt earlier. Couldn't just say "I'm sorry." Not Margaret. I drove and said nothing, still slightly injured, but soothed by her voice, giving me the story; giving a good deal, really, more than the story.

She said, *The Mists of Shanghai* takes place in nineteenth-century China during the opium wars, when low-quality opium, harvested from British poppy fields in India, was thrust upon the Chinese people. "Isn't that interesting?" she said. "A novel should teach you something. I learned that the production, transportation, and distribution of opium, just as today, was controlled by Western military and intelligence agencies, there were black slaves in Macao, and eunuchs were very powerful figures in government."

The central story of the novel, said Margaret, which is told by an evil eunuch named Jujuzi, who is an addict and a dealer, is about two lovers— a woman named Neiping and a man named Goo. First we hear about Neiping's childhood. She is the youngest in a large, very poor family. Her parents sell her to an elegant brothel in Shanghai, where the madam buys little girls, selected for brains and beauty. She tells Neiping that she will be taught to read, and eventually, she will participate in conversation with patrons. Though only eight years old, Neiping has a strong character, learns quickly, and becomes psychologically mature. One day a new girl arrives and refuses to talk to anyone. She cries quietly to herself at night. Neiping listens to her crying and begins to feel sorry for herself. But she refuses to cry. She leaves her bed and crawls into bed with the crying girl, who then grows quiet. Neiping hugs her and says, "I am Neiping. What's your name?"

She says, "Dulu."

They talk for hours until they both fall asleep. She and Neiping become dear friends.

It happens that a man named Kang, a longtime patron of the brothel, arrives one evening. He is a Shanghai businessman, dealing in Mexican silver. He also owns an ironworks, and has initiated a lucrative trade in persons, sending laborers to a hellish life in the cane fields of the Pacific Islands and Cuba. Kang confesses to the madam that he is very unhappy. He can't find anyone to replace his recently deceased wife as his opponent in the ancient game of *wei-ch'i*. The madam tells Kang not to be unhappy. She has purchased a clever girl who will make a good replacement. Kang can come to the brothel and play *wei-ch'i*. She brings little Neiping into the room, sits her at a table with Kang, a playing board between them. Kang has a blind eye that looks smoky and gray. He is unashamedly flatulent, and he is garishly tattooed. All in all, rather a monster. Pretty little Neiping is terrified. She nods yes, yes, yes as he tells her the rules of the game, and he explains how one surrounds the opponent's pieces and holds territory on the board. When he asks if she has understood everything, she nods yes again. He says to Neiping, "If you lose, I will eat you the way a snake eats a monkey."

Margaret said, "This is supposed to be a little joke, see? But, since Kang looks sort of like a snake, it's frightening."

Kang takes the black stones and makes the first move. Neiping, in a trance of fear, recalls his explanation of the rules, then places a white stone on the board far from his black stone. They play until Kang becomes sleepy. He goes home. The game resumes the next night and the next. In the end, Kang counts the captured stones, white and black. It appears that Neiping has captured more than he. The madam says, "Let me count them." It also appears that Neiping controls more territory than Kang. The madam counts, then looks almost frightened. She twitters apologies, and she coos, begging Kang to forgive Neiping for taking advantage of his kindness, his willingness to let Neiping seem to have done well in the first game. Kang says, "This is how it was with my wife. Sometimes she seemed to win. I will buy this girl."

The madam had been saving Neiping for a courtier, highly placed, close to the emperor, but Kang is a powerful man. She doesn't dare reject the sale. "The potential value of Neiping is immeasurable," she says. Kang says Neiping will cost a great deal before she returns a profit. "The price I am willing to pay is exceptionally good."

The madam says, "In silver?"

Kang says, "Mexican coins."

She bows to Kang, then tells Neiping to say goodbye to the other girls.

Margaret says, "I'll never forget how the madam bows to Kang."

Neiping and Dulu embrace. Dulu cries. Neiping says they will meet again someday. Neiping returns to Kang. He takes her hand. The monster and Neiping walk through the nighttime streets of Shanghai to Kang's house.

For the next seven years, Neiping plays *wei-ch'i* with Kang. He has her educated by monks, and she is taught to play musical instruments by the evil eunuch Jujuzi, the one who is telling the story. Kang gives Neiping privileges of a daughter. She learns how he runs his businesses. He discusses problems with her. "If somebody were in my position, how might such a person reflect on the matters I have described?" While they talk, Kang asks Neiping to comb his hair. He never touches her. His manner is formal and gentle. He gives everything. Neiping asks for nothing. Kang is a happy monster, but then Neiping falls in love with Goo, the son of a business associate of Kang. Kang discovers this love and he threatens to undo Neiping, sell her back to the brothel, or send her to work in the cane fields at the end of the world. Neiping flees Kang's house that night with Goo. Kang wanders the streets of Shanghai in a stupor of misery, looking for Neiping.

Years pass. Unable to find a way to live, Goo and Neiping fall in with a guerrilla triad. Neiping becomes its leader. Inspired by Neiping, who'd become expert in metals while living with Kang, the triad undertakes to study British war technology. Neiping says they can produce cannons, which could be used against opium merchants. The emperor will be pleased. In fact, he will someday have tons of opium seized and destroyed. But there is no way to approach the emperor until Neiping learns that Dulu, her dear friend in the brothel, is now the emperor's consort. Neiping goes to Dulu.

"The recognition scene," said Margaret, "is heartbreaking. Dulu has become an icy woman who moves slowly beneath layers of silk. But she remembers herself as the little girl who once cried in the arms of Neiping. She and Neiping are now about twenty-three."

Through Dulu's help, Neiping gains the emperor's support. This enrages Jujuzi, the evil eunuch. Opium trade is in his interest, since he is an addict and a dealer. Everything is threatened by Neiping's cannons, which are superior to the originals, but the triad's military strategy is betrayed by Jujuzi. Neiping and Goo are captured by British sailors and jailed.

Margaret said, "Guess what happens next. Kang appears. He has vanished for three hundred pages, but he's back in the action."

The British allow Kang to speak to Neiping. He offers to buy her freedom. Neiping says he must also buy Goo's freedom. Kang says she has no right to ask him to buy her lover's freedom. Neiping accepts Kang's offer, and she is freed from jail. She then goes to Dulu and appeals for the emperor's help in freeing Goo. Jujuzi, frustrated by Neiping's escape, demands justice for Goo. The British, who are in debt to Jujuzi, look the other way while he tortures Goo to death.

The emperor, who has heard Neiping's appeal through Dulu, asks to see Neiping. The emperor knows Goo is dead. He was told by Jujuzi. But the emperor is moved by Neiping's beauty and her poignant concern to save the already dead Goo. The emperor tells her that he will save him, but she must forget Goo. Then he says that Neiping, like Dulu, will be his consort. In the final chapter, Neiping is heavy with the emperor's child. She and Dulu wander in the palace gardens. Jujuzi watches the lovely consorts passing amid flowers, and he remembers in slow, microscopic detail the execution of Neiping's lover.

"What a story."

"I left most of it out."

"Is that so?"

"You think it's boring."

"No."

"You do."

"Don't tell me what I think. That's annoying."

"Do you think it's boring?"

"Yes, but how can I know unless I read the book?"

"Well, I liked it a lot. The last chapter is horribly dazzling and so beautiful. Jujuzi watches Neiping and Dulu stroll in the garden, and he remembers Goo in chains, bleeding from the hundred knives Jujuzi stuck in him. To Jujuzi, everything is aesthetic, knives, consorts, even feelings. He has no balls so he collects feelings. You see? Like jewels in a box."

Lights went up in the midst of the applause. Margaret said, "Aren't you glad you came?" Claude Rue bowed. Waves of praise poured onto his head. I applauded, too, a concession to the community. Besides, Margaret loved the lecture. She watched me from the corners of her eyes, suspicious of my enthusiasm. I nodded, as if to say yes, yes. Mainly, I needed to go to the toilet, but I didn't want to do anything that might look like a negative comment on the lecture. I'd go when we arrived at the reception for Rue. This decision was fateful. At the reception, in the Faculty Club, I carried a glass of white wine from the bar to Margaret, then went to the men's room. I stood beside a man who had leaned his cane against the urinal. He patted his straight blond hair with one hand, holding his cock with the other, shaking it. The man was, I suddenly realized, himself, Claude Rue. Surprised into speech, I said I loved his lecture. He said, "You work here?"

Things now seemed to be happening quickly, making thought impossible. I was unable to answer. Exactly what was Rue asking—was I a professor? a men's room attendant? a toilet cruiser? Not waiting for my answer, he said he'd been promised a certain figure for the lecture. A check, made out to him from the regents of the university, had been delivered to his hotel room. The check shocked him. He'd almost canceled the lecture. He was still distressed, unable to contain himself. He'd hurried to the men's room, after the lecture, to look at his check again. The figure was less than promised. I was the first to hear about it. Me. A stranger. He was hysterical, maybe, but I felt very privileged. Money talk is personal, especially in a toilet. "You follow me?" he said.

"Yes. You were promised a certain figure. They gave you a check. It was delivered to your hotel room."

"Precisely. But the figure inscribed on the check is less than promised."

"Somebody made a mistake."

"No mistake. Taxes have been deducted. But I came from Paris with a certain understanding. I was to be paid a certain figure. I have the letter of agreement, and the contract." His green stare, fraught with helpless reproach, held me as he zipped up. He felt that he'd been cheated. He dragged to a sink. His cane, lacquered mahogany, with a black iron ferrule, clacked the tile floor. He washed his hands. Water raged in the sink.

"It's a mistake, and it can be easily corrected," I said, speaking to his face in the mirror above the sink. "Don't worry, Mr. Rue. You'll get every penny they promised."

"Will you speak to somebody?" he said, taking his cane. "I'm very upset."

"Count on it, Mr. Rue."

"But will you speak to somebody about this matter?"

"Before the evening is over, I'll have their attention."

"But will you speak to a person?"

"Definitely."

I could see, standing close to him, that his teeth were heavily stained by cigarette smoke. They looked rotten. I asked if I might introduce him to a friend of mine. Margaret would get a kick out of meeting Claude Rue, I figured, but I mainly wanted her to see his teeth. He seemed thrown off balance, reluctant to meet someone described as a friend. "My time is heavily scheduled," he muttered; but, since he'd just asked me for a favor, he shrugged, shouldering obligation. I led him to Margaret. Rue's green eyes gained brightness. Margaret quickened within, but offered a mere "Hello," no more, not even the wisp of a smile. She didn't say she loved his lecture. Was she overwhelmed, having Claude Rue thrust at her like this? The silence was difficult for me, if not for them. Lacking anything else to say, I started to tell Margaret about Rue's problem with the university check. "It wasn't the promised amount." Rue cut me off:

"Money is offal. Not to be discussed."

His voice was unnaturally high, operatic and crowing at once. He told Margaret, speaking to her eyes—as if I'd ceased to exist—that he would spend the next three days in Berkeley. He was expected at lunches, cocktail parties, and dinner parties. He'd been invited to conduct a seminar, and to address a small gathering at the Asian Art Museum.

"But my lecture is over. I have fulfilled my contract. I owe nothing to anybody."

Margaret said, "No point, then, cheapening yourself, is there?"

"I will cancel every engagement."

"How convenient," she said, hesitated, then gambled, "for us."

Her voice was flat and black as an ice slick on asphalt, but I could hear, beneath the surface, a faint trembling. I prayed that she would look at Rue's teeth, which were practically biting her face. She seemed not to notice.

"Do you drive a car?"

She said, "Yes," holding her hand out to the side, toward me, blindly. I slipped the keys to my Volvo into her palm. Tomorrow, I'd ride to her place on my bike and retrieve the car. Margaret wouldn't remember that she'd taken it. She and Rue walked away, but I felt it was I who grew smaller in the gathering distance. Margaret glanced back at me to say goodbye. Rue, staring at Margaret, lost peripheral vision, thus annihilating me. I might have felt insulted, but he'd been seized by hormonal ferocity, and was focused on a woman. I'd have treated him similarly.

Months earlier, I'd heard about Rue from Margaret. She'd heard about him from her sister May, who had a Ph.D. in library science from Berkeley and worked at the university library in Beijing. In a letter to Margaret, May said she'd met Professor Claude Rue, the linguistic historian. He was known in academic circles, but not yet an international celebrity. Rue was in Beijing completing his research for *The Mists of Shanghai*. May said, in her letter, that Rue was a "womanizer." He had bastard children in France and Tahiti. She didn't find him attractive, but other women might. "If you said Claude Rue is charming or has pretty green eyes, I wouldn't disagree, but as I write to you, I have trouble remembering what he looks like."

Margaret said the word "womanizer" tells more about May than Rue. "She's jealous. She thinks Rue is fucking every woman except her."

"She says she doesn't find him attractive, doesn't even know what he looks like."

"She finds him very attractive, and she knows what he looks like, what he sounds like, smells like, feels like. May has no respect for personal space. She touches people when she talks to them. She's a shark, with taste sensors in her skin. When May takes your hand, or brushes up against you, she's tasting you. Nobody but sharks and cannibals can do that. She shakes somebody's hand, then tells me, 'Needs salt and a little curry.'"

"All right. Maybe 'womanizer' says something about May, but the word has a meaning. Regardless of May, 'womanizer' means something."

"What?"

"You kidding?"

"Tell me. What does it mean?"

"What do you think? It means a man who sits on the side of the bed at two in the morning, putting on his shoes."

"What do you call women who do that? Don't patronize me, Herman. Don't you tell me what 'womanizer' means."

"Why did you ask?"

"To see if you'd tell me. So patronizing. I know exactly what the word means. 'Womanizer' means my sister May wants Claude Rue to fuck her."

"Get a dictionary. I want to see where it mentions your sister and Claude Rue."

"The dictionary is a cemetery of dead words. All words are dead until somebody uses them. 'Womanizer' is dead. If you use it, it lives, uses you."

"Nonsense."

"People once talked about nymphomaniacs, right? Remember that word? Would you ever use it without feeling it said something embarrassing about you? Get real, Herman. Everyone is constantly on the make—even May. Even you."

"Not me."

"Maybe that's because you're old-fashioned, which is to say narrow-minded. Self-righteous. Incapable of seeing yourself. You disappoint me, Herman. You really do. What about famous men who had bastards? Rousseau, Byron, Shelley, Wordsworth, the Earl of Gloucester, Edward VII."

"I don't care who had bastards. That isn't pertinent. You're trying to make a case for bad behavior."

"Rodin, Hegel, Marx, Castro—they all had bastards. If they are all bad, that's pertinent. My uncle Chan wasn't famous, but he had two families. God knows what else he had. Neither family knew of the other until he died. Then it became pertinent, everyone squabbling over property."

"What's your point, if you have one, which I seriously doubt?"

"And what about Kafka, Camus, Sartre, Picasso, Charlie Chaplin, Charlie Parker, J.F.K., M.L.K.? What about Chinese emperors and warlords, Arab sheiks, movie actors, thousands of Mormons? Everybody collects women. That's why there are prostitutes, whores, courtesans, consorts, concubines, bimbos, mistresses, wives, flirts, hussies, sluts, etc., etc. How many words are there for man? Not one equivalent for 'cunt,' which can mean a woman. 'Prick' means some kind of jerk. Look at magazine covers, month after month. They're selling clothes and cosmetics? They sell women, stupid. You know you're stupid. Stupid Herman, that's you."

"They're selling happiness, not women."

"It's the same thing. Lions, monkeys, horses, goats, people . . . many, many, many animals collect women animals. When they stop, they become unhappy and they die. Married men live longer than single men. This has long been true. The truth is the truth. What am I talking about? Hug me, please."

"The truth is, you're madly in love with Claude Rue."

"I've never met the man. Don't depress me."

"Your sister mentions him in a letter, you imagine she wants him. She wants him, you want him. You're in love, you're jealous."

"You're more jealous."

"You admit it? You've never before conceded anything in an argument. I feel like running in the streets, shrieking the news."

"I admit nothing. After reading my sister May's gossipy, puritanical letter, I find that I dislike Claude Rue intensely."

"You never met the man."

"How can that have any bearing on the matter?"

As for the people in the large reception room at the Faculty Club—deans, department heads, assistant professors, students, wives, husbands—gathered to honor Claude Rue—he'd flicked us off like a light. I admired Rue for that, and I wished his plane back to Paris would crash. Behind me, a woman whispered in the exact tone Margaret had used, "I dislike him intensely."

A second woman said, "You know him?"

"Of course not. I've heard things, and his novel is very sexist."

"You read the novel. Good for you."

"I haven't read it. I saw a review in a magazine at my hairdresser's. I have the magazine. I'll look for it tonight when I get home."

"Sexist?" said the first woman. "Odd. I heard he's gay."

"Gay?" said a man. "How interesting. I suppose one can be gay and sexist, but I'd never have guessed he was gay. He looks straight to me. Who told you he's gay? Someone who knows him?"

"Well, not with a capital K, if that's what you mean by 'knows,' but he was told by a friend of Rue's that he agreed to fly here and give this lecture only because of the San Fran bath houses. That's what he was told. Gossip in this town spreads quick as genital warts."

"Ho, ho, ho. People are so dreadfully bored. Can you blame them? They have no lives, just careers and Volvos."

"That's good. I intend to use it. Do look for conversational citations in the near future. But who is the Chinese thing? I'll die if I don't find out. She's somebody, isn't she? Ask him."

"Who?"

"Him, him. That man. He was standing with her." Someone plucked my jacket sleeve. I turned. A face desiccated by propriety leaned close, old eyes, shimmering liquid gray, bulging, rims hanging open like thin crimson labia. It spoke:

"Pardon me, sir. Could you please tell us the name of the Chinese woman who, it now seems, is leaving the reception with Professor Rue?"

"Go fuck yourself."

Margaret said the success of his lecture left Rue giddily deranged, expecting something more palpable from the night. He said, she said, that he couldn't have returned to his hotel room, watched TV, and gone to sleep. "'Why is it like this for me, do you think?'" he said, she said. "'It would have no style. You were loved,'" she said, she said, sensing his need to be reminded of the blatant sycophancy of his herdlike audience. "'Then you appeared,'" he said, she said. "'You were magnificently cold.'"

Voilà! Margaret. She is cold. She is attentive. She is determined to fuck him. He likes her quickness, and her legs. He says that to her. He also likes the way she drives, and her hair—the familiar black Asian kind, but which, because of its dim coppery strain, is rather unusual. He likes her eyes, too. I said, "Margaret, let me: 'Your gray-tinted glasses give a sensuous glow to your sharply tipped Chinese eyes, which are like precious black glittering pebbles washed by the Yangtze. Also the Yalu.'"

Margaret said, "Please shut up, dog-eyed white devil. I'm in no mood for jokes."

Her eyes want never to leave Rue's face, she said, but she must concentrate on the road as she drives. The thing is under way for them. I could feel it as she talked, how she was thrilled by the momentum, the invincible rush, the necessity. Resentment built in my sad heart. I thought, Margaret is over thirty years old. She has been around the block. But it's never enough. Once more around the block, up the stairs, into the room, and there lies happiness.

"'Why shouldn't I have abandoned the party for you?'" he said, she said, imitating his tone, plaintive and arrogant. "'I wrote a novel.'" He laughs at himself. Margaret laughs, imitating him, an ironic self-deprecatory laugh. The moment seemed to her phony and real at once, said Margaret. He was nervous, as he'd been onstage, unsure of his stardom, unconvinced even by the flood of abject adoration. "'Would a man write a novel except for love?'" he said, she said, as if he didn't really know. He was sincerely diffident, she said, an amazing quality considering that he'd slept with every woman in the world. But what the hell, he was human. With Margaret, sex will be more meaningful. "'Except for love?'" she said, she said, gaily, wondering if he'd slept with her sister. "'How about your check from the university?'"

"'You think I'm inconsistent?'" He'd laughed. Spittle shot from his lips and rotten teeth. She saw everything except the trouble, what lay deep in the psychic plasma that rushed between them.

She drove him to her loft, in the warehouse and small factory district of Emeryville, near the bay, where she lived and worked, and bought and sold. Canvases, drawings, clothes—everything was flung about. She apologized.

He said, "'A great disorder is an order.'"

"Did you make that up?"

He kissed her. She kissed him.

"'Yes,'" he said. Margaret stared at me, begging for pity. He didn't make that up. A bit of an ass, then, but really, who isn't? She expected Rue to get right down to love. He wanted a drink first. He wanted to look at her paintings, wanted to use the bathroom and stayed inside a long time, wanted something to eat, then wanted to read poetry. It was close to midnight. He was reading poems aloud, ravished by beauties of phrasing, shaken by their music. He'd done graduate work at Oxford. Hours passed. Margaret sat on the couch, her legs folded under her. She thought it wasn't going to happen, after all. Ten feet away, he watched her from a low-slung leather chair. The frame was a steel tube bent to form legs, arms, and backrest. A book of modern poetry lay open in his lap. He was about to read another poem when Margaret said, in the flat black voice, "'Do you want me to drive you to your hotel?'"

He let the book slide to the floor. Stood up slowly, struggling with the leather-wheezing-ass-adhesive chair seat, then came toward her, pulling stone foot. Leaning down to where she sat on the couch, he kissed her. Her hand went up, lightly, slowly, between his legs.

"He wasn't a very great lover," she said.

She had to make him stop, give her time to regather powers of feeling and smoke a joint before trying again. Then, him inside, "working on me," she said, she fingered her clitoris to make herself come. "There would have been no payoff otherwise," she said. "He'd talked too much, maybe. Then he was a tourist looking for sensations in the landscape. He couldn't give. It was like he had a camera. Collecting memories. Savoring the sex, you know what I mean? I could have been in another city." Finally, Margaret said, she screamed, "'What keeps you from loving me?'" He fell away, damaged.

"'You didn't enjoy it?'" he said, she said.

She turned on the lamp to roll another joint, and told him to lie still while she studied his cock, which was oddly discolored and twisted left. In the next three days, the sex got better, not great. She'd say, "'You're losing me.'" He'd moan.

When she left him at the airport, she felt relieved, but driving back to town, she began to miss him. She thought to phone her psychotherapist, but this wasn't a medical problem. The pain surprised her and it wouldn't quit. She couldn't work, couldn't think. Despite strong reservations—he hadn't been very nice to her—she was in love, had been since she saw him onstage. Yes; definitely love. Now he was gone. She was alone. In the supermarket, she wandered the aisles, unable to remember what she needed. She was disoriented—her books, her plants, her clothes, her hands— nothing seemed really hers. At night, the loneliness was very bad. Sexual. Hurt terribly. She cried herself to sleep.

"Why didn't you phone me?"

"I knew you weren't too sympathetic. I couldn't talk to you. I took Gracie out of school. She's been here for the last couple of days."

"She likes school."

"That's just what you'd say, isn't it? You know, Herman, you are a kind of person who makes me feel like shit. If Gracie misses a couple of days it's no big deal. She's got a lot of high Qs. I found out she also has head lice. Her father doesn't notice anything. Gracie would have to have convulsions before he'd notice. Too busy advancing himself, writing another ten books that nobody will read, except his pathetic graduate students."

"That isn't fair."

"Yes, it is. It's fair."

"No, it isn't."

"You defending Sloan? Whose friend are you?"

"Talking to you is like cracking nuts with my teeth."

She told me Rue had asked if she knew Chinese. She said she didn't. He proposed to teach her, and said, "'The emperor forbid foreigners to learn Chinese, except imperfectly, only for purposes of trade. Did you know that?'"

"'No. Let's begin.'"

Minutes into the lesson, he said, "'You're pretending not to know Chinese. I am a serious person. Deceive your American lovers. Not me.'"

She said, "Nobody ever talked to me like that. He was furious."

"Didn't you tell him to go to hell?"

"I felt sorry for him."

She told him that she really didn't know a word of Chinese. Her family had lived in America for more than a hundred years. She was raised in Sacramento. Her parents spoke only English. All her friends had been white. Her father was a partner in a construction firm. His associates were white. When the Asian population of the Bay Area greatly increased, she saw herself, for the first time, as distinctly Chinese. She thought of joining Chinese cultural organizations, but was too busy. She sent money.

"'You don't know who you are,'" said Rue.

"'But that's who I am. What do you mean?'"

"'Where are my cigarettes?'"

"Arrogant bastard. Did you?"

"What I did is irrelevant. He felt ridiculed. He thought I was being contemptuous. I was in love. I could have learned anything. Chinese is only a language. It didn't occur to me to act stupid."

"What you did is relevant. Did you get his cigarettes?"

"He has a bald spot in the middle of his head."

"Is there anything really interesting about Rue?"

"There's a small blue tattoo on his right shoulder. I liked it. Black moles are scattered on his back like buckshot. The tattoo is an ideograph.

I saw him minutely, you know what I mean? I was on the verge of hatred, really in love. But you wouldn't understand. I won't tell you any more."

"Answer my question."

She didn't.

"You felt sorry for him. I feel sorry for you. Is it over now?"

"Did it begin? I don't really know. Anyhow, so what?"

"Don't you want to tell me? I want to know. Tell me everything."

"I must keep a little for myself. Do you mind? It's my life. I want to keep my feelings. You can be slightly insensitive, Herman."

"I never dumped YOU at a party in front of the whole town. You want to keep your feelings? Good. If you talk, you'll remember feelings you don't know you had. It's the way to keep them."

"No, it isn't. They go out of you. Then they're not even feelings anymore. They're chitchat commodities. Some asshole like Claude will stick them in a novel."

"Why don't you just fly to Paris? Live with him."

"He's married. I liked him for not saying that he doesn't get along with his wife, or they're separated. I asked if he had an open marriage."

"What did he say?"

"He said, 'Of course not.'"

Margaret spoke more ill than good of Rue. Nevertheless, she was in love. Felt it every minute, she said, and wanted to phone him, but his wife might answer. He'd promised to write a letter, telling her where they would meet. There were going to be publication parties for his book in Rome and Madrid. He said that his letter would contain airline tickets and notification about her hotel.

"Then you pack a bag? You run out the door?"

"And up into the sky. To Rome. To Madrid."

"Just like that? What about your work? What about Gracie?"

"Just like that."

I bought a copy of *The Mists of Shanghai* and began reading with primitive, fiendish curiosity. Who the hell was Claude Rue? The morning passed, then the afternoon. I quit reading at twilight, when I had to leave for work. I'd reached the point where Dulu comes to the brothel. It was an old-fashioned novel, something like Dickens, lots of characters and sentimental situations, but carefully written to seem mindless, and so clear that you hardly feel you're reading. Jujuzi's voice gives a weird edge to the story. Neiping suffers terribly, he says, but she imagines life in the brothel is not real, and that someday she will go home and her mother will be happy to see her. Just as I began to think Rue was a nitwit, Jujuzi reflects on Neiping's pain. He says she will never go home, and a child's pain is more terrible than an adult's, but it is the nourishment of sublime dreaming. When Dulu arrives, Neiping wishes the new girl would stop crying. It makes Neiping sad. She can't sleep. She stands beside the new girl, staring down through the dark, listening to her sob, wanting to smack her, make her be quiet. But then Neiping slides under the blanket and hugs the new girl. They tell each other their names. They talk. Dulu begins slowly to turn. She hugs Neiping. The little bodies lie in each other's arms, face to face. They talk until they fall asleep.

Did Claude Rue imagine himself as Neiping? Considering Rue's limp, he'd known pain. But maybe pain had made him cold, like Jujuzi, master of sentimental feelings, master of cruelty. Was Claude Rue like Jujuzi?

A week passed. Margaret called, told me to come to her loft. She sounded low. I didn't ask why. When I arrived, she gave me a brutal greeting. "How come you and me never happened?"

"What do you mean?"

"How come we never fucked?"

She had a torn-looking smile.

"We're best friends, aren't we?"

I sat on the couch. She followed, plopped beside me. We sat beside each other, beside ourselves. Dumb. She leaned against me, put her head on my shoulder. I loved her so much it hurt my teeth. Light went down in the tall, steel-mullioned factory windows. The air of the loft grew chilly.

"Why did you phone?" I asked.

"I needed you to be here."

"Do you want to talk?"

"No."

The perfume of her dark hair came to me. I saw dents on the side of her nose, left by her eyeglasses. They made her eyes look naked, vulnerable. She'd removed her glasses to see less clearly. Twisted the ends of her hair. Chewed her lip. I stood up, unable to continue doing nothing, crossed to a lamp, then didn't turn it on. Electric light was violent. Besides, it wasn't very dark in the loft and the shadows were pleasant. I looked back. Her eyes had followed me. She asked what I'd like to drink.

"What do you have?"

"Black tea?"

"All right."

She put on her glasses and walked to the kitchen area. The cup and saucer rattled as she set them on the low table. I took her hands. "Sit," I said. "Talk."

She sat, but said nothing.

"Do you want to go out somewhere? Take a walk, maybe."

"We were together for three days," she said.

"Did he write to you?"

"We were together for hours and hours. There was so much feeling. Then I get this letter."

"What does he say? Rome? Barcelona?"

"He says I stole his watch. He says I behaved like a whore, going through his pockets when he was asleep."

"Literally, he says that?"

"Read it yourself."

"It's in French." I handed it back to her.

"An heirloom, he says. His most precious material possession, he says. He understands my motive and finds it contemptible. He wants his watch back. He'll pay. How much am I asking?"

"You have his heirloom?"

"I never saw it."

"Let's look."

"Please, Herman, don't be tedious. There is no watch."

With the chaos of art materials scattered on the vast floor, and on tabletops, dressers, chairs, and couch, it took twenty minutes before she found Claude Rue's watch jammed between a bedpost and the wall.

I laughed. She didn't laugh. I wished I could redeem the moment. Her fist closed around the watch, then opened slowly. She said, "Why did he write that letter?"

"Send him the watch and forget it."

"He'll believe he was right about me."

"Who cares what he believes?"

"He hurt me."

"Oh, just send him the watch."

"He hurt me, really hurt me. Three days of feeling, then that letter."

"Send it to him," I said.

But there was a set look in Margaret's eyes. She seemed to hear nothing.

viva la tropicana

BEFORE WORLD WAR II, Cuba was known for sugar and sex, but there was also a popular beach with sand imported from Florida, and grand hotels like the Nacional, where you could get a room with a harbor view for ten dollars, and there were gambling casinos organized by our glamorous gangsters whose faces appeared in *Life* magazine, among them Meyer Lansky and my uncle-by-marriage, Zev Lurie, a young man who could multiply giant numbers in his head and crack open a padlock with his hands. *Habaneros*, however, celebrated him for his dancing—rumba, mambo, cha-cha—rhythms heard nightly in New York, Miami, Cuba, Mexico, Central America, and much of South America, where Zev toured as an exhibition dancer before he went to Cuba and caught the fancy of big shots in the mob.

The first time I heard mambo, I was in a Chevy Bel Air, driving from Manhattan to Brooklyn with Zev's son, my cousin Chester. We'd just been graduated from high school and were going to a party. To save me the subway ride, Chester came to pick me up. He wore alligator shoes, like Zev's dancing shoes, and a chain bracelet of heavy silver, with a name tag, on his left wrist. It was a high school fashion, like penny loafers and bobby socks. Chester had spent time in Cuba, but mainly he lived with his mother in Brooklyn and hardly ever saw his father. Uncle Zev, I believe, didn't love Chester too much, or not enough. This accounts for an eccentric, showy element in his personality, which distinguished him in high school as a charming ass, irresistible to girls, obnoxious to boys. As we drove, he flicked on the radio. The D.J., Symphony Sid, began talking to us, his voice full of knowing, in the manner of New York. He said we could catch Tito Puente this Wednesday at the Palladium, home of Latin music, Fifty-third and Broadway. Then Symphony Sid played a tune by Puente called "Ran Kan Kan."

Chester pulled the Chevy to the curb, cut the motor, and turned the volume way up. "You know what this is?" I shrugged, already afraid Chester was about to do something show-offy. He lunged out of the car and began to dance, his alligators flashing on the asphalt. "Cuban mambo," he cried, pressing his right palm to his belly, showing me the source of the music, and how it streams downward through your hips and legs into your feet. He danced as if he had a woman in his arms, or the music itself was a magnificent woman, like Abbe Lane or Rita Hayworth, with mammalian heat and substance, as required by the era. Chester's every motion displayed her with formal yet fiery adoration. His spine was straight, shoulders level, and his head aristocratically erect, the posture of flamenco dancers, but the way he moved was more fluid and had different hesitations. "This is Cuba, baby. *Ritmo caliente.*" He looked very macho. I could see why girls liked him.

I envied his talent and succumbed to his love of this music and dancing, in which I saw the shadow of Uncle Zev, greater dancer and friend of gangsters, who moved in a greater life, far away in the elegant casinos of Havana, where beautiful women and dangerous men took their nightly pleasure. I began yearning to go to Cuba, but over thirty years would pass before I had the chance. America was almost continuously at war or on the verge of war, and there was the revolution in Cuba. Then, in 1987, I was invited to a film festival in Havana. I'd be in the American contingent, which included film directors, screenwriters, photographers, and journalists.

The night before I left, I received a phone call from Uncle Zev, who for the past twenty years had lived in Brooklyn with his wife, Frances, my mother's sister. I lived in Berkeley.

"You're going to Havana."

"How did you know?"

"I know."

In this way, with his old-fashioned gangsterish manner, he intimidated me.

"I need a favor," he said.

"Of course. Anything."

"There's a woman in Havana. Consuelo Delacruz. I am saying this once, which is already too much, so listen. Go to Consuelo. Identify yourself. Get down on your knees. Then say . . ."

"I think you said get down on my knees."

"Say that your Uncle Zev continues to worship the ground she walks. Say he kisses her feet. Get a pencil and paper and I'll tell you how to say it in Spanish."

"I already feel guilty. Chester and I used to be close. We went to high school together."

"Chester is in the construction business. A Manhattan contractor. Last month was very bad. He made two hundred fifty thousand. You think he gives a shit about human feelings? I'm telling you about undying love in the heart of an old man. Are you a sensitive writer or what?"

"Should I kiss her feet, assuming I find her?"

"She works at the Tropicana. I'll fill in the background. Listen."

In a few minutes he'd told me a long story . . .

Zev worked in Havana from the late forties to the mid-sixties. When Fidel made his triumphant progress through the streets, with Che Guevara and Celia Sánchez, a doctor and the daughter of a doctor, Zev stood in the delirious crowds, trying to figure out what to do with his life. Not political, he was indifferent to the revolution, except that it cost him his job, but he was madly in love with Consuelo Delacruz, who refused to leave Cuba with him. To struggle with English, in a Brooklyn grocery store, would be an insufferable humiliation. Besides, Zev was married.

He lingered in Havana, doing this and that, and didn't leave until obliged to do so by the revolutionary government. In 1966, the Ministry of Economics unearthed ledgers in the Hotel Capri, where George Raft once had the penthouse suite, and discovered Zev's initials beside certain figures, again and again, right up to New Year's Eve, 1959, suggesting that he had been in possession of great sums of gambling money, not only from the Capri, but from the Nacional and Tropicana, too. The revolution wanted it. He showed them a receipt, the same he'd shown the mob, proving he'd turned over the money to Batista before his flight to the Dominican Republic. In a fit of moral disgust, Fidel personally ordered Zev's expulsion. He said, "I wanted only to burn the money in your face."

Zev had been a runner between the casinos and Batista's officers. On the night Batista fled, Zev rushed with conga drums on his shoulders down O'Reilly Street to the docks and then into a receiving shed. Two soldiers emerged from behind crates, took the drums, which contained over a million dollars, and gave Zev a photo of Batista. This was the receipt. Across the eyes of the photo, Batista always signed his mother's name. The photo was signed, but across the mouth, not the eyes. Zev understood that the soldiers, whom he'd never seen before, intended to hand the money over to the revolution and thereby escape Fidel's tribunals and the firing squad. Neither here nor there, as far as Zev was concerned. He had to present the authentic receipt to parties who also had firing squads. Zev laughed. "I see it's over with Batista, eh, *amigos*?" The soldiers laughed, too, and Zev broke the neck of one with a forearm blow and disemboweled the other with a knife even as their laughter resonated in the shed. Searching their uniform pockets, he found the authentic receipt. He spent that night with Consuelo, in her apartment, brooding.

"Return the money, or give it to the revolution."

"The soldiers are in a crate at the bottom of the harbor. I have the receipt. The money is for you and the child."

"Nobody will need money anymore. What child do you mean?"

Now, 1987, considering the economic misfortunes of the revolution, Zev figured Consuelo would be glad to have the money, but he wanted her to come to the States. I was to explain this to Consuelo, reading from the Spanish dictated to me by Zev over the phone. She knew about the money. She didn't know what Zev had done with it.

That night in Havana, twenty-eight years ago, lying in the arms of Consuelo, Zev made a plan—to be put into effect only if he continued to love Consuelo. "I am a realistic person. Feelings die," he said. Seven years later, a few weeks before Zev was deported, his child was born. He was still in love with Consuelo.

From the pattern of whorls in the tiny thumbprint, Zev worked out a formula. It translated into a graph. This graph described the proportionate distance between peaks and valleys along the shaft of a key that opened a bank box in Zurich. The original key was destroyed. To reconstruct it, Zev's child—now twenty-one years old—had to supply the thumbprint. That's how Zev planned it in 1959. Only one person in the world, his Cuban love child, could lay hands on the money. Zev had waited seven years in Cuba and loved Consuelo. He'd waited over twenty years away from her. He loved her no less. The old man cried himself to sleep at night.

On December 22, at 10:00 p.m. I walked into the Tropicana and began looking for Consuelo Delacruz to tell her that she and the child were rich in dollars and the undying love of my uncle Zev Lurie. I imagined he was at that moment huddled in a heavy wool coat, his face bent against the blades of winter, hustling through freezing New York streets from his office to his limousine. My heart went out to him. I was delivering warmth to the lonely winter of his life and I was glad. He'd confessed to me. I felt honored, grateful. I valued his intimacy.

I passed through an entranceway of pointed arches, then a lobby, and entered the largest outdoor nightclub in the world. Tiers of white tablecloths, in a great sweep of concentric circles, descended toward a vast curved stage. There were trees all about, tall palms and flamboyants, the towering walls of a natural cathedral open to the nighttime sky. I went to a table near the edge of the stage. A waiter approached. I pulled out my notebook and asked, *"Dónde puedo encontrar Consuelo Delacruz?"*

"Ron y Coca-Cola," he said.

Music started, lights began flashing, dancers appeared onstage.

I raised my voice. *"Consuelo Delacruz. Ella trabaja aquí."*

"Cuba Libre?"

"O.K.," I shouted. He left. Was I reading incorrectly? Mispronouncing? I'd try again when the drink came.

The Marxian adage "Nothing can stop the course of history" is incontestable, but here was the Tropicana, in a Havana suburb, the creation of fifties architecture, airy and geometrical, and, on its stage, just as in the prerevolutionary days, the garish, glitzy artificiality of Las Vegas tits-and-ass dance routines.

At the next table, two men in identical white shirts, with pale, expressionless robot heads, from East Germany, were sipping beer. Beyond them, on platforms built high in the air, on either side of the stage, appeared an orchestra, chorus, and dancers, performing in the trees, with the fantastic sensationalism of show-biz Americana. *Viva la Tropicana!* I said to myself, and looked about for my waiter and my drink. It was coming to me in the hand of a tall, slender black woman, very handsome, about fifty or so. I got right down on my knees and started reading the Spanish in my notebook. When I glanced up, she was half smiling, her eyes softly inquisitive.

"Zev?"

I nodded. She set the drink on the table, tugged me to my feet, kissed me, and pulled me after her along the aisle that curved with the stage front, and then behind it into darkness tangled with wires. We stopped only to gape at each other, to see what couldn't be said. She asked fifteen questions. Spanish is the fastest language in the world. Cuban Spanish is even faster, but if she'd spoken with the slow lips of death, I'd have understood none of it. She continued to hold my hand, hers quivering with eagerness to know what I couldn't tell her. Gradually, she made out in my eyes no hope, no Spanish.

"*Norteamericano?* Brook-leen?"

Then, more strongly, she pulled me after her through the dark and around behind the stage into an alley, like another part of the city, no longer the Tropicana, and pulled me toward two near-naked women, their heads glorified by mountains of feathers, their bodices all spangles. They practiced dance steps together, not noticing our approach until Consuelo thrust me in front of one of them. To me she said, "*La niña*, Zeva." To her she said, "*Tu padre lo mandó. Anda hablar con él. Háblale.*" *La niña* looked from her mother to me, then just at me, fixing me with large dark eyes rich in incomprehension. Words came, as if experimentally. "You are from Zev?"

"He sent me to see your mother."

She was Chester's half-sister, Zev's love child, my cousin. I had to tell this to myself, review the facts, before saying, "I am your cousin." She told this to her mother, who, while she'd had no trouble kissing me earlier, seemed now to show faint reserve, though she smiled and said, "Ah." Zeva stepped toward me. In a sweetly formal way, she kissed my cheek, whispering, "Did he send us money?" I whispered, too: "More than you can imagine."

After the last show, I waited for them at the front gate. Zeva emerged wearing blue jeans, a white T-shirt, and sandals. She looked like an American college student. Consuelo had gone ahead to get their car, an old Chevy, like the one Chester drove years ago, but very rusted, battered, and loud. We drove along the Malecón, where waves smashed against the seawall, stood high in the air, and collapsed along the sidewalk and onto the avenue. Facing the ocean were rows of old, grim, suffering buildings, arcades and baroque ornamentation, much decayed, and very beautiful in decay. I had glimpses of Arabic tile work and the complicated glass of chandeliers hanging amid clotheslines in rooms where the rich once lived. We turned right, passing through a large square, then along empty streets with hardly any lights. The Chevy sounded very loud, echoing in the darkness, because there were no other sounds, no voices, no music, and nobody about.

This was the Old Town, where Zeva and Consuelo had an apartment in a three-story building with a much broken façade, elaborate mortar work along the balconies fallen away, iron railings loose in their moorings, and tall windows eaten up by water and fungus. The apartment was long and very narrow, with a linoleum floor throughout. Lights hung from the ceiling by naked wires. Chests and tables were loaded with porcelain figurines, ashtrays, framed photos, and innumerable bright little cheap glass nameless things, like junkshop memorabilia. We sat in the kitchen at an oval Formica-topped table. The surface was imitation gray marble with an aluminum border. The pipe·legs were also aluminum. Right out of the fifties. In an L.A. antique shop, it would sell for about a thousand bucks—with the four chairs.

Zeva looked at her hands when I finished the story and said, "Which one?"

"Aren't they the same?"

"Maybe only one is good. I could give you impressions of both thumbs, or I could cut them off and you bring them to him."

"He wants all of you," I said.

Consuelo, respectful of our deliberations, waited for us to conclude. Zeva told her where we stood. Then an argument started. I couldn't understand it, but it touched old disagreements. Zeva wanted to go to the States. Consuelo didn't. Consuelo rose, stood with arms folded across her chest, looking down at us. Then, from her angry rigidity, she bent abruptly and hugged me. She did the same with Zeva, then walked off down the narrow hall to a bedroom. Zeva said, "She's tired. She's going to sleep. You stay here tonight. She wants you to. I'll fix a bed for you by the windows, or take my room. I won't be able to sleep, anyway. This is terrible. Terrible. I don't know Zev, but he must be a thoughtless man. How could he do this to me? To us? We have lived for years with promises. This apartment is ours. Almost ours. We are buying it slowly. Now you bring new promises from him. She wants to tell the authorities. It won't be too good for you. I'm sure you'll be detained. Come, I'll show you."

I followed her to the window.

The street was empty except for a man at the corner, ordinary-looking, wearing a hat, brim pulled down front and back.

"The police?"

"They will want to know what we talked about."

"We're cousins. We talked about Zev. You told me about yourself, how you learned English. How did you learn English?"

"I don't really know."

"You don't?"

"After Zev was thrown out, my mother was in ill favor. She lost her job at the Tropicana. They gave it back to her later, but for years she did other work, mainly cooking and cleaning for the family of a diplomat. She took me with her every day. I played with their children. They spoke English. I spoke English. When they switched to Spanish, so did I. There were also other languages. The family had lived in different countries. I spoke maybe five languages. It was all language to me and I never knew which I was speaking."

"You don't speak a child's English."

"I studied it later in school. If you speak one language as a child, then another, you are left with a child's knowledge of the first. Like changing lovers."

"Have you changed many lovers?"

"I can count them on one thumb, but I imagine you grow and mature with the next lover, and the next. With the first you are always a child. I wanted to be in the foreign service, so I studied English. I would like to travel. I'm good at languages, but I'm a little too black, a little too much like a woman. Opportunities didn't come my way. My mother says Zev speaks nine languages. She refuses to admit she understands a word of English."

"Zev still loves her."

"She obliged him to speak to her in Spanish. If a man loves you, she says, he must prove it every day. When Zev spoke to her, always in Spanish, he reminded himself of what he felt for my mother. She's a real Cuban, very warm and loving, but when she tells me what Zev did to Batista's soldiers, there is no pity in her voice. I ask her why not. She says, Your father is a man."

The man in the street lit a cigarette and glanced up; the flare of the match revealed his eyes. I waved to him. He looked away.

She said, "Americans think anything can be made into some joke. Do you like rice and beans? If not, you may have to learn."

We stood near each other, easy in our nearness, familial. It wasn't an American feeling. My cousin was very attractive, but I had no trouble with that. I put my arm around her shoulder. She leaned against me, as if we'd grown up together, two Latin kids, always touching. "I like rice and beans," I said.

I wasn't detained in Cuba. Nothing was done to me; nobody asked questions. On the last night of the film festival, I was invited to a grand dinner, with hundreds of others, at the Palacio de la Revolución. Long tables in parallel lines, with wide aisles between them, were laid out with Cuban foods. Guests walked the length of the tables, loading their plates, then returned for more. At the end, they served cakes and excellent Cuban ice cream. Without announcement, Fidel appeared and the crowd swarmed toward him, surrounding him, but this was an elegant crowd of well-dressed people, and they felt the necessity of leaving him a little space in front. I couldn't approach closely, but I could see his head and shoulders, the top of his green army uniform, his beard and intense black eyes. He was the tallest man in the hall, perhaps six-foot-five. His head was large, leonine, heroic, bending slightly toward those who asked questions, listening with utter seriousness. I saw a monument, not simply the man called Fidel, but the living monument of himself. He seemed, in that instant, while talking to a man in the crowd, to be talking beyond that man to me. "Of course," he said, "we would publish the works of Kierkegaard. If somebody came to me with the manuscript, say, of his great work *Either/Or*, I would think it is worth a million dollars."

When my plane landed in Miami, I went to a phone and called Zev. It was 5:00 a.m., but he'd said to phone him the moment I arrived. I was sure he'd want to hear from me. Besides, I was too excited to wait. As soon as he said hello, I began telling him I'd met Consuelo, and I told him about his brilliant daughter, Zeva, how she spoke several languages, how well she danced, though I'd seen her only as a spangled figure among others, all burdened by colorful feathers. "Zev, why didn't you say the baby was a girl?"

"I couldn't remember for sure."

"Oh, come on."

"When you get a little older, the differences between boys and girls matter less."

I told him Fidel is willing to let them go to the States, but with conditions. *Either* the million dollars is returned to the revolution, *or* Zev's women never leave. "It's up to you."

"He spoke to you personally?"

"Not exactly. It was indirect, but we were in the same room. I'd been followed by the police. He certainly knew who I was."

"Right, right. Well, I have the bank and the number, but only Zeva can open the box. The key is her thumb. Wait in Miami. I'll catch a plane this afternoon. Stay with my friend Sam Halpert. I want you to call him, but listen carefully. When you hang up, look around, look at the people. Look good. Then take a walk. Make four or five turns like you're lost, you don't know the airport. Don't go into toilets. Stay in plain sight. Then find another phone and call Sam—Sam Halpert—and then look around again. You'll recognize the one who's following you. Describe the guy to Sam. Whatever he tells you, do it."

"Zev, you're scaring me."

"I'll see you soon."

The phone went dead as I shouted, "Wait a minute." I dialed him again. What the hell did he think I was, a person with nothing to do but hang around Miami? The phone rang at his end. Nobody answered. Too damn bad. Zev would fly here for nothing. I slammed down the receiver and started toward my San Francisco flight, so angry that I forgot to look around at the faces, but there were none, anyhow, just a man lying on a bench with a *Miami Herald* covering his face, sleeping.

I didn't notice him.

I didn't notice his white shoes, either.

Blind with feeling, I thrust along the passageways where slender neon tubes of pastel light floated, a modernistic touch, suggesting a chemical bloodstream fed the airport's extremities. My big leather shoulder bag slammed against my hip, my breathing was loud. I talked to myself, finishing the conversation with Zev, telling him he was my favorite uncle. I'd admired and loved him since I was a kid, but . . . I owed him a lot, nevertheless . . . I'd never forget that he paid my college fees, still . . . that he pulled strings in New York to get me summer jobs, and, when my high school sweetheart became pregnant, Zev found us the doctor in New Jersey and paid for the operation. Then I stopped raving and let myself wonder if maybe it wasn't anger that I felt but fear.

The philosophers say nothing in the mind is inaccessible to the mind. They are wrong. The mind is promiscuous. It collects more than you can ever possibly know. *It*—not me—had seen white shoes, and taken in the man on his back, sleeping under the newspaper. Minutes after the phone call, as I stood at a coffee counter, still tumultuous, I saw white shoes dangling from legs on either side of a stool and I remembered—I'd seen them before—remembered what I didn't know I knew. I remembered the newspaper, too, which the man was now reading.

I left my coffee untasted on the counter, went to a phone, trying to be efficient, though hurried and frightened. I dialed Information, then

Sam Halpert. Not once did I glance back at White Shoes, but I'd have bet a million dollars his eyes were set high in his head, which I'd seen as a blondish blur, complexion pocked and gullied from cheek to neck, as if he'd been washing in acid. Somebody picked up the phone, and, without any hello, said, "Can you hear me good?"

I said, "Yes. Sam Halpert?"

"Start laughing."

"I have nothing to laugh at, Mr. Halpert."

"This is a hilarious phone call, if somebody is watching you."

I laughed, laughed.

"Don't overdo it, kid. What does he look like?"

"Blond. Ha, ha, ha. Maybe six feet tall. Late twenties. Your average white trash." The expression surprised me. It came flying out of fear, as if to strike the man. "Ha, ha, ha. Blue-and-white Hawaiian shirt, white slacks, white shoes with pointed toes. Ha, ha, ha. I'm scared out of my mind."

"I want you to talk to me. Move your mouth, shake your head, laugh. Then hang up and go look for a taxi. Don't run. Don't dawdle. Don't get ideas about calling a cop. Tell the taxi driver to go to Bayside, and to drop you at the flags."

"The flags?"

"You'll see like a park, flags at the entrance. An aisle of flags. Walk through the flags. There's shops on either side. Go straight, straight, straight till you're standing on a concrete ledge facing the bay. Below the ledge you'll see a parapet. Go down to it and walk right. Repeat what I said."

"Taxi to Bayside. Aisle of flags."

"Laugh."

"Ha, ha, ha. Through flags to water, down to parapet, walk right. Ha, ha, ha, ha, ha."

"The taxi will cost maybe fifteen bucks. You got fifteen bucks?"

"Yes. What if you're not there? It isn't even 6:00 a.m. I'll be alone, Mr. Halpert. Wouldn't it be advisable to wait a few hours until there are people in the streets? Ha, ha."

"Am I here?"

"Yes."

"I'll be there."

"But wouldn't it be advisable . . ."

"I gave you the best advice you'll ever get." He hung up.

Another outrage. Zev had told Sam Halpert to expect my call. He'd known this would happen. I wasn't living my own life. Walking, talking, laughing, but it wasn't me. There was no trouble getting a cab. Maybe Zev had arranged that, too. I was driving through Miami followed by a creep.

Minutes later, I dragged my shoulder bag out of the backseat of the taxi, paid the driver. He abandoned me in the tremendous and brilliant emptiness of a business center, tall new buildings amid older ones alongside the park and Bayside, a mall built at the edge of Biscayne Bay. The aisle of flags marked a wide bleak walk into the mall. I was entering it when I heard a car door slam. I turned, saw a taxi and the blue-and-white shirt moving free of it. I thought to drop my bag and run, but I wasn't supposed to know I was being followed. It wasn't advisable.

The water lay before me, black but for the lights of slow-moving boats way out and city lights skimming the surface, defining the shore. Where concrete ended and became a ledge, I saw the parapet, wide enough for two men walking side by side. A stairway took me down. I walked right, doing everything right. Below, water slapped listlessly at the wall. It didn't give a damn about me. There was nobody in sight along the parapet, but after a few yards I saw a man up ahead descending a stair toward a small dock, taller than the blond, wearing a Windbreaker, jeans, and tennis shoes. He stopped to light a cigar, all very casual. A local yachtsman. He started toward me along the wall to my right. I had to keep to the water side, which unnerved me, though there was room to pass each other easily. He walked in a loose, loping, athletic way, slightly tipped forward. I assumed he was Sam Halpert, but maybe he wasn't Sam Halpert. As we drew close, he looked for my eyes and said, "Good morning, kid," and passed me. Then I heard a cry, and turned. The blond in the Hawaiian shirt, kicking and flailing, sailed off the parapet through the air.

The tall man, his arm thrust out with the shove he'd given the blond, flicked his cigar into the water. The flying blond, having hit with a great splash, thrashed toward the wall, slapping at its slimy face, seeking a fingerhold. There was none. He couldn't drag himself out. Halpert came toward me. "Forget him. Let's go."

The blond thrashed in the water, mouth a black O closing, going under, then bobbing up, opening to an O again, as if swallowing a pipe, his eyes wild with lights of fear.

"He's drowning," I said.

"You kidding? This is Miami. Everybody here is a fish. Let's go." He began tugging at my arm. I pulled it away.

"That man is drowning, Mr. Halpert."

"Call me Sam."

"You and Zev have your ways and I have mine, Sam."

That instant, a chunk of concrete broke from the wall above my head, leaving a hole big as a grapefruit, and I heard the gunshot—much louder than I'd have expected—and I saw the blond go under again, black booming steel in hand.

Sam said, "I'll hold your bag, kid. Jump in after him."

We took off along the parapet as I yelled back at the water, "Drown, fucker. I hope you drown."

Sam drove, sometimes stopping at stop signs, sometimes not. I wasn't concerned. Little concerned me. The shot missed my head and left me with a sense of my potential for instant nothingness. The blond face lingered in memory, mouth and eyes wide open, begging life to enter, aware it was drowning, but I couldn't feel for his terror, too much awed by myself being alive, strangely humiliated, but alive.

We cut through residential areas heavy with the sweetness of flowers. I lay back against the seat. A dark sensuous weight of air and silence lingered before morning, neither dark really nor yet morning, and I took in solemn banyan trees beginning to emerge, hulking, elephantine, streaming tendrils, and I saw white houses set back from the road.

"I could go Dixie Highway," said Sam, "but I figured you'd want to look at the neighborhoods. Ever been to Miami?"

"No."

"You'd never guess how little it costs me to live here."

"Probably not."

"I don't live like the dancing man. Never stops, that guy. I told him I play tennis on the local courts. He says, 'You don't own a court?'"

"That's Zev."

"Not in the mood to talk? You can't believe Sam is blabbing."

"I can't believe it."

"We'll talk later. No hurry. It's beginning the way Zev figured. Fidel made his move. Now we make ours, and play it through to the end. Fidel never quits. Blood of the conquistadors."

"What if he drowned?"

"Fidel is a great swimmer."

"I mean White Trash."

"What I'm about to say is not an insult, but you're an asshole."

"Do you carry a gun, Sam?"

"Am I an American?"

"I keep seeing his face go under."

"A face like that should go under. You told him to drown. Don't you say what you mean?"

"You sound like my girlfriend Sonny. She expects to see me tomorrow, but I'll be in Miami. She'll say, 'If you wanted to be here, you'd be here. Don't you say what you mean?'"

"She talks like that to you? Let me ask you a question, man to man. Is the screwing you get worth the screwing you get?"

"Yes."

He laughed. "We have different needs."

"What do I smell?"

"Mango. We're passing an orchard."

"I don't see it."

"Most of the trees have been cut down. Beautiful trees. I love mango. Very good for your digestion. Do you know the death rate in Florida is higher than the birthrate, but the population is growing. Five thousand new residents a week. They need houses. Goodbye mangos. There's money around to build a lot of houses."

"*Drogas?*"

"I don't know from *drogas*. Ask your uncle. He owns a bank in Miami. I'm just his lawyer."

"I'm dying to sleep, but I'm afraid I'll dream. That guy's face. I'm still watching it."

"It could have been him watching you. You never saw a man die. Don't worry. You came to the right city."

"I'm flying out of here."

"I know what you mean. It's a rude introduction to the life, but Zev needs you. There's my house. You sleep. Later, we'll talk. Work things out."

"Why does Zev need me?"

"There's a hundred guys who would kill for Zev."

"Like you?"

"Like me."

"So why me?"

"You're family, people he trusts."

"He's got a son."

"Zev wouldn't want Chester to do it. The kid is too eager to please. He's a crook. He'll see chances for himself, lose sight of the goal. Anyhow, Zev doesn't want to owe him anything. We talked about you for a long time before you got that call. You're not a crook. There's nothing you want. You're perfect."

"For what?"

"We'll talk later."

We were in the driveway to Sam's house, parked beside a wood fence about seven feet high.

"I want to go home."

"You want to be with your girlfriend, what's her name. I know how you feel. Hungry?"

"I couldn't eat. I haven't slept for two or three nights, partying in Havana. Then this. I expected to sleep on the flight to San Francisco, but look where I am. Where the hell am I?"

"South Miami, at the edge of Dade County. It's good you're sleepy. That's an animal feeling. You're going to like it here. Hey, do you like mud wrestling? We got that in Miami Beach. We'll go tonight. What do you say? Twenty-five naked girls wrestling in the mud. It'll take your mind off your problems. Tell me, kid, what's not to like in Miami?"

"I must be out of my mind, feeling depressed in Miami."

Sam's house, a stucco box with a flat roof, had a red tile floor in the living room and very little furniture—rattan couch, rattan chairs, a coffee table, and a dining-room table. No curtains, no rugs. A bachelor's house. Some full-page cartoons, cut from magazines, were pasted to a wall in the living room, perhaps hiding cracks in the Sheetrock. There was a kitchen, dining room, and two bedrooms.

He showed me into one of the bedrooms. I dropped my shoulder bag, took off my clothes, and lay down on a thick foam mat on a plywood base. It felt good, but I could have slept on the ground. I didn't wash, didn't want to move. I sprawled on my back beneath a light wool cover, in my underwear, and shut my eyes.

Sam began making phone calls in the living room, beyond the wall, door shut, but I heard every word. It was early, too early for phone calls. He talked to an international operator, then people overseas, in different time zones, making hotel reservations. Somebody was going to travel "overseas." Beautiful word. It named a feeling. Sorrow at not going home. I missed Sonny and thought again of the man's face, drowning.

Sorrow attached to the face more strongly than would a feeling in waking life; weepy pressure, as if I were about to cry, but I was tired and slid into dreaminess. I never act out in dreams. Doing nothing, I've come, not even touching the woman. Sonny once said she'd come during a lecture, toppling out of her chair, moaning. I teased her. She said men have impoverished lives. So much they don't feel. How much did a man need? My feelings reduced to her. She was wearing her black leather miniskirt, sitting in the front row, naked legs crossed. She leaned over the armrest where it expanded into a table for her notebook and uncrossed her legs. The flash of her underpants shocked the professor, made him brilliant, made her go toppling out of her chair. Seeing her taken like that, we came together, she on the floor, me in South Miami, loving her feelings, but, in the bowels of sleep, Sonny on the floor, ravished, unconscious, it wasn't her. It was Zeva. How an innocent moment becomes another, which is depraved, I don't know. Sam's voice returned to me, saying, "Don't worry, kid, you'll see her again."

I felt light without opening my eyes—the way an amoeba sees—through skin. I knew it was afternoon.

"Was I talking in my sleep?"

He stood beside the bed. Sam. No dream. I hadn't yet seen him in natural light—tall with dark little close-together eyes and the sloping shoulders of an athlete, holding a glass of orange juice in a long hand. "I never met Zev's kid," he said. "She got to you. Have some orange juice from my trees. Zev calls her 'it.' The poor bastard doesn't even let himself call her a her. He's been dying twenty years, telling nobody. Did you fuck her?"

"I didn't hear you say that." I sat up and took the juice from his hand. "I told her what I was supposed to, that's all. About the money. Then we just talked. I liked her a lot and felt very happy for Zev. I didn't know what's what. I still don't."

"This has nothing to do with money. Let's go eat. I'll tell you what's what." He put my bag in his car. Apparently I wasn't coming back.

I recognized neighborhoods we'd driven through earlier in the semi-darkness. Then we were near the center of town and out of Sam's car, walking through the funereal lobby of a hotel. Somebody was shoving a vacuum cleaner across the rug. It droned, abdominal and despairing in the shadowy cave of the lobby. A buffet had been set up in the dining room. We loaded trays, took a table in a corner beside a long window, light filtering through gauzy white curtains, bathing us in a smoky glow; its quality came to me, as had odors in the night air, mixtures of perfumed decay, but the light wasn't as palpable. It stirred different nerves, like desert light, with holy intimations. Sam and I ate in silence, soldiers on a lonely mission. Coffee was served.

Sam looked to see if I was ready to listen. I avoided his look, but felt its pressure. He would talk, tell me what's what, whether or not I was receptive. There was no forgetting what had happened, trying to enjoy sensations of light, as if I had time for the mere luxury of being alive.

He said, "This is about women and power, kid. They need each other, like Samson and Delilah, or Zeus and Leda. In Cuba, Fidel is known as the Bull. A force of nature, you know what I mean? Like he told Khrushchev to grow balls—bomb New York, vaporize Washington? What a guy."

Sam had shoved a man into Miami Bay and been indifferent. Now he leaned toward me, grinning, glee in his eyes, loving the great destroyer. He expected me to relish the idea of Fidel. I could only nod, which wasn't enough for him, but he continued to lean toward me, grinning, urging me to feel something in myself that wasn't there.

"When Fidel was in the mountains, there was a shortage of women. What did he do? He didn't do anything. They came to him."

"They came to him?"

"Naturally. But some didn't go because they wanted to fuck a god. They were sent. You think this is incredible? See it. The afternoon is hot. You can hardly breathe. Mosquitos cover your skin like hair. Fidel and the others have just returned from patrol. They squat in a clearing in the woods, too tired to worry about Batista's police. A woman steps out of the woods. She doesn't say a word. She's gorgeous. The men wait for Fidel to acknowledge her. What does he do? He does nothing. He's Fidel. So she goes to him and stands until he feels that her claim on his *cojones* is not inconsistent with his revolutionary principles. 'Are you the only one?' he asks, thinking of his men. She says her colleagues wait in the woods. He nods to his men. They go into the woods. Listen, kid, it is the common practice. The shah of Iran had high-class whores sent to him from Paris, and he couldn't always get it on, let alone up. Fidel never paid a cent. Women wanted to go. Their motivation was basic to the universe, like the law of gravity. Every woman wants to fuck a god. No exceptions. Here is where Zev comes in."

"I can guess."

"You're a quick study." He looked pleased and disappointed at once. "Go ahead. Guess."

"Zev was already in the business."

"You and me will have conversations at a high level, but you look like you tasted something distasteful, not familiar to your mind."

"I thought Zev's business had to do with gambling. I never asked what else."

Sam shook his head, then blinked and rubbed his eyes, as if he'd developed a tic. He was trying too hard. This wasn't exactly the conversation he'd expected. I felt dim regret. He was doing his job. He wanted to come through for Zev, but I wasn't listening to him in the right spirit.

"Your uncle was in the business," he said quietly, no longer working on me. "Gambling, drugs, whores—so what? He's diversified since Cuba, but he's still in the business. You see in the newspapers how a cabinet official is getting off a plane in Berlin with fifteen advisers wearing suits and ties. To you they look important. Compared to Zev, they are errand boys. You will never see Zev stepping off a plane in Berlin, Beijing, Dakar, or Teheran on anybody's business but his own. Before the government types get on their planes, they phone Zev, ask if he's free for lunch. Maybe he'll give them some phone numbers in Helsinki. Sure, they're going to talk about arms control, but there's talk and there's talk, and nobody ever talks to anybody except in bed. Departments of the CIA and KGB are run by whores, many of them supplied by Cherchez La, Zev's international information service. For you, he got on a plane. He'll be at the airport in a little while."

"All right, he's big, he's important. He came to America as an immigrant kid. Life was tough. He made his way. It's the common story. I didn't ever want to know everything. He's been good to me. Look, Sam, I get your point. I believe you. But it makes no difference. I don't care how important he is. I don't admire his line of work, and I don't think he's flying down here for me."

"Why not? It's been a long time since he's seen you. Remember what you said when I asked if you fucked Zeva? You said, 'I didn't hear you, Sam,' or something like that." His tone was melancholy and nostalgic, as if he'd referred to the distant past.

"I remember. So do you. You have an ear for facts. What are you getting at now? Are you setting me up for something? I don't like the feeling, Sam."

His ears—I hadn't noticed until that instant—protruded slightly; long and batlike; fact-catchers. He dipped his head, in a tiny, sheepish, Oriental bow, to concede the point.

"When I was a boy, I knew the statistics for every player in the major leagues. I could name the capital of every country in the world. I love facts. Do you know, in the state of Florida, you're never more than sixty miles from water? Don't get so excited. You feel strongly for the Cuban bitch. I approve. You want to protect her honor. Maybe you have Latin blood. Maybe you'd die for *la familia*. But right now you're suffering from culture shock." He stabbed the tabletop with his fingertip. "Here, you're in America, not Berkeley. Miami is America and I'm trying to tell you something. I don't think you can hear me. Let me—please—tell you something. In the human brain there are two major centers. One is for sex, the other is for aggression. They lie side by side. Cut the links between them and a natural human person becomes a fucking liberal. Somebody cut your links?"

"What the hell are you talking about?"

"César Chávez says, 'Don't eat grapes,' so you don't eat grapes?"

"Damn right I don't. You've got my number. Is it all right to change the subject now, or do you intend to finish the story?"

He sighed, rubbed his eyes again. As though much discouraged, he continued. His voice went flat and thick.

"The rest is obvious. Some women were sent by Zev. When they came down from the mountains, Zev put them on airplanes to places like Zurich, Caracas, Stockholm. Different ambassadors helped him. The same later, after the revolution. The women still live in distant places with their sons. We call these women Vessels. The sons we call Potentates."

"That's very poetic."

"Everything is in Zeva's thumb."

"That sure isn't what I told her. I feel like a liar. Fidel knows about his *familia*?"

"He has received photographs. He sees boys becoming young men. No question who is the father. Fidel is prepotent, you know what I mean? It's a technical fact."

"What do you mean?"

"If the stud is prepotent, it doesn't matter what the woman looks like. Fidel's baby grows up big, handsome, smart, with a memory for detail. It talks when it's six months old and never stops. By the time it's six years

old, it's kicking ass. No kid on the block can handle it. Beat it with a baseball club and it comes off the floor fighting. You follow me? I'm talking
about a hero."

"Sounds like a pit bull."

"Fidel is no longer young. The revolution no longer feels to him like
his personal expression. He finds himself looking at the photos. He cares.
He needs these sons. He is ready to deal. That guy in the water bothers
you, but we had to send a strong message. No other way. He was dead
before he left Havana. Or you were dead."

"Zev risked my life to send a message?"

"It was the first stage of our negotiations. The last is when the
Potentates go to Havana, and Zev's women leave."

"What about his daughters? He had none?"

"Sure he did. There's one right in Havana. He sends her Christmas
presents. That's a fact. But he'll bargain only for Potentates. Zev wants you
to find them. You won't talk to reporters, won't sell the story, won't make
deals on the side with the Vessels, or subcontract with other operatives.
You won't even think about that kind of shit. We'll have Zeva in a couple
of days and you two will fly to Zurich. You go to the bank and open the
box. You'll find cash and bankbooks in the names of the Vessels. Give the
bankbooks to the manager. He'll show you the status of each account
along with addresses in different cities. With the cash you and Zeva play
while you find the Potentates and put them on planes to Havana.
You have a month. After that Zeva's passport is invalid. If she isn't back in
Havana, Consuelo is dead."

"I can imagine us playing. How many sons?"

"Some Vessels miscarried, and some, like I told you, had daughters.
Of twenty-eight babies, fifteen sons."

"Zev wants me to find fifteen men I never saw in my life, who could
be anywhere in the world, and put them on planes to Havana?"

"They won't be so hard to find. They look like him. Maybe a couple
are dead. There could be a few it wouldn't be wise to send to Fidel. You
have to study them; use good judgment. Figure, eleven. Maybe less. Look,
Consuelo is already in jail. You understand? It's under way."

"What if they won't go?" I said, panic in my heart. "Not everybody is
like me."

This was like agreeing that I might go. Unthinkable, but I'd said the
words. Not everyone is like me, including me, but I'd been shoved over

the edge with news about Consuelo. Sam picked up the implicit agreement. As if the main issue were settled, his mood changed. Encouraged,
he said, "Tell a guy in France or Norway he's won a free trip to Cuba,
and you think he won't go? Miami is full of European tourists and Latin
Americans. Not only drug barons. We've also got former dictators and
their dependents who are to a high degree scumbags. They drive around
in fancy cars, wearing gold chains and no shirts. Like the guy who lives
across from me. He parks on my grass. I asked him nicely not to do it, but
he keeps on doing it."

"Must be a scumbag."

"I've been feeding broken-glass hamburgers to his watchdog."

"Sam, I have an idea. You and Zev write letters to the Potentates and
stick plane tickets to Havana in the letters. I'll help."

"We don't know who they are. And maybe you're right, some won't
go. We'll tell you how to encourage them."

"You think I'm a travel agent."

"That could be your cover—a business card, official papers, home
office in Miami, secretaries answering the phone."

I detected in Sam's long narrow face, broken by the glint of small dark
eyes, an *idea* of me passing across his features like a breeze across a lake.
It touched the strong nose, the sensuous droop of his lower lip. But it
wasn't me. He saw the travel agent. There'd been a flash of intenser concentration on my presence, like an animal fixed in his gunsight stare,
through which I could see Zev's stare, his invincible determination of
how things will be; and I saw that I had nothing to say about it, only to
behave as Zev assumed I would, because I wasn't a crook and there was
nothing I wanted.

I said, "There are chores I have to do in Berkeley. Not very important,
but they're my life, such as it is. Otherwise, I'd leave for Zurich this minute.
What the hell. Why not? Zev is my favorite uncle. I owe him plenty."

"What do you have to do? I mean *have to do*. Like pay some bills?"

"That's right. Like pay some bills. Telephone, gas, electric . . ."

"Like pick up your car at the dealership?"

"Yes, as a matter of fact."

"The new clutch was five hundred and seventeen bucks. We paid.
The car is sitting outside your place. Your landlady will drive it around
the block every couple of days. Your other bills are also paid. As for your
girlfriend's birthday present . . ."

"Oh God."

"You forgot, didn't you? Don't even know your own fucking life. Lawyers, accountants, and car mechanics—total strangers—are living your life. We bought your girlfriend a pair of earrings at Gump's. Antique jade. They go with her eyes. She'll be pleased. There is nothing left for you to forget. You're a free man."

"What about my new glasses? They're waiting for me this week in Berkeley at Dr. Schletter's office."

Sam shoved a brown leather glasses case across the table. I took out the glasses, tried them on. They seemed correct. He called for the check.

A free man, I never felt more helpless except in dreams where I'd want to scream or run and couldn't. I followed him to his car.

"A million bucks to spend traveling around the world with a beautiful girl, and he worries about his glasses. What a putz. Wait till Zev hears this. He'll change his mind about Chester."

"No, he won't."

Sam laughed. "He thinks you're perfect."

Zev's plane was a silver twin-engined jet with two pilots. The first to emerge was a light-skinned black woman. For an instant I thought she was Zeva. The same size as Zeva with her dancer's legs, strict posture, aristocratic neck. She wore a one-button jacket and short tight skirt. High heels forced emphasis into her calves. The power and shape of her thighs were evident in the skirt, green-gray cotton, same as the jacket. Her blouse was lavender, like her shoes. She stood in the door and looked about the tarmac. Spotting Sam's car, she called into the plane, no doubt telling Zev we were here.

"Zev's pilot?"

"Also driver, bodyguard, business manager," said Sam. "You want my opinion, she's his sickness. Penelope de Assis. Reminds you of someone?"

"Except for the eyes."

They were mounted on the flared branches of her cheekbones, birds fashioned by a diamond cutter. Fifty feet away, I could tell they were blue.

"Where did Zev find her?"

"In Rio, dancing in the street for tourists. She was eight years old, shaking her ass to a conga drum. She's been with him fifteen years. She signs his checks, kid, so be polite. Her name, let me repeat, is Penelope. Don't call her Penny. Don't suppose any other familiarity is allowed. She's the one who fixed your life in Berkeley."

"Nobody knew about the glasses except me and Dr. Schletter."

"She saw a photo in a writer's magazine. You're at the typewriter working on a screenplay, but she could tell you weren't reading the type, so she phoned every optometrist within a mile of your house, to ask if your glasses were ready. Your girlfriend was easier. Penelope needed only her license plate number."

"How does she feel being a surrogate daughter?"

"She feels that Penelope de Assis—nobody else—is the daughter of the yid from Odessa, Zev Golenpolsky Lurie. That's how Zev once wanted it. Now he wants a little distance—room for the other women, you know what I mean? Is it too much to want? Penelope says no, no, no. She'd love to have a sister. She'd love to kill her."

"Let's push Penelope into the bay."

"Try it. I've seen her kick out a man's teeth. There's Zev."

He was coming down the steps from the plane, Penelope, at the bottom, watching. I saw his age in Penelope's tension—as if braced to save him should he lose his balance—and also in his slowness and caution. He glared at her, despising her concern or his dependency. The cossack-yellow hair was still yellow, straight, thick as honey and brushed back flat in the old fashion, appropriate to a dancing dandy. When he looked toward us and grinned, terrific peasant teeth appeared in the square, heavily structured Russky head, built for hard blows. He wore a black linen suit, pink shirt, gray tie. He carried nothing. I hadn't seen him for over twenty years—our dealings were by phone, me asking for favors until he asked—not that I'd understood—for my life. He looked much as I remembered. Sam and I got out of the car. Zev came toward us. Then I could see more indications of age—seams in his neck and a downward pull about the wide, heavy mouth—but still, in his sixties, Zev could pass for a younger man, even here in the Miami sunlight through which he approached with a strong step, the blue-eyed Penelope de Assis at his side.

He embraced me, then shoved me back, arm's length, his hands lingering on my shoulders.

I said, "You betrayed me, Uncle Zev."

He shook his head, sighing. His words came slowly, with the weariness of ancient disappointment.

"You did me a favor unknowingly. Is that what you call betrayal?"

"Yes."

"I'm sorry that's how you feel, but I can understand. I won't ask more of you. Say 'No, Uncle Zev. You ask for too much,' and I will walk right back into that airplane and there will be no hard feelings."

His green-and-yellow flecked eyes stayed strictly on mine as he extended his left hand toward Penelope, palm upward. "You have a reservation on the next flight to San Francisco. It leaves in two hours and forty-five minutes."

Penelope put an air-ticket envelope into his palm. He rattled it in my face.

"Say no. Use this ticket. You fly first class. Say it—'No, Uncle Zev. I feel deeply how much this means to you, but my answer is no.' A chauffeured car will meet you in San Francisco and drive you home. Phone your girlfriend. Take her to dinner at Jack's. It's on me."

"Uncle Zev, give me a chance to—"

"I'm still talking. Should you say yes, I have also made a reservation for you at my hotel in Key Biscayne. They're holding a bay-view suite. A speedboat is at your disposal. It's got a thousand horses. Penelope will drive you to the hotel and buy you decent clothes in the shop. To these old eyes, the way you're dressed, you look like a piece of shit."

"Uncle Zev, please, this isn't about clothes and speedboats."

"You got something better in your miserable life? What? Writing a screenplay? It's digging a ditch. They make a movie, the ditch becomes a sewer." He squeezed my shoulder. "Soft as a fairy."

"All right, enough." I snatched the ticket out of his hand and tore it in half. My freedom had been compromised by neediness and favors, but the trouble was deeper—in the chemistry. I stared at the epicanthic folds that lay on his tigerish, Genghis Khan eyes, the grainy texture of his heavy skin, the yellow hair—each of the billion strands an expression of his soul—and I was hypnotized by the force, the mystery of his particular being, which I couldn't reconcile with the idea that he was a son of a bitch. Penelope took the torn ticket from me and slipped it into her jacket pocket. Frugal.

"All right, what?"

"Introduce me to your daughter."

Having said "daughter," I glanced at her. There was no gratitude in her face. If she felt anything, it looked like anger. Maybe Sam hadn't told me enough. Zev's voice, now low and harsh, as if I'd kicked him in the groin, said, "Penelope de Assis, meet my nephew."

We shook hands. She said, "I'd like to talk to you."

"Listen to her," said Zev. "She knows more about you than you. Sam and I must have a short conference in the plane. We'll meet you later at the hotel and go to dinner. You'll be there. I like a Spanish restaurant on Calle Ocho. You know it, Sam?"

"The Malaga."

Zev snapped his fingers. "Correct." Turning to me, he said, "Afterward, we'll go dancing. What do you say?"

"What's the difference?"

"Truer words were never spoken. Buy clothes. Look good. Take a ride in the speedboat. Penelope, show my nephew how to live." Sam handed Penelope the keys to his car.

Driving to Key Biscayne, Penelope concentrated on the road and, it seemed, didn't want to speak. I figured I knew why. She'd witnessed my confrontation with Zev and decided she had nothing, after all, to say to me. With an apologetic and resentful tone—coming out of an irrational need to be polite and make her approve of me—I began to apologize for causing her trouble, though I was more sinned against than sinning—"I had no idea of the complications in my Cuba trip. I didn't even know you existed until a few minutes ago"—when she grunted and swung her arm, like a backstroke in tennis, banging my jaw with the heel of her fist. Blindly, reflexively, my hands flew up, catching the next blow on my wrists. The car swerved left and right as she overcorrected, hitting the brakes, tearing gravel. We stopped. A fiend with searing cold blue eyes screamed at me:

"Why didn't you just say no and get the fuck out of here?"

Then she stiffened, pressing herself back against the seat, and breathed deeply. A hundred cars and trucks passed before she restarted the engine, reentered traffic. We sped on to Key Biscayne.

My jaw was hot. I wanted to touch it, but I sat like a dummy, not looking at her legs, the skirt awry, pulled up to her crotch. Dummy or not, I was alert and feverish. Only she and I existed in Miami. Pray, I told myself, for patience. Be silent, strong, clean of heart. You don't know what's going on. A wrong word and she might drive into a palm tree.

As we pulled into the hotel grounds, she said she would go to the shop, buy some clothes, bring them to me. "You will keep whatever you like. I'll return the rest." She would choose the clothes alone. Her tone was cold and curt. No talk of styles, colors, materials. She didn't ask for my sizes. Go to my suite, sit in the bar, take a walk about the grounds, look at the trees, flowers, shorebirds, or ride in the speedboat. If I preferred, she would ride with me later. "I assume you'll want me," she said matter-of-factly, without the coyness or arrogance of a good-looking woman, or any apparent suspicion that I might prefer to strangle her. The boat ride didn't matter to her one way or the other. Please myself. She'd see me in an hour.

I went to my suite, lay down on a couch, got right up and looked out the window. Looked, didn't see, lay down again, shut my eyes, waited, waited, waited. There was a knock at the door. Penelope came in with jackets, shirts, pants, socks, shoes, and bathing trunks. She dropped everything on the couch, smiling faintly, as if amused by the colors and variety. I was glad to see this other face. It was possible almost to like her. But, far more important, despite her volatile personality, I was oppressed by desire. "Try this on," she said, holding up a jacket. I took it from her.

With Penelope looking, I stood before a mirror staring at my reflection. The clothes were horrible and exciting, too gorgeous, flashy, expensive-looking, designed. Penelope said, "That looks good. Return these shirts. Keep the two jackets. I like those shoes." She tossed clothes onto the couch, one pile to return, the other to keep. I was proud when she liked something, embarrassed when she didn't. Putting clothes on, taking them off, I began to sweat. It was hard work; her eyes on me. I said, "I can't stand this anymore."

"Let's go for the boat ride. I'll meet you at the dock in fifteen minutes." She snapped up the clothes to be returned. The door shut behind her. I waited ten minutes, opened the door, and walked out to the dock.

She was at the wheel of a speedboat, standing barefoot, in a black bikini and black sunglasses, not watching for me, just standing there, waiting. I climbed in and stood beside her, holding on to a rail. She turned on the engines and maneuvered slowly into the bay.

The Miami skyline was suspended in the enormous trance of late afternoon as we picked up speed heading into the heart of space. Then she cut the motor and the choppy, pummeling flight gave way to stillness and silence. Stillness and silence, deep and abrupt as when passing through the door of a cathedral into sanctified vacancy, but this was towering air above vast waters.

I wondered, as I often had, why falling in love is so important to everybody—since the invention of the feeling—but, in the ambient

grandeur, sense became sensation, and I entered a zone of blood, exceedingly alert, no thoughts. An airliner, lifting slowly above the city, seemed
motionless, like our drifting boat in the quiet afternoon. Penelope wasn't
in any hurry to talk. Neither was I. I waited as if for a degree of darkness
to descend and make words. Lights went on here and there among far-
away buildings, and a moon appeared. Penelope removed her sunglasses.
"Please forgive me for what happened earlier. I know what you think of
me," she said.

"I've forgotten the business in the car."

"That's good of you, but I would do it again. What I'm thinking
about, really, is that Sam told you I'm jealous and afraid I'll be shoved out
in the cold, didn't he?"

"He didn't say that."

"Yes, he did. I know the man. He had to say it. Perhaps you don't
listen carefully. He takes the simplest view of everything. That's what
makes him useful to Zev and also dangerous. Well, he's wrong about me.
I've no reason to be jealous or afraid. See that one and that one." She
pointed to a cluster of tall buildings. "I own them. I own buildings in New
York and Los Angeles, too, and a ranch in New Mexico and a chain of car
washes. Except for my brains and my ass, everything I own cometh from
Zev Lurie. But I am the owner. And there is always more, more, more. Zev
puts a paper in front of me and says, 'Sign.' I sign."

"Why does he do that?"

"So he won't be responsible for anything. Nobody can sue him, he
says, and take his property. But I believe he wants only to feel young. Like
a baby. Irresponsible. Property makes you age. So he's still a baby and I'm
five hundred years old—I own so much. Do you know why I'm telling
you this?"

"No."

"Guess."

"Your heart is broken."

"You're less stupid than I thought. What's she like?"

"You could be friends."

"What makes you think so?"

"She's very, very nice, but what's wonderful is . . ."

Penelope was wrong. I'm very stupid. I've said very stupid things. I've
lost sleep thinking about them. In a rush of pity—sympathy, affection,
hope—I said the most stupid thing ever. Her hands whitened on the

wheel. Tendons stood forth in her neck. Her eyes were huge, shining with pain.

"What do you mean, she looks exactly like me?"

"I don't mean anything. I am too enthusiastic. I exaggerated a trivial coincidence." I was almost shouting, as if to crush her anger before it gained momentum.

"What do you mean, coincidence? What the hell do you mean? This face? This neck? These arms and legs? What? She has these breasts?" She tore off the top of her bikini and pulled down the pants, flung the pieces at her feet, screaming, "This is me. This is me, not her."

There wasn't a lot more to see, seeing her naked. She was less modest than a three-year-old. Desire fled.

"I'm sorry," I said, stooping to pick up the bikini pieces at her lovely narrow feet; from there on up, trembling stone flesh. I slipped the bikini top over her head. She didn't do the rest, just let it hang like a rag necklace. Down on one knee, I held the bottom for her to step into it. She did. I drew it up her legs. We stood face to face.

Desire returned in a rush.

I looked away with a cry, looked back, kissed her, and—to my embarrassment—she merely said, "What's that noise?"

I let her go instantly and listened.

There was a bumping like my heart against the boat, though duller and trailing hollow reverberations along the bottom, irregular and persistent. We leaned over the side, peering into the water. "Must be a flashlight in the console," she whispered, as if someone were around to hear us. We didn't need the light. Sliding into view from beneath the boat, bobbing and bumping against the side, came the head and the gaping, glossy, moon-foiled eyes of White Trash, mouth open as if to suck the world. His right arm was gone, the stump stringy and red.

Penelope groaned, "Sharks," as a smooth gray snout, tiny eyes and undershot maw, burst from below and took White Trash's head away in a quick shake and a noise like tearing silk, then a slither, an arcing plunge into oblivion. I grabbed my neck, gagging as if it had happened to me. Penelope staggered to the wheel.

Engines coughed, grumbled, propellers took purchase on the bay. We lurched between white plumes lifting on either side like wings, as we raced toward the lights of Key Biscayne, me yelling against the rage of engines. "I know him, I know him. That's White Trash," I yelled, as if it were a great boast, my claim to a life of action. I yelled the whole story, how he followed me from the airport, how he ended in the bay, and then, having spent myself, I said, "I make trouble for everybody, don't I?"

She laughed. "Not the sharks." In a sweetly bemused tone, she added, "I hope you haven't made us late for dinner."

It occurred to me she was joking. I answered seriously, "You're going too fast and I don't want dinner. I don't want new clothes. I don't want speedboats. Zev can go to hell with his property. I don't want any of it—not even you. Tell him that. No, I'll tell him myself. I see what you're all doing and I don't want any of it. NOT EVEN YOU."

"Don't say that." Her voice was low, faintly reproachful. She slowed the boat. "I was only teasing, because I'm turned on. Aren't you? Don't bullshit me about your fine character. Tell me the truth."

What I felt of exhilarating horror diffused into a generalized vibrancy. "I could fuck a seagull," I said with eerie tenderness, never more depraved or truthful.

"It's nothing personal?"

The speedboat drifted. Her eyes were strange diamonds, their authority not to be denied.

That night, sharks feasted in the fateful bay, and I loved her and loved the loving of her, which seemed very obvious, perhaps too obvious. She said, "What keeps you from loving me?"

Occasional clouds crossed the moon and were bleached to a glow.

Did she expect an answer?

I thought of Zev and Sam. The desk clerk would say I had gone for a speedboat ride with Penelope and never returned. Zev would be alarmed.

The enveloping night came down like a swirl of black camellias, except for stars and moon and the electric syllables of the Miami skyline singing cheerily against the blackness.

Penelope lay in my arms.

I hadn't forgotten what she said.

Gradually and gradually, it came to me that Zev wasn't alarmed. Not at all. My providential uncle hadn't gone to the hotel. If he'd bothered to phone the hotel desk, it was to confirm what he supposed.

However my life swerved, it answered to his remote determinations even as the fragrant waters of Penelope opened to me in widening circles like the Red Sea for Moses.

She said, "Do you like my body?"

"Can't you tell?"

"Why don't you say it?"

"I see that you aren't a monster."

"How sweet of you. But what if I were?"

"It would be a hard test."

"Then you don't love me."

"Not like that. You aren't my child."

"I'm young."

"Make me young."

It was better the second time. I was better, less eager, and her body spoke to mine in easy dreamy pleasure that seemed to rise from the very navel of the cosmos, flowing through her into me.

Holding my face, looking into my eyes, she said, "Your turn."

"No."

"Didn't you say that you wanted everything?"

"No."

"Can I give you something? How about a building?"

"No."

"Then take them all."

"That's nice of you, but I'm not a landlord."

"Not one little building? Tell you what, I'll give you five percent of one. You claim depreciation and never pay taxes again in your life. Spend the money on me."

"Who are you?"

"You're being cruel."

Labor and spin, yet everything returns from whence it came in the night. I found myself thinking, yeah yeah, in the manner of Uncle Zev—so who was I falling in love with? A mulatto from Rio—arms, legs—who? Aside from the delicate sweetness of her breathing, who?

The ogling moon hung upon my question. I kissed her neck, which answered me little.

Zev found her dancing in the street.

Now he had visions of a lonely deathbed in Brooklyn, wanting flesh of his flesh beside him.

"It's nothing personal?" she'd wittily said.

I licked her ears, then she put her tongue in my mouth. Dark, delicate scholarship.

I wondered if there would be another time. There wouldn't ever be everything, or enough, but there could be more. She lay on her back, eyes shut. She didn't have to see. I was there, like the night, completely given to her. I sat up and looked around.

A white star burned on the water, as if it were the *more* I had in mind. It was far away, growing bigger and brighter, an immense dazzling. Then it came toward us, shooting lights, searching the bay. I realized it was no star but some kind of ship, brighter than the stars, too bright to see in detail. Penelope sensed my tension, and sat up, too. We watched it approach.

"Good or bad?" she whispered.

I made out a high sharp prow and three tall masts strung with lights, a great steaming funnel among them, everything blazing white, beautiful as the Taj Mahal. Then I heard the doon-doon throb of conga drums and the sinuous elegance of a Latin flute. With the schooner almost upon us, I read, painted on the side, *El Señor*.

Two men at the stern leaned over a rail. One was Sam. The other was Zev. Zev shouted, "We've been looking for you two all over the bay. Come aboard. We're going to Cuba." He said it the Spanish way, "Cooba," shouting again, "Cooba." He and Sam laughed as powerful lights spun around our speedboat in crazily hilarious blinding celebration.

Penelope stood up and waved and laughed with them, marveling at the schooner, long and high and glacial, shining on the black water. "Isn't Zev certifiably insane?" she said, an awestruck child in her voice, very plaintive and adoring. She didn't care, but I covered her with my shirt anyway.

the nachman stories

nachman

IN 1982, RAPHAEL NACHMAN, visiting lecturer in mathematics at the university in Cracow, declined the tour of Auschwitz, where his grandparents had died, and asked instead to visit the ghetto where they had lived. The American consul, Dirk Sullivan, was surprised. Didn't everyone want to tour Auschwitz? He probably thought Nachman was a contrary type, peculiar, too full of himself. As for Nachman, he thought Sullivan was officious and presuming. Sullivan said he would call the university and arrange for a guide to meet Nachman at his hotel.

At eight o'clock the next morning, Nachman left his room and passed through the small lobby on his way to the still smaller dining room for coffee. He noticed a girl standing alone beside the desk. Her posture and impassive expression suggested she was waiting for somebody. She didn't glance at Nachman as he approached, so he assumed the girl wasn't his guide, but he asked anyway, "Are you waiting for me, miss? I'm Nachman."

The girl said, "Yes, I know. How do you do? I'm Marie, your guide."

She knew? She didn't smile, but Nachman told himself Poles aren't Americans. Why should she smile? She was here to do a job. She'd been sent by the university, at the request of the American consul, to be his guide. Perhaps she'd have preferred to do something else that morning. So she didn't smile, but neither did she look unhappy.

They shook hands.

Nachman invited her to join him for coffee. She accepted and followed him into the dining room.

Nachman wasn't inspired to make conversation at eight o'clock in the morning, but he felt obliged to do so out of politeness, though Marie looked content to sit and say nothing. After sipping his coffee he said, "I like Cracow. A beautiful city."

"People say it is a small Prague."

"From what I've seen, there has been no destruction of monuments and buildings."

"Russian troops arrived sooner than the Germans expected."

Nachman now supposed she would tell him the story of Cracow's salvation. She didn't. Again, he was slightly disconcerted, but the girl was merely terse, not rude. Her soft voice gave Nachman an impression of reserve and politeness.

"How fortunate," he said. "The city remained undamaged."

"There was plunder. Paintings, sculptures . . . Is 'plunder' the word?"

"Indeed. Are you a student at the university, Marie?"

"Yes. I study mathematics."

"Of course you do. They sent me someone in my field. I should have thought so."

"I attended your lectures."

"You weren't too bored?"

"Not at all."

"That's kind of you to say."

"You talked about the history of problems, which is not ordinarily done. A student might think all problems were invented the day of the lecture. I wasn't bored."

"Your English is good. Do you also speak Russian?"

"I was obliged to study Russian in high school."

"So you speak Russian?"

"I was unable to learn it."

"English came more easily?"

"Yes."

"What else were you obliged to study?"

"Marxism."

"Did you learn it?"

"I was unable to learn it."

"Why not?"

"I'm not very intelligent."

Nachman smiled. She'd said it so seriously.

"How old are you, Marie?"

"Nineteen."

"Are you from Cracow"

"No. A village in the country. The nearest city is Brest Litovsk."

"I've heard of Brest Litovsk."

"You would never have heard of my village."

It would be easier to study the girl if she talked and he listened, but Nachman asked questions mainly because he felt uneasy. It was a defensive approach.

The American consul had warned Nachman about Polish women and the secret police. It seemed unlikely that the secret police had employed this girl—less than half Nachman's age, a peasant with a solemn face—to compromise him and make him vulnerable to their purposes. She claimed to be a student of mathematics. Nachman could have asked her questions about mathematics and would discover quickly if she was the real thing, but it would be awkward and unpleasant if she wasn't. She didn't seem to be lying about her failure to learn Russian or Marxism.

So Nachman lit a cigarette and sipped his coffee. He never smoked at home in California, but it seemed appropriate to his sojourn in the old world, within the shadow of death.

Nachman didn't test Marie's knowledge of mathematics, and he decided not to ask anything further about her failure to learn Russian and Marxism. She was neither a police agent nor a village idiot. Beyond that, Nachman assumed, considering her manner, he wouldn't learn much about her. Not that it mattered. She had answered his questions sufficiently and complimented his lecture. At worst she made his American friendliness seem clumsy and naïve, or somehow irrelevant to the purpose of their meeting. If she didn't trust Nachman, she probably had good reasons, but it was awkward. He couldn't get his bearings.

The American consul, in his way, had also unsettled Nachman during their interview, and the memory lingered strongly. Nachman had said, "My field is mathematics. Nothing I do is secret, except insofar as it's unintelligible. I'm of no conceivable interest to the secret police. If they want to ask me questions, I'll give them answers. I'd do the same with anyone."

"You know many people, Professor Nachman."

"They are almost all mathematicians. Our work means nothing to the majority of the human race. I invent problems. If I'm lucky, I solve one and publish the solution before another mathematician. My publications are available to everybody who has access to a library and understands numbers. You needn't call me professor. Nachman will do."

"You're modest, Professor Nachman. You were invited to Cracow because your work has important implications . . ."

"What important implications?"

"I'm sure you know. Be that as it may, a casual remark about any of your colleagues or acquaintances is recorded and filed. There are listening devices everywhere. Even in my car. I'm sure they are in your hotel room."

"I don't gossip, and there is no one in my hotel room but me. I don't talk to myself. In my sleep, maybe, but I wouldn't know about that."

"I believe you, but if you were to say in conversation at a cocktail party, in all innocence, that So-and-so is a homosexual, or a heroin addict, or badly in debt, your comment would enter his file at the headquarters of the secret police. You might compare it to academic scholarship. With such innocent comments, gathered in different cities—not only in Poland—a detailed picture of So-and-so is eventually developed."

"For what purpose? It seems utterly mindless."

"Who knows what purpose will emerge on what occasion?"

"I never heard of a homosexual mathematician. Could you name one?"

"Yes, I could, and so could you, Professor Nachman, but my point is, we are not to name any. As for Polish women, they have destroyed American marriages more often than you might imagine."

"Are you married?"

"My marriage is in no danger, but thanks for your concern, Professor Nachman. The allure of Polish women is considerable. They are the most gorgeous women you will ever meet. I'm sure you noticed Eva, the receptionist."

"Does she destroy marriages?"

"With her, a man could fall in love in two minutes, perhaps sooner. It has been known to happen in Poland. Even a sophisticated executive of an international corporation, falling in love, soon forgets the distinction between matters of the heart and corporate information of a privileged and sensitive kind. Believe me when I say it has happened more than once. I will not name names, but I could tell you about one in particular. Every word he said was reported. The destruction of his marriage was incidental."

"I'm not married. I have no secrets. I don't gossip. I didn't come to Cracow for romantic adventures. It's arguable that I'm a freak. You're wasting your time, Mr. Sullivan, unless you want to make me frightened and self-conscious."

"My job is to welcome American visitors like you, Professor Nachman, and to mention these things. Bear in mind that your value to the secret police is known to them, not you. By the way, I have your ticket for the tour of Auschwitz. Compliments of the State Department."

Nachman said, "Thank you. I don't want to tour Auschwitz. I would like to see the ghetto, particularly the synagogue."

Marie said they could walk after breakfast from the hotel to the ghetto. She added, as they left the hotel, "On the way, we can see an ancient church. Many visitors ask to go there."

Like the consul, she was telling him where to go, but she seemed less personal and intrusive. Nachman didn't object.

It was an extremely cold morning. Marie walked with a long stride, easily and steadily. Nachman supposed that she could walk like that for hours and remain indifferent to the cold. He found himself adjusting to her rhythm, though he was hunched up in his overcoat, chin buried in his scarf, his arm muscles tight against his ribs. He didn't walk as smoothly as Marie. The pain of freezing air in his face was relentless. It got to his feet, too; made them blocklike.

"Do you go to church regularly?" he asked.

"I haven't been inside a church since I was a child," said Marie. "This one is famous, visited by many foreigners. I thought you might want to see it, but we can go directly to the ghetto. The church isn't important."

"Do you want to see the church?"

Marie became silent and for a moment seemed to wonder if she wanted to or not. Then she said, "Do you want to see the synagogue?"

It wasn't an answer. Maybe Marie felt she'd answered enough questions, or maybe he'd been mildly reproached. She seemed to resist conversation as if it were a distraction from the main thing. The girl had a strong character, but Nachman wondered if it was merely a kind of psychological narrowness or limited imagination. Look how she walks. No dreamer, this girl.

"My grandparents lived in the ghetto," said Nachman. "I don't know where, of course, but I want to see the synagogue. My grandfather was known for his piety. It is possible that he worshipped in that synagogue. But I know almost nothing. My parents saw no reason to talk to me about their life in Poland."

The way they walked in the cold seemed to shape Nachman's remarks, each phrase or sentence the length of a stride, more or less.

"You know almost nothing about your grandparents?"

"I have some old photos, so that's something, but I know very little. My grandmother died young, I think. In the photos she seems much younger than my grandfather."

"They didn't go to America with your parents?"

"My parents never forgave themselves. I suppose they didn't care to remember Poland and preferred that I never think about it. How much could they say that a child should hear?"

"I see. As a result, your life has been spared bitter memories."

"As a result, not a day passes that I don't think about it."

"You're more than curious about your grandfather. You want very much to know."

Nachman said lightly, "It's why I do mathematics."

The words surprised him. They sounded so simple and light, rather as though he merely meant what he said. He had intended to be ironic.

Marie glanced at Nachman, as if she had a question in mind, but decided not to ask it. Nachman continued, "As for my grandfather, he was frequently mentioned, but always in a mythical way. I heard that he was consulted by Polish nobility for his business acumen—what business, I don't know—and respected by the Jews for his piety and learning. What does piety mean? I'm sure many Jews observed the rituals, but only a few were respected for their piety. How is it recognized?"

"He must have been an interesting person."

"He was also a musician, and he was good at numbers. I heard that he could speak well on ceremonial occasions. I was told he was witty. But all of this is mythology. When I asked what instrument he played, I was told, 'Many instruments.' When I asked what he did with numbers, I was told, 'He did everything in his head and never used pencil or paper.' I don't know what he spoke about in public, or on what occasions. I was told that I look like him. I inherited his name, Raphael Nachman."

"The Germans didn't destroy Cracow, only your family history. That's why you came to Cracow."

"I was invited to lecture at the university. I wouldn't be here other-wise. If I learn something here it will be entirely by chance. Everything I know, I have always learned by sitting in a room with a pencil and some paper. My grandfather could do everything in his head. I'm not as good as he was. Maybe the problems have become different, or more complex. I'll tell you something strange. Ever since I arrived, I've had an uncanny sensation. It's as if I'd been here before. When I walk around a corner I expect to know what I'll see. I couldn't tell you in advance, but when I see it—a small square with a church and a restaurant or a theater—I feel I've seen it before. Cracow is a small city, but even so, one could get lost. I've walked around several times without a map and I get lost, but not for long. I have no sense of direction, yet sooner or later I find my way back to the hotel. Even the pavement has a strange familiarity. It seems to recognize me. It pulls at my feet."

"You don't need a guide."

"I certainly do. I don't know where things are."

"We will go directly to the synagogue."

"No, no. Take me to the church first. I would like to see what is interesting to visitors. We'll go first to the church, then to the ghetto and the synagogue."

Nachman was aware that he'd talked extravagantly, precisely what the American consul had warned him against. But Nachman wasn't in love, and he was talking more to himself than to Marie.

She seemed to listen to him with the most serious concentration, her expression so intense it was almost grim. She respected Nachman as a mathematician, no doubt. Perhaps she was now fascinated by his personal revelations. Maybe she felt privileged to hear about him in a personal way, but her feelings were of no consequence to Nachman. Still, he wanted her to be less reserved, perhaps to suggest that she liked his company and wasn't merely doing a job. She was a kid from the countryside, not a world-class Polish beauty like Eva, the receptionist at the American Consulate. There was no danger that Nachman would fall in love in two minutes. He felt free to talk, despite the consul. After today, he'd never see the girl again. No, he wasn't in love.

Nachman had never been in love for long, perhaps never at all, and he sometimes wondered how people knew they were in love. He'd had girl-friends, but the idea of any passionate derangement had never appealed to

him. He played the violin and he solved problems in mathematics. His
need for ecstasy was abundantly satisfied. Nachman wasn't especially
sensual. Two or three bites took care of hunger. The rest was nutrition. He
considered himself a congenital conservative, which is not to say anything
political. He was frugal by nature, and had no lust to consume the world,
and he didn't feel one was enlarged or made wise by experience. He'd
been outside the United States only once before, to attend the funeral of
an aunt in Toronto. This was his first trip to Europe. He walked to work
and hardly ever went anywhere farther than a mile from his house in
Santa Monica, though he visited his mother regularly in San Diego. Every
morning in Cracow he made the bed in his hotel room and cleaned up
after himself in the bathroom. The room looked as if Nachman weren't
guilty of existence.

If you said he was dull, many would agree, especially his American
colleagues at U.C.L.A. They were rarely excited by Nachman's mind in
action. While some mathematicians went flying toward proofs, Nachman
demanded tedious repetition. He was slow in conversation with colleagues, which was unusual for a mathematician, but the published work
of Slow and Repetitious Nachman was distinguished. Some colleagues
suspected that he wasn't slow, only perverse. Like a crab, Nachman
seemed to go backward while others were flying toward solutions, yet he
often arrived before them.

"Here we are," said Marie.

"This is a church?"

"This is the synagogue. We'll go to the church later."

Nachman shrugged. Marie was willful. She did what he wanted,
though it wasn't what he said he wanted.

An empty old building, heavy with abiding presence; certainly old,
older than mere history. Old in the sense of having long been used. Even
the large, flat, soot-blackened stones that formed a rough path to the door
had presence as opposed to history. The stones seemed alive to Nachman,
more alive than himself. He felt apprehensive, though not about anything
he might see, only about what he would feel. The hollow interior, which
reminded Nachman of the inside of a wooden ship, a caravel with a spacious hold, made an effect of stunning emptiness, as if recently and tem-
porarily abandoned by the mass of passengers, who would soon return
and fill the big, plain wooden space with the heat of their bodies and their
chanting. The congregation was gone, annihilated at a date memorialized

in books, but Nachman, overwhelmed by apprehensions and sorrow, felt he had only to wait and the books would prove wrong, the Jews would return and collect in this room, and he would find his grandfather among them and his grandfather would tell Nachman the names of all the people.

Nachman entered deeply into the space, and stood there with Marie beside him, neither of them speaking. Then they heard a noise, a cough or a sneeze, and turned toward the rear of the room. A man stood not far away, partly in the shadows, looking at them. He was less than average height and had a large head and broad shoulders. His neck was bound in a red silk scarf. It had once been an elegant scarf. The color still lived, but the silk was soiled by sweat and grease, and it was frayed. His gray wool coat seemed barely to contain his bulk, and his arms were too long for the sleeves. Presumably, the caretaker. He walked toward them, rude physical authority in his stride. Though he was far from young, there was vigor and strength in his torso and short bowed legs.

Marie spoke to him in Polish. He answered in a rough and aggressive voice from his chest, a voice so much unlike hers that he seemed to speak a different language. Then Marie said to Nachman, "He says there is no fee. It is all right for us to stay until he closes the building in the afternoon."

Nachman said, "Ask him questions."

"What questions?"

"Anything you like."

Marie spoke to the man again, and a conversation ensued that was not the least intelligible to Nachman, but he listened to the words as if he could follow them, and he heard his name mentioned by Marie. After a few moments, Marie said, "He has been the caretaker of the synagogue for more years than he can remember, from before the war. He says he remembers your grandfather. You look like him."

"You told him who I am?"

"I only mentioned the name Nachman. He said he remembered such a man, and you look like him."

"Ask him more questions."

"What more questions?"

"I don't know. Please just ask."

Marie spoke to the man again. He seemed to liven as he answered, as if this was an opportunity he longed for, his words like rocks tumbling from the crater of his chest. He made gestures with his thick hands to emphasize what he said. His face, which was a broad bone with small blue eyes and a wide mobile mouth, took on different expressions, each swiftly replacing the last. There was so much motion in his features that Nachman wasn't sure what the man looked like, only that it was a big face with small animalish blue eyes and a thick nose with burst capillaries along its length. He was full of talk, full of memories. They seemed to lift from within and push behind his eyes, as if they intended to burst through and be seen.

Nachman waited and watched, his heart thudding palpably. He listened so hard that he became dizzy with anticipation, as if at any moment he would understand Polish and know what the man was saying. Nachman hesitated to make a sound. He didn't dare ask Marie to tell him anything until the man said as much as he wanted. Marie finally turned to Nachman and said, "We should go now."

"But what did he tell you?"

"He told me that your grandfather Nachman was gifted. People would cross the street to touch his coat and then run away. His gift was mysterious and frightening. People came to him for advice, often about money matters, but also about love affairs and sickness."

"He had some kind of medical knowledge?"

"He knew herbs that could cure skin diseases. He helped Poles and Jews, but it was dangerous for him. He was afraid of his own powers, and would often suffer worse than the people who came to him with their problems and sickness. This fellow himself, the caretaker of the synagogue, says he once came to Nachman with a broken leg that wouldn't heal. The pain was indescribable. He says Nachman went into a trance. He suffered as if his own leg were broken. In his trance, he made strange sounds, as if he were talking to somebody in an unknown language, but not with words, only cries and grunts and shrieks. Let's go, Professor Nachman. We've heard enough."

Nachman didn't want to go.

"So what happened? Did his leg heal?"

"Yes."

Nachman stared at the man, much taken by a sudden affection for him. He wanted to hear more, but Marie was insistent.

"We can come back, if you like. Let's go now."

"What else did he say?"

"I'll tell you later."

"I must give the man something."

Nachman pulled bills from his pants pocket.

"Is American money acceptable? I have fifty dollars."

"Give him a dollar."

"That's not enough."

"He'll be happy with a dollar. Give it to him and let's go."

Nachman was trembling. Was this girl a guide, or some kind of Polish despot? He'd admired her strength of character, but at the moment it seemed more like obstinate and imperious willfulness. Nachman recalled the way she walked, her long, tireless stride. He thought suddenly it was consistent with her whole character, the stride of a warrior, a conqueror. It measured land. Wherever she strode she seized and possessed. Her voice was soft, but the softness enclosed a wire of steel. She was abrupt and terse. Her figure was lean as a fashion model's, but not languid. It had moral stiffness, military tension, as if built to endure. She was willful; pigheaded; less sensitive than even the oxlike caretaker. Nachman had asked for a guide, not a descendant of Genghis Khan. The Mongols had overrun Poland. Of course she could do math. The Chinese were great mathematicians.

Nachman gave the man five dollars, and then shook his hand. The man grinned and nodded thanks. Then, to assert himself against Marie's desire to leave, Nachman smiled at the man and embraced him.

Marie sighed. "He's not a Jew, Professor Nachman."

Nachman was startled by the remark.

Walking away from the synagogue, again with her rhythm, Nachman said, "I didn't care if he was a Jew. I hadn't thought he was a Jew or not a Jew. Why did you say that?"

"It seemed relevant. Perhaps I was mistaken."

"He was eager to talk about my grandfather. I learned something. I was grateful to him. If you don't mind, please tell me everything he said."

"He said your grandfather could play musical instruments, and he could sing Polish folk songs. He said a few other things."

"What other things? Please try to remember."

"He could juggle."

"Juggle? My grandfather was a juggler?"

For the first time that morning Marie raised her voice. "He said your grandfather could bend nails with his teeth. He could fly."

Understanding came to Nachman slowly, against strong resistance in his feelings.

Nachman was silent for several blocks. He was upset and confused, and the morning felt colder, though the sun was brighter and sharp, making the streets dazzle and every shadow black. The long walk hadn't warmed his body. When they came to the ancient church, he followed Marie inside, as if without personal will. It was less cold than the street, but far from warm.

The church was small and unusually dark, despite the tall windows that glared with color. There was a great deal of elaborately wrought gold and brass. It seemed to writhe and it gave off a dull hard shine, which intensified rather than dispersed the darkness. Clots of shadow formed about small flames of candles along the walls and in niches. A priest was conducting a service, and a dozen or so elderly men and women were gathered in the pews before him, some on their knees, some standing.

Nachman wandered away from Marie, retreating into the general darkness, absorbing the sensation of deep shadows and scattered brilliance of flame and metal, all of it enclosed in cold, heavy stone. He felt his isolation, his separateness within the church. He settled into the feeling, as if into the obscurity of a densely woven cloak. Long minutes passed before he remembered Marie and looked about for her. She was standing near the door, leaning against a pillar, looking at the priest, apparently absorbed by the ritual. Nachman approached her slowly and stopped a few feet away, waiting for her attention. She looked at him finally, and then moved toward him. As they walked together toward the door, she said, "Maybe I'll return. I don't know." Nachman understood that she meant return to the religion of her childhood.

Outside, Nachman lit a cigarette, his second of the day. He said, "Would you like to eat something? You must be hungry."

"There are no luxurious restaurants."

"Any place with heat will do. I'm cold."

"It's still early, but I know where we can have vodka. Eel, too, maybe. The owner is a distant relation. Would you like vodka? You can pay him in dollars."

"Vodka would be a blessing. I never in my life felt so cold."

The restaurant, a fair-sized, square room with pretty gold-hued wallpaper, was warmer than the church, but Nachman didn't remove his coat. The two waiters wore dinner jackets and ties. But there were no customers aside from Nachman and Marie. One waiter approached their table and presented menus and left. The other then came to the table. Nachman realized that the waiters were sustaining a ritual of service, for lack of knowing what else to do.

The menu was printed on large sheets of good, thick paper, and it listed a considerable variety of dishes, but Marie told him not to bother ordering any of them. It would embarrass the waiter. She said, "The dishes don't exist. If you like to feel nostalgic, you may enjoy reading the menu, but it will have no practical purpose. Vodka and eel. Would that be all right?"

"Yes, all right."

Nachman cared less about eating than simply sitting inside a fairly warm room, at a table with a clean white cloth. Glasses of vodka were set before him and Marie. Nachman picked up his glass and drank it all at once. The vodka went down in a delicious searing flow. He wanted another glass immediately. Two plates of eel, chopped into small sections, were set before them. Nachman ate a section. It went well with vodka.

Marie finished eating before he did. She sipped her vodka slowly.

Nachman urged her to take what remained of his plate of eel. She accepted.

"And two more vodkas."

With his third glass Nachman became high, and felt better, almost good. His vision seemed to improve, too. Marie's plain face took on a glow and looked rather beautiful. What is plain, anyway? Nachman asked himself. Her features were nicely proportioned. Nothing was ill-shaped. Others wouldn't call her beautiful, but it was a good face, beautiful enough for Nachman. Where you expected a nose, she had a nose, and a mouth, a mouth. Her face looked fine to him. A bit long, perhaps, and somewhat solemn, but normal and unobjectionable, however plain. Nachman was sure he would remember her face with pleasure. Her brown eyes were intelligent and kind. What more could a man want? A beautiful face, afflicting people with passionate love, must be a tragic burden. But why was he thinking this way? In a city where his grandparents had been murdered, and the history of his family lost. The irresponsibility of feelings was a serious problem. But Nachman felt no obligation to define the problem, let alone solve it. For an instant, Nachman wished that he could love Marie, feel what a man is supposed to feel for a woman, but not for the sake of ecstasy. He would have liked something real, true, consistent with his nature, like the vodka, maybe. Pain, but a good pain. After today he'd never see Marie again. He already felt the poignancy of her absence from his life. She'd been an excellent guide. He wanted to kiss her.

"Would you like another vodka?"

"No thank you," her voice was soft and polite as usual.

He remembered how she said, "He's not a Jew, Professor Nachman," and how she'd raised her voice to him in the street walking away from the synagogue. She'd known what Nachman was feeling under the spell of the caretaker and had wanted to protect him. But from the way she looked at him now, he could tell that she had no idea what he was feeling. For her, ordinary life had resumed. She simply looked as if, even in her personal depths, she was polite. She accepted what was there, didn't wonder. It wasn't in her to be intrusive, to speculate about his soul, and yet when it mattered, she'd understood and been with him. Nachman knew he was being sentimental, indulging a feeling. It was partly due to the vodka, but Nachman was suddenly awed by this plain girl, and it didn't seem unrealistic or foolish or morally dubious, and he knew the feeling would outlast this moment.

nachman from
los angeles

IF NACHMAN WAS GIVEN fifteen cents too much in change, he'd walk half a mile back to the newsstand or grocery store to return the money. It was a compulsion—to make things right—that extended to his work in mathematics. He struggled with problems every day. When he solved them, he felt good and he also felt that he was basically a good man. It was a grandiose sensation, even a mild form of lunacy. But Nachman wasn't smug. He had done something twenty years before, when he was a graduate student at U.C.L.A., that had never felt right and still haunted his conscience. The memory of it came to him, virtually moment by moment, when he went to the post office or when he passed a certain kind of dark face in the street. And then Nachman would brood on what had happened.

It had begun when Nachman saw two men standing in front of the library on the U.C.L.A. campus. One was his friend Norbert, who had phoned the night before to make a date for coffee. Norbert hadn't mentioned that he was bringing someone, so Nachman was unprepared for the other man, a stranger. He had black hair and black eyes, a finely shaped nose, and a wide sensuous mouth. A Middle Eastern face, aristocratically handsome.

Better-looking than a movie star, Nachman thought, but he felt no desire to meet him, only annoyance with Norbert. He should have warned Nachman, given him the chance to say yes or no. Nachman would have said no. He felt the beginning of a cold sore in the middle of

his upper lip. Nachman wasn't vain, but the stranger was not merely handsome. He was perfect. Comparisons are invidious, thought Nachman, but
that doesn't make them wrong. Compared with the stranger, Nachman
was a gargoyle.

"Nachman, this is Prince Ali Massid from Persia," Norbert said, as if
introducing the prince to a large audience and somehow congratulating
himself at the same time. "The prince has a problem. I told him you
could help and I mentioned your fee, which I said is in the neighborhood
of a thousand bucks."

Nachman assumed that Norbert was joking, but the prince wasn't
smiling. With modest restraint, the prince said, "Norbert thinks of me as
an exotic fellow. He tells people I am from Persia or Jordan or Bahrain.
I've lived mainly in Switzerland. I went to school in Zurich, where there
were a dozen princes among my classmates. I have noble relations, but
in America I am like everyone else. My name is Ali. How do you do,
Nachman? It is a pleasure to meet you."

Nachman said, "Oh?"

The little word "Oh" seemed embarrassing to Nachman. What did
he mean by "Oh"? He then said, "How do you do? I'm Nachman from
Los Angeles."

Norbert said, "What is this, the UN? Switzerland, Persia, Jordan—
who cares? Ali's problem is about a term paper. He'll explain it to you."

Norbert walked away, abandoning Nachman and Ali. Nachman
grinned at Ali and shrugged, a gesture both sheepish and ingratiating. "I
don't always know when Norbert is joking. I thought I was meeting him
for coffee. He didn't mention anything else."

"I understand. Norbert was indiscreet. He is like a person at a
séance who speaks beyond himself. He has no idea how these things are
done."

What things? Nachman wondered.

Ali smiled in a knowing manner, and yet he seemed uncertain. The
smile flashed and, before it was fully formed, vanished. "Norbert is in my
city-planning class, and we talk about this and that. The other day, I mentioned my problem, you see, and Norbert said that he had a friend who
could write papers. He insisted that I meet his friend. So here I am—you
know what I mean?—and here you are. I want to ask you to write a
paper, you see."

"I see."

"I cannot write well, and I have done badly in one class, which is called Metaphysics. I should never have taken this class. I imagined it had to do with mysticism. Please don't laugh."

"Who's laughing?"

"It happens that this class has nothing to do with mysticism, only with great thinkers in metaphysics. I am not interested in metaphysics, you see."

Ali nodded his beautiful head as though he were saying yes, yes, making a gentle obbligato to his soft voice, and his hands made small gestures, waving about and chasing each other in circles. It was distracting. Nachman wanted to say, "Stop doing that. Talk with your mouth." Only Ali's eyes remained still, holding Nachman's eyes persistently, intimately, in their darkness.

"But I don't write well about anything, not even about mysticism, you see, and I have no desire to try to write about metaphysics."

"Why don't you drop the class?"

"Good question. I should drop the class, but it's now too late, you see. I was hoping the professor would eventually talk about mysticism. There are people, you know, who talk and talk and never come to the point. The professor is a decent man and he is doing his best, but if I fail I won't graduate. This would ruin my plans. Your friend Norbert said that you would be sympathetic. He said that you could write about metaphysics."

"I don't know anything about metaphysics. I don't even know what it is. I'm a student in mathematics."

"Norbert said you could write about anything. He was sincere."

Ali sounded as if he were sliding backward down a hill he had just struggled to climb. Nachman felt sympathy. Ali had persuasive force, because of his looks, but also because he seemed to engage Nachman personally, irresistibly. It wasn't strictly correct to write a paper for someone else, but Nachman already knew that he was willing to help.

"I'm sure Norbert was sincere," Nachman said. "Norbert wants to start a paper-writing business. Did he tell you that?"

"No. But I applaud this idea. Many students need papers. You will be partners with Norbert?"

"I never said that, but you have to let a friend talk. Talking is Norbert's way of life. He is always broke, but he doesn't think about getting a job. He schemes day and night. And he dollars me. You know the expression? 'Nachman, lend me a dollar.' He never pays me back. He had the idea about the paper-writing business. I don't need the money. I have a scholarship that covers books and living expenses."

"Even so, you must go into business with Norbert. Because of your friendship. Norbert loves you, and he had a splendid idea. Norbert brings you poor students like me, and you write the papers. He gets a percentage, and soon he will owe you nothing. Will you do it? A thousand dollars."

"It's not a question of money. If I write a paper, it will be a good paper."

"So you will help me?"

"What was the assignment? Let me think about it."

"I need a paper on the metaphysics of Henri Bergson. About twenty pages. It's due in three weeks."

"Bergson writes about memory, doesn't he?"

"See, Nachman, you already know what to write. If a thousand dollars isn't enough, I'll pay more. Will you do it?"

"I don't know."

"Don't know if you will do it? Or if a thousand isn't enough?"

"One, I don't know. Two, I also don't know. The money is Norbert's department. Talk to him about the money."

"So we have a deal?"

With a fantastic white smile in his dark face, Ali put forth his hand. Reflexively, Nachman accepted it. A line had been crossed. Nachman hadn't noticed when he crossed it. Maybe Ali had moved the line so that, to Nachman's surprise, it now lay behind rather than in front of him. Ali's expression was deeply studious, as if he were reading Nachman's heart and finding reciprocity there, a flow of sympathy equivalent to Ali's need. For Nachman the reciprocity was too rich in feeling and too poor in common sense. He felt set up, manipulated. But he'd shaken hands.

"I'll phone you," Ali said. He nodded goodbye. Nachman nodded, too, and walked into the library, went to the card catalogue, and pulled out a drawer. He found cards with the name Henri Bergson printed on them, and he copied the titles of several books onto call slips. Half an hour later, Nachman left the library and went to his car, a blue-and-cream-colored Chevy Bel Air.

Nachman's apartment was in the basement of a house in the Hollywood Hills, near Highland Avenue. It had a bedroom and living room, a tiny

kitchen, a bathroom, and low ceilings. It was cramped, but not unpleasant. The windows, approximately at ground level, looked down a
steep hillside to a narrow winding street. Nachman could see ice plants,
cacti, rosebushes, and pine trees.

Sitting at the kitchen table, Nachman picked up a book by Henri
Bergson. According to the jacket, Bergson had won a Nobel Prize in
Literature and had influenced the intellectual and spiritual life of the
modern age. He'd intended to convert to Catholicism, but when the
Nazis invaded France and began rounding up Jews, Bergson elected to
remain what he was, a Jew. His story was heartbreaking, but seemed
irrelevant to Nachman from Los Angeles. To Nachman, all religious insti-
tutions were frightening. Read the books, Nachman thought, just read
the books.

That evening when the phone rang, Nachman picked it up and
shouted, "Norbert, are you out of your mind?"

"A thousand dollars, Nachman."

"Ali wants me to write a paper about Henri Bergson."

"Who is Henri Bergson?"

"You wouldn't be interested and I don't want to talk about him. If
you think writing a paper is easy, you do it."

"Nachman, I once tried to keep a diary. What could be easier?
Little girls keep diaries. Every night I opened my diary and I wrote 'Dear
Diary.' The next thing I wrote was 'Good night.' Nothing comes to me.
I'm a talker. Believe me, Nachman, I can talk with the best, but I can't write."

"What does that have to do with me, Norbert? You did a number
on me."

"Come on, man. A thousand dollars. We'll take a trip to Baja, hang
out on the beach. It'll be great."

Norbert's voice had a wheedling, begging tone. It was irritating, but
Nachman forgave him. Although he came from a wealthy family in Beverly Hills, Norbert needed money. He carried books around campus and
even went to classes, but wasn't a registered student because he couldn't
pay his fees. His father had cut him off when he'd gotten a small tattoo on
the side of his neck. There had been a dreadful scene. Norbert's father, an
eminent doctor, considered tattoos low class. Norbert still lived at home
in Beverly Hills and drove one of the family cars, a Mercedes convertible.
He paid for gas with his mother's credit card. But until the tattoo was removed he wouldn't get a cent. For months he'd wandered around campus

with his tattoo and no job. He didn't want a job. He could survive in an original manner. He had business ideas.

"I don't know anything about metaphysics," said Nachman.

"What do you have to know? It's all in a book. You read the book and copy out sentences and make up some bullshit. *Finito*. That's a paper. Do me a favor, Nachman, look at a couple of books. Flip through the pages and you'll know all you need."

"I've been reading for hours."

"That's good, that's good."

"Norbert, have you ever read a book?"

"Ali told me you promised. He is very happy."

"It's not for the money, and not because I want to go to Baja and hang out on a beach."

"I understand."

"I'm doing it because I like Ali. He's a nice guy."

"I feel the same way about him."

"After this, no more. I'll do this one time."

"You're O.K., Nachman."

"You're an idiot, Norbert."

"I'm glad you feel that way. But don't get too sentimental about Ali and forget the money part. Ali is very rich, you know. I would write a paper for Ali every day, but I can't write. You should see Ali's girlfriend, by the way. Georgia Sweeny. You ever go to football games? She's a cheerleader. An incredible piece. I'd let her sit on my face, man."

Nachman hung up.

Norbert was shockingly vulgar. Nachman felt resentful, unwilling to write the paper, but then he remembered the look in Ali's eyes. It had nothing to do with the cheerleader or with being rich. Nachman's resentment faded. He went back to the books and read through the night.

For the next three days, he did none of his own work. He read Henri Bergson.

At the end of the week, Ali phoned.

"How are you, Nachman?"

"O.K."

"That's wonderful news. Have you given some thought to the paper?"

"I've been reading."

"What do you mean, reading?"

"I can't just start to write. I'm in math. It's not like philosophy. Math you do. Philosophy you speculate. Did you ever hear of Galois? He was a great mathematician. He fought a duel. The night before the duel, he went to his room and did math, because he might be killed in the duel and not have another chance."

"Was he killed?"

"Yes."

"What a pity. Well, I agree completely. You must read and speculate. But is it coming along?"

"Don't worry."

"I'm sorry if I sound worried. I am confident that you will write the paper. A good paper, too. Do you mind if I phone now and then?"

"Phone any time," said Nachman.

He liked Ali's voice—the way feelings came first and sense followed modestly, a slave. The voice was consistent with Ali's looks. Nachman wanted to ask, jokingly, if he had a sister, but of course he couldn't without embarrassing Ali and himself.

"Can I invite you to dinner?" Ali asked. "You can't speculate all the time. It will give us a chance to talk."

"Sure. Next week."

Nachman went back to the reading.

Metaphysics was words. Nachman had nothing against words, but as a mathematician, he kept trying to read through the words to the concepts. After a while, he believed he understood a little. Bergson raised problems about indeterminate realities. He then offered solutions that seemed determinate. Mathematicians did that, too, but they worked with mathematical objects, not messy speculations and feelings about experience. But then—My God, Nachman thought—metaphysics was something like calculus. Bergson himself didn't have much respect for mathematics. He thought it was a limited form of intelligence, a way of asserting sovereignty over the material world, but still, to Nachman's mind, Bergson was a kind of mathematician. He worked with words instead of equations, and arrived at an impressionistic calculus. It was inexact—the opposite of mathematics—but Bergson was a terrific writer, and his writing was musical, not right, not wrong.

By Monday of the second week, Nachman had read enough. He would reread, and then start writing. He would show that Bergson's calculus was built into the rhythm and flow of his sentences. Like music, it was full of proposals, approximations, resolutions—accumulating meaning, building into crescendos of truth.

Ali phoned.

Nachman said, "No, I haven't started, but I know what I'm going to say. I love this stuff. I'm glad I read it. Bergson is going to change my life."

"I'm glad to hear that. You are marvelous, Nachman. I think the writing will go quickly. Perhaps you will be finished by tomorrow, almost two weeks ahead of time. I never doubted that you would do it."

Ali's faith in Nachman was obviously phony. He was begging Nachman to start. Despite his assertions, Ali lacked confidence. More troubling was Ali's indifference to Nachman's enthusiasm. That he didn't care about metaphysics was all right, but he also didn't care that Nachman cared. Nachman's feelings were slightly hurt.

"It's only been a week, Ali. Tomorrow is too soon. I still have two weeks to write the paper. I could tell you what I'll say. Do you want to hear?"

"I am eager to hear what you will say. So we must have dinner. The telephone is inappropriate. At dinner you can tell me, and I can ask questions. How about tonight? We will eat and talk."

"I'm busy. I have my own classes to think about. My work."

Surprised by his reproachful tone—was he objecting to a dinner invitation?—Nachman tried to undo its effect. "Tomorrow night, Ali. Would that be good for you?"

"Not only good, it will be a joy. I will pick you up. I have in mind dinner at Chez Monsieur. The one in Brentwood, of course, not Hollywood."

"I never heard of Chez Monsieur in Brentwood or Hollywood. But no restaurant music. I can't talk if I have to hear restaurant music." Nachman sighed. He was being a critical beast. Couldn't he speak in a neutral way? "Oh, you decide, Ali. If you like restaurant music, I'll live with it."

"I'll tell the maître d' there must be no music. Also no people at tables near ours."

"Do you own the place?"

"Tomorrow night I will own the place. Have no fear. We will be able to converse. When I make the reservation, I will also discuss our meal with the maître d', so we will not have to talk to a waiter. What would you like, Nachman? I can recommend certain soups, and either fowl or fish. Chez Monsieur has never disappointed me in these categories. I don't want to risk ordering meat dishes. I've heard them praised many times by my relatives, but personally, I'd rather not experiment."

"Ali, please order anything you like."

"But this is for you, not me. I want you to enjoy the meal."

Ali's solicitousness made Nachman uncomfortable. He wasn't used to being treated with such concern for his pleasure. "I'll trust your judgment."

"And the wine?"

"The wine? You would like me to decide on the wine? If they run out of wine, I'll settle for orange soda."

"That's very funny. I'll come for you at eight. Give me your address."

Promptly at eight, Nachman stood outside the house. The limousine appeared one minute later. A door opened. Nachman saw that Ali was wearing a dinner jacket. Nachman was wearing his old gray tweed jacket, jeans, and a white shirt open at the collar. He hadn't been able to find his tie. In jacket, shirt, jeans, and no tie, Nachman climbed into the limousine.

Ali greeted him in a jolly spirit, "As you see, Nachman, I'm incapable of defying convention. Not even in California, where defiance is the convention. I must tell you a story. It will make you laugh."

There was no uncertain, embarrassed smile flashing and vanishing in the dark face. There was nothing apologetic or needy in his manner. The limousine went sliding down Highland Avenue into the thrill of the city's billion lights, and Ali talked cheerily. Nachman sank into the embrace of soft gray leather and studied the back of the driver's head. The limousine smelled good. It seemed to fly. Tinted windows made Nachman invisible to the street. Such privilege and sensuous pleasure. He felt suspicious of it, as if he were being made to believe that he liked something he didn't like and could never have.

Ali said, "One evening not long ago—this was after I came to America—when I first started to go out with Sweeny . . . Have I told you about Sweeny?"

"No."

"She is my girlfriend. Do you go to football games? You would know who she is."

"She plays football?"

Ali paused. He lost his storytelling momentum and seemed to sneer faintly, but the expression quickly changed, became a smile.

"Sweeny is a cheerleader."

Nachman had been unable to resist the joke. The limousine, Ali's dinner jacket, and Nachman's embarrassment at his inappropriate attire had made him feel—yes, he named it—like a jerk. Hence, he became a comedian, keeping his dignity by sacrificing it.

"As I was saying, Nachman, I picked her up at her apartment and I arrived wearing jeans. Sweeny shrieked. Why is Sweeny shrieking? I asked myself. It was because my jeans had been ironed, you see. I laughed. I was being a good sport, laughing at myself. In my heart, I was bitterly ashamed. When she stopped shrieking, Sweeny was able to explain. Ironed jeans, you see, are horrifying. An American would know this, but I had just arrived and I had never before worn jeans. Naturally I had had them ironed. Can you imagine my shame?"

Ali wanted to make Nachman feel that his outfit was all right. Nachman appreciated his intention, but the word "shame" was telling. Ali thought Nachman looked shameful.

The limousine stopped in front of a white stucco building with a tile roof. There was no sign, no window, no doorman. Ali led Nachman through an ordinary wooden door, and *voilà*! Chez Monsieur, a restaurant reserved for those in the know. It was two rooms, one opening into the other, neither very large. The decor was subtly graded tones of gray and ivory. A panel of black marble, like a belt, swept around the rooms. Nachman instinctively recoiled, but tried to cover by asking, "Do you come here often?"

Ali seemed not to have heard him. Maybe the question was contemptible. A man appeared and shook hands with Ali, then led them through the first room, which had a bar and several tables occupied by men and women in beautiful evening clothes. Not one head turned to look at Nachman, despite his shameful attire. This crowd, Nachman thought, is as cool as the decor. In the other room, Nachman saw empty tables. All had cloths and plates and napkins, but only one was set with silver and glasses. Ali had reserved the entire room.

Waiters came and went. Dishes were placed before Nachman, wine was poured, dishes were removed. Everything was done with speed and grace, in silence. Ali chattered happily from one course to the next, describing the preparation of the soup and fish. He was playing the gracious host. Nachman glanced up now and then and said, "Good."

"I'm so pleased you like it," Ali said.

Nachman was beginning to feel resentful again. He disliked the feeling. It had surprised him repeatedly in the past few days. That afternoon, before meeting Ali, Nachman had imagined with excitement how he would talk about the paper. But Ali was absorbed by the food and the sense of himself as a man who knew where and how to eat. Nachman thought the restaurant seemed too old for Ali, who was in the prime of life, the lover of the mythical Georgia Sweeny. Did he really care so much about food? Nachman remembered Norbert's comment about Georgia Sweeny. It now seemed less vulgar than healthy.

They finished a bottle of wine. Another bottle was set on the table. Ali had signaled for it with a nod or a glance. Nachman hadn't noticed. He'd already had a lot to drink. His attention was diffuse. He forgot about the paper. Ali now talked about Sweeny. He wanted to spend some years in Teheran, but Sweeny refused to live with restrictions on how she could dress. It was a perplexity. The chador was peasant attire, of course, but even at the higher levels some women found it pleasing. Ali laughed at the idea of Sweeny in a chador. After all, she appeared nearly naked before a hundred thousand people on Saturday afternoons. Nachman laughed, too, though he wasn't sure why. Intermittently, he said things like "I see" and "Is that so?" He was hypnotized by pleasant boredom. It struck him that lots of people go through life without ever talking seriously about anything, let alone Bergson's metaphysics.

The table was cleared, the cloth swept clean, and reset with fresh glasses and an ashtray. Ali ordered port. He settled back in his chair. A fine sheen of perspiration appeared below his dark eyes. The port arrived in a black bottle with a dull yellow label. It was held over a small flame and decanted. The taste was thick and sweet, sliding along the tongue. Ali offered Nachman a cigar. Nachman didn't smoke cigars, but he accepted it anyway. They clipped the ends. Ali held a cigarette lighter to Nachman's cigar and said, "Tell me, Nachman. It must be nearly finished, am I right?"

Nachman drew against the flame. He flourished the cigar and exhaled a stream of white smoke. "It's finished," he said, an air of dismissive superiority in his tone.

"Marvelous. I've been dying to hear about it."

"Hear about what?"

"The paper."

"Right. Well, it's coming along."

"You just said it was finished."

"I mean in my head. Writing is a tedious chore. I'll put it in the mail by Friday."

Ali reached into the inside pocket of his jacket and withdrew a small card. He handed it to Nachman. Ali's name, address, and telephone number were inscribed in brilliant black ink. He said, "Could you give me a sense of the paper?"

Nachman cleared his throat, then laid the cigar in the ashtray and brushed his napkin across his lips. Earlier, he'd been eager to talk about the paper. He had no heart for it now. Ali sensed Nachman's reluctance. His dark eyes enlarged by a tiny degree and his mouth shaped itself with feeling. A subtle swelling, almost a pout, appeared in the lower lip. Nachman suddenly felt an intense desire to give Ali a pleasure that was worth ten thousand dinners, the undying pleasure of an idea. Nachman decided to say everything, to make it felt.

"I will begin the paper with a discussion of Zeno's paradox, then move swiftly to Leibniz's invention of calculus. Then, then comes the metaphysics, but a good deal, Ali, depends on how I imitate Bergson's musical style, particularly as I elucidate his idea of intuition. I could put it all in a simple logical progression, but the argument would be sterile, unnatural, and unconvincing. Don't misunderstand me. Bergson is not some kind of rhetorician, but it is critical to understand what he means when he talks about intuition, and for this you must see why his style, his music, his way of advancing an argument by a sort of layering . . ."

Ali interrupted: "I told Sweeny about your extraordinary grasp of metaphysics."

Nachman hesitated. Ali raised an eyebrow and smiled. His expression intimated that, speaking man to man, Sweeny was relevant to metaphysics.

"She said she would love to meet you."

"Me?" A sensation of heat suffused Nachman, filling him with a confusion of hurt and rage.

"It isn't inconceivable that you would enjoy her company."

The remark had a provocative thrust.

"I don't object to meeting Sweeny."

"You sound reluctant, Nachman." Ali was teasingly ironic, with an edge of contempt.

"I wasn't thinking about meeting anyone."

"Sweeny would be the first to admit that she isn't an intellectual. Don't imagine otherwise. She has no pretensions of that sort. Perhaps you object to wasting time with people who aren't intellectuals."

"I know plenty of people who aren't intellectuals."

"Sweeny has other virtues. There is more to life than intellect."

"I'm not crazy about intellectuals. Norbert is my best friend and he is an idiot. What are Sweeny's other virtues?"

"She is a woman who exists for the eyes. Some things shouldn't be described in words; among them are women like Sweeny. It cannot be done without desecration. That's the reason for the chador. A man shouldn't share his woman with other men, but I will make an exception for you. The three of us will go out some evening. Do you like to dance?"

"I can't dance."

"Perhaps it isn't intellectual enough."

"I also can't swim. These things are related."

"How are they related?"

"I'm deficient in buoyancy, you know what I mean? To dance you must be light on your feet. Buoyant, as in water."

"There is something heavy in your nature, Nachman."

"I can't even float, Ali. If I lie down in the water, I sink."

"Well, Nachman, you don't have to dance. It would be enough to talk to Sweeny about metaphysics. She has never met a man who could tell her about metaphysics."

The conversation was more like Ping-Pong than a fight with knives, and yet the hostility was obvious. Ali didn't want to hear about the paper. Ali didn't want to hear about Bergson or metaphysics. He was flaunting Sweeny, even giving her to Nachman, though not quite as he had given him the superb dinner. Ali's generosity had been reduced to an insulting message. Nachman could have wine and port and a Cuban cigar. Some

night he could dance with Sweeny. But with all the metaphysics in the
world, he could never have a girlfriend like her.

There was no business with the check. There was no check. Ali simply
stood and walked away from the table. Nachman followed him. The
limousine was waiting. They climbed inside. It slipped away from the
building and gained a dreamlike speed. Nachman felt an impulse to lean
over the seat in front of him and look at the driver's face. But what if there
were no face, only another back of a head?

He wondered how much Ali had paid for the dinner. The room
at Chez Monsieur must have cost at least a few thousand dollars. And
the dinner itself? Another two thousand? A bottle of wine could be five
hundred. Nachman was guessing, but he couldn't be far off. Two bottles
of wine, and then the port. There was also the tip.

"Ali, do you mind if I ask a question? How much did you tip the
headwaiter and the others?"

"One doesn't tip servants."

Nachman should have known that waiters were servants. He was
embarrassed, but he was also high, and he continued blithely thinking
about the cost of dinner. Even if Ali didn't tip servants, he'd probably spent
five thousand dollars, and not even the faintest shadow of a thought related to the cost of anything had appeared in his eyes. Nachman suddenly
felt illuminated by a truth. Why not spend five thousand dollars on dinner? They had eaten well. The service had been magical. They had sipped
port and puffed on their cigars, which must have cost a fortune, perhaps
even the lives of Cubans who smuggled them past the Coast Guard.
Nachman felt that he was on the verge of grasping the complexities at the
highest levels of the universe.

Ali looked splendid and triumphant. He had allowed Nachman to see
him as a man who knows how to live and how to include a person like
Nachman in the experience of living. He hadn't listened to anything
about the paper. He'd made Nachman feel meaningless. The idea of
himself as meaningless compared with Ali made Nachman chuckle.

Ali said, "What's funny?" He was smiling, ready to enjoy Nachman's
funny thought.

"I've never had an evening like this. Thanks, Ali."

"We must do it again soon. With Sweeny."

Nachman was awakened the following day by the telephone. He slid out of bed and stood naked with the phone in his hand.

"I wish you had been there, Norbert," he crowed. "You wouldn't believe how much Ali spent on dinner."

"How much?"

"Eleven, maybe twelve."

"Twelve hundred. Wow."

"Thousand."

There was silence.

Nachman continued, "As for the paper, by the end of the week it will be in the mail to Ali."

"That's fantastic, Nachman, but don't bother mailing it. I'll come pick it up. You've done enough."

Nachman detected a strain of reservation in Norbert's voice. What a person says isn't always what a person means. If Norbert said what he was thinking, fully and precisely, he might have to talk for an hour. And yet Nachman heard everything in that tiny reservation. Norbert was jealous. Ali had spent thousands on a dinner for Nachman. Norbert wanted to be the one to give the paper to Ali. Personally.

"No trouble, Norbert. Besides, I'm going out of town on Friday. My mother moved to San Diego. I have to see her new house. I'll stick the paper in the mail. When I return, say late Monday, Ali will have read the paper, and you'll have a thousand bucks."

"A percentage."

"Fifty percent."

"Too generous."

"I wouldn't have met Ali, if not for you. What's money? It's soon spent. A friendship never. What a dinner."

"Nachman, I don't know what Ali spent, but it wasn't eleven thousand dollars, so don't jerk me off. I'm not stupid. I'll accept an agent's percentage. Say twenty-five percent."

"Are we in business, Norbert? If we're in business, we're partners."

Nachman enjoyed the heat of his feeling long after he said goodbye.

On Friday, he didn't leave town. He hadn't finished writing the paper, but that was only because he hadn't begun.

Ali phoned on Monday.

"It didn't arrive?" Nachman said. "I mailed it from my mother's house in San Diego. She had a nice house in Northridge, but decided to sell it because real estate in her neighborhood went way up in value. She said to sleep in Northridge was like snoring money away. I used the address on your card. Is it correct?"

"Why would I put the wrong address on my card?"

"You sound angry."

"I am not a person who feels anger. Do you think the postal service is reliable?"

"We will go to the post office and initiate a search."

"The paper is lost?"

"Ali, if the paper doesn't arrive tomorrow, we will go to the post office and you will see a man who feels anger."

"I appreciate your sincerity."

Nachman stayed home the next day waiting for the phone to ring. The phone didn't ring. Nachman began to wonder why not. He was tempted to phone Ali and ask whether the paper had arrived. He glanced at the phone repeatedly, but didn't touch it.

Late in the afternoon, there was a soft knock at the door. Nachman hurried to open it. It was a girl. She was average height, blond, very pretty. If Nachman had had to describe her to the police ten minutes from then, he could have said only that. Average height, blond, very pretty. She wore a blue cardigan the color of her eyes. She had left the cardigan open, revealing a skimpy, bright yellow cheerleader's outfit.

She said, "Hi."

"Hi."

"Are you Nachman?"

"Yes."

"Do you know who I am?"

"He sent you?"

"Can I come in?"

Nachman stepped back. She walked in, glanced around the apartment, and said, "This isn't bad. I mean, for a basement apartment. The light is nice. It could be real dark in here, but it isn't."

"Have a seat," said Nachman.

She sat on Nachman's sofa, her purse in her lap, her posture rather prim. She smiled pleasantly at Nachman and said, "Ali doesn't know

what he did or said to offend you. But he is sorry. He hopes you'll forgive him."

"He is sorry?"

"Yes, he is sorry. He wants the paper."

"The paper didn't arrive?"

"Is this happening, Nachman?"

"What are you talking about?"

"What do you think? What am I doing in your apartment? Isn't this
crazy?"

She laughed. Her expression became at once pathetic and self-
mocking. "Two men who, as far as I can tell, aren't brain damaged can't
talk to each other plainly. And I'm late for cheerleading practice."

"Go, then," Nachman said.

"Don't you think you owe Ali something? He took you to dinner. He
intends to pay you a thousand bucks for the paper."

"It's in the mail."

"Nachman, come on, be nice. Ali has an embassy job. We can't leave
the country until he graduates. The paper is his passport. Won't you give
it to me?"

"It's in the mail."

"Even a rough draft would do."

"Let's go to the post office."

"Oh, please, Ali went yesterday. I've been there twice today. Look, I
brought a tape recorder." She took it from her purse and held it up. "See
this little machine? You talk to it. Tonight I'll type up what you said."

Sweeny was trying to seem amusing, but her voice was importunate and
rather teary, and then she bent forward, her face in her hands. "I'm not good
at this," she said. "It happens all the time. We go for a drive and Ali gets lost,
so he pulls over at a street corner and tells me to ask some guys for directions. Man, we're in the barrio. I don't want to ask those guys anything. He
says, 'You're a blond girl. They will tell you whatever you want to know.'"

Nachman wanted to embrace her and say, "There, there," but worried
that she would misinterpret the gesture.

She said, "I'm in the middle of this, Nachman. I don't even know
what's going on. Ali is being mean to me. All I know is, it's your fault. Do
you hate Ali? He's suffered so much in his life."

"Suffered? Ali is a prince, isn't he?"

"Ali descends from the Qajar dynasty. It was deposed in 1924 by the shah's father, Reza Shah. Ali's father owned villages, and beautiful gardens around Teheran. So much was taken away. They're still multimillionaires, but they have sad memories. Can you imagine how much they lost? It's really sad. Don't laugh. How can Ali think about schoolwork? You're laughing, Nachman. Please give me the paper. I'm really late for cheerleading practice."

"I'm sorry."

Sweeny was on her feet. She said, "I guess I should go," and gave her head a small defeated shake. "Ali tells me you're a smart guy, but I don't believe you understand the simplest thing."

Nachman said, "Practice can wait. I'll tell you about the paper."

Sweeny pursed her lips and frowned. "All right."

"Let's start with the idea of time. Tick tock, tick tock. That's how we measure time. With a clock. Do you follow me?"

"Yes."

"Each tick is separate from each tock. Each is a distinct and static unit. Each tock and tick is a particle that does not endure. It is replaced by another particle. Like cards shuffled in a deck. Do you see?"

"This is intense." She grinned. Her mood changed radically. She was playing the moron for him. Nachman felt charmed, beginning to adore her a little bit.

"Each particle occupies the space occupied by the previous particle, or card or tick or tock. Do you follow me?"

"Like 'Hickory, dickory dock.'"

"But the point is that 'tick tock' is an abstraction. A spatial idea about measuring time. It's nothing at all like the real experience of time. Real experience is fluid, as in a melody—la, la, la. Real human experience is different from an idea of experience. When you make love, time doesn't exist, isn't that true?"

Her mouth dropped open with mock amazement, and Nachman smiled and wondered about what could never happen between them.

"Making love is an example. I just thought of it. The nursery rhyme 'Hickory Dickory Dock' is funny. It's mechanical. Love isn't funny. Love is an example of what's real."

"I'll just turn on the tape recorder."

"Sit down."

Sweeny sat.

Nachman was startled. He hadn't intended to order her to sit. But he had, and she had obeyed. There she was, a pretty blond Sweeny sitting on his sofa. Nachman felt a surge of gratification. Also power. He blushed and turned away so that she wouldn't see her effect on him.

She continued to sit and watch Nachman, entirely natural except for the tape recorder which lay in her lap, waiting upon his next words.

"As I was saying," Nachman said, now addressing the ceiling, "we measure time by dividing it into tick tock, and this has nothing to do with . . . Look, if you can measure a thing, then you are talking about something that can change. Anything that can change is subject to death. The opposite of death is not life, it's love. How can I talk to you about Bergson? This won't do, Sweeny."

"Why can't you talk to me?"

"No damn tape recorder."

Nachman's voice had become hoarse. He felt a warmth in his chest and face, as if something had blossomed within because of this girl with her naked thighs and short yellow skirt. What he felt was the most common thing in the world, but Nachman didn't think it was uninteresting. He was inclined to do something. What? He could sit down beside her. The rest would take care of itself.

"Why not?"

Nachman was jarred. The question returned him to himself. He didn't sit down beside her.

"Why not?" Nachman sighed. "I don't know why not. I suppose it's because I want you to understand me. I mean, I want you to get it. This is all about intuition, which is about real experience, where everything begins. You simply have to get it. I don't know what I mean. Maybe I don't mean anything." Raising his voice, Nachman said, "Please put the tape recorder away."

Sweeny stood up, aghast, the tape recorder in her hand. She whispered, "Do you have something to say or not?"

Nachman shouldn't have said "please." He should have ordered Sweeny to put the tape recorder away. He'd been cowardly, unsure of his power. Now he had no power. He reached for the tape recorder and drew it slowly from her hand. She let it go. In the gesture of release, Nachman felt their connection falter. Sweeny's eyes enlarged as if to make a sky, a vastness wherein Nachman felt minuscule. He was a dot of being that subsisted within her blue light. A dot; no Nachman at all beyond what Sweeny perceived. He'd never been looked at that way by a woman. His knees trembled. He couldn't think. She said, "I don't believe you are interested in talking to me," and started toward the door.

Nachman called, "Wait!"

Sweeny stopped and looked back at him. He held the tape recorder toward her. She took it and said, "Ali ought to have his head examined." An instant later, she was gone.

Nachman sat at his small kitchen table and looked out the window. He rarely had visitors in his apartment, and yet he had never felt so alone. As the light failed, the trees became darker. Soon they were black shapes against the pink-green glow of sunset. Just before twilight became full night, a ghostly-looking dog appeared, sniffing about amid the ice plants. It sensed Nachman's eyes and lifted its head and faced him. Nachman realized that it was a coyote, not a dog. His heart beat with excitement, and his eyesight sharpened. He could see a glistening patina of moonlight on the coyote's nose. Nachman's neck muscles stiffened as he met the coyote's stare.

The next morning, Nachman went to the post office. He asked about an envelope addressed to Prince Ali Massid. The clerk was unable to find it, and called for the supervisor. Nachman told the supervisor about the envelope. The supervisor said he would initiate a search. Nachman returned the next day. There was no envelope. There was nothing the next day, either.

Nachman went regularly to the post office in the weeks that followed. He asked Norbert to go with him a few times. Norbert trudged sullenly at Nachman's side. There was hardly any conversation. Once, Nachman said in a soft voice, "Did you really need that tattoo?"

"Did Ali really need a paper?" said Norbert. He sounded unhappy.

Eventually, Norbert stopped going to the post office, and Nachman went less and less frequently. Then he, too, stopped. But over the years, he continued to remember Ali's handsome face and Sweeny's beseeching expression, and he remembered the supervisor who had looked at him suspiciously and asked with a skeptical tone, "You're sure you mailed it?" Nachman wasn't sure, even now, but then he hardly remembered having written the paper, not one word.

nachman at the races

PEOPLE CALLED NACHMAN NACHMAN, as if he were a historical figure. He couldn't remember anyone ever using his first name, not even his
mother. Maybe there were some kids in elementary school, but that was
long ago. Now that he was a professor of mathematics, forty-eight years
old, the name was famous among mathematicians. "Nachman," they said,
and that's all, as if to use his title would diminish him. Having never been
called by his first name, Nachman felt he'd never had a childhood, and he
sometimes thought he was compensating for it by going to the races. It
was a kind of playing, the only kind he knew—playing the horses.

Being a mathematician, naturally Nachman had a system for betting,
but he considered it sufficient to believe his system worked. He never
tested it scientifically. He was confident of its power. It even frightened
him a little to think he could name the winning horse almost anytime.
Occasionally, after reading the *Daily Racing Form* and tip sheets, Nachman
felt tempted to name the winner—but only out of curiosity—and he'd
been right often enough to believe he could be right almost always. He
had no intention of exerting himself further, and actually applying his
knowledge.

After looking at the forms, Nachman always walked to the ring
where he studied the horses being displayed just before the race. In his
eyes there was nothing more beautiful than a racehorse. The line of its
neck and rump, the colors of its coat, the elegance of its slender ankles,
and the light flashing along its muscles as it moved, and simply the way it
moved. This collection of living elements, this singular and splendid life,
this was a racehorse. Nachman knew the names of hundreds of race-
horses, and he could tell you the statistics associated with their careers.

He loved everything about an afternoon at the track, from the display of the horses to the sight of them walking to the gate and then the race itself. It was a grand ritual, and it stirred the deepest sense of gratification in Nachman. He loved the trumpet, the sound of the announcer's voice, the people in the stands, and even how they lined up at the betting windows.

As for Nachman's system, it had simply come to mind one day. He wasn't trying to invent a system. It had presented itself to him. This isn't remarkable, he thought. Ideas come and go. The mind is an independent operator. But peculiar to Nachman's mind was its recognition of problems, and its systematic attack on the unknown. Whether he liked it or not, his mind had produced a system. It was a matter of statistics, which were supplied by the *Racing Form* and various tip sheets. The statistics were based on different sorts of measurements, but Nachman didn't need a computer to reconcile one set of statistics with another. He didn't even need pencil and paper. His eyes took in the numbers, his mind adjusted the averages, and the winner emerged—almost always, it seemed, if he bothered to think about it and do the calculations.

You could say, "Nachman, if you have a system and you don't use it, you're betting against yourself." He would agree. But there would be no pleasure, no drama, no excitement in the betting. The races would be just a way to make money. Nachman cared little about money. His university salary was more than he could use. He also made money when he traveled and gave lectures. An unmarried man who lived alone, with no expensive tastes, Nachman had enough money.

He went to the races and, unthinkingly, placed his bets like someone without a system, giving himself only as much chance of winning as anyone else. Sometimes he won, sometimes he lost. This is how it should be, he thought, and he cheered and shouted with everyone else, the regular people. It was Nachman's deepest pleasure to feel like everyone else, regular, not like a freak, a mental monster, who, because of his mechanical gift for numbers, could know the winners before almost every race.

It was also Nachman's pleasure to say hello to people who recognized him as a regular at the track. He knew few of their names, but he recognized their faces and they recognized him, which made him feel at home. A black man named Horace sometimes called out to him: "Hey, Nachman, how you doing?" or "Hey, Nachman, that's a snazzy tie." Once, Horace bought Nachman a drink between races. There wasn't much to talk

about, but the company feeling was good. "Let me get the next one," said
Nachman. He found out that Horace was a deacon, and his church was in
Hollywood. He invited Nachman to attend some Sunday, and Nachman
said, "I'd like that. Thank you." Soon afterward they separated and were lost
to each other in the crowd.

When a race began, Nachman was thrilled by the sight of the horses
lunging out of the gate, then flowing along the rail at the far turn, and
then the sight of them coming around the turn in his direction, a flurry
of churning legs, hooves pounding the track, jockeys bent low to the
horses' necks, whispering to them like lovers.

Since Nachman believed he could know which horse was likely to
win, it took a little bit from the thrill. If you told Nachman, "You could
enjoy the full thrill if you didn't let yourself read the *Racing Form* and tip
sheets. Then you wouldn't know anything," Nachman would agree. He
would even confess that he felt hypocritical, pretending that he didn't
know more than the next guy. But Nachman was fascinated by the *Form*
and tip sheets. The information, the innocent scholarship, the whole idea
of such literature was fascinating to Nachman. It intrigued him that you
could publish a tremendous amount of statistical information about the
horses and yet not reveal the name of the horse that would almost always
win the race.

People believed too many indeterminable factors enter into a horse
race. Nachman was aware of this belief, and he also knew that skeptical
philosophers, including the genius Hume, said the same thing as people
who bet on horse races. Regardless of statistics, the future is a mystery.
You can't even be sure the sun will rise tomorrow. Nachman wished it
were true. He was confident that it was mainly untrue.

A jockey could ride badly, or a horse could get sick, or a race could
even be fixed, but it was mainly untrue that the winner couldn't be pre-
dicted much of the time, if not always. Nachman wasn't a man who
turned his back on truth, but he only played the horses, betting intuitively,
making his choices by the look of a horse, the reputation of the jockey,
the prevailing odds, and other considerations, what Nachman called
"deep imponderables." What a horse eats, for example, can affect performance, and who knows if a horse feels depressed? In short, Nachman had
respect for the unknown. But he'd been born with a mind, and it had a
great potential to know the truth. The truth was that many races were
over before they started.

In today's last race, a horse named Frenchy was listed at twenty to one. Such pessimistic odds were embarrassing. Why had Frenchy been entered at all?

As usual, Nachman looked at the *Racing Form* and tip sheets, and then looked at the magnificent horses, particularly Frenchy. His color was mahogany with a strong reddish tint. He was big, with a deep chest and long legs. There was exceptional snap and vibrancy in the muscles of his flanks and shoulders. If you laid your ear against him, thought Nachman, you'd hear a humming. What a pity that such a grand horse was a loser. Even as he thought this, Nachman's system pressed into mind with strange information. Frenchy would win. Nachman hadn't wanted to know, but willy-nilly, his system said Frenchy would win, though it was statistically impossible. Nachman knew about the horse. Frenchy was clocked at record-breaking speed during workouts, but after a few early wins he'd come in fourth and fifth, out of the money. He'd lost heart for winning. This happens to a horse, Nachman believed, just as it happens to a person. There were gifted mathematicians who never achieved what was expected of them. High expectations, not mathematical problems, led to mental impotence. Frenchy was like them. He knew he was expected to win, so he couldn't win. Frenchy was worse than a loser.

But maybe something had changed. Maybe it was the new jockey, a Mexican named Carlos Aroyo whom the owners had brought up to the States to ride Frenchy. Aroyo was reputed to understand problem horses. Knew how to talk to them. Won a lot of races. A great jockey. You could bet on him, if not the horse, but not at twenty to one. Nachman's system couldn't handle psychological mysteries. Problems, yes. Mysteries, not likely.

Nachman must have made a mistake in the calculations, or there were subtle factors, implicit in his system, that he'd failed to notice. An honest mistake. But maybe there was something else at work. Nachman wanted Frenchy to win because the horse was beautiful. Frenchy's beauty and Nachman's yearning had entered the calculations, and come up with a sentimental assertion. Dishonest but not deplorable. Merely human.

Some of the greatest mathematicians had thought, because their proofs were beautiful, they revealed the secrets of God. Nachman was moved by their visionary enthusiasm, but he wasn't mystical. Frenchy's numbers were simply wrong. His beauty was irrelevant. Nachman's yearning was irrelevant. His system had exceeded itself. He wanted to figure out why, but he couldn't do it now. The race was minutes away.

Nachman joined the line to the betting window, a twenty-dollar bill in his hand, prepared to bet on a horse named Night Flower, not Frenchy, of course. In front of Nachman stood Horace and a little girl, about nine years old. She had the same skin tone as Horace, the same eyes and mouth. Obviously Horace's daughter. She noticed Nachman smiling at her and said, "My mom is in the hospital. That's why I'm not in school."

Horace turned and said, "How are you doing, Nachman?"

"All right. I'm sorry about your wife, Horace."

"Everything is fine. Don't listen to her."

The girl said, "He won't let me go to school because he's scared to be alone."

Horace said, "Be quiet, Camille. And tie your shoelaces." Then he looked Nachman in the eye and said, "If I stay home I'll go crazy."

"You don't have to explain. It's none of my business."

"We went to the hospital this morning."

The line moved. Horace turned away to the betting window and said, "Fifty bucks on Ladies' Man to win."

Impulsively, Nachman said, "No. Fifty bucks on Frenchy."

Horace pulled his money back, as if he'd burned his hand.

The betting agent said, "Which is it?"

Horace said, "Give me a second, please," and then to Nachman, "Frenchy is twenty to one. You know something I don't?"

Nachman said, "Frenchy."

Nachman's voice was strong with authority, as if he knew what he was talking about. In fact, he'd never been less certain of himself, but he wanted to give something to Horace. Frenchy was all he had.

Horace turned back and slid the money across the counter. Nachman placed his own bet, then joined Horace and his daughter. They walked down the steps and worked their way through the crowd to the rail. Horace didn't look at Nachman.

"You don't win, I'll give you fifty dollars," said Nachman, regretful and anxious. It became worse when Horace said, "I made the bet. I lose, I lose. Any other day but today, Nachman. Any other day."

"What?"

"I wouldn't have done it."

"You did the right thing," said Nachman, bluffing, unable to shut up. "When Frenchy wins, you'll make a thousand dollars."

"I don't need a thousand dollars."

"What do you need?"

Horace didn't answer, which made things still worse. Apparently, the race now meant a great deal to him. The race was on. Nachman had to force himself to look.

The pack bunched up coming out of the gate and stayed tight until Night Flower took the lead. Nachman couldn't see Frenchy, but he heard the announcer say Frenchy was running fifth. Nachman stared strictly at the horses. He thought he could feel Horace glance at him. Then the announcer said Frenchy was coming up through the pack, running fourth, running third. Camille began screaming, "Frenchy, Frenchy," as the horses came into the stretch. Horace placed his fists on the rail and hammered it slowly, methodically. Nachman looked at him, hoping for a connection, anticipating Horace's disappointment and maybe anger. Frenchy couldn't win. At least he looked better than usual, thought Nachman. Horace's face showed nothing, but Nachman saw terrible intensity in his fists. In the stretch, Frenchy pulled ahead fast and won by three lengths.

Nachman said, "Thank God."

Horace was grinning and shaking his head. "I don't believe it."

"Believe it. Frenchy could have won by more," said Nachman with a knowing tone.

"He won good enough."

Horace took Camille's hand, then headed off to collect his winnings. He glanced back and nodded, and his eyes said thanks to Nachman.

Nachman went toward the exit. He'd bet intuitively on Night Flower. The horse came in last. As he entered the vast parking lot, he stopped to light a cigarette and collect himself. People streamed by on either side. Then Nachman heard his name called and saw Horace coming toward him through the crowd with Camille.

Horace said, "I don't believe I said thanks."

"Please don't mention it. I'm glad I could help."

"How'd you know he'd win?"

"A feeling."

"Don't give me that jive, Nachman. You knew something, didn't you?"

"I had a strong feeling."

"You had a strong feeling."

"Yes."

"Maybe you had a strong feeling, but I think it wasn't about a horse. It was about me. I needed a sign and you gave it to me. Maybe the Lord sent you and you don't even know that, but I appreciate what you did, and I thank you."

"Everything is going to be all right," said Nachman, overwhelmed by affection and sympathy. He wanted to hug Horace, but he hardly knew the man. Besides, the affection he felt was mainly for himself. Nachman said again, "Everything is going to be all right."

"I know it is."

They shook hands, said goodbye. Nachman walked away purposively, like a soldier. You could even say he marched, exhilarated, down a long aisle of cars, feeling too much to think clearly. He'd mistrusted his system, but it had been right, which was wonderful, if somewhat unnerving. Maybe he was a better mathematician than he knew. When he got home he would take pencil and paper to the numbers, try to figure out what happened. No. Best to leave well enough alone. Nachman suddenly realized he was marching aimlessly, not purposively. He didn't remember at all where he'd parked. There were thousands of cars. He was confused, helpless as a lost child, and yet no less happy. Sooner or later his car would turn up. The feeling wasn't so bad, the feeling of being lost.

the penultimate
conjecture

FROM THE BEACH IN SANTA MONICA, Nachman could look across the water toward LAX and watch airplanes take off and land. The sight reminded him that he hated to travel. Nevertheless, he'd decided to make the short flight to San Francisco, where he would attend this year's meeting of the Pythagoras Society, an international organization dedicated to pure mathematics. Nachman wanted to hear the featured talk on the Penultimate Conjecture. It would be given by the Swedish mathematician Bjorn Lindquist.

Nachman packed a clean shirt, a razor, a toothbrush, and a change of underwear and socks, though he planned to return the same day. He didn't expect to become involved in a discussion and could think of no friends he might meet in San Francisco who would cause him to prolong his stay, but any trip held unpredictable elements. Every time you walk out of your house, thought Nachman—and then let it go. He was aware of a compulsive strain in his thinking.

Razor, toothbrush, underwear, socks, and shirt went into his briefcase, along with a writing pad and some ballpoint pens. He added a bottle of aspirin, too, as if he expected to have a headache. At the airport, he bought a package of chewing gum to help relieve the anticipated pain in his ears on takeoff and landing. He particularly disliked flying, with its discomforts and terrors; also having to breathe unhealthy gases.

The flight was uneventful except for ten minutes of turbulence. However, shortly before landing, an argument erupted a few rows behind Nachman. A passenger and a flight attendant were yelling. It was about something serious. When the plane landed, police rushed into the cabin. Nachman heard shouts amid the commotion of a struggle as he shoved past the passengers in the aisle who were gaping toward the rear.

"What the hell happened?" asked a man at the front of the plane, his eyes wild and prurient, crazed with desire for information.

"How would I know?" said Nachman, pulling his arm free of the man's grip and pushing by him. He didn't know because he'd been thinking about the Penultimate Conjecture, and scribbling notes throughout the commotion. He continued thinking about it as he walked through the airport to the taxi stand. Television reporters, lugging a camera, went by, rushing in the direction Nachman had come from.

The problem of the Penultimate Conjecture was formulated during the Second World War by brilliant English cryptographers who broke the German code Enigma. Germans, also brilliant, broke English codes. Obscure men, and some women, who had a knack for solving puzzles, analyzed the coded messages of the enemy so that nameless soldiers, sailors, and airmen could be blown to bits, drowned, burned alive. A proof of the Penultimate Conjecture would have no such practical consequences—at least none yet known—but for mathematicians, it was a glamorous problem indirectly associated with horrendous violence. As a graduate student, Nachman had brooded over it. The problem was exceedingly difficult. He was afraid he might spend years on it and fail to prove anything. A mathematician had only so much time. Nachman then turned to other problems, and built a reputation for solid, indispensable work. Bjorn Lindquist would know the name Nachman.

As for Lindquist's reputation, it rested on a number of dazzling publications, all co-authored. Mathematicians worked together more than they had in previous years. Lindquist's name appeared first on the publications he co-authored. He was considered a genius for his ability to see the implications of the work of others, and also for his devastating questions. In San Francisco, Lindquist would be the one who was questioned. The sole author of his lecture on the Penultimate Conjecture, Lindquist had taken the risk Nachman cautiously declined, making a bid for greatness, something beyond mere reputation.

Nachman, who was unusually slow, was never asked to collaborate. It didn't much matter. He preferred to work alone. He had sometimes wondered about returning to the Penultimate Conjecture, but he assumed that even if many mathematicians engaged it seriously, none would be successful. When he was ready, Nachman imagined, the problem would be waiting for him like Penelope watching for Odysseus. Suddenly it was too late.

According to gossip, Lindquist had an amazing proof. As if the problem had been stolen from him, Nachman was somewhat hurt and suffered a touch of jealousy, but he felt no ill will toward Lindquist. He wanted only to see Lindquist demonstrate his proof. Nachman was extremely curious. He didn't want to wait for Lindquist to publish his proof on the computer or in a paper, but wanted to see him do it in person, in public. Nothing else would have made Nachman buy his own ticket to go to San Francisco in a terrifying airplane, breathing plague.

The taxi from the airport arrived at the hotel an hour before Lindquist's scheduled talk. Nachman sat in the lobby, reviewing the notes on the Penultimate Conjecture that he'd made feverishly during the hour-long flight. He'd worked more quickly than ever before, as if fueled by drugs, and it almost seemed, now that it was too late, that Nachman was approaching a solution to the problem. It was rather like racing west, as the sun goes down, to make the day longer. If he only had a little more time—but why should he care? The problem had been solved by Lindquist. In a sense, there was no longer any problem. Immersed in the nonexistent problem, Nachman noticed a crowd of people heading toward the auditorium where Lindquist would talk. Thrusting his notes into his briefcase, he joined the crowd. He felt humble, like a member of a religious congregation. The room was large, and almost every chair was taken. A blackboard had been wheeled to the front. As in a theater before the curtain rises, the crowd was full of spirited chatter.

Nachman took a chair beside a skinny young man who wore a blue suit of cheap synthetic material. He noticed that the jacket was too big in the shoulders and the lapels seemed asymmetrical, but it was a new suit and the young man obviously felt good in it. He smiled at Nachman, revealing large, vigorously thrusting teeth. His eyes were greenish yellow, a feral hue, and slanted. They had a strange intelligence, and a fine hot savoring look.

The man said, "You're Nachman."

Nachman nodded.

"I'm Nikolai Chertoff. How do you do? I heard you lecture in Cracow."

They shook hands, Nachman muttering for no reason, "I don't like to travel." Chertoff's eyes were unnerving. To turn away or modify their attention, Nachman asked, "Where are you from, Chertoff?"

"Moscow Communication Labs. You know me?"

The eyes and their attention were unchanging.

"I'm sorry."

"Don't be so sorry. Nobody knows me. I published one paper in a Russian journal of robotics. Who read it? Nobody."

"What is the paper about?"

"Of no importance. Who cares? But everybody knows Nachman. It should be Nachman who solved the Penultimate Conjecture."

"I walked away from it many years ago. Lindquist solved it."

"If you say so."

"What do you mean—if I say so?"

"Do you believe Lindquist solved it?"

"Of course."

"If I were you, I would be inclined to kill, not believe."

"Kill?"

"Look, here he is. Your worst enemy."

There was a flurry of applause as Lindquist walked to the front. Nachman was startled, but with a surge of anxious pleasure, he joined the others, including Chertoff, in applause. Nachman whispered, "Why did you say that? My worst enemy."

"If he's a mathematician, what are you?"

Chertoff's face assumed an expression of disdain, pretending to the attitude he expected in Nachman.

"There's room for more than one mathematician, Chertoff."

Chertoff grinned. "Sure, sure. You're in the same field, and you do the same work. But why not? Like Newton and Leibniz. Maybe five other mathematicians also discovered the calculus. Plenty of room."

The greenish-yellow eyes narrowed with laughter. As Chertoff's head tipped back, his sharp, prominent teeth pointed at Nachman.

Nachman laughed, too, though with imperfect delight. Chertoff's comments had touched a nerve. In truth, Nachman's feelings toward Lindquist were darkened by thoughts of himself. He should have taken the risk. He should have been more like Lindquist, more manly. "Enough, Nachman," said Nachman to himself. "You didn't fly to San Francisco to reproach yourself." Letting it go and getting free of himself, Nachman got hold of himself.

Lindquist was tall and lean and pale. His blond hair was streaked grayish-white. He had cold, light-blue eyes and a wide tragic mouth, bent at the corners as if it might release a wail. He began abruptly, pacing before the blackboard as he talked, stopping to write equations. Evidently, Lindquist had chosen to suggest the nature of his proof rather than exhibit it in exhaustive detail, but each time he wrote an equation he was taken by a rush of excitement. Unable to contain himself, he proceeded to offer more, then more. His fingers squeezed the chalk hard, and it broke. He continued with the broken piece, and then it, too, broke, and he snatched up a fresh stick. His English was first-rate, Oxford faintly mixed with Stockholm. The audience, submerged in silence, was like a many-eyed crocodile, the body suspended underwater, inert. The chalk squeaked and pulverized as Lindquist dragged it against the board.

Beautiful work, thought Nachman. Tears formed, blurring his vision slightly, but then—actually, within the first two minutes of Lindquist's demonstration—even as Nachman thought it was beautiful, he'd begun to suffer a dark excitement. He tried to ignore it as Lindquist progressed. He even nodded once or twice, a motion of assent to Lindquist's voice, and he exerted himself to focus strictly on Lindquist's demonstration. But the excitement persisted, clutched Nachman like a nameless, primordial apprehension.

Nachman had seen where Lindquist's proof was going, and truly wanted to witness its evolution passively, like someone in a train, face pressed to a window, watching the countryside go by. But in the matter of numbers, Nachman was among those who see actively, even aggressively. There are things one knows—who knows how?—and Nachman felt in himself a shadow passing through his cells. He knew Lindquist had failed. In his bones and blood, in his teeth and the roots of his hair, Nachman sensed the conceptual error.

He might have raised his hand and stopped the demonstration, but it would have been disruptive, unmannerly, immodest. He'd be obliged to make a show of himself and indicate Lindquist's mistake. Nachman's sense of it was instinctive, not yet analyzed, but he'd have bet his life that, if he tried, he could specify it. He would say, "I think I could suggest . . ."

Stammering, apologetic, even pretending not to have a good grasp of the problem, Nachman calculated that it would take him about five minutes to demolish the proof and Lindquist.

Nachman couldn't do it. Not to Lindquist, not to anyone in public. But the feeling was there, a blood-ferocity. It shocked him. In his silence, doing nothing, he felt as if he'd struck a blow. It didn't make Nachman feel good. The opposite was true. Nachman felt very bad. Lindquist was handsome. Heroic facial bones made him look like a courageous knight. Nachman, a lowly foot soldier, had knocked Lindquist off his horse. On his back, pinned to the earth by the weight of his armor, Lindquist was helpless. Nachman kneeled above him with a dagger. Lindquist said, "Spare me, Nachman. I'll give you Chantal."

"Who?"

"Chantal. My slave girl."

Thus, Nachman drifted from mathematics. He no longer cared about the demonstration, though he sat like everyone else and watched as if the evolving proof were valid. Lindquist's chalk continued striking and squiggling rapidly, trailing equations, shedding streams of fine white powder. Wrong, thought Nachman. The word beat tremendously in his heart, and the desire to speak raged in his bowels against an unrelenting force of polite repression. An unknown mathematician could gain a reputation in minutes if he had the courage to speak up and undo Lindquist. None spoke up. Lindquist talked and scribbled. Silence prevailed as if everyone were hypnotized, possessed by the Swede's fame and extraordinary presence. The mouth was a curve of ancient solemnity. Gaunt, large-boned, his pallor belonged to a man of vision.

The talk ended. Nachman participated in the applause, showing respect for his colleagues and for Lindquist's fine qualities. He even felt affection for Lindquist, and hoped somebody would give the Swede a prize. But the Penultimate Conjecture remained a conjecture. Nachman couldn't deny that he wasn't displeased. There were only a few questions from the audience, and then it was over. Chertoff stood up. Nachman noticed that his bow tie was fixed to his collar with metal clips. His neck was skinny, and his Adam's apple slid up and down when he said, "If you visit Moscow, Nachman, please do ring me." Reaching into the inside pocket of his hideous jacket, Chertoff withdrew a business card. Nachman took it.

"I must smoke a cigarette," said Chertoff. He drew one from a pack and lit it, then sighed smoke. "What a proof."

Nachman said, "Were you pleased?"

"Lindquist did good work. What did you think?"

"Same as you."

Nachman had hoped that they might share a moment of mathematical brotherhood. Instead, like everyone else, Chertoff assented to the demonstration. Nachman felt himself closing within, shrinking from connection with Chertoff. It had always been like this. Nachman worked alone, lived alone, thought alone. He didn't need solidarity with Chertoff, such a peculiar fellow.

"I see it in your eyes," said Chertoff. "You think I let you down."

"Nonsense."

"Not nonsense. To me the proof is good. I'm not you, Nachman. How many numbers have chosen you as a friend? Fifty? Seventy-five? I have maybe five, and I'm not always too sure of their friendship. How many, Nachman? Ninety. Sure, you have ninety. Negatives, fractions, rational, complex—they come when you call. For you mathematics is a big party. But I am like most people—only five. Less is revealed to us, so we think the proof is good. You want to know something—it might as well be good. For six months, a year—good or no good—we'll think it's good. This is the common fate. But you, Nachman, you don't think it's good. You're alone. Worse yet, you're frightened."

"Excuse me. I must give my congratulations to Lindquist."

"You must run away. See?"

"I see that you're impertinent, Chertoff."

"Go, run to him, give him a kiss. When you're in Moscow, ring me. We'll talk about real things."

Chertoff's feral eyes surrendered their interest in Nachman as he glanced toward the corners of the room. He half-smiled, then winked slyly at Nachman. "There are more women here than I expected."

Nachman joined the group that had formed around Lindquist, and immediately forgot Chertoff while trying to think how to make a pleasant remark, with perhaps the slightest hint, giving Lindquist pause. Someone whispered to Lindquist, and he looked toward Nachman, spotting him at the edge of the group. Lindquist extended his hand, urging Nachman forward. "Thank you for coming to hear my talk, Nachman. I feel honored."

Shaking Lindquist's long, cool surgeon's hand, Nachman decided not to give any hints. Lindquist was disarming in his friendliness, which made it harder, not easier, to suggest his failure. Besides, Lindquist was extremely quick. He might see everything instantly, regardless of how subtle the hint, and he'd be furious because Nachman hadn't been forthright. Others would sympathize with Lindquist. Even when they saw that Nachman was right—no, especially when they saw he was right. Better to keep his mouth shut. Nachman knew what he knew. A difficult knowledge. Why bring himself into bad odor? People need to believe, which requires an irrationality, a suspension of critical faculties, an abnegation of will, a spreading of the thighs. Nachman's colleagues, like Saint Teresa, had been ravished, penetrated with belief. Between a mistake and madness, there was a nourishing relationship. If they knew what Nachman thought, they'd despise and revile him. Chertoff was right. Nachman was frightened.

The Swede looked with blue incisiveness into Nachman's brown eyes. "What do you say, Nachman? It was all right?"

As if speaking from a trance, Nachman said, "Wonderful."

"Wonderful? Did I play the cello? I only did mathematics. I saw you in the audience and watched your face. It didn't look full of wonder."

Nachman shouldn't have said "Wonderful." A bleat of mindless enthusiasm. Helpless to undo the word, Nachman repeated it, "Wonderful."

Lindquist nodded gravely. "All right, then, wonderful. Such praise coming from you is . . ." He made a noise, not an intelligible word. His tone was grim, as if he detected in the word "wonderful" a form of contempt. "Do you have time to talk, Nachman? If you want to say something, I want to listen."

"Now?" Nachman had intended to say he had nothing to say. With the question—"Now?"—he surprised himself. Where did the word come from? It made him feel like a liar.

"Lunch tomorrow. Could you call my room in the morning?"

"You're staying at this hotel?"

Another question. Of course Lindquist was staying at this hotel. The whole conference was here. Lindquist looked puzzled and mock-injured, pouting as if Nachman's question were an oblique insult. "Are you being evasive, Nachman? Would you prefer not to meet for lunch?"

"I will," said Nachman. "I'll call." His voice was eager, compensating for the imagined insult. The talk had been stressful, making Lindquist hypersensitive, but there had been no insult. Unless he'd been struck by a critical thought-ray from Nachman's subconscious, a flow of searing deadly brainlight. Nachman remembered Chertoff's question, "If he's a mathematician, what are you?" He'd meant that Lindquist's existence, merely that, threatened Nachman's, and vice versa. Confused and embarrassed, Nachman backed away, repeating, "I'll call," and turned, hurrying out of the lecture hall, then to a men's room, where he shoved into an empty stall, dropped his briefcase, and—no time to spare—threw up. Weak and dizzy, he washed his face. He did it to clean himself and also not to let himself think. It came to him that he, too, was a believer. He believed there is good and bad. He'd been bad not to speak up when Lindquist asked for his reaction. Nachman saw again the solemn handsome face and heard the simple appeal: "It was all right?"

Bad not to answer. Bad not to tell the truth. But how could it matter if Nachman's mere existence was potentially lethal. Nachman dried his face, and then, staring into the mirror above the sink, said to himself, "Let him have the solution. I'll settle for the slave girl."

Nachman left the men's room and wandered into the hotel lobby, dazed and disoriented. He looked about for people he knew. Where was Chertoff? To see the hideous blue suit, the ferocious eyes and teeth, would be a blessing. Nachman badly needed someone to talk to. Moving through the crowd, he sensed people turning in his direction. He knew he was being recognized, but he recognized nobody. The crowd seemed too young. The conversations on every side—in Italian, French, German, Russian, Japanese—were estranging. Mathematicians had flown in from everywhere. Nachman had surely met many of them, but he'd never been a sociable fellow, never made sure to remember names. Groups of two and three clustered about the lobby, talking with frenzied energy, as if desperate for communion. Nachman wandered among the groups, feeling awkward and self-conscious, scrutinizing name tags, which he considered rude. Some faces were familiar, but no names. He couldn't bring himself to approach a familiar face without knowing the name that went with it. With exasperation, he asked himself why he was in this hotel lobby. Nobody was talking to him. Nachman supposed he looked forbidding, unapproachable. He had no reason to stay.

Planes left for Los Angeles every half hour. Nachman could be in Santa Monica, in his own house, well before midnight. Tomorrow he'd phone the hotel and leave a message at the desk for Lindquist, apologizing. Not for missing their lunch, but for what Nachman couldn't tell him, though he'd say it was for missing lunch. Nachman remembered saying, "I will."

He felt like a criminal, as if he were fleeing, when he saw the taxis at the curb in front of the hotel, but he stepped quickly up to one of them and jumped inside. "The airport," he said. The taxi nudged into traffic. Minutes later it was free of city streets, passing other cars along the highway. Nachman sat with his briefcase in his lap and looked across the gleaming blue of San Francisco Bay to the tawny hills in the east. He wasn't sorry he'd made the trip, yet his heart was fraught with regret even as it swelled and beat against the bone cage, Nachman's chest, with triumph.

Abruptly from this beating and swelling issued a strangled cry, "Turn around, please, I must go back."

Nachman was more embarrassed than surprised by his outburst. Would the taxi driver think he was crazy? They drove now in loud silence. Nachman sat rigidly, as if braced to receive a blow. His eyes were fixed on the back of the taxi driver's head, expecting him to question the order, or simply to ignore it and drive on to the airport. But the driver took the first exit off the highway, smoothly reversing direction, and headed back to San Francisco. Then he said, "You forgot something at the hotel?" The voice was a gentle tenor and seemed incongruous with the man. He was big, heavy, broad-shouldered, and black.

"Yes," said Nachman.

"Happens."

"I'm sorry. I feel very foolish."

"No problem. Maybe you don't really want to leave the city."

"I don't always know what I want."

"That sounds like my wife. We go out for ice cream, it's always a crisis. I say, 'Pick any flavor. You don't like it, we'll throw it away and get another. Just pick.' But she stands at the counter having a nervous breakdown over vanilla or pistachio."

"That's it. I'm having a crisis," Nachman said to himself.

At the hotel, Nachman went to the desk. He intended to phone Lindquist's room and ask if they could meet that evening, but before he could get the clerk's attention, Chertoff appeared.

"Nachman, you're still here. It was my impression that you were leaving."

"What do you want?"

"Want? Nothing. Are you angry, Nachman?"

"What do you want?"

"I believe you are angry."

"Are you going to tell me to kill Lindquist?"

"Did I upset you?"

"Yes, you upset me."

"I meant no harm. My way of speaking is too strong on occasion. Forgive me. What I said is only because I am your great admirer. I would like to be your friend. Let me buy you a drink. Over there is a pleasant bar."

"I have to phone Lindquist."

"Of course, but later. Even next week the bad news will not be too late."

"How do you know I have bad news?"

"As a mathematician, I don't hope to know what you will say. As a man, I know everything. Please," said Chertoff, taking Nachman's arm, drawing him away toward the bar. Nachman didn't resist.

Chertoff asked what Nachman would have, then ordered. Shoulder to shoulder at the bar, with drinks before them, Nachman felt an intimacy he needed very much, and yet it seemed he was being subjected to it, somewhat like a child, as if for his own good. Neither of them spoke for a minute. Then Nachman said, "I should tell him. Do you agree?"

He turned to look directly at Chertoff's face. Chertoff, looking with equal directness at Nachman, produced a ferocious smile, as if he'd been given permission to be fully himself. His eyes, in the smiling pressure, narrowed with catlike satisfaction. His lips swept wide over the large, thrusting teeth. He said, "Nachman, I don't give a shit."

"You're some friend, Chertoff."

"A good friend. I think only what you think—which is that you should solve the problem."

"When I was young . . . maybe."

"Do you have a better reason to live?"

"What a question! It reminds me, I dreamed during Lindquist's lecture. Only a few seconds, but I dreamed that I was about to kill him. He begged me to spare his life. He promised me his slave girl."

"I am touched that you are—how do you say it?—sharing this dream with me."

Nacham shrugged. "You know what it means?"

"The spoils of war, Nachman. It is about the spoils of war. Remember the *Iliad*? Since childhood I have loved and yearned for Briseis. You know the poem is even more wonderful in Russian than in Homeric Greek." Chertoff boomed the opening lines in Russian. Heads turned along the bar to stare at him. Then he whispered, "Nachman, you must take the slave girl."

"I must?"

"And you must kill Lindquist, too."

"It's not in my nature."

"You have no choice, my friend," said Chertoff as he put an arm around Nachman's shoulders, and drew him close, and kissed him on the cheek in the Russian manner.

nachman burning

NACHMAN HAD THE BLUES. Maybe it was the weather, cold and gray, unusual for Santa Monica; or maybe it was a change in Nachman's bodily chemistry, or maybe it was a psychological problem below consciousness. Maybe it was just being over fifty, or the fact that he needed a haircut. Two months since the last one. Nachman telephoned Felicity Trang.

She said, "Felicity Hair Salon."

Nachman said, "I want to make an appointment."

"We have free time at noon. O.K.?"

"O.K."

"Which girl you want?"

"I want Felicity."

"O.K. What name?"

"Nachman."

"How you spell?"

Nachman spelled his name.

"Oh, Dr. Nachman. How nice."

"Not doctor. Nachman is good enough. I'll see you at noon, Felicity."

"Yes. Thank you, Not doctor, ha, ha, ha . . ."

Felicity's laughter, excessive yet pleasing, continued to stir Nachman after he put down the phone. He already felt better. A degree of anxiety mixed with his pleasure, but there was no doubt that he felt better; hopeful. He imagined himself tipped back in the chair, surrendering his head, a hairy bundle of complexities, to Felicity's ministrations.

There were other ways of dealing with low spirits, but Nachman wouldn't take drugs and rarely exercised. He'd told himself more than once that Felicity cost less, for the same amount of time, than a psychiatrist.

She compared well with any doctor. A haircut was a visible, tangible result, and Nachman would feel reborn. Hair grew back, but psychological problems also returned. In essence, nobody changed. Don't think that way, he told himself, teetering at the edge of a mental hole. Walk briskly. He was almost there, and looked forward to the shampoo. He loved the shampoo. To Nachman, it was worth the price of the whole haircut. Then would come the skull massage. Before the haircut itself, before she picked up her comb and scissors, Felicity always stood beside his chair, her shoulder pressed gently to his. Together they looked at Nachman's face in the mirror and Felicity asked how Nachman would like her to cut his hair. Her voice was sweetly deferential, her expression rapt with concern to please. She was more than a barber. Like a sister, a confidant, or even a lover, she was involved. Nachman always said the same thing, slightly choked by self-consciousness:

"Not too short."

"This long you like?" she responded, always touching the top of his ear, and ever so lightly fingering it.

"Yes, about right there."

"Layered?"

"Yes. Small scissors. No electric clippers."

"Oh no, no machines. Only small scissors and comb. Comb O.K.? Ha, ha."

Nachman felt gooseflesh along his arms, and then a general surge of pleasure, like a mass of troops racing across a field, overwhelming their enemy, anxiety, vanquishing it. The battle of such emotions, thought Nachman, is what a man feels when he is about to get married. In short, approximately every two months, Nachman married Felicity Trang for about forty-five minutes.

Caressed by the rush and swirl of warm water, head cradled in Felicity's hands, the delicate perfume of shampoo, and then the massage with Felicity's strong fingers, and then the sweet seriousness of her voice:

"You like to part your hair on the right?"

Nachman opened the door and entered the barbershop. Four Vietnamese women barbers were at work. Felicity was free, sitting at the cash register near the door. She smiled at Nachman and stood right up. He followed her to a chair, sat down, and abandoned himself to the ritual, becoming oblivious to everyone in the barbershop except Felicity and himself; and time was abolished for Nachman. He imagined their marriage, mediated by his hair, as heavenly, an eternal condition, though he knew, when Felicity fashioned the ultimate shape of his hair with a comb and a blow dryer, the marriage was over. He also knew he wouldn't look good. She was a terrible barber.

To know the consequences of an action is one thing. To eschew the action is another. Who would smoke cigarettes if this wasn't true, let alone have casual sex—thought Nachman somewhat irrelevantly—Nachman who, despite his susceptibility to women, was a strict observer of limits. He didn't fool around. For forty-five minutes every two months— you couldn't call it fooling around—Nachman was in no danger of compromising himself. Better to burn was Nachman's motto. A haircut was inconsequential, erotic, not sexual. Thus tumbled the thoughts of a serious being. By pleasure deranged, maybe, but no longer depressed.

In Nachman's life, Felicity was an anomaly—a silliness—depending on how you thought about it, but should Nachman think about it? Nachman thought too much about everything; even in the throes of his abandonment he couldn't entirely stop thinking, lest he die or cease to exist or relinquish his grip on the real. Not to think would be like an astronaut separated from his rocketship, adrift in space with nowhere to go and no means of propulsion. Nachman had seen that condition often in a person's eyes.

When Nachman explained how he wanted his hair to look, Felicity had nodded and nodded to show that she listened carefully, and then she went to work and tried to do what Nachman wanted. Meticulous, diligent, infinitely concerned to do right and good. But Felicity had no art in her soul, no feeling for the shape of Nachman's hair in relation to his face. The haircut "styled" by Felicity would look as if it had been inflicted, and it would bring to mind images of poor laboring men.

So?

It looked honest enough, and the point cannot be made too strongly that Nachman loved the feeling of Felicity's hands soaping his hair, then massaging the skull behind his ears, and, with a subtle circular movement, his occipital bump. She knew how to touch a man. As for doing the actual haircut, it would have been wise to call in a different barber, or anybody passing in the street, but even so, when Felicity stepped back and tilted her head as she studied the progress of her work, Nachman saw that she considered herself a first-class barber and his heart went out—no, it rushed—to her. He would never say a word that might suggest reservations or criticism.

Near the end, Felicity would say, "You like O.K.?"

Nachman would say, "Perfect." He would sound drowsy.

Later, he always tipped generously and smiled, saying, "Thank you," and walked giddily home, supposing that his head might now look appropriate on a pedestal in his garden, with a grin on his lips, expressing blissful indifference to the fluttering doves and jays, lighting and asquat, shitting on his haircut. But where else, for twenty-two dollars (four for the shampoo, thirteen for the haircut, and a five-dollar tip), could Nachman get such relief from low spirits and uncomplicated satisfaction? He'd have paid more.

Regardless of Felicity's butchery, then, Nachman could live with the result. A stupid-looking haircut didn't make him miserable, and he soon forgot about how he looked, anyway. He had plenty else to think about, such as math problems, lectures, and politics at the Institute of Higher Mathematics, where Nachman worked in a bare office at a gray steel table with pencil and paper. The problems he dealt with were so difficult that Nachman sometimes cried. Nearly unbearable frustration attended his mathematical struggles until he suffered the piercing joy of an illumination. Sometimes he'd find himself sitting up in bed in the middle of the night, sweating and feverish, and he'd thrust out of bed and stumble to the table where he kept pencil and paper for such unpredictable moments, and he'd scrawl the solution to a problem, and then fall back into bed and was instantly asleep. In the morning, he'd find his scrawled solution. He'd then remember having awakened and, as if he were taking dictation from a nightmare, recording the solution. The look of the haircut was not important to Nachman.

Felicity, a small woman about forty years old, had a complexion slightly ruined by acne, and a figure slightly ruined by childbearing. Color photographs of her three children were pasted to the mirror. Nachman always asked about them. Felicity told him they spoke Vietnamese as well as English. Lowering her voice to a whisper, as if she feared the evil ear, she said her children were excellent students, the two boys and the girl were first in their respective classes. She also talked about her husband, who refused to let her invite friends to dinner, or attend night school to study English, or drive the family car. She walked to shopping. Walking to work took over an hour. Without a car, in Los Angeles, it was impossible for her to visit people. The few women she knew at the church, to which she walked once a week, lived too far away. Felicity said, "I hope someday I have more friends."

Nachman wondered if Felicity hoped he would be her friend. Probably not, but the idea embarrassed him. He felt a touch of anxiety. The haircut was friendship enough. Felicity lived in a different world. She went to church, unimaginable for Nachman. They could probably never have much to say to each other. A few questions, a few answers. Felicity once asked what kind of work Nachman did. He told her he was a professor of mathematics. She once asked if he was married. He told her he was not married. Today she asked if he lived alone. He told her he lived alone. This was the furthest they had gone conversationally, and Nachman didn't expect or want them to achieve a higher level of generalization, or deeper level of intimacy.

"No girlfriend?" said Felicity, as if the idea took her breath away.

"No."

Did she have someone in mind for him? Nachman continued to wonder what her gasp could mean, but at the moment, Felicity's small scissors, working about his ears, pleased him to the point of stupefaction, and he enjoyed the ripping sensation as she pulled the comb through lengths of wet hair caught between her middle and index finger before she snipped and snip-snipped, and in the shallow depths of a semi-sleep, he liked the way she then released his hair with studious and insensitive attention to its layers, mutilating it. Nachman felt no annoyance or despair, only the musical nature of the occasion. In the sound and pull of the comb drawn through his hair came the rich tones of a cello pulling against the flight and flash of scissoring violins, and spinning high and away in thought, Nachman wished he had a ton of hair so this fine delirium could last longer than forty-five minutes. Hair, he thought, is basic to erotic connections between a man and a woman, usually the woman's hair, and, and, and—what follows? Nachman didn't know, but he pursued the thought—no—the thought pursued Nachman as he felt a pressure against his elbow which rested on the arm of the barber chair. Felicity leaned over it, her pelvis inadvertently brushing against the bone.

Felicity was no more than five feet four, if that tall. Her arms weren't long. She had to lean with her whole torso as she moved about the chair. Her pelvis brushed against Nachman's elbows, on either side of the chair. Merely inevitable given Felicity's build, thought Nachman, but thinking about it, he wondered if there wasn't a suggestion in her pelvis as she said, "My husband never talks to me. He comes home late. Tired. Never talks."

Nachman's heartbeat could be detected pulsing in the cloth that lay across his chest, and he felt himself hardening. He assumed Felicity meant that she had something in common with him: Nachman had no girl and Felicity had no man to talk to.

"Never talks?" said Nachman.

"Not touched me for many months."

Nachman's pleasure, which had been diffuse, suddenly concentrated. It became a feeling of urgency, as if Nachman was about to do something. He felt a rush of energy, a strong intention, a strong disposition to act. Nachman to the first power was becoming Nachman to the second, an entirely different creature, a stranger to himself, the agent of a potentiality. His hand jerked spasmodically and seized Felicity's upper thigh, just below her crotch.

Hardly breaking the rhythm of her work, she twisted her hip to the side, and Nachman's hand fell away. She'd experienced this before, apparently, and knew how to deal with it. There was nothing to say. She didn't even interrupt her work. Nachman sat in the chair, rigid, vibrant, pulsing, burning with the unconsummated violence that had taken his hand, and burning with shame. In the mirror he and Felicity were all that he could see. The other chairs and customers and women didn't exist.

Felicity said, "I could meet a friend sometimes, maybe."

"Yes."

"A man who would be gentle."

Her voice was so gentle that Nachman hardly felt the reproach. He almost imagined that she was hinting, encouraging him to entertain a romantic supposition.

Soon the haircut was finished, and Felcity stood beside the chair as she had at the beginning, intently looking at Nachman's head in the mirror.

"O.K.? Not too short?" she said cheerily.

Nachman said, "Perfect."

He followed her to the cash register, his hand in his pants pocket feeling for bills. He felt a stick of gum, too, and pulled it out, nervously unwrapping it, and started chewing the stick of gum as he counted two tens and a five. She had appealed for a friend, and Nachman groped her. Money might make things worse, but he dropped the bills on the counter beside the cash register, and as Felicity started to give him his change, he said, "No, keep it," and he looked at her with the face of a man chewing gum—somewhat cool, somewhat moronic—but Nachman didn't know how to look at her, or what to do or say. His eyes were silent beggars.

Felicity said, "Oh, ha, ha. I like gum, too."

She understood what he felt. Nachman realized she was trying to connect; trying to make him feel all right. Instantly Nachman searched his pockets for another stick of gum. He found none. Felicity's smile saddened and became an ironical little pout, and she opened her eyes wide and shook her head No, No, as if sympathizing with a child, and then said, "Ha, ha, ha," a high and utterly artificial laugh, but with such goodwill that Nachman laughed, too, and they laughed together as Nachman said goodbye, leaving the barbershop with a sense that he'd been forgiven.

# of mystery
there is no end

TRAFFIC MIGHT MOVE AT ANY MOMENT. He might still get to the dentist on time, but Nachman was pessimistic and assumed he would miss his appointment. He imagined himself apologizing to Gudrun, the dentist's assistant, a pale Norwegian woman in her forties with white-blond hair. Nachman could almost hear his ingratiating tone. He was begging Gudrun to forgive him, swearing it would never happen again, when he felt himself being watched. He looked to his left. From the car next to his, a young woman stared at him. She looked away immediately and pretended to chat on a cell phone, as though indifferent to Nachman, who now stared at her. He saw heavy makeup and chemical-red hair. She was smoking a cigarette and tapping the steering wheel with her thumb, keeping time to music on her car radio. Nachman imagined reaching into her car, snatching away her cell phone and cigarette, turning off her radio, and ordering her to sit still. She would soon be reduced to quivering lunacy. Drivers in Los Angeles shoot each other for no reason, let alone rude staring.

Of course, Nachman would never shoot anybody. He pitied the woman who encumbered her head with a cell phone, cigarette, music, and unnatural colors. Compared to her, Nachman was a sublime being. He could sit for hours in silence, alone in his office, with only pencil and paper. Thinking. In fact, there was pencil and paper in the glove compartment. Nachman's car could be his office. He would do math problems. Millions were stalled and rotting in their cars in Los Angeles, but Nachman had internal resources.

He leaned toward the glove compartment, and just as he touched the release button, his eye was drawn by a flash of black hair. He looked. Adele Novgorad, the wife of Nachman's best and oldest friend, Norbert Novgorad, was standing on the sidewalk. Nachman wanted to cry out her name, but hesitated. He was sure it was Adele, though she was turned away from him. Few people in Los Angeles had such wonderfully black hair or skin so white. She was talking to a man who had an unusually large and intimidating mustache, and they stood close together—too close—facing each other in front of a motel, about ten yards from Nachman's car. Horns blared behind Nachman. He heard the horns, but they meant nothing. Adele and the man had begun kissing.

Horns screamed, and at last they pierced Nachman's trance. He looked away from Adele to the road, but for Nachman, still shocked by what he had seen, the avenue, the traffic, the buildings were all meaningless. He clutched the steering wheel. Fairfax Avenue was clear for a thousand yards straight ahead, but he didn't step on the gas pedal. He looked back at Adele. She had stopped kissing the man, though she still clung to him; the man had now heard the horns and was looking over her shoulder at Nachman's car. When the man's eyes met his, Nachman stepped on the gas pedal and released the clutch. In the rearview mirror, he saw Adele separate from the man. He was pointing at Nachman's car. Adele looked. Having seen too much, Nachman had been seen.

Driving south down Fairfax Avenue, Nachman felt something like the thrill of departure, as when a boat leaves the shore, but the thrill was unpleasant. He seemed to be departing from himself, or everything familiar to himself. Through the blur of feeling, a voice spoke to him: "You must tell Norbert what you saw on Fairfax Avenue." It was Nachman's own voice, commanding and severe.

He could drive to the community college where Norbert was a professor. And then what? Interrupt his lecture or a department meeting to tell him that he had seen Adele kissing someone? How ridiculous. Besides, if he told Norbert, Adele would hate him. She, too, was his friend. She had invited Nachman to dinner many times, and she always gave him a tight hug and a kiss when he arrived and again when he left, pressing her warm lips against his cheek. She cooked special dishes for Nachman. To please her, he cried out with pleasure at the first bite, and when she looked gratified, he took more delight in her expression than in the food. With her cooking and hugs and kisses, Adele made Nachman feel very important to her. He liked Adele enormously. The way she walked with her toes pointed out like Charlie Chaplin was adorable. He also got a kick out of her smile, which was usually accompanied by a frown, as if happiness were a pleasant form of melancholy. Nachman wanted sometimes to lean across the dinner table and kiss the lines in her brow. He suddenly heard himself speak again, in a cruel voice, as if he were a stranger to himself and had no regard for his feelings about Adele: "You must tell Norbert what you saw on Fairfax Avenue."

Nachman hammered the dashboard with his fist and shouted an obscenity. In the twenty-first century, in Los Angeles, a great city of cars where no conceivable depravity wasn't already boring to high school kids, Nachman, a grown man, found himself agonized by an ancient moral dilemma.

Was it his duty to tell Norbert or to protect Adele? Would it make any difference if he told Norbert? Yes, it would make a difference. Nachman would seem like a messenger worse than the message. The friendship would be ruined. Nachman forced himself to ask: did he want to hurt his friend Norbert? There was no reason to tell him unless he wanted to hurt him. People who told unbearable news to friends, as if it were their duty, then felt very good about themselves while their friends felt miserable— Nachman was not like those people. Besides, to feel good about oneself was important only to narcissists, not Nachman. Nachman loved his friend Norbert and would sooner cut off his own arm than hurt him just to feel good about himself. In the righteous fervor of his thinking, Nachman forgot his dental appointment.

He drove to the ocean and turned toward Malibu. He barely noticed that he was driving well beyond his house. After a while, he saw a place to stop. He parked close to the beach and left his car. In his shoes, he trudged along the sand. The ocean was a sheet of glinting metallic brilliance. Gulls were dark blades soaring in the white glare of the afternoon sun. For the gulls, light was no different from air. For Nachman the difference between one thing and another was the most serious consideration in life. The gulls brought this home to him with terrible poignancy. He remembered his first lesson in mathematics, when he learned about differences.

After his parents divorced, when Nachman was five, his mother's aunt Natasha Lurie had moved in with Nachman and his mother. She was a small elderly woman from Saint Petersburg, Russia, and had been a well-known mathematician in her youth. She decided to teach Nachman mathematics, and began the lesson by asking him, in a soft tired voice, to write the word "mathematics." Nachman wrote it phonetically, with an *a* in the middle. Natasha, who reminded him of clothes hanging on a line, susceptible to the least touch of the wind, took Nachman's pencil out of his fingers. Pinching the pencil between her own skinny white fingers, she dragged the eraser back and forth on the paper, back and forth, until the *a* was obliterated. Then she drew a round and perfect *e*, pushing the pencil point into the fiber of the paper and pulling the shape of the letter, like a small worm, slowly into view. More than four decades later, trudging on the beach in Malibu, Nachman saw again the red rims of Aunt Natasha's ancient eyes. She looked at Nachman to see if he understood. The lesson had little to do with spelling or mathematics. She taught him there is a right way. It applied to everything.

He thought of Adele smooching on Fairfax Avenue as he trudged back to his car and drove to Santa Monica and then to his house. When he opened the door, Nachman heard the phone ringing. It continued to ring while he looked through the mail he had collected from the box attached to the front of his house. He entered his study and sat down at his rolltop desk. The phone continued ringing.

Nachman put the bills in one pile and dropped junk mail, unopened, into a wastebasket. Then he opened his personal mail. He found a request: Would Professor Nachman read the manuscript of a proposed mathematics textbook? It was being considered for publication by a major East Coast firm. The job would take many hours. Nachman would be paid five hundred dollars for his opinion and suggestions. It wasn't much money, but he supposed he should feel honored by the request. He then found two invitations. One was to a conference on mathematical physics, in Indiana. Why had they invited Nachman? It wasn't his specialty. The appropriate mathematicians had probably turned them down. The second invitation was for a defense job. It had to do with antiballistic-missile systems and would pay ten times what Nachman was making at the Institute of Mathematics. It was a job, Nachman supposed, that was held only by third-rate mathematicians and spies. Antiballistic missiles, indeed. Nachman felt insulted. What a terrible day. The phone was ringing. Nachman went to the bathroom and swallowed an aspirin. He then went to the bedroom and sat on the edge of his bed and took off his shoes and socks. The phone on his night table was ringing.

Late-afternoon light, filtered by the leaves of an avocado tree outside his bedroom window, glowed on the pine floor and trembled like the surface of a pond. It was a beautiful and deeply pleasing light, but the roots of the magnificent avocado tree had been undermining the concrete foundation of Nachman's house for years. He thought about that almost every day. Sooner or later, he would have to choose between the tree and the resale value of the house.

There was sand in his shoes and socks, and sand between his toes. On the night table beside the bed, the phone was ringing. Nachman lay down on his back and placed his right forearm across his eyes.

Let the foundation be torn apart. Let the house fall down. Let the phone ring. Nachman would sleep. Let the phone ring . . . It was impossible to sleep. Nachman sat up on the edge of his bed and lifted the receiver. He didn't say hello.

"It's me," she said.

"Goodbye," said Nachman.

"Don't you dare hang up. You knew it was me. You could hear the ringing. You're the only person in California who doesn't have an answering machine. You heard the phone. Why didn't you pick it up?"

"Between you and me, Adele, a certain subject does not exist."

"If any subject doesn't exist, no subject exists."

"So we have no subjects."

"I caused you pain. Is that it?"

"I live a simple life. Like a peasant. I go to work. After dinner I go to sleep. I have no interest in adventures."

"We have different needs. I'm not you, Nachman. And you are not me. I couldn't live without an answering machine or a television set."

"O.K., leave it at that and let's not plunge into a discussion of electronics. I have a headache."

"I don't want to leave it at that. I want to understand. I have great respect for your opinions."

"Adele, I am not in the mood for a confessional orgy. I will say only this—I don't believe that experience, for its own sake, is the highest value. Kissing in the street, in the middle of Los Angeles . . . For God's sake. How could you?"

"You saw me kissing a guy. Was it a threat to your peasant simplicity?"

"In the middle of the afternoon, on Fairfax Avenue, with the *bubees* and *zeydes* walking home with grocery bags. There are limits."

"I think you mean morals."

"O.K., morals. Yes, morals. You have something against morals?" Nachman heard himself shouting and felt his breath coming faster.

"Morals-shmorals. It sounds to me like you think I did something to you personally.

"I saw you kissing some guy who isn't Norbert, my best friend, who happens to be your husband. It was a spectacle of irresponsible lust performed in public, in my face—Norbert's best friend."

"Nachman, get ahold of yourself! How the fuck would I know that Norbert's best friend was stopped in traffic, twenty feet away."

"You trivialize my feelings."

"What is it that you feel? Tell me exactly."

"This minute, talking to you, I feel exactly as if I were betraying Norbert."

"Oh please. Every time you look at me, you betray Norbert. When I stroll down Wilshire Boulevard, Norbert is betrayed sixty times a minute. I answer the door to the postman, Norbert has horns. This is California, not Saudi Arabia. I'm a woman on display, front and back. Do you know it's been said that a modern woman can neither dress nor undress."

"Who said it?"

"I don't know, but it's true. Look, all that matters is you and me, Nachman—we're friends. Our conversation is not a betrayal of anybody. Aren't we friends? I thought we were friends."

Adele was crying.

"Of course," said Nachman, his voice hoarse, on the verge of failure.

"Nachman, are you in love with me?" said Adele. "Is that the real problem?"

"I love many people."

"Liar. You love your mother in San Diego, and you never talk about your father or your colleagues or the women you date. Anyhow, I said 'in love with me.'"

"What does that have to do with anything?"

"It has to do with everything. Norbert is the injured party, not you. Don't you hear yourself?"

"What should I hear?"

"Don't be a mystery to yourself, Nachman. Maybe we all walk in darkness, shadows, mystery—I wouldn't deny it—but you must try to understand. Of mystery there is no end. Of clarity, there is precious little."

"Adele, you're raving. Stop it."

She now spoke in a rush, sniffling and sobbing, "O.K., I'll stop, but I want to make things clear to you. The telephone is no damn good. Let's meet at Calendar's, near the La Brea Tar Pits. It's a few blocks from my office. I go there for lunch. One o'clock tomorrow. If you don't show up, Nachman, I'll understand that you didn't want to betray Norbert. But please do show up."

After the phone call, Nachman felt better. Nothing had actually changed, and yet he could think more liberally about what hadn't changed.

He continued to sit on the edge of his bed. He didn't want to move. It seemed he could still hear Adele's unmelodious voice, made ragged by cigarettes. Adele had urged him to examine his feelings, but he didn't care to know too much about what he felt. After all, as soon as you know what you feel, you feel something else. No. There would be no such examination. It would end in confusion. It was enough that he felt cheered by Adele's phone call. He admired her daring. He liked her sluggish, heavy carriage. She walked as if she had large breasts, though they were average, proportionate to her height, which was about five feet five inches. Her hips seemed to lock slowly, and then reluctantly to unlock as she walked, toes pointed outward. Nachman wanted, mindlessly, to hug her.

O.K., he thought, energized, returning to himself, the moral being. Look at the issue analytically, from Adele's point of view. As Adele had said, people have different needs. So let's be fair to Adele, a green-eyed Hungarian woman of considerable intelligence and nice hips. God knows why she married Norbert Novgorad.

It was obvious, Nachman suddenly realized, that the unrelenting repetitiousness of domestic life was destroying Adele. So the poor woman had been unfaithful. What was infidelity, anyhow? What was it precisely that Adele might have done? Let's get that straight. She kissed a man? Big deal. Perhaps she had sexual intercourse? Oh, who cares? It was an imaginative experience, a mental tonic, like a trip to Paris, except of course you don't bring back photographs of yourself in a motel room performing fellatio to show your friends. But who cares? With stunning visionary force, a picture burst into Nachman's mind. Adele was naked, lying on her back

with her wrists tied to bedposts. She smiled with vague, soporific satisfaction at Nachman, her green eyes glazed by a delirium of pleasure as she
said, in her cigarette voice, "Morals-shmorals."

The picture vanished. Nachman looked down at his shoes, which he
had dropped beside the bed. He felt an extraordinary need for ordinari-
ness. His shoes were British. Hand-sewn, soft reddish-brown leather. He'd
worn them for years and he'd had them resoled and reheeled at least
three times. He kept them oiled. They were molded perfectly to the shape
of his feet and so pliant they felt buttery. It occurred to Nachman, though
he hadn't been thinking about it, that maybe Norbert knew about Adele's
lover.

If Norbert knew, and if Nachman told Norbert what he had seen, it
might be grotesquely embarrassing. Boundaries are crucial to the integrity
of relationships. That settled it. He wouldn't tell Norbert and he wouldn't
meet Adele for lunch. It was an enormous relief to have arrived at this
understanding of his situation.

Traffic moved normally the next afternoon, so Nachman was on time
when he parked his car in the lot near the La Brea Tar Pits. Calendar's was
crowded. Waiters rushed down the aisles, with expressions of intense
concentration, as if solving puzzles. There was ubiquitous chatter and
laughter. Nachman looked about for Adele. When he saw her, he took a
breath and started toward her table. She was wearing sandals, jeans, a
celadon-green tank top, and a thin beaded necklace of primary colors.
Beside her wineglass was a newspaper, which she pressed down with her
hand as she read it. She glanced up as Nachman approached. She smiled,
folded the newspaper, and dropped it beneath her chair. She continued
smiling as Nachman sat down opposite her. He looked at her tank top and
necklace. He looked at her wedding ring, a barrel of dull yellow, and then
at her watch. It had a large face, etched with black numerals, and a clear
plastic band. Adele continued smiling. Nachman shook his head ruefully
as he finally looked directly at her face.

Her black shining hair was pulled back severely, and tied with a red
ribbon. She wore assertive poppy-red lipstick. In gold-framed glasses, her
eyes, related to the color of her tank top though much brighter, accepted
Nachman's attention, but he could see their uncertainty. Her smile became
tentative. Quizzical.

"Order something," she said, unable to bear Nachman's silence.

"I don't want anything."

"Won't you have a glass of wine?" she implored, as if it would do her good if Nachman had a glass of wine. Her smile was weak.

"All right."

Adele raised her hand. A passing waiter stopped. Adele said, "Two more," pointing to her wineglass. The waiter nodded.

"I shouldn't have another," said Adele. "I have to work on a difficult case this afternoon. I hired a new assistant. A gay kid named Geoffrey Horley Harms. He has two degrees. Three names and two doctorates, can you believe it?" She paused, then said, "What are you thinking?"

"I wasn't thinking."

"You've never been married. You don't know what it's like."

Nachman looked around at the action in the restaurant and sighed.

Adele said, "This is going nowhere. Look at me, please. I want to talk to you. I wasn't raised by Protestants. I'm not a nice person. Do you follow me? I'm a very direct person."

"What are you talking about?"

"I want your full attention."

"O.K."

"I'm glad you saw me outside the motel."

"I was stuck in traffic. I'm sorry."

"Don't be sorry. I'm grateful. What you saw has been going on for a long time, but I could never tell anybody. If I told my girlfriends it would be unfair to Norbert. I'm bad, but not evil. The guy you saw me with—Ivan—is from another life. I was in high school when we met. I was a kid. Ivan was already out of college, working. His mustache got to me. I don't know why. It made his face so fierce. But Ivan is very kind. He is in the insurance business, a claims adjuster. He doesn't live in Los Angeles. Sometimes he disappears for two or three years, then he phones me as if we were still together. As if I had never married. People stare at him because of his mustache. When he wears dark glasses he has no face, just a nose."

"Adele, what did you want to talk about?"

"I'm talking about it."

Nachman shut his eyes for a second, as if things would be different when he opened them. Nothing was different.

"Ivan phoned again a few days ago. Believe me, I was very clear and firm. I said I wouldn't meet him. I said that I felt bad about having done so in the past. I told him exactly how I felt. He started begging. I said no, no, no. The next day, he walked into my office. I almost fainted. He looked worse than shit. But the mustache was there, and old feelings were stirred. I was transported. What could I do? Even if I were a happily married woman, the old feelings would be there. I was helpless."

"Helpless? You?"

"Give me a break, Nachman."

"All right, you were helpless."

"So we went to a motel . . . Try to understand, Nachman. It's been going on for years, and I never told anyone. Motels. You wouldn't believe how many motels I've been in. Did you know that a lot of Indians are in the motel business?"

"I can't begin to tell you how interesting that is to me. Hindus or Muslims?"

"That's enough. I don't like being teased. So we went to the motel, a squalid dump at the edge of a trailer park."

A picture came. A motel room. The walls are water-stained and the paint is peeling away. Adele is standing beside a bed where a man lies. His eyes peer over a huge mustache, gazing at Adele as she steps into her panties. She pulls them up, then plucks the material free of the crease in her behind. At that instant Nachman's wineglass was set before him. He reached too quickly and knocked the glass over. Wine splattered Adele.

Nachman said, "I'm sorry. I'm sorry."

Adele's tank top bore dark splotches like the shadows of maple leaves.

"They once threw stones," Adele said. "I'm getting off easy."

"What can I say?"

"I wanted you to listen. You don't have to say anything."

Adele swept her tongue across the front of her teeth. A tiny dark green shape, perhaps a piece of arugula, was plastered against Adele's front tooth. Nachman ordered another glass of wine.

"If I hadn't seen you yesterday," he said, "nobody would ever have known."

"These things often come out. I told Ivan it was over. I think he heard me this time. Why don't you order a sandwich or something? I already had a salad."

Nachman didn't want anything.

Outside the restaurant, they stopped for a moment in the sunlight and looked up the avenue toward the County Museum.

"We should go there someday," said Nachman. "See the show and then go somewhere and have lunch."

"I'd like that."

Nachman kissed Adele on the cheek. She said, "Do you think I should . . . now that I've told you."

"Yes. Tell Norbert."

Nachman sounded principled, but he was already worried about whether Adele would invite him to dinner again. It would be a great loss if she decided that she had said too much and would prefer not to have Nachman around at the same time as her husband.

She had said she was bad, but not evil. Nachman wasn't sure what she meant. He supposed it had to do with Norbert's integrity. How he lived, consciously or not, in the eyes of other people. That was important to Adele. She wanted to protect Norbert. It was an aesthetic as well as a moral consideration. She'd had a long affair with Ivan, the mustache, but everything had ended in the motel. Nachman decided that bad Adele remained lovable.

A week later, Norbert phoned. It was late evening. Nachman heard fatigue and displeasure in Norbert's voice. It sounded like anger or controlled pain. All that had troubled Nachman earlier rushed into mind. He felt regret and shame. He braced internally, expecting to hear Norbert say, "You're a rat, Nachman. I'm furious at you."

Nachman hadn't told Norbert what he'd seen on Fairfax Avenue, and he'd met Adele for lunch, thereby making himself complicitous. Nachman had agonized over those things, but to know what you're doing is not the same as fully appreciating the terribleness of it. Nachman pressed the receiver hard against his ear. He'd never felt worse. If punishment were available to people the moment they deserved it, Nachman would have been punished days before. He could then show Norbert the receipt. Nachman suddenly realized that every move a person made was to one degree or another criminal, and that there was a great shortage of punishment. These thoughts occurred in the instant before Norbert said, "Would you like to go for a drive? I bought a new car."

Norbert hadn't denounced him, thank God, but Nachman didn't look forward to the drive. Who knows what might be said? Who knows what lies Nachman might be obliged to tell? Nachman put down the receiver. He had been holding it in a sweaty clutch. His heart was beating quickly and heavily.

Fifteen minutes later, Norbert came by in his new car. It had a big engine and a dashboard like the flight panel of an airliner. Nachman had no idea what company made the car, and he wasn't curious. If the car nourished Norbert's spirit with fantasies of power, that was good.

"I like your new car," said Nachman. "Really great. Beautiful."

"Umm," said Norbert, as if distracted.

Norbert drove out of the city along the San Diego Freeway. When a stretch of open road appeared, he stepped hard on the gas pedal. Nachman's spine pressed against the seat.

"Too fast, don't you think?" said Nachman.

"Are you serious?" There was contempt in Norbert's question. He continued, "I do a hundred and fifty in the desert."

Nachman glanced at the speedometer, saw that it read ninety-five, and then glanced at Norbert. What was he thinking? Norbert sat rigidly, staring down the road as if hypnotized by a point far off in the darkness. He was driving toward that point at greater and greater speed. But he was getting no closer, because the point existed only within Norbert, and they would probably be dead before he reached it. Minutes passed with only the drone of the big engine. The road rushed toward them and was swept under the devouring hood. Nachman watched cars and trucks far ahead loom suddenly and vanish in a blur and whoosh. Lights of oncoming traffic slashed by, going the other way. Slower lights of houses in the distance, along either side of the highway, moved like ships at sea. Norbert was driving well over a hundred miles per hour, speeding deeper into the night. Nachman was terrified, but trying to be a good friend, he said nothing to ruin Norbert's mood. Norbert needed to drive fast, needed to terrify Nachman. If Nachman demanded to be let out, Norbert would doubtless slow down and apologize. Maybe he was waiting for Nachman to lose his composure. Nachman forced himself to abide silently in terror. He deserved it; he accepted it. Part of him imagined that he wanted it.

Norbert seemed abruptly to soften, to relent. He continued to stare straight ahead and was no less self-absorbed, but he slowed the car, then left the highway and returned to it in the direction of Santa Monica.

"Let's have a drink," he said.

With no enthusiasm, Nachman said, "Do you know a place?"

"I know a place."

Norbert drove into Venice, and then to a bar in the middle of a long, poorly lighted street. It was a dark room with low ceilings and sawdust on the floor. Surfer types were shooting pool in the rear. Their girlfriends, scrawny blond kids who looked much alike, sat on a bench against a wall and smoked. Men in motorcycle leather were drinking beer at one end of the bar. Nachman would never have come to this place alone. But Norbert had a thick neck and broad shoulders. He was also fearless. He descended from Russian peasants. Shrewd, strong, dark, stocky, he had never once been sick, and never had a toothache. He'd played rugby in college, a game where men hurtle against one another, as in American football, but with no girlish helmets or shoulder pads. The atmosphere of the bar, like driving fast at night, suited Norbert's mood. Nachman didn't want to stay, but felt he owed his friend company the way convicts owe a debt to society. Norbert said, "I want a vodka martini. You, too?"

Nachman nodded yes, though he would have preferred a Coke. The bartender sneered, "Vodka martini?" as if Norbert had asked him to dance naked on a table. Norbert stared with no expression and said nothing, waiting for the bartender's next remark. There was none. The bartender made the drinks. Norbert carried them to a booth.

"Here's to life," he said, his tone sour.

"Are you troubled about something?" Nachman blurted out the question.

"That's how I seem to you?"

"Is there a problem?"

"Not my problem."

"Whose, then?"

"A guy in my department. You wouldn't understand."

"So it's an academic problem?"

"The most academic problem."

"What do you mean?"

"You heard of Plato? The ancient Greeks talked about this problem in their philosophy departments. It's about epistemology and fucking."

"Come on, Norbert, spare me the lecture. What about this guy in your department?"

Norbert shook his head, evidently overwhelmed by the prospect of telling Nachman about the guy. Muscles began working in Norbert's jaw, as if balls of feeling were being chewed. He had too much to say.

Nachman urged gently, "Tell me. What is the guy's problem?"

"I already told you too much. I shouldn't have said anything."

"You said almost nothing."

"All right, a student came on to him. That's the problem. O.K.?"

"Could you say a little more?"

"Forgive me for saying this, but you live a small life. Somebody gives you a pencil and a piece of paper and you are a happy Nachman. Like a kid on a beach. Give him a pail and he is king of the sand, ten billion tons of sand. You follow? The sand is like life, but all you need is a pail."

"Is this about me?"

"Of course not."

"But you sound angry. Are you angry?" Nachman asked, risking the worst possible. He couldn't go on with so much bad feeling suppressed.

"I'm angry at the guy with the problem. What a jerk. Imagine you are in your office, and a beautiful girl in a miniskirt is standing two inches from your nose. She is looking into your eyes and she smells good."

"Why is she standing two inches from your nose?"

"It isn't because she is nearsighted. She has no idea that anything she does has consequences. She is a girl."

"All right, go on."

"This girl is asking for advice about her major. Naturally, given such a provocative question, blood begins bulging in your manly part."

"So what did this guy do?"

"He told her to get the hell out of his office and phone in her question."

"I'm beginning to see the picture."

"You disapprove? This is a story about nature. To you, maybe, nature is a foreign language."

"Finish the story. What happened with the girl?"

"This guy kissed her and he put his hand between her legs."

"Just like that? What did she say?"

"She said, 'Ohhhhhh.'"

"I see the picture."

"The guy can't eat. Can't sleep. He is crazy with jealousy because she sleeps with other guys. Look, it's late. Do you want to get out of this dump and go home? You must want to go home. Say the word. Whatever you want."

"If it helps you to talk, Norbert, I'll listen all night. But there is something I must tell you."

"You needn't bother. I know you feel compromised. Adele told me about the mustache. She told me everything. It's not your fault that you saw her on Fairfax Avenue."

"So you're angry at Adele?"

"I love Adele. Who wouldn't love her? I asked her why is the mustache so important? Why do you need him? She says she doesn't know why. Nachman, you live with numbers. One plus one is two. It was always two, and it will always be two. For you there are problems, but no mysteries. The solutions exist, so take a vacation."

"Don't say another word. A vision is coming. I see a man who looks like me walking on an empty beach. He is on vacation. I know this because he is barefoot, collecting seashells. Now he is holding a shell to his ear, listening to the ocean, the chaos in which this shell was born. He knows that it was shaped according to a law which is expressed in the ratio of the rings on the shell. My God, he realizes the shell can be described mathematically. The shell is a resolution of chaos, a mathematical entity. Do you understand?"

"Yes. You are constitutionally incapable of taking a vacation."

"What's real is numbers. When I solve a problem, I collect a piece of the real. Other men collect paintings, cars, Hawaiian shirts. They even collect women. So I'm a little different. You're angry at Adele, but why at me?"

"You need to believe I'm angry at you?"

Norbert was clearly angry at Nachman. The feeling was mixed, but anger was there. He was angry because he had felt obliged, as a matter of pride, to confess the affair with the student. His confession sounded like boasting. It was forced, somehow unconvincing. Nachman understood that Norbert was embarrassed as well as angry, and he was concerned to protect his wife.

"Does Adele know about the guy who kissed the girl?" asked Nachman.

"A man is a man."

"He doesn't have to account for himself?"

"There is always something for which there is no accounting. Take, for example, the whole world."

"This is between you and me, not you and the whole world. If you're angry at me, you should tell me why."

"Let's go. I'll drive you home."

Norbert got up and strode to the bar. He reached into his pants pockets, fingers scrabbling along his thighs, searching for money to tip the bartender. There had been ugly tension between them when he ordered. The gesture meant Norbert was leaving with no hard feelings. It also meant that Norbert had forgiven Nachman.

They drove in silence to Nachman's house. As Nachman got out of the car, Norbert said, "Come to dinner this Friday. Adele told me to invite you." Norbert's expression, in the glow of the dashboard, was unreadable. His big head and the wide slope of his shoulders resembled a pit bull's. The shape was very familiar to Nachman. Even if he saw only Norbert's head, at a distance, in a crowded street among a hundred moving heads, it would be enough to recognize his old friend. Nachman said, "I'll look forward to dinner."

Later that night, as always before going to sleep, he sat in bed reading. The book was called *Die Innenwelt der Mathematiker*. Nachman read German slowly and with difficulty, struggling with the sentences, consulting a dictionary every few minutes. Five pages took him nearly an hour, but he persisted. The book examined the question of whether mathematics is a social creation or a mysterious gift offered to certain individuals. Nachman didn't see how it could be a social creation. Mathematicians collaborated sometimes, but he had never heard anyone say, "We solved the problem." Nachman had never even met a mathematician who could tell you how a solution came to him or her. It just came or it didn't. The great genius Ramanujan said the goddess of Namakkal came to him in his dreams bearing formulas. Well, no goddess had ever come to Nachman. But he did occasionally awake at night and stumble from his bed to a nearby table where he kept a pencil and paper. In the morning, when he discovered that he had scribbled the solution to a problem, he didn't always remember having done so. What could be less social? It couldn't even be said Nachman socialized with himself. In truth, he didn't really know what "social" meant. He and Norbert were the closest of friends, but were they social? Norbert was Norbert. In his pit-bull head, he dreamed of cars. Nachman was Nachman. He dreamed of numbers.

With the *Innenwelt* book open in his lap, Nachman fell asleep and had a vivid, frightening dream. He saw Adele kissing the mustache man. Nachman ran desperately toward them to pull her away. "No!" he cried, and he found himself awake, crying, "No, no, no!" his feet churning beneath the blanket, running nowhere.

Shaken by the dream, Nachman turned off the lamp and lay staring into the darkness. He didn't know what, if anything, his dream had revealed to him. He was aware only of a certain tumultuous feeling. He'd been aware of it before, when Adele had asked if he was in love with her. He saw the silent question in her green eyes, and he heard her cigarette voice say, "I thought we were friends." Nachman suddenly felt very lonely, lying in the darkness, wondering if he was in love with Adele.

cryptology

NACHMAN HAD ARRIVED IN NEW YORK the previous evening, and was walking along Fifth Avenue when she came up behind him, calling, "Nachman, Nachman, is that you?" He looked back and saw a woman shining with happiness, for which he, apparently, was responsible. His mere existence had turned on her lights. Nachman kissed her on both cheeks, and then they stood chatting at the corner of Forty-second Street, the millions passing with the minutes. When Nachman parted from her, he was holding her business card and the key to her apartment in Chelsea, having promised to join her and her husband for dinner that evening.

"If you arrive before us, just wait in the apartment," she had said. "It's been so many years, Nachman. I'm Helen Ferris now. Do you know my husband, Benjamin Strong Ferris? He's a lawyer. Also a name in computer science and cryptology. I assume you're in New York for the cryptology conference. Benjamin goes there to find geniuses like you for his company."

"As a matter of fact . . ." Nachman had said, but she was still talking.

"It would be wonderful if we could have a drink, just you and me, and remember the old days, but I have to run. There'll be time to talk later. I can't tell you how glad I am that we ran into each other. Actually, Nachman, I followed you for about five blocks. I couldn't believe it was you. Benjamin will be so delighted. He's heard me talk about you so often. Should I cook, or should we have dinner out? Oh, let's decide later."

When she had stopped talking, Nachman said he didn't know the name Benjamin Strong Ferris, and he didn't consider himself a genius. "I'm a good mathematician," he added. "Good is rare enough."

Helen Ferris smiled with affectionate understanding, as if his modesty amused her, but there was also something more. She seemed to believe a special bond existed between them. While Nachman's every word nourished her smile, her dark brown eyes bloomed with sensual anticipation, as if at any moment Nachman might do something very pleasing. To disguise his ignorance—what special bond was there between them?—Nachman became expansive, even somewhat confessional.

He told Helen Ferris that he was indeed in New York for the cryptology conference; he'd been invited to a job interview by a representative of the Delphic Corporation. But whoever had invited him hadn't given his name.

Helen Ferris obviously took great pleasure in listening to Nachman, and yet, in the center of her rapt, almost delirious focus, Nachman saw a curious blank spot, as if she were not conversing so much as savoring. Her brown eyes devoured his, and her smile suggested a rictus in its unrelieved tension and shape. This intensity, and her alarming red lipstick, made Nachman think she wanted to eat him. A smile is a primitive expression, he supposed, carried in the genes, the reflexive anticipation of a meal—not necessarily of people, but who knows the ancestral diet? Nachman smiled in response, but felt no desire to eat her.

"So the person who invited you didn't give his name?" she prompted.

She'd repeated the information, presumably, to hold Nachman a moment longer and give him a chance to say something more. Her devouring smile made him nervous, and he astonished himself by talking like a man making a police report, obsessed with facts.

"The letter was signed by a secretary. Abigail Stokes. She just gave me the name of the hotel and a date and time for the interview. To tell the truth, I didn't really come to New York because of the interview—I wanted to visit my father, who lives in Brooklyn. I haven't seen him in years. And since Delphic was paying for my plane ticket and hotel room, why not? The interview was set for one o'clock this afternoon, and I figured they were taking me to lunch, but nobody was there to meet me. No one at the hotel desk had heard of the Delphic Corporation, and my room had been paid for by someone whose name they weren't free to disclose."

He paused after his recitation of the facts, then gave her a last little personal tidbit to chew on. "So, since then I've been walking around feeling a bit . . . I don't know what. Weirdly disappointed."

"It is weird," said Helen Ferris. "But why feel disappointed? You got a free trip to New York. How clever of you! The airline ticket was prepaid?"

"If I had to put down one cent to fly three thousand miles and meet a nameless person, I wouldn't be here," said Nachman, with indignation. "I hate to travel, but I showed up for the interview. The other party didn't."

"I see. You were hurt. You're sure there was no other name at the bottom of the letter? It didn't say something like 'Abigail Stokes for Joe Schmo'?"

Nachman wondered fleetingly if Helen Ferris thought he was an idiot.

"No Joe Schmo. Somebody anonymous wanted to interview me for a job. I have a job. I'm not looking for another one. But I agreed to come. Why not? I figured I might even learn about cryptology, an exciting field. A good mathematician could make a lot of money fooling with codes."

"But that's not like you. Would you really have considered taking the job?"

"I guess not, though it might be fun to be a millionaire. I fancied myself buying things like a dishwasher, but I don't work for money. You know what I mean. My salary check pays my bills. I work like most people, not to waste my life."

Nachman had begun to relax into his subject. "Have you been to Santa Monica? That's where I live. On the beach you see people with nice bodies and no jobs. Also no brains. Life is too short to waste a minute getting a sunburn. I've never even taken a vacation. I don't know why anybody would want to. Anyhow, as I said, I wanted to visit my father. This was an opportunity. Expenses paid by the Delphic mystery man."

"You don't own a dishwasher?" Helen Ferris asked, giggling. "That's also mysterious. I bet I know what happened. Delphic sent out a form letter signed by Abigail Stokes. The letter went to a hundred mathematicians like you. A few of them accepted the invitation and came to New York. Before you arrived, Delphic decided to hire one of these. So you no longer existed as far as they were concerned. They simply forgot about you."

"But they paid for my ticket and hotel room."

"Just the cost of doing business. You feel disappointed, but it isn't the least bit personal. You mean nothing to them."

"I'm meaningless?" This was the one clear thought that emerged from her pelting of words.

"Not to me," Helen Ferris said. Was she teasing him? Or was she right?

"I've got to go," she said, touching his chest lightly. "I'm so excited. We'll have fun tonight."

When they parted, Nachman wondered how long it had been since he'd last seen Helen Ferris. He also wondered who, exactly, was Helen Ferris?

She remembered him so well. She had called out his name in the street. How could he say, "Who are you?" Another man might have been able to say it. Not Nachman. In a few hours, she would expect him to show up and meet her husband. The prospect of joining strangers for dinner had something adventurous about it, even devilish and appropriate to New York. Nachman didn't know anyone in the city who was as friendly as his old friend Helen Ferris, whoever she was. Any moment it would come to him. Her wide cheekbones and dark, roundish, somewhat fleshy face, with its maternally sexy brown eyes, looked Semitic, maybe a little Asian, but she might just as easily be Mexican or Puerto Rican. He'd known women who looked like her, but remembered none named Helen. She was quite attractive, though a little scary. You'd think he'd remember her for that reason. Had she noticed his confusion? People can tell if you recognize them or not. They see it in your eyes, hear it in your voice. If she knew Nachman didn't recognize her, then she was complicit in his failure to admit it. Oh well, Nachman would get the question out of the way when he saw her again. It would be more embarrassing later than it would have been a few minutes ago, but he would show up for dinner and confess. The key to Helen Ferris's apartment was in his pants pocket. Her card was in his wallet. It said Helen Ferris, Editorial Consultant, but it told him nothing about who she was.

Dinner was still a few hours away. Nachman continued walking aimlessly, trying to remember. How do you try to remember? You make yourself passive, receptive, available. If it comes it comes. A strange kind of trying. He wondered if there had been a clue to her identity in what she'd said. Unfortunately, Nachman had done most of the talking. The look in

Helen Ferris's eyes and her red smile came to him; nothing else. She refused to step from the shadows of his mind.

The late-October weather felt summery, but as the afternoon wore on, Nachman detected a quality in the breeze that was too poignant for summer, had too fine an edge. Another year was almost over. Nachman liked the poignancy, could almost see it in the changing light. The sun would soon be lower in the sky. Shadows would grow longer. Darkness and cold would invade the streets and challenge people's energy, give steel to their thoughts. Nachman felt as if he were walking heroically into the heart of the drama, the adventure of the city, and not just because of the season. Helen Ferris was part of New York's endemic adventurousness. The crowds, the traffic, the buildings, the changing weather, the city's infinite complexity, its unknowability—who could comprehend it? Nachman felt exhilarated. From a certain point of view, there was even adventure in being stood up at the cryptology conference. Invited, all expenses paid, to come three thousand miles, only to find nobody who gives a damn whether you came or not. No explanation, no apology. Not even a note at the hotel desk. This couldn't have happened in small-time towns like London, Paris, Rome, Berlin, and Tokyo. That's what made New York great. Nobody gives a shit about anybody.

The truth is that Nachman was enraged. He had smiled as he talked to Helen Ferris. He hadn't let her see his anger. She might have thought he was angry at her.

Nachman then chuckled to himself, and shook his head ruefully, as if he required a moment of private ironic theater. His mood became philosophical. After all, he was morally compromised. He'd agreed to the interview in bad faith. He had no intention of changing jobs and had wanted only to visit his father. In fact, he had planned to go directly from the airport to his father's apartment, but when he phoned—once from the plane, then, again, from the airport—nobody had answered. His father was old and forgetful. He might have gone out. He might even have left town to visit relatives in Connecticut. So Nachman had taken a cab to the hotel. He'd visit his father tomorrow, if the old guy answered the goddamn phone. If not, he'd fly back to California, feeling he'd wasted his time.

As for the sense of adventure, the weather and all that, it was a fantasy, a kind of lie. Nachman had been trying to give value to his trip. He could kid himself only so long before self-contempt made him see things as they were. Only a fool would accept an invitation to meet somebody who had no name. Nachman was a fool. That was now an established fact. Good. He felt much better.

A few hours later, Nachman entered a building in Chelsea. The doorman, who had been given Nachman's name, said, "Go right up. Apartment 14-B." The elevator was brightened by three half-mirrored walls. Nachman could see himself from head to waist in triplicate. Three half-Nachmans made him feel less, rather than more, visible. The reflections seemed mental rather than physical, mere versions of himself. He felt suddenly claustrophobic, as if the elevator were overcrowded.

Below the mirrors, there was a walnut-stained surface embossed with carved flowers. A brass strip marked the place where the wood met the gray industrial-carpeted floor. The elevator door was two panels of brown enameled steel. They slid separately, one behind the other. Nachman studied the light fixture directly above his head. A fat bulb glowed through a bowl of cloudy glass that was subtly textured with incisions radiating from the center. The elevator spoke for the building, thought Nachman—a confusion of materials suggesting luxurious waste. It carried him slowly to the fourteenth floor, then stopped with a jerk. Nachman had the familiar sensation of a lightness in his belly and lead in his feet.

Nothing about Helen Ferris had come to him. Nachman supposed he must have known her when he was a graduate student at U.C.L.A. He'd had quite a few acquaintances then, men and women with whom he'd since lost touch. There had been parties where he'd fallen into intense and transitory intimacy with people to whom he'd only nodded as they passed on campus later, avoiding eye contact. Wait a minute. Hadn't he once left a party with a dark girl who had been too drunk to drive? Hadn't he driven her in her white Jaguar to her parents' house in Beverly Hills? Hadn't they . . . what? The elevator doors opened. No, her name was Dolores. She looked nothing like Helen Ferris. The elevator doors slid shut behind him, and the elevator descended, taking Dolores to oblivion.

There were four apartment doors, two on either side of the hall, which was carpeted in the same way as the elevator and was stunningly silent. Dim lights, set in elaborate brass sconces, trailed along the walls. Nachman found the door marked 14-B. He looked at a brass-rimmed eyehole as he pressed the black nipple-like bell. He heard a muffled gong inside the apartment. He waited. Nobody answered. He pressed the bell again and waited. Nobody answered. The key worked. The door opened into a large room.

"Hello," said Nachman, careful not to shriek. "Anybody home?" No one responded. He stepped inside, shut the door, and realized that he wasn't alone. An odor of perfumed soap lay on the air, which was faintly moist and warm. He heard water running and glanced at what he guessed was a bathroom door. It was partly open. Someone was taking a shower and had heard nothing because of the noise of the running water. Nachman was reluctant to shout. People taking a shower feel defenseless and are easily frightened.

Nachman stood in the large room. It was maybe forty by twenty feet, with a gleaming maple floor. No rugs. A bar counter separated a kitchen area from the rest of the room. Furniture was clustered in the middle, floating in space. A glass-topped coffee table was set lengthwise between two red sofas, with black chairs at either end. Nachman noticed an imposing desk against a wall, and a library table carrying stacks of papers. The room had tall windows that looked across the avenue toward the windows of other buildings. Near the farthest wall there was a dresser and a bed with night tables and reading lamps. To the right of the bed a spiral stair led to an opening in the ceiling, apparently the second floor of the apartment. A suitcase was on the bed. It sat in the middle of a bulky white comforter that had been flung back, revealing silky cobalt blue sheets. At the foot of the bed was a large television on a wheeled aluminum stand that held magazines on a shelf above the wheels. In the ceiling there were two rows of track lights.

Who was in the shower? Helen or Benjamin Ferris? In answer to his question, Nachman heard voices. They were amplified in the largely hollow space of the room, as in the barrel of a drum. The man's voice was emotionally neutral. The woman's voice was strained, higher pitched. It was Helen Ferris. "I'm not finished. Why don't you get out and let me finish."

They are showering together, Nachman realized.

"I don't want to have to talk to him alone."

"Oh, for Christ's sake. You can talk to him until I come out. Fix him a drink. Turn on the TV and watch the ball game. Men like sports. You won't even have to talk to him. Be nice for once in your fucking life."

"Hey, hey, hey. *I'm* supposed to be nice? Like *I* invited the schmuck to the apartment? I'll pick up the check at dinner, baby, but that's where it ends. This is your affair."

"Don't start with the affair business. He's not my type."

"You have types?"

"I'm nice to your friends, Benjamin, even when they bore me to death."

"Friend? You said he didn't even recognize you."

"So what? He's drifty. Not your average New York cocksmith, like some persons I could name. I'll remind him who I am at dinner."

"I'll be sitting there, for Christ's sake. He'll die."

"He won't know I told you anything. Besides, he probably doesn't remember that, either. He's practically certifiable. I think his fly was unzipped."

"Don't make me jealous."

Helen Ferris laughed.

Benjamin Ferris went on: "What's the guy's name? Nachman?"

"What's wrong with Nachman?"

"I didn't say there was anything wrong with it."

"It's your tone. You think Ferris is so beautiful? People are always saying, 'Like the Ferris wheel?' It bores me."

Nachman walked past the bathroom, crossing the thirty feet or so to the television set. He put the key on top of the TV. He'd heard enough. He was leaving. As he drew his hand away, the key fell to the floor. It had stuck to his fingertips, which were slightly damp. So were his palms. He was perspiring. The key made a sharp clink when it hit the floor. Nachman bent quickly to retrieve it, as if to undo the noise. If they had heard the key, they knew he was in the apartment. He couldn't leave. He would have to confront them. No. He would shout hello, pretend he'd just arrived. They would pretend that they didn't know he'd heard them talking about him. Every word the three of them said would be a lie. He put the key back on the television, and it remained there as he drew his hand away.

He'd never before overheard people talking about him. It was unnerving. He'd been radically objectified, like an insensate rock, while his soul floated in the air. A general hurt spread within his chest and began to seep like a poison throughout his body. He couldn't think clearly. It was hard to breathe. Again Nachman felt an impulse to leave, but he couldn't simply walk back to the door. If they heard the door shut behind him, they'd feel terrible, knowing Nachman had heard them. Why should he care? Nachman cared.

The open suitcase on the bed was large and old-fashioned, made of yellow leather like a beautiful Gladstone, with straps and metal corners. Looking at the suitcase, Nachman felt as if he were doing something, not merely suffering. What he saw in the suitcase told him that Helen and Benjamin were packing for a trip. How nice. They did things together—showered, traveled, bickered, and said vile things about people who had never done them any harm. Their conjugal solidarity was daunting.

If Nachman had stayed in California, he'd have gone to work in his office at the Institute of Mathematics and never heard himself described as a drifty man who walks about with his fly unzipped. Nothing she had said was true, but she had said it. She actually said it. We were all going to die, but Helen Ferris had to kill people.

The voices persisted, but Nachman focused on the suitcase and tried not to listen. Shirts, underwear, dresses, trousers, and tennis shoes lay in a confused pile, and a stack of papers had been tossed on top. Nachman admired the indifference with which the expensive-looking clothes had been flung into the suitcase. He saw passports and airline-ticket envelopes among the papers and reached out to open them. His hands were shaking. His heart swelled as he intruded upon the privacy of strangers. How could he do this?

Before he'd engaged the question, he felt a soft pressure against his lower leg. He looked down and saw an exceptionally fat Siamese cat. It must have hidden under the bed, frightened of Nachman, but then decided he was no threat and emerged to brush against his leg. The cat leaped onto the bed and stepped into the suitcase, settling on top of the papers, as if it knew that Nachman had been about to look at them. The cat wanted Nachman's attention. Nachman stroked its back. A fat purring friend come to comfort and console him. While he stroked the cat with one hand, he tried to lift the corners of the papers with the other.

There were no rugs or drapes in the room, nothing to absorb the voices, and the moisture in the air only sharpened them. Nachman wasn't listening, but then, abruptly, the water noise ceased.

"He's had a hard time," Helen Ferris said. "He flew across the country to meet someone at the conference and he was stood up. I felt sorry for him."

"If I were stood up, I wouldn't tell anyone. Word gets around. People think you're a schmuck."

"He tried to be cheerful, but I could tell he was furious. The minute I said hello, he started venting like a maniac."

Helen Ferris's voice changed, becoming husky and teasing.

"Tell me, Benjamin," she said.

"What?"

"That I am beautiful."

"Come here."

She laughed. "No, no, no."

Nachman glanced toward the bathroom door. He imagined Helen Ferris's dark-brown hair, cut level with her chin, now a wet black shining cap about her eyes and cheeks. Her mouth, free of lipstick, was softened and bloated by hot water. Nachman thought she'd look better without lipstick. He remembered her motherly sexy eyes. Barefoot, she was maybe five two. She stood as high as his chest. She had wide hips. Did she have large breasts?

She squealed. The note was pitched so high that Nachman thought—terrified—that she had entered the room and was staring at him with shock and revulsion.

He shut the suitcase instantly. On the cat. It thrashed against the leather. Instead of flipping the case open, Nachman pressed the lid down harder, as if to hide the evidence. Not too hard, not hurting the cat, but thus, unintentionally, Nachman gave it time to piss.

When he realized that he was alone and hadn't been seen, he opened the case. The cat sped across the blue silk sheet and leapt onto the maple floor, trailing turds of fear. It vanished behind the bar in the kitchen area, and Nachman saw that it had deposited about a gallon of liquid in the suitcase. Letters and legal papers had softened and wrinkled, edges curling as urine attacked their fibers. Trapped in the suitcase, the cat had spun beneath Nachman's hands, hosing in all directions.

In the elevator, Nachman kept his eyes on the doors and didn't glance at the mirrored walls. He didn't want to see his reflection. In a spasm of superstitious dread, Nachman thought that if he saw it he might be obliged to leave it behind. He wanted to get entirely out of the building, taking himself and his reflection far away from the Ferris couple, particularly the naked, squealing Helen Ferris. The Ferrises had taken something from him, torn a hole in his existence. Out of the corner of his eye he saw the doorman nod. Nachman went by with no acknowledgment and was immediately outside in the anonymous street. He wanted no human recognitions, however minimal, as he headed downtown. Strangers passed like ghostly shapes in the night. Nachman walked mindlessly, block after block until, gradually, he stopped feeling devastated and, in the cool night-time air of the city, recovered the good simplicity of being himself. "A fool," he said, "but mine own."

He thought about finding a restaurant and having dinner. But he decided he wasn't hungry and continued walking. In Washington Square Park, Nachman came to an empty bench and sat down. The paths were shadowed by trees, through which lamplight shone brokenly. He couldn't make out the features of passersby, and assumed that he was more or less invisible to them, too. Alone, unknown, unseen, he became deeply peaceful and free in his thoughts.

He thought about Helen Ferris. Her smile, which Nachman had read as anticipation, he now understood had meant something different, like expectation. Nachman had been expected to light up just as she had, but he'd failed to recognize her. He was no longer the person he had been. A part of his life was gone.

She'd given him her card, though God knows what she thought of him now. Perhaps she believed Nachman, not the cat, had pissed in her suitcase. He could phone her tomorrow, or perhaps the following day from California, and explain what had happened. He could ask her to tell him her maiden name. If he finally remembered who she was, he might then be enriched by memories of himself. Memories are far superior to photographs, for example, which are good only for nostalgia, not under-standing. But did Nachman want those memories? The Nachman he no longer remembered was certainly himself. After all, who else could it be?

It's been said the unexamined life isn't worth living. Nachman wasn't against examining his life, but then what was a life? The day before yester-day he'd been in California, and tomorrow he could be almost anywhere on the globe. He could change his name, learn a new language, start a new existence. He could go to an exotic place, get married, have children of various colors and surprising features. It was easy enough. People did it all the time. He could herd yaks in Mongolia, or be a slave trader in Sudan. It took no courage to consult a travel agent. Such metaphysicians were in the phone book. "Get me a flight to Mongolia," said Nachman to himself. "One way."

But Nachman wasn't adventurous. He had no passion for change. As for "a life," it was what you read about in newspaper obituaries. The history of a person come and gone. Nachman would return to California and think only about mathematics. Numbers have no history. For history something has to disappear. Numbers remain. Just wondering about Mongolia, with its bleak and freezing plains, made him homesick. He yearned for his office and his desk and the window that looked out on the shining Pacific. He'd never gone swimming in the prodigious, restless, teeming, alluring thing, but he loved the changing light on its surface and the sounds it made in the darkness. He didn't yearn for its embrace.

On a bench nearby, partly obscured by shadows, a man began playing a guitar. The tune was a bossa nova, haunting, something like a blues, only more finely nuanced and not at all macho. The rhythm was subtly engaging and it seemed to caress Nachman's heart. He thought again about phoning Helen Ferris. He'd apologize, certainly, for not waiting until she and her husband came out of the bathroom. Vaguely, he supposed that they might have a lot to say to him. His thoughts became still more vague as they surrendered to the bossa nova, and soon he wasn't thinking at all, only following the tune. It made a lovely, sinuous shape, and then made it again and again, always a little differently and yet always the same, as the rhythm carried its exquisite sadness toward infinity.